Slick
RUNNING
SATAN'S DEVILS #3

Manda Mellett (signature)

MANDA MELLETT

Published 2017 by Trish Haill Associates
Copyright © 2017 by Manda Mellett

Edited by Brian Tedesco (pubsolvers.com)

Book and Cover Design by Lia Rees at Free Your Words
(www.freeyourwords.com)

www.mandamellett.com

Disclaimer

This is a work of fiction. Names, characters, businesses, places, events
and incidents are either the products of the author's imagination or
used in a fictitious manner. Any resemblance to actual persons, living
or dead, or actual events is purely coincidental.

Warning

This book is dark in places and contains content of a sexual nature. It
is not suitable for persons under the age of 18.

ISBN: 978-1-912288-03-8

AUTHOR'S NOTE

Slick Running is the third in the Satan's Devils MC Series, but can be read as a standalone.

I've been overwhelmed by the reception given to the first two books in the series, *Turning Wheels* and *Drummer's Beat*, and the support and encouragement to continue with the Satan's Devils. I'm having as much fun writing these as I understand you are reading them.

If you're new to MC books you may find there are terms that you haven't heard before, so I've included a glossary to help along the way. I hope you get drawn into this mysterious and dark world in the same way I have done—there will be further books in the Satan's Devils series which I hope you'll want to follow.

If you've picked this book up because, like me, you read anything MC, I hope you'll enjoy it for what it is, a fictional insight into the underground culture of alpha men and their bikes.

GLOSSARY

Motorcycle Club – An official motorcycle club in the U.S. is one which is sanctioned by the American Motorcyclist Association (AMA). The AMA has a set of rules its members must abide by. It is said that ninety-nine percent of motorcyclists in America belong to the AMA

Outlaw Motorcycle Club (MC) – The remaining one percent of motorcycling clubs are historically considered outlaws as they do not wish to be constrained by the rules of the AMA and have their own bylaws. There is no one formula followed by such clubs, but some not only reject the rulings of the AMA, but also that of society, forming tightly knit groups who fiercely protect their chosen ways of life. Outlaw MCs have a reputation for having a criminal element and supporting themselves by less than legal activities, dealing in drugs, gun running or prostitution. The one-percenter clubs are usually run under a strict hierarchy.

Brother – Typically members of the MC refer to themselves as brothers and regard the closely knit MC as their family.

Cage – The name bikers give to cars as they prefer riding their bikes.

Chapter – Some MCs have only one club based in one location. Other MCs have a number of clubs who follow the same bylaws and wear the same patch. Each club is known as a chapter and will normally carry the name of the area where they are based on their patch.

Church – Traditionally the name of the meeting where club business is discussed, either with all members present or with just those holding officer status.

Colours – When a member is wearing (or flying) his colours he will be wearing his cut proudly displaying his patch showing which club he is affiliated with.

Cut – The name given to the jacket or vest which has patches denoting the club that member belongs to.

Enforcer – The member who enforces the rules of the club.

Hang-around – This can apply to men wishing to join the club and who hang-around hoping to be become prospects. It is also used to women who are attracted by bikers and who are happy to make themselves available for sex at biker parties.

Mother Chapter – The founding chapter when a club has more than one chapter.

Patch – The patch or patches on a cut will show the club that member belongs to and other information such as the particular chapter and any role that may be held in the club. There can be a number of other patches with various meanings, including a one-percenter patch. Prospects will not be allowed to wear the club patch until they have been patched-in, instead they will have patches which denote their probationary status.

Patched-in/Patching-in – The term used when a prospect completes his probationary status and becomes a full club member.

President (Prez) – The officer in charge of that particular club or chapter.

Prospect – Anyone wishing to join a club must serve time as a probationer. During this period they have to prove their loyalty to the club. A probationary period can last a year or more. At the end of this period, if they've proved themselves a prospect will be patched-in.

Old Lady – The term given to a woman who enters into a permanent relationship with a biker.

RICO – The Racketeer Influenced and Corrupt Organisations Act primarily deals with organised crime. Under this Act the officers of a club could be held responsible for activities they order members to do and a conviction carries a potential jail service of twenty years as well as a large fine and the seizure of assets.

Road Captain – The road captain is responsible for the safety of the club on a run. He will organise routes and normally ride at the end of the column.

Secretary – MCs are run like businesses and this officer will perform the secretarial duties such as recording decisions at meetings.

Sergeant-at-Arms – The sergeant-at-arms is responsible for the safety of the club as a whole and for keeping order.

Sweet Butt – A woman who makes her sexual services available to any member at any time. She may well live on the club premises and be fully supported by the club.

Treasurer – The officer responsible for keeping an eye on the club's money.

Vice President (VP) – The vice president will support the president, stepping into his role in his absence. He may be responsible for making sure the club runs smoothly, overseeing prospects etc.

Brothers protecting their own

Contents

CHAPTER 1

Ella

Four months ago

I'd defy anyone who's a resident of Tucson not to be aware of the Satan's Devils Motorcycle Club, whether they regard them with fear and hide in the shadows as the sound of thunder announces their approach, or, like me, eyeball them with a mixture of intrigue and curiosity.

Maybe it's down to the parts of the city that I frequent, but I often see them on my side of town, wearing leather vests proudly claiming their loyalty to the Tucson chapter. My interest in them is, at least in part, inspired by me being a hopeless romantic and spending far too much of my time with my nose in my e-reader devouring MC romance novels as though they were going out of fashion. My imagination fuelled by the rough but tender outlaw bikers I read about, making me wish for an opportunity to discover if fiction bears any similarity to the flesh and blood men I see riding around on their Harleys in real life.

It's rumoured they own the Wheel Inn Restaurant and Bar, and whether they do or don't, it's an excellent place to find tall, ruggedly handsome, muscular, and tattooed members of the club who regularly drop by, presumably, if the gossip is true, to check in on their investment. Though I'd never gone inside— let's face it, I can barely afford a takeaway from McDonald's—I often manage to find an excuse to walk past on my way to work, if only in the hope that I'll bump into the man of my dreams.

Just a distant sighting of one of them on their gleaming machines is sufficient to make my mouth and lady parts water, something to store up for the lonely nights in my bed.

Until one day when I was passing and, so intent on letting my eyes feast on a pair of bikers standing talking, I tripped on the kerb and fell into leather-clad arms. As I flushed red I made the mistake of glancing up into a pair of the most beautiful eyes I'd ever seen. To be met with a smirk. He'd righted me, patted me on the shoulder and sent me away with a little slap to my butt. *I was dismissed.* I'd walked on fast to put distance between us, berating myself as to how stupid I was to think little plain old me would ever attract their attention. Shit! I'd literally fallen at his feet and thrown myself at him, but he'd barely noticed, not even pausing his conversation, showing discussing bike parts was clearly far more interesting than me.

After that, embarrassment had me changing my route, no longer taking the detour past the establishment they apparently own, relegating thoughts of devastatingly handsome bikers to where they belonged. In my dreams.

And there I thought they would stay, until the day I bump into Jill.

The spring sun is gleaming down, a perfect temperature to sit outside and treat myself to a cup of coffee bought with the extra tips I'd earned last night. Leaning back, my eyes closed, a rumbling sound roars up the road, echoing around the buildings until suddenly cutting off. Straightening, I sit up and, shading my eyes with my hand, see a vision parked up on the other side of the road. *It's one of them.* The Satan's Devils. Unable to tear my attention away, I watch as the biker removes his sunglasses and slips them into a pocket in his leather vest before disappearing into to the hardware store.

2

Honestly, I need to fan myself. *They're just so hot!* I'm still gazing across at the black and chrome monster parked up at the kerb, keen not to miss seeing him re-emerge when I hear a sudden shout.

"Hey! It's Ella, isn't it? My God! It is! I haven't seen you for fuckin' years!"

Slightly annoyed at the untimely interruption and at the person who blocks the sight of the bike, my eyes are drawn to an attractive woman wearing almost indecent shorts that showcase legs going on for miles, and a tight tee that brazenly outlines her braless breasts. The sun shining directly in my eyes, I need a second look before I recognise her.

"It is, isn't it? Fuck me! How have you been?" As she pulls out a chair opposite me and without waiting for an invitation sits down, her face becomes clear, and it's only then I'm able to place her.

My voice comes out as a squeal when I grasp who it is. "Jill! For heaven's sake. I can't believe I've bumped into you."

At once we both stand, pulling each other in for a hug, exchanging comments of "how have you been" and "what have you been doing", both talking at once and laughing as the words tumble out.

I haven't seen her for years. We'd gone to school together and were on the cheerleading team. Always the pair getting into mischief, the ones who'd got the notice of the boys. Well, her at least, me not so much. My role was normally just tagging along. I'd acted as look out on more than one occasion. But remembering the fun we'd had together, before we lost touch, my friendship with Jill has to be one of my best memories about my teenage years.

Grinning at each other, we sit down again. Now I'm in for my second surprise of the morning. My attention being focused on my companion, I hadn't noticed the biker leaving the store.

But I certainly don't miss him dodging through the traffic and coming over to this side of the road, approaching us, then curling his hand around the back of Jill's neck, tipping her head back and giving her deep kiss on her mouth. It's like a scene out of one of my novels, and now I really do need to wave my hand briskly in front of my face to cool myself down.

As my eyes open wide he murmurs, "Later doll." He gives her a wink that holds promise, then he disappears back to his bike, throws his leg over the seat then looks back over and lifts his chin before starting the engine and heading up the road with an ear-shattering roar.

"Hell, Jill. Is that your boyfriend?" My eyes are still staring in the direction where he's disappearing into the distance.

When I look back it's to catch her smirking. "Not exactly." Her enigmatic reply is all that she says.

"Well...?" I prompt her, hoping she'll say more. Christ, I'd give my back teeth to be the subject of a display like the one I'd just witnessed. *Who is he to her?*

She shakes her head dismissively and won't be drawn. Instead, she changes the conversation back to the rather more boring subject of me and how my life's turned out. It's fairly simple to sum up. Boring.

After another cup of coffee she gets up to leave. "Hey, I've had fun reminiscing about old times. Do you come here often? Shall we meet up again?"

When I can afford it. "Yeah. I'd like that." *Especially if your boyfriend, or whoever he is, turns up.* I've enjoyed myself too. And I'll jump at the chance to find out just how well she knows the man in black leather. And whether she can introduce me to his friends.

It quickly becomes habit for us to get together. I spend far too much on coffees I can't really afford, but it's pleasurable to renew our friendship. However, much to my disappointment, as the weeks pass, while she's managed to extract the uninteresting facts about my job and my life, she gives little away about hers. And I don't see her biker friend again, nor can I get her to talk about who he is or how she knows him. But I enjoy her company, and she appears to like mine.

Gradually, as we continue to meet and start to regain the easy relationship we'd had when in high school, her tongue loosens until eventually, to my delight, she begins to open up. Over a second cup of coffee that has me counting my remaining cents in my head, she begins to explain exactly what her relationship with the Satan's Devils entails. I'd started with an innocent enquiry about her address, and my eyes opened wide as, with a wary glance around her, she whispers conspiratorially and lets it all out.

"You really live at their compound? For *free?*" It's the words she's just spoken, but I don't understand. "What, are you a waitress or cleaner or something?" It's all I can think of when she explains they provide her accommodation and food for nothing, as well as making sure she's got money in her pocket to cover her expenses. "Shit, Jill. That sounds like a dream."

She stares into my face as though waiting for my reaction, then prepares to clarify her role. She straightens her back and shakes back her hair, then after a moment of silence, which I start to think she's not going to fill, she tells me the truth. "I'm what's called a sweet butt, Ella. I make myself available to the men…"

"You what?" My coffee spits out of my mouth and my eyes almost pop out of my face. "When you say…"

"I fuck them." Her eyes narrow, as if in challenge.

Using a napkin to wipe up my spilled drink, and then looking down into my half-empty cup, I try to process what she means. But the coffee provides no other interpretation than what she's just said.

"All of them? You're a *whore*? How can you do that?" My voice is low as I breathe the words out. To say she's shocked me would be the understatement of the year. Of the century, come to that.

She leans forward, her face splitting into a grin as she laughs. "Girl, how can I do that? Have you seen them around? Boy, are they something. And do they have some cock. Biker cock, babe. Best there is." The last she whispers conspiratorially.

I'm shocked but intrigued, and must admit, a tiny bit jealous. Going through a particularly dry spell myself, I'm becoming increasingly certain my girly parts are starting to forget what they were made for, I listen with my jaw dropping as she elucidates the reasons for her fascination with these men.

"They live fast, hun, on the edge. They don't bide by no citizen—that would be the types of you—rules. They fuck hard too. And there's this one, Tongue, well, he'll go down on you for hours and I can't even start to tell you what he can do with his stud." She glances at me, her eyes are half-lidded, her lips turning up in a smile. "Can't explain, El, what it's like to have such power over these men. I have them in the fuckin' palm of my hand."

She sleeps with all the bikers? I'm still trying to get my head around that. What if she doesn't find one or more attractive? "Do you get any say? What if you don't like one of them?" I take a sip of my now cold coffee to give my fidgeting hands something to do and my eyes something else to look at. My face burns red and it's not from the heat of the sun.

She looks smug and not overly offended by my inquisitive questions and shrugs. "It's no hardship. They all know how to fuck. So why not? I'm not ashamed to admit that I enjoy sex. Sure, one or two I might need to keep my eyes closed, but the rest. Mmm, mm. And if they're coming at you from behind it's their cocks that matter, not their face." Her eyes glaze over dreamily. "And sometimes there's one that prefers to keep to one girl, you know, you get to know what each other likes. And maybe in time there'll be that special one who'll make me his old lady." Her lips curl up as though she's putting them through their paces in her mind. "It's mind-blowing sex on tap, twenty-four-seven. What citizen boyfriend would be able to offer that?"

Certainly none I'd ever come across.

It's probably one of the strangest and most enlightening conversations I've ever had. And one it seems I'm unable to get out of my mind. Over the next few days I keep remembering how she'd shown no shame in being what I would term a whore. But then, my knowledge of prostitutes is limited to films like *Pretty Woman*, where girls sell their bodies on the streets to anyone who comes along, longing for a chance to get out of that life, preferably by being swept away by a millionaire. Or hookers needing money for drugs. What she'd described was something very different. While at the heart of it she's still selling herself, it is to a limited pool. And if she's right about them all being well-endowed and knowing what to do with their endowment, she probably sees more action in a week than I have my whole life. She certainly seemed to enjoy what she does. Hmm.

Her description of the way she lives gets stuck in my head. While remaining uncomfortable at the thought of being at the beck and call of a group of men—what if you weren't in the mood, for example? I find myself envying her as I compare her life to my own. Is the way I live so much more admirable? I've got a go-nowhere job in a sleazy bar and a shithole of an apart-ment I share with Tilly, my human companion, and several of the animal variety that I try not to think about. I've no man interested in me—if you exclude the shady offers whispered in my ear along with the drinks that I serve, and there's certainly been none which have tempted me to follow up.

The thought starts to sneak up on me. *Could I do what she does?* Of course I couldn't. *Don't be ridiculous.* I'm worth much more than that. Standing at the sink washing up after my messy housemate *yet again*, I dismiss the idea as outrageous. She's bound to have made it sound far more glamourous than it actually is, maybe as an excuse to justify how she's sunk so low.

So low? She didn't look like she was down on her luck. Her eyes sparkled with fun, and her clothes, while minimal, don't look like they've come from a thrift shop.

Me on the other hand? I just manage to scrape by.

You'll never amount to anything. Oh yeah, my mom never held back. Part of the reason I moved out of home, only to live a life which seemed to prove her correct. Glancing around me, I see it as she would. I'm living in a hovel—and even that's almost more than I can afford—with a woman I'm fast coming to dislike. If I'm going to get out of here I've got to do it myself, and I've limited options. I've no chance of fulfilling my dream and going to college, and even finding a new, better paying job has proved impossible.

I think back to the bikers I'd seen around town and a shiver goes through me at the thought of letting them do anything they want to me. What if, as Jill had suggested, there'd be that special man, that someone who'd want only me. *Maybe the biker who'd caught me in his arms that day?* Oh, it's obvious why he didn't find me attractive. Not when he'd got the likes of Jill back at base, ready and waiting.

Without really realising it's happening, the idea starts cementing in my head, justified the next time I meet Jill and enviously note the glow of satisfaction on her face, which certainly isn't on mine. Having now opened up, she revels in telling me such stories she makes my toes curl with her descriptions of the bikers and life on the compound. I find myself feeling jealous at the differences in our lives.

It takes just one more bad night at the bar, together with a re-examination of what little I've got, for me to summon up enough courage. At the coffee shop the next Saturday, I pick up my cup and speak over the top. "Are they looking for another girl?" As the words leave my mouth I immediately regret them, covering my lips with my hand. *I didn't mean to say that. I'm not whore material.* Surely I can't be that desperate? But the memory of the foul-breathed man who'd lent over the bar to grope me last evening reminds me that perhaps I am.

She doesn't seem surprised, just laughs and waves her hand. "You fancy yourself some biker cock, do you? Well," she looks me up and down as if seeing me for the first time, "you've kept yourself in shape. The men would definitely go for that rack." Her visual inspection makes me want to squirm. "I could ask for you. Be good to have you there, El. The others are okay, there's Chrissy, Pussy, and Allie, and they're alright, but we," she points to me then to her, "we go way back." She breaks off and then gives me a broad smile. "Yeah, I'll put your name forward and see how it goes." Her tongue flicks out to catch a stray drop of coffee as she leans forward and continues, "You'll probably have to come around as a hang-around first off."

"Hang-around?"

"Yeah." She shrugs, "We have girls up from Tucson every Friday night, sometimes Saturdays too." Her mouth twists as she continues, and her little frown shows me she doesn't approve of them very much. "The boys go with whoever happens to take their fancy."

That might be a good place to start. A chance for me to give them an informal interview as well as the other way around. A flicker of excitement warms me from the inside. Sex hasn't been anything great for me before. Oh, I've done it, sure. Many times, even had a few one-night stands. But now hearing about the type of experience she has with men who know how to use the tools God gave them, I suspect the ones that I've been with weren't so accomplished. When we part it's with her promise to float the idea back at the club.

What the fuck am I doing? I leave the coffee shop bemused. What the hell made me even ask? *Is this what I want out of life?* My mother would have conniptions. The thought makes me smile as I think of seeing her face. *You might not have thought much of me to start with, Mom, but just wait until I tell you I'm thinking of becoming a whore.* She'd have a fit. Or then again, maybe not. Sometimes I don't think she cares very much at all.

Returning home, I search with the remote until I find a rerun of *Sons of Anarchy* and settle back to watch, my mouth dropping open as the scenes play out. *There's so much fighting and violence.* Satan's Devils aren't like that, are they? *But oh, my. That Jax Teller.* Now if they were like him... I get engrossed by the way his tight ass moves as he fucks his old lady, muscles rippling as he drives into her, that rapturous look on her face. That night I use my vibrator.

Come the next morning, I take a real good look at myself in the mirror, lifting my boobs in my hands, and glancing down—they're firm, not too large, not small and perky though, and from this angle look a bit lopsided. Looking lower, my stomach's flat, my bush is neat and tidy, but don't men like that prefer it bare? Well I don't. Pursing my lips, I decide to give it a nice trim, but not go any further. Not unless I'm asked to. I move my eyes up again and bite my lip. Jill's so pretty, you could see why anyone would want her. Me? I decide after my inspection I'm very ordinary. Nothing special at all. Nothing to attract the likes of Jax Teller here.

Would they even want me? I'm suddenly nervous that even if I did get an invite to the club I may end up the girl sitting in the corner with none of the men showing any interest. Now that would be embarrassing. *You don't know until you try.*

Now that I seem to have made the decision and have taken the first step, I start to fear rejection more than acceptance. My life continues to slide downhill. Tilly's being more of a slob than ever, and I'm desperate enough to do just about anything to get out. The next time we meet I pester Jill almost before she's got her ass on the seat.

With a smirk, she assures me she's mentioned my name, but hasn't yet had a response. When we part I leave dissatisfied, knowing once my mind is made up, very little can change it, and the delay's only making it worse. The following nights I continue to pleasure myself, my inspiration that elusive biker cock.

CHAPTER 2

Ella

Four months ago

For the next week life goes on much as normal, my tedious job still as boring as hell. Excited and hopeful, I go to the café the next Saturday, but Jill doesn't turn up. Disappointed, I wonder whether anything's happened, but then convince myself it must be a sign they don't want me and she's too embarrassed to tell me to my face. And that's probably a good thing, isn't it? Am I really cut out for the sort of life she described at the Satan's Devils' club?

By the following Tuesday I've almost given up on the idea, when there's a knock at the front door. Flinging it open I'm expecting to find Tilly's latest layabout boyfriend and am about to give him a piece of my mind for forgetting his key, when I shut my mouth fast. It's no one for my housemate. Instead, to my astonishment, I see Jill standing there with a Satan's Devil's biker waiting behind.

After a wide-eyed nod to my friend I study her companion. My eyes go up, and up, eventually meeting the grinning face of one of the most striking men I'd ever seen in my life. Not classically handsome, and a bald head which I don't normally like, but with piercing blue eyes which seemed to see right through me. Full lips I just long to kiss. He leans with his hand on the top of the doorframe, his elbow resting on the side.

Rendered completely speechless, I stand with my mouth gaping like a fool.

"Gonna invite us in?" he prompts at last with a smirk.

After swallowing a couple of times I find the right words. "Yeah, come in. Er, it's not much." I step aside and look around, seeing the place as it would look to others. Secondhand furniture sourced from the thrift store, and not looking particularly clean. To call my housemate a slob is to give her a compliment, and after months of becoming tired tidying up after her, I'd become that way too. Dirty cups, glasses, empty bottles, and takeaway bags litter the floor. I feel shame at the way I've started to live. They pretend not to notice, and without making a fuss clear a space and sit down.

Once seated, the biker makes no attempt to hide his blatant visual inspection, his sharp eyes making me flush. *He's checking me out.* Although his intense gaze makes me uncomfortable, I realise it's all part and parcel of what I'm looking to become, and can probably expect more in the future if I make it through this first test. Hoping I will pass muster because, by Christ, if this is an example of who I'd have to make myself available to, I'll be all for it. Straightening my back, I ignore my discomfort and let his eyes roam.

In turn I'm giving him a good once-over too, coming to the conclusion I don't think I've ever met a man who made me feel so immediately turned on in my life. As his eyes lazily examine me, my underwear begins to feel damp, my nipples start peaking, and it's on the tip of my tongue to invite him into my bedroom to give me a trial run. Embarrassed, I look down, then dare glance at him again, and a shiver runs through me as my eyes drop to the apex of his jeans. Hell, Jill hadn't been lying. He's hiding one hell of a package under the denim. And it seems to be growing in front of my eyes.

"Like what you see?"

Going red, I turn away fast, hating I've been caught. I don't know where to look, or what to do with my hands.

"The name's Slick." He takes pity on me. "Jill, here," he nods at his companion, "said you're hankerin' to join us as a sweet butt. That right?"

He's certainly direct, and faced with the plain-spoken question I'm suddenly flummoxed. *Am I really going to admit I want to be a whore?* But as I step back my foot kicks at a bottle, it rolls away and hits the table leg with a thud, reminding me of my current circumstances. *Have I any other option?* Living like this isn't what I'd planned. Anything has to be better. And it's the handsome biker in front of me that helps me decide.

Being so tall, when Slick stands up he looms over me. Reaching out his hands, he wraps his large fingers around my arms. "Look, Ella, isn't it?" When I nod my confirmation he continues, "I need an honest answer." His eyes flick to Jill. "Sweet butts live at the club. We provide comfortable and," he pauses and looks around the room, his face wrinkling in disgust, "clean accommodation. And everything you need. You'll get money to spend. In return, you'll do whatever the brothers want from you. You'll become property of the club. In essence, that means you look after us, and we look after you." He finishes with a wink, leaving me in no doubt what he means.

Property? I'm not sure I like the sound of that. "What if I don't like what they want?"

He offers that panty-melting smirk once again. "Oh, I think you'll find you like it, darlin'. Look, it's fuckin' darlin'. You like to fuck?"

I've never heard it put so crudely. I gulp, and just about manage to nod my head.

"They'll expect you to give head. You up for that?"

Christ! He's being too frank. With a boyfriend I don't mind, with just anyone I'm not sure. I suppose I'd have to try. I bite my lip, not knowing what to say.

"Hmm. Well, most of us use condoms to be careful."

I raise my eyebrows. I'd expected I'd have to take charge of birth control. And I probably will, in case. Then it dawns on me why they use condoms. I'll probably be going from one man to another. Hastily I start to rethink.

He chuckles. "Biker fuckin', baby. It's not one sided. You'll come so many times you won't know which way is up."

And my traitorous womb clenches. *Just how many times could he make me come?* Once has been a bonus in my past.

My face must give my thoughts away. Another close examination, then he seems to come to a decision with a nod. Speaking over his shoulder, he throws out an instruction, "Jill, get lost."

Obediently my friend gets to her feet, she casts a look at me I can't quite interpret, picks up her jacket I hadn't noticed her take off, and steps to the door.

"Er…"

I'm not sure about this turn of events. *She's going to leave me alone with this big burly biker?*

She must notice my confusion, but she just shakes her head. "It's club business, and I can't be involved." Her eyes flick toward Slick. "You'll be fine with him, Ella. He just wants to talk."

I look in the same direction, only able to see this hunk of a man standing in front of me. *And if I want to do more? Who's going to protect him from me?* Shit, woman, get a hold of yourself.

He chuckles and seems to read my mind. "This isn't a practical, Ella. I won't be tryin' you out." Then his levity disappears and the corners of his mouth turn down. "There's a conversation we need to have."

15

Again, I look at Jill, but she simply shrugs. She looks puzzled as though this isn't the normal way they go about things, but what would I know? I've never previously auditioned getting into someone's bed before.

And she's going to leave anyway. His strong hands are still holding me, and I realise I don't have a choice. The door bangs behind her, and I'm left alone with a man I don't know.

Slick looks at me carefully, then gives a jerk of his chin. "Ella, I'll be straight with you. Usually you'd come to a party or two. If the brothers like you, and you're okay with their demands, then we'd talk about allowin' you to stay after that. But fuck it, this situation ain't fuckin' normal."

One of his hands moves down and wraps round my fingers. He encourages me over to the couch and sits beside me, his body twisting so he can look me in the face. "You're a good-lookin' woman, Ella. Wouldn't be any hardship havin' you in the club. You hear me?"

I jerk my head. *Is he offering me a job?*

"Jill reckons you're trustworthy. That right?"

Pleased that she's vouched for me, I tell him I am. Well, I always turn up on time and have never stolen anything.

"Won't kid you, Ella. You let slip one word of what I'm gonna tell you to anyone else, well, let's say it would probably end up being the last thing you say."

Another shiver, this time from nerves, and I try to pull my hand away. *I can't do this.* I've heard rumours about the club, anyone living in Tucson knows their reputation. They're not people you'd cross lightly.

"I don't think I want you to tell me anything more." What if I inadvertently gave something away, even if I don't mean to? Reading between the lines, he's just told me I'd end up dead.

Ignoring my protest, he continues, "We have a problem." Now he lets go of my hands, and rough fingers push a strand of my long auburn hair over my shoulder. For a second he glides it between his fingers. "We think you might be the person to help us. And in return, you get all the biker cock you could want."

I can't say he's not being forthright and upfront about everything. And there's a tingle of excitement that I could help them out. *Just think how might they reward me!* My conversations with Jill come into my head. *Oh, I'll take this man's cock any way he wants me to.* Even in my mouth. There's just something about him. A rush of arousal influences my response.

"Okay…"

"Okay," he parrots, putting his hand to his head, smoothing over the shaved dome, and is quiet for a while, then, "I said the situation isn't normal. Thing is Ella, we need someone just like you. We need an attractive woman to go into another club and plant some tiny cameras for us."

What? I look him straight in the face, trying to ignore that he called me attractive and focus on the more important part. Giving an incredulous laugh, I respond, "You're asking me to spy for you? I think you've got the wrong person, I'm not James Bond."

He snickers. This conversation might be easier if that sound didn't go straight to my already very wet nether regions. As he reaches for one of my hands and brings it to his lips, it's at that moment I decide whatever he wants me to do I'd do it, just for the chance to experience his undivided attention for the night. A niggling doubt at the back of my head reminds me it's usually men that are led by their dicks, and here I am letting my pussy have far too much influence on the matter.

"Ain't gonna kid ya. Going into another club? They'll expect the same as we would."

His deep voice affects me on some subconscious level, making me dream of being in his bed. And all I have to do to reach this utopia is go to another biker club, and, by the sound of it, break myself in on a different biker's cock. *But isn't that exactly what I was planning to do anyway?* But Slick, now I've met him… I don't want to lose the chance with *him*.

"If," I cough to clear my throat, which seems to have seized up, "if I do this, will you…?"

"Will I fuck ya, darlin'?" He gives a low laugh and his eyes rake my body, lingering unashamedly on my tits before coming back to my face. "You can count on that."

Before I can reconsider it, I blurt out the words, "You would? Even if I've been with another biker first?"

A strange look passes over his face before he recovers and laughs loudly. "I think you could say that's part of the job description, darlin'. No, it wouldn't matter one fuck to me."

Again, without thinking the words come out. "I'll do it." What? I'm not sure I meant to say that.

But his expression of pleasure means I can't take it back. "You will?" Sounding surprised, he turns my head to face him. "I can't tell you how much this would mean to my club." Then his smile fades. "Ella, I have to be honest with you. You do everything I say, else it could get dangerous. You'll need to be careful."

Dangerous? I don't like the sound of putting myself in danger. But I'm not one to go back once I've committed. I just mentally note I'll listen to his every instruction. "I will."

"Okay." He sits forward and clasps his hands between his knees. "This is how it's going to play out. The club we want you to go to is in Phoenix. We'll rent a small apartment in your name so it won't look like you come from out of town. We'll provide a small junker to get you to and fro."

So far it sounds brilliant. To get out of here, and to be given a car? Bring it on!

"You'll have to try and get into one of their parties. You'll need to look sexy for that." He glances at me again. "Not that you'll need to do much."

I preen at his compliment.

"The cameras are tiny. We want you to plant as many as you can. Shouldn't be too difficult, especially later on when they're drunk. Don't try to be clever, El. Don't be tempted go into their church." At my look of confusion never having thought bikers would be a religious lot, he explains, "It's where they hold club meetin's."

Ah.

It all sounds so simple, until I remember the catch. "I'll have to, er..."

"Yes, Ella. You'll have to fuck whoever wants you. But that won't mean anything, will it? It's no different to what you're wantin' to do for us."

That was before I met you. I don't say that out loud. Then I rationalise it. He's the first biker I've spoken to. Maybe my lady parts would start singing for another if they were anything like him. After a moment I nod.

"Ella, darlin'. You get can't get caught. If it's too risky, don't place the cameras."

"But if I don't, there's not much point to going there at all." I swallow and then put more force in my voice. "I won't let you down, Slick. I'll get it done."

"Don't take chances. They'll kill ya without turnin' a hair." His stare tries to impress that he's deadly serious.

Shivering, I stand and walk away from the couch, rethinking my hasty agreement. When I turn around I catch the look on his face. It's one of hunger, and is directed at me. I felt a twinge as my muscles clamp down. *He's so sexy it shouldn't be allowed.*

"What if they get suspicious?"

"Then get out of there right away. I'll be stayin' close, a phone call away. If you need to get out, or the moment you've been successful, I'll swing by and pick you up."

"You?"

He gives a quick grin. "Yeah, darlin'. I'll be there. And I won't leave you stranded."

I can only hope the flush on my face doesn't give away that the assurance of his personal attention pleases me far too much.

CHAPTER 3

Slick

Present day

"Hey, Beef!" Seeing him enter through the front door, I wave him on over.

"Slick." Giving a chin jerk, my brother crosses the busy restaurant, joining me at the bar at the Wheel Inn, the business that's owned by the Satan's Devils MC. Recently we purchased the building next door and have expanded, adding a bar where people can just come for a drink and get bar snacks instead of, or in addition to, having a full-on sit-down meal.

We keep a light presence here, just enough to make citizens feel safe, but not outnumbered, and not enough for them to think they were in a biker bar if they didn't already know.

Beef surveys the full tables around us and motions toward them with his hand. "Seems like we've hit it about right here."

He's not wrong, both bar and restaurant are heaving. A good crowd for a Saturday night. Some attracted, of course, by flirting with the edge of danger being in the rumoured biker-owned premises. And it's that thought that has my eyes returning to a woman who I've been watching for a while, debating whether she's here for that very reason. Her mode of dress seems to scream she may very well be out for a walk on the wild side tonight. And the glances she's been throwing my way suggest she's equally interested in me. If I'm reading it correctly, and I'm rarely wrong on these things, I'll be getting lucky later. Who am I to turn down something offered on a plate?

I nudge Beef. "Think I might have it fuckin' made tonight."

He barks a laugh as he looks over to where I'm pointing my beer. "I could so hit that."

"I'm gonna, Brother."

As he raises a quizzical eyebrow, I narrow my eyes. I was here first. Judging the situation correctly, he snorts and offers a good-natured grin. "Looks like it's the sweet butts for me, back at the compound. See you later, Brother, and don't forget to glove up."

As if I would. I'm never going to get caught in a trap. Nor have an old lady. Been there, done that, and won't be risking it ever again.

When Beef leaves I shoot the shit a little with the bartender, not wanting to approach too soon, which might make me appear too over keen or needy, using the time to pointedly survey all the women before making my move. I order another beer and ignore her for a time, while taking the opportunity to check her out in the mirror over the bar. When she starts to fidget and her face falls, it's then I drain my beer and go over.

As she looks up her face splits into a relieved smile. Checking I've read all the signals right, I lean down and speak into her ear. "Name's Slick. You want it?"

At her nod, I curl my hand round her arm and lead her through the now emptying restaurant, steering clear of the staff closing up for the night. Using the staff entrance at the back, I take her outside, pausing once in the fresh air to light up a cigarette. I offer the pack, but she declines. Blowing out smoke I notice her eyeing up my bike. *Woman, you've got no chance.* I'm not letting a skank I don't know anywhere near that—or any woman I do know for that matter. If she wants to experience biker cock it's going to be up against the nearest discreet wall which happens to be just around the corner of the building and where I'm leading her now. Yeah, I might have done this a time or two before.

"You ready for me sweetheart? Am I gonna find you wet?" I don't wait for her answer, just throw down my half-smoked light, the end burning amber on the ground. Her jagged breathing is the only encouragement I need, signalling her excitement at the coarse words I used. She gasps as I slide my fingers up under her short skirt and into her already dripping slit, every sign showing she's thoroughly turned on at the thought of such illicit activity.

I circle her clit, my fingers expertly slipping inside and finding that spot that will make her go wild. Her pussy's not exactly tight, but it will do for a quick fuck. She closes her eyes and her head rolls back as she spasms around my fingers. Okay, job done, that didn't take too long. Now for my turn. Undoing my jeans, I release my cock and have it covered with latex before her breathing evens out. I lift her against the wall, her legs go around my waist and then, without fanfare, I thrust inside.

She gasps and I grin. *Yeah, lady. That's what you wanted, wasn't it?* A long, thick biker cock. Holding her up with one arm, my other hand against the wall, I start thrusting, my balls already boiling with the need to come.

Fuck! That phone vibrating in my pocket alerting me to a text is putting me off my game.

There it goes again. And again. How many fuckin' people are trying to message me? *Shit, just give me a fuckin' minute will ya? I'm kinda in the middle of something here.* I try to ignore it, and hammer in once again.

Another vibration! Fuck, it better be something fucking urgent else someone's going to get their head torn off for this. And right now they can take that to the fucking bank. Frustrated, I let my cock slip out of her cunt.

"What the fuck?"

"Sorry babe. Gotta look at this." Easing my phone out of my jeans when they're shrugged down over my hips isn't easy. Swearing, I pull them up and finally succeed in sliding the damn thing out, my engorged angry dick knocking against my hand as if showing he's extremely unhappy about the interruption. Peering down I read the message which has already been sent half a dozen times by the prez, the VP, and a number of others.

Code Red. Followed by the name of a hospital in the south of Tucson.

Fuck! My cock instantly starts to deflate as I feel a sharp pain, like a punch to my gut. There's not enough information, and immediately I'm imagining the worst. Damn Mouse and his fucking insistence on using codes. Red means a brother is down, but gives me no clue as to who it is, or how serious. Quickly tucking my now flaccid cock away, I zip myself up.

"Slick?"

I look down at the woman whose name I didn't bother to discover, she's still leaning against the back wall of the Wheel Inn, her dress pushed up to her waist, her panties hanging off one ankle. "Sorry babe, gotta run."

Leaving her with her mouth gaping open, I run to my bike, step astride, take out and put on my safety glasses in a quick practiced move, the woman already forgotten. *Who the fuck has been hurt? And how badly?* Unable to consider it might be anything worse, starting the engine I roar off into the night, twisting the throttle and knocking up through the gears fast. Whoever it is, it must be serious, otherwise they'd have just called Doc to come to the clubhouse. This must be beyond anything the ex-Army medic can treat.

As I ride I think over what had been planned for today, but can't think of anyone who might have been heading into danger. No runs scheduled which would leave us exposed. Nothing had been discussed at church last night which had bothered us, or nothing out of the ordinary. No, today's been a usual Saturday, brothers relaxing and doing the shit that makes them happy. *What the fuck has happened?*

Arriving in record time, I'm chilled to see the number of Harleys parked outside the emergency room. *It looks like everyone's here.* Backing in on the end of the line, I switch off my engine and listen to the cooling engine ticking, rubbing my hand over the smooth bald dome of my head as I try to prepare myself for bad news.

Taking a breath, knowing I'll be getting no answers sitting out here, I get off and go toward the entrance, in two minds as to whether I want to hurry or not, not overly eager to hear what I suspect won't be good.

If you can believe what you see on television, you'd expect an emergency room to be a hive of activity—trolleys being pushed, people shouting orders, medical staff running around, patients bleeding over the floor, and relatives screaming and crying. But here everything appears to be orderly. There's even a couple of nurses standing chatting, laughing, and sharing a joke. My fists clench at my sides. If one of my brothers has been hurt, why the fuck aren't they doing anything other than hanging around? But causing a commotion won't help me get answers. I satisfy myself with a glare in their direction as I smartly step up to the reception desk.

I don't have to say anything. One glance at my cut and, with a look which I can interpret as thinly veiled disgust, the man behind the computer screen doesn't wait for me to speak before telling me in a bored voice, "Family room. Down that corridor, take a left, then third door on the right."

Suspecting it's not the first time tonight he's give the parroted instruction, I spin on my heels and follow the direction he's pointed. Opening the door, I notice immediately the room's far too small to comfortably hold the number of people waiting inside.

My eyes scan quickly, calculating who's here and who's missing, but with all the bodies milling around, sprawled over the available chairs and spilling onto the floor, it's not easy to immediately spot the omission. It looks like everyone's present, including the old ladies, and even little Amy, who's snuggled up on the president's old lady's lap. An undercurrent of low conversation comes across as a background murmur, and Carmen and Sandy are sniffling. Sophie's leaning against Wraith, her eyes rimmed red.

Drum's eyes flick to me and he raises his chin, then stands and comes over. I see lines etched deep on his forehead. "What, who is it, Prez?" My voice breaks with emotion.

With his hand on his beard, he gives a shake of his head and swallows before giving me the answer. "It's Heart and Crystal. They're in a bad fuckin' way."

"What the fuck?" My eyes widen. "What's fuckin' going on, Prez? What's happened?"

Now his hand touches my arm, a gesture of comfort. "We don't know what the fuck happened, Slick. They were out for a ride, citizen reported it in apparently. The bike was down, off the road, Crystal and Heart both unconscious. They haven't come round yet, far as we've been told."

Turning, I slam my fist into the wall, my breath catching in my throat. "Fuck, they gonna be okay?" But one look back at Drum and I know he can't reassure me. "Fuck." My eyes go to little three-year-old Amy. Both her fucking parents? Life wouldn't be so fucked up as to take them both away, would it? "Was it an accident...?" *Or did someone deliberately run them off the road,* I finish the thought in my mind.

The prez shakes his head when he speaks it's through gritted teeth. "We don't know anything. I'll take a couple of the brothers and run out there in the mornin' and see what we can find. The citizen who called it in didn't see it happen."

"I'll come with." If this was done on purpose the motherfucker who did it will pay.

As Drum jerks his head in recognition of my offer, Blade comes over, followed by Dart, and both nod at Drum. "We're goin' for a smoke. Wanna come, Slick?"

Having only just got here, I need a second to get my head around what's going on. But as I open my mouth to refuse the suggestion, a man in a white coat appears in the doorway.

"Family of Crystal Norman?"

Brothers stand up, or at least give him their attention. Drum takes the lead, his hand circling around. "That's all of us."

"That's me," a new voice interrupts.

From my vantage point by the doorway I see the doctor's been followed by a middle-aged woman. She's scruffily dressed, a woollen cardigan wrapped around her that's seen better days, dirty and worn with burn holes from cigarette ash. Her hair's in a mess as if it hasn't been brushed, and her face is pinched, her lips thin. I immediately dislike her.

"I'm Crystal's mother," she states as I finish making my inspection.

"Right, er..." The man, who I assume is a doctor, looks flummoxed.

"Any news, you tell us together." From the sneer on his face, Drummer cares about as much about the newcomer as I do. If she's not an addict I'll eat my fucking hat. The doctor pushes back his hair, at a loss what to do. He glances down at the woman and wrinkles his nose. Yup, he's caught a whiff of her too. I feel fleeting amusement expecting he's wondering what's worse, a roomful of bikers or this distasteful woman.

"Crystal," Drum prompts, using the voice no one with any sense would argue with. "How's she doin'?"

After a quick nod to show the prez's encouragement has worked, the doctor looks down and composes his face into the one he probably always wears when delivering sad news. When he peers back up he tells us, "I'm sorry to inform you that Mrs Norman didn't make it. There was excessive bleeding on her brain. We did what we could to relieve it, but she died on the operating table."

Female gasps and cries of despair, bitter denials from my brothers. I put my hand against the wall to hold myself up. *Crystal?* No! There must be some mistake. He must be wrong. My eyes go to Drummer, and then to Blade and Dart. The expressions on their faces must match the one on mine. *Crystal? Dead? I ate the breakfast she cooked only this morning.* Shaking my head in disbelief, I look behind the doctor to the woman who'd introduced herself as Crystal's mother, quickly realising there's far more emotion in the room than outside in the hall.

"You could have told me that on the phone," she sneers. "And saved me a trip down here." As she glares at the doctor she continues, "And what about that piece of shit with her? He dead too?"

His eyes widening, the doctor turns around. "Ma'am, we contacted you as you were on her records as her family. We need someone to identify the body."

"I'll do it." I don't know why I jumped in, but I had the sudden feeling I should be the one to do that service for my club brother, not this woman who clearly hadn't been distressed at hearing the terrible news.

The doctor looks sharply at me. "And you are?"

"Heart—Dale's brother." For me it's true in every sense of the word.

28

"Ah, her brother-in-law. That will be acceptable." He nods and seems relieved. I don't bother to correct his erroneous assumption, doubting he'll probe further. It's clear he's not too keen to spend longer in this woman's company either.

"What about her husband, Dale? Any news of him?" While Carmen's bitch of a mother had asked the question in a different way, Prez wants the answer we all need to hear.

"I'm sorry. I'm not treating him. I can't tell you anything."

Fuck. It's bad enough to lose Crystal, the vibrant young mother who not only loved and cared for her husband and daughter, but all of us in the club. To think I'm never going to see her cheerful, smiling face again. The thought tears me inside, and I'm not ashamed to say I feel my eyes leaking. *We can't lose Heart as well.*

Suddenly Crystal's mother pushes in through the door, squeezing past the doctor and pushing Drum aside. She marches into the room and stands in front of Sam and points to the sleeping child in her arms. "I'll take the brat."

"What?" Sam's arms tighten around Amy. "No. No way. She stays here with us." Sophie moves closer, looking prepared to physically help the prez's old lady keep hold of the child should the woman try to take her by force.

"I'm her grandmother. Her mom's gone, so she belongs with me." These are not caring words. She sounds cold and callous.

"Her dad is still alive. And until we know anythin' fuckin' different, she stays with us." Drummer's voice is low but fierce. He's going to allow no argument.

The raised voices have woken the kid. Amy looks up, her eyes bleary, little fists come up to rub them. Pain slams into me once more. How the fuck do you tell a child, just turned three, that she'll never see her mother again? Gazing up at Sam, Amy cries in her innocent high-pitched voice, "Where's mommy? I want my mommy." Well, even if she doesn't understand what's going on her distress isn't surprising, she's in a strange place at a time she should be asleep in her bed.

Sam's at a loss what to say and just shakes her head.

"Yer mom's gone. You're comin' with me."

"Gramma?" She might recognise her grandmother, but from the way she snuggles further into the protection of Sam's arms, she clearly doesn't have much liking for her.

Seeing the woman standing her ground, Drum steps close enough to wrap his hand around the scrawny arm of Crystal's mother. "Her parents left us in her care, and that's where she's fuckin' stayin'. At least until we know what's happenin' with Heart," he growls menacingly. I nod my head, he's made the right call. Letting that sweet little kid go with a woman like that? No fucking way. There's something off about her, and I don't just mean what I can smell.

With narrowed eyes, Crystal's mom silently challenges the prez. It's a battle of wills and, as I expect, Drum wins. She looks around and must see she's outnumbered. With a sneer, and a mumbled, "You haven't heard the last of this," she turns on her heels and goes out. I swear the air in the room becomes easier to breathe as soon as she's gone.

I watch as the doctor, still standing in the doorway, follows her with his eyes as she disappears down the hall. After a few seconds, he turns back and lifts his chin approvingly toward Drummer. Then, addressing me, says, "I'll get someone to let you know when Mrs Norman's been taken to the morgue. I'd appreciate you identifying her formally." And with that he leaves.

"What the fuck was all that about?" Blade's shaking his head.

But before anyone can answer him, the door opens again, and this time two people step in. Neither of whom I've ever seen before, but their air of suspicion immediately gives them away. It's the heat.

Drum's on the uptake as quick as myself, and from the stiffening of postures around the room, we're not alone. As they walk in their eyes glance warily around. The prez steps forward, immediately taking charge. "Drummer, President of the Satan's Devils." Then he waits.

"Detective Archer," the man starts, then indicates his companion, "and Detective Hannah." He pauses for the information to sink in. "There was an accident tonight out on the highway. A fatality and severe injury we understand. Members of your gang were involved."

"We're a club not a gang." Drum's eyes blaze in response. "And that's not news to us. Why the fuck else d'ya think we'd all be here?"

The man I take an immediate dislike to, the woman, Hannah, he'd called her, well, maybe I'm influenced by the fact I wouldn't kick her out of bed, or not too fucking fast, but she looks okay for a pig. She looks sympathetically at the women, who are crying, and when her eyes fall on the child her face softens.

And it's the female detective who speaks next, taking the lead. "Well, Drummer, we don't know much at the moment, such as whether there was any other vehicle involved. We need to find out if it's a case of reckless driving or whether there could a charge of manslaughter or murder. We're here as a courtesy to inform you we'll be investigating. It will help us to know any information you might have." She pauses and looks around. My brothers and I stare back with shielded expressions. She nods slowly. "Anything you may know could assist as we try to piece together what happened. We're taking this seriously. A young woman has died today."

Fuck, that's all we need. Fucking law investigating us.

When Archer opens his mouth I know I'm right to be concerned. My eyes half close as he says with a sneer, "Yeah, we need to know what enemies your, er, club's got."

I see Drummer take a deep breath before he replies, and in my view quite honestly, "We've no enemies that would run a brother off the road." Yeah, we had in the past, but not recently, or none I can immediately think of. My brow creases as I wonder whether there could be someone gunning for us. Could Heart have upset someone we don't know about? It seems unlikely. For a biker he's a mild-mannered man.

But even if there was, we'd handle it ourselves and not give any intel to the cops. Our methods of retribution would be quicker and more permanent than theirs.

Hannah's lips thin as she turns to her companion, and I get the impression there's something on which they don't agree. After staring at him for a second, she nods toward Drummer and passes him a card. "If you can think of anything that can help, that's where you can contact me." As Drum puts it in his cut without looking at it she adds, "Mr Norman's motorcycle is in our shop, we'll be assessing the damage."

"You'll let us know what you find?"

She points toward his chest and the pocket he's just secreted the card in. "My number's on there."

Interesting.

My phone rings as the police leave. Fuck, that thing's getting a work-out tonight. Taking it out, I see there's no number displayed. I hover my finger over the disconnect key, and then have second thoughts. With all the shit going around it's best that I answer. Going out in the hallway, half watching Archer and Hannah retreat, I answer. "Yeah?"

I grow cold as I recognise the voice, and it's the last fucking straw I need tonight. "Fuckin' get off the line, bitch. I've got nothin' to say to ya. I don't fuckin' care whatcha got goin' on. I ain't helpin' ya with fuckin' nothin'."

I end the call fast, leaning my forehead against the wall. Why, after all this time, is that bitch contacting me now? With Crystal gone and Heart's life hanging in the balance there couldn't be a worse fucking time for her to get in touch. Does she want to come crawling back to me? She's got no fucking chance.

Footsteps approaching have me turning fast. *Fuck, this place is busier than downtown Tucson at rush hour.* It's another damn doctor approaching. I step back inside, leaving the doorway free in case it's our room she's heading for. And it probably is, everyone else has made a beeline for it.

She acknowledges me with a tired smile as Drum crosses over. It looks like he's met her before. "Doc, any news?"

Her face looks grim, and I close my eyes. Not him too. No. That would be too much to fucking take. Not Heart. I can't lose my brother.

"Mr Norman's still with us," she starts, and when I glance over at what at first sounds like a positive update, I see she looks exhausted, lines on her forehead, her eyes reddened, cheeks flushed. "We lost him, but managed to bring him back." As she pauses she brushes back a strand of hair that's escaped from her bun. "I won't lie to you, it was touch and go for a while, and he's got a long way to go if he even manages to make it out of the woods." Her face looks full of sympathy as she adds, "I'm sorry to say this, but you should be prepared. He might not make it."

Dismissing her warning with a wave of his hand, as though he knows Heart will pull through, Blade asks, "What we dealin' with?"

She lifts her shoulders. "He's got a broken leg, broken ankle on the same side. Fractured ribs, he lost a lot of blood, and we had to remove his spleen. But it's the head injury that's worrying us. We've got him in an induced coma for now, and we'll keep him under for a couple of days while we try to reduce the swelling. When we bring him round we'll be able to tell a bit more." Breaking off, she looks around, her eyes taking us all in. Unlike the receptionist earlier, there's no judgement in her face. "Look, I can see the love you all have for him, and I assure you we'll be doing our best."

"Whatever it takes, Doc." Drum's hand brushes down his face, coming to rest on his salt and pepper beard. "Bring in consultants, don't worry about the cost. Transfer him to a specialist unit if you need to. The club will pay whatever." Murmurs of agreement meet his pronouncement.

A quick quirk of her lips, she replies, "That's good to know, Drummer. And we'll bear that in mind. For now I assure you he's in the right place. We'll know more… when he comes round."

The slight gap shows she was thinking if. My breathing falters. Heart. Heart's not only a member of the club, an officer, and our secretary. He's the one who's always there behind us giving silent support. He got his name for his gentleness, his generosity. As Crystal would have said, he's got a big fucking heart. And if his own stops beating, it will create a hole so big it will take us a fuck of a long time to recover.

The loss of any one of us would hit the club hard. But if we lose Heart? Some of the soul will go out of the club.

CHAPTER 4
Ella

Four months ago

In the seven days between meeting Slick that evening and him returning to pick me up, I must have rethought my impulsive decision a hundred or more times, not at all certain I'm cut out for a career in espionage. Entering enemy territory and infiltrating the club of the Satan's Devils' rivals? That's just not me. But it's difficult to back out as Slick keeps in touch by regularly calling, his wry humour and deep velvety voice resonating through me, helping me keep my resolve. When he emphasises how grateful he and his club will be, I can do nothing but lie and assure him I haven't reconsidered. Then when I put down the phone I have more second thoughts. But as time passes, it becomes too late to back out.

All too soon, Slick's plan gathers a momentum all of its own. Before I'm anywhere near ready, I find myself packing a bag, giving a mumbled excuse to Tilly to explain my absence for a few days, and opening the door to Slick. The first thing I notice as he leads me out to an SUV is he's not wearing his black leather vest with the colourful patch on the back.

It strikes me as significant. I've never seen any of the club's members without one before. Pointing at him I ask, "Where's your vest?"

He laughs, his rumbling chuckles having the predictable result. "It's called a cut darlin', and I'm drivin' a cage today. The club would fine me if I disrespected our colours and wore my cut while I'm drivin'."

"A cage?" My eyes narrow, it sounds like he is talking a different language.

"A car." He sighs. "Come on, it's a two-hour drive to Phoenix, we can talk on the way. Seems like you're needin' a bit of biker education before you go into the Rock Demons' club."

Buckling up the seat belt, I settle in to enjoy the journey. Listening to his deep tones washing over me is no hardship at all. Trying to remember everything he's telling me is a little more difficult. "Okay, so there's a president, officers, and non-ranking members. And prospects who do the drudge. Got it, I think."

My ignorance has been showing, but he's been patient with his answers. There so much to learn. Their way of life seems so very different, the strict hierarchy and rules alien to me. But by the time we get to our destination I feel about ready to take a text.

While I'm nervous about the end game, I'm also excited about what seems like a mini vacation. I'm going to have a couple of days in an apartment I don't have to share with anyone else, and where the furniture is clean, if not new. I wave away Slick's apology for the sorry excuse for a car they're providing. As I've never owned one, having any vehicle to myself even if it's only a heap, and just for a short time, it feels like I have true independence at last. In Tucson, I borrow Tilly's if she's not using it when I need to go out. Which means I rarely have the opportunity to drive.

Slick drops me off, hands over the necessary keys that I'll need, then quickly leaves. As I watch his tail lights disappear I feel a moment of loneliness, and concern returns as to what I'm doing. *Treat it as an enjoyable break.* Following my own good advice, I decide to make the most of it and, going inside, get unpacked and settled in. Noticing the cupboards are empty, I venture out into what he'd assured me is a relatively safe neighbourhood and, with the money he gave me, I buy food. Returning home, I cook a half-decent meal for myself. And wash up my own plates and pans immediately afterwards.

For those first few days I'm happy. Slick stays away, not wanting to risk being seen visiting, but checks in by phone. As far as I know he's holed up in a nearby motel.

The time on my own passes quickly. Too quickly. Come Friday evening I'm a bundle of nerves as I doll myself up, slapping on more makeup than I usually wear. I open the bags of new clothes that I'd bought and put on the sluttiest things I can find. A short skirt that's almost indecent, and a tight top without a bra. When I lean over to look in the mirror while applying bright red lipstick, my boobs spill out of the top. Just the right look I've been trying to achieve, but one I'm not entirely comfortable with.

I pause, blusher in hand, gazing at my reflection. *I'm going to get laid tonight. By a biker.* But with surprise as I realise whatever Jill said, the tantalising picture she'd drawn has become tarnished. I don't want any old biker cock, the idea of allowing strangers to pore over me no longer appealing. The reason for my change of heart is simple—the only biker I want is Slick. Fuck! What am I doing? I won't be able to go through with this. I must tell him...

I can't. If I back out now I won't get to have him. I'd be letting down both him and his club, which will hardly endear me to him. And if I go through with it, any attraction he has toward me might disappear—I'll have slept with his enemy after all. It's a wicked conundrum. I'm damned if I do or if I don't.

In the end it's the thought of letting Slick down and how disappointed he'll be that provides the incentive. His club is depending on me to carry this through, and it must be important for them to stoop to asking a virtual stranger to help. Slick's got confidence I can carry this off. And how hard can it be? There might be a way to plant the cameras without having to get close to any of the men. And if not, there must be someone there who would tempt me. They're bikers after all. Maybe there'll be someone just like Slick? After all, he's the only biker I've spoken too. And in Jill's view, they've all got something to offer. But despite my pep talk, my lady parts remain dry, my nipples drawn tight against my breasts. *I don't want to do this.*

I've left myself no choice. The Satan's Devils have housed me, temporarily given me a car, a taste of freedom such as I've rarely enjoyed. They've given me money for food and for clothes, a short space of time where I'm not afraid to open my wallet. If I don't go ahead with this I'll anger both Slick and his club. I shudder, realising I wouldn't want to know what would happen to me if I pulled out. *I know too much about their business.*

I ring Slick just before leaving, needing to hear his voice, while a large part of me hopes he'll offer me a reprieve. "I'm going in now." I hold my breath, waiting for him to give me the chance to abort.

But he's fixed on the plan. "Be safe, Ella. Don't take any fuckin' chances. And remember, let me know as soon as you're out. We're relyin' on you, darlin'. I know you can do this."

His voice and his confidence bolsters me, but the mission's an obvious go, and my brief newfound courage wears off almost as soon as I put down my phone.

With shaking hands on the steering wheel, and my foot slipping the clutch as I fumble with unfamiliar gear changes, I managed to get to the club and eventually find a place to park.

My hands tremble as I lock the car, leaving it in a side street with a pang of regret. If my assignment's successful I'll not be driving it again. *Slick will be driving me home.* That's the thought that encourages me most. Just a few more hours, then when the cameras are planted I'll be on my way back to Tucson. *With Slick.* Just the evening to get through, surely there can't be too much problem with that?

My stomach churns with nerves as I approach the building ahead, a tumbledown warehouse which has seen better days. *It's a biker club.* And all I've got to do is go in and flirt. They'll do the rest. Then I'll hide the tiny devices currently hidden in my fuck-me-heels and get away fast. That doesn't sound like much work.

Walking up I slow, apprehensively eying the number of Harleys parked up. Then with a deep breath to fortify myself I step forward. Exuding a confidence I don't feel, I come up to the entrance, tagging behind another scantily clad female entering ahead of me.

"Hey, you. You're new."

An arm whips out to block my way. I stop and tilt my head to one side, giving the man a flirtatious smile. I lick my lips with my tongue. *I can't fail at the first hurdle.*

My actions have the desired effect. He laughs and steps aside, waving me past. And as easy as that I walk in through the gates of hell.

Early the next morning I dislodge the heavy arm holding me captive, carefully trying not to disturb the sleeping body snoring by my side. I'm grabbing my clothes when, to my dismay, the man wakes up and stirs, his eyes watching me suspiciously.

"Where ya goin'?"

It hurts to breathe, but I try to keep it together as I answer, "I've got to ring my mom. She likes me to check in."

Fuck knows they must be used to this, using women so cruelly. He doesn't say anything, just allows me to move, then turns over and almost immediately the rasping snores start ringing out again. Moving silently and painfully, checking no one else is stirring, I go behind the bar and plant the miniscule cameras I've removed from my shoes.

Then I ring Slick, praying he'll answer the phone.

Another biker appears, he's standing with his arms folded, mistrustfully listening to my call.

"Mom, I... Oh, my. Are you alright? I'll come now."

Turning to the onlooker, I shrug. "My mom's real poorly, she's had a fall. I've got to go to her."

Shaking his head as though he couldn't give a damn, he turns away. Holding my shoes in one hand, I tiptoe around sleeping bodies, making my way outside, pausing to gulp as much sweet-smelling air into my lungs as I can. It's not much, I'm too sore to take deep breaths.

I tentatively nod at the prospect manning the gate, relieved when he slides it open allowing me to pass. I see the black SUV waiting just a little way down the road.

Expecting shouts to come after me any moment, I force myself to walk calmly, hiding my pain both inside and out, concentrating on putting one foot in front of the other. I stagger slightly as I come to the door. It's opened from the inside, and awkwardly I ease myself in.

My words tumble out of me, my tone full of hate. "Just tell me, Slick, whatever you're doing. You're going to rain Satan's wrath on those fuckers back there."

He gives me a sharp look as he wastes no time moving off. "What the fuck did they do to you, Ella?"

I can't tell him. "Let's just say they were rough."

Thumping the steering wheel, he jerks his foot on the throttle making the car lurch forward. I let out a groan.

"You're hurt." It's a statement, not a question, he can see that I am. "Ella, I'm so fuckin' sorry." His voice is full of regret.

"It's done, Slick. I did what you asked me to do." I sound emotionless.

"I didn't want them to harm you." Glancing sideways, I see he's gripping the steering wheel so hard his knuckles are white. Then he tells me through gritted teeth, "You're gonna be alright, Ella."

It's a platitude, a weak promise that he'll be unable to follow through. I don't think I'll ever be alright again.

"Just take me home, Slick."

"No can do, darlin'. You're comin' back to the compound until we finish our business with the Demons." He takes his hand off the steering wheel and squeezes mine. I flinch, rubbing my fingers as though to wipe away his touch. Slick growls as he notices and slams his hand back on the wheel.

"Fuck!" he swears loudly, but I know he's not cursing at me.

Another few miles pass. "Ella, we owe you one fuck of a lot." His eyes flick toward me before returning to the road. He doesn't miss the way my mouth is pursed, my arms folded protectively over my middle. "Don't worry, darlin', we'll get Doc to the club. He's a medic and will look after you." He mutters something inaudible under his breath.

For the remainder of the journey we drive on in silence, me lost in my pain, him in simmering anger. When we arrive at the compound I start to shiver as the gates slide shut behind us, locking me in. The last place I want to be is in another biker club. I'd much prefer to take my chances at home.

Slick parks the car and, coming around to the passenger side, offers a hand to help me out. I'm biting my lip, my eyes wide open and looking around, then anchoring back on him as though he's my rock.

His brow creases as he senses my uneasiness. "Look, darlin', I know you'd rather go back to your place. But it's possible they clocked you plantin' the cameras, and we want to keep you safe. We owe you," he repeats, then gestures to my ribs. "Stay until you feel better. Least we can fuckin' do for ya. I promise we'll keep you safe."

I'm scared of being here, but his suggestion the Phoenix club might find the cameras I planted and come after me is just as terrifying, if not worse. Now I know just how much Jill had misled me, at this point I'll be happy if I never see another biker for the rest of my life. My teeth start chattering even though warmth of the sun is permeating the car.

"Come on. Let's get you looked at. Doc should be here soon." Slick tries to encourage me, his voice is gentle but his jaw is set.

"Slick, I..." *I can't, I'm screaming inside.* I don't want to take a step into his club.

"Come," he urges again, indicating the building we've parked alongside, drawing my attention to it for the first time. Even from my quick glance it's obvious the Satan's Devils clubhouse is a million miles away from the one I went to last night. Bizarrely, the front façade resembles a foyer and reception of a hotel. Apart from the row of Harleys parked outside, it doesn't look much like a home for bikers.

The striking difference is what gives me the courage to get out of the car. Slick puts his hand to my back to encourage me inside. I pull away, preferring to move of my own volition. Once through the doors he leads me over and seats me on the couch. My shoulders are hunched over, protecting my ribs, and my right arm is hugging my stomach. My cheek throbs from where I was hit.

"Hey, VP, come 'ere a sec." Slick's voice washes over me. As I hear footsteps approach he continues, "Wraith, this is Ella."

A stranger hunkers down in front of me, lifting his hands as if to push back my hair to get a better look at my face. I flinch before he can touch me, and then feel Slick putting his arm around me possessively, and I shudder at his touch. He lets me go immediately.

"Sorry, darlin'," the man called Wraith says to me, then looks up at Slick. "She get caught?"

With a shake of his head, Slick tells him, "No. She did what she went there to do. Cameras should be transmittin' now well enough. This," he waves his hand down to emphasis the state that I'm in, "this is just how they treat their women."

Their VP swears softly, then asks, "Doc look at her?"

"I've called him, he's on his way in. Reckon you've got a broken rib, don't ya, babe?"

I nod and Wraith growls, "Fuckin' bastards." Turning back to Slick, he asks, "Told Drum yet?"

"Haven't had a chance, I was just goin' in to see him."

Suddenly the clubroom doors swing open, and in walks a familiar face. As soon as she sees me Jill runs over, her eyes widening in horror as she takes in the state I'm in. When she demands to know what happened, I make something up on the spot.

"I was mugged."

"Oh, Ella!" She goes to hug me, but mindful of my ribs I back away.

"You take care of her," Slick tells her. "I'm off to see Drum. Doc will be here in a bit. Get her set up in my room, got it?"

His room? No! But before I can protest he's disappeared down a corridor. One by one bikers follow him, and I suspect they've got some kind of meeting. Probably to discuss the devices I'd planted. I should be proud of myself for having completed my task, but I'm not. Success had come with far too high a cost.

Jill leaves instructions with a biker manning the bar to have Doc follow us, and then helps me walk to a bloc further up the compound.

"Where did it happen, Ella? Did you have much taken?"

I wouldn't be in this state had I not listened to her, and I'm mindful I need to keep quiet on all that had happened. I shudder, remembering Slick's threat if I disclose anything that he told me—if he'd wanted her to know, he wouldn't have sent her away that night. I ignore her inquisition as we walk past interlinked units and, to take my mind off the pain, and hers off my predicament, I ask about my surroundings.

"What is this place?"

"It's an old vacation resort," Jill informs me. "A fire destroyed it, the club bought it up cheap and rebuilt. Each of these units has two suites. Up the top there's some houses as well, where I live with the girls." She pauses for a moment. "Not sure why Slick wanted you in his room and not with us."

As I glance at her face, she seems to be frowning. "I'd rather be with you," I gasp out. The last thing I want to do is stay with a biker who might expect to make good on his promise to reward me for the job I'd done. But then again, I don't want to stay with the sweet butts and give the wrong impression.

When the slight incline makes me winded and I have to stop, her expression turns to one of concern. "Look, Slick's is the next unit. He shares it with Wraith. Or did, before Wraith got an ol' lady. He's got it all to himself now. Not far to go."

Staggering on the last few steps, I follow her in through an entrance. She opens one of the two doors and I get a first look inside. Slick's huge room looks clean and tidy. It's dominated by a large bed, and there's a desk, a wardrobe, and a couple of comfortable looking chairs by a window. Outside there's a balcony looking over the desert. While not in the state to appreciate it, I can tell it's a glorious view in a beautiful spot. You can see for miles. Right over to a range of mountains in the distance. "Chair or bed?" she asks as I pause before entering.

"Chair," I respond, not knowing how long Slick will be and not wanting to look like I'm issuing an invitation if he finds me lying flat out. "I won't be staying here. I'll be off home later after I've been fixed up." *I can't stay. Being in the compound's bad enough. Slick's room is even worse.* And any notion of being a sweet butt has been knocked on its head. Despite Slick's warnings, my fear of him and his Satan's Devils brothers outweighs the unlikely possibility that the Rock Demons could find out who I am or where I live.

A rap at the door and a man enters. He's not wearing a cut, although he's dressed as a biker. He's carrying a bag in his hands.

"This is Doc." Jill confirms my suspicions.

With a nod to her, wasting no time, he comes over. Gentle hands touch my face, becoming insistent when I try to back away.

"Easy, sweetheart. Just let me see what I'm dealin' with here." He holds my chin in one hand, probing my cheek with his other. "Nasty bruise here, darlin', but yer cheek bone's intact. Now where else are ya hurting?"

"I think I've broken a rib."

"Can I see?"

Jill's face seems full of encouragement, clearly seeing there's nothing wrong with his request. As he is acting so professionally, I slowly lift my t-shirt, exposing the darkening area on my ribs. He looks into my eyes, his head tilted in question. Preparing myself with as deep a breath as I can, I let his hands probe lightly, unable to suppress a squawk of pain.

"Hmm, I think you've definitely broken a couple, and that must be painful. I'll give ya some painkillers."

"Gonna strap them up?" Jill asks.

He shakes his head. "Strappin' can do more damage than good," he tells us. "They'll heal on their own if you just take it easy. If you cough or sneeze, try and lean forward to keep the pressure off, okay?"

Jill's looking concerned. "I thought they had to be taped or something." She frowns as though she doesn't think he's doing his job properly.

With another dismissive shake he says, "Tape them up and you could force a jagged end into the lungs. I know it looks like I'm doing nothin' for ya, but here time will be your best healer. And being careful. Do ya work?"

"In a bar."

"You'll need to take time off and rest."

"She will, Doc." My eyes widen as I hadn't heard Slick entering. My heart begins to beat faster as he enters the room, but it's not with desire. It's with terror. *What will he expect from me?* Back at my house I'd all but begged him to fuck me. Now that's the last thing I want. I shudder.

"Are you hurtin' anywhere else?" Doc's watching me carefully, and I hide the lie as I deny any other injury. Then he rummages in his bag and pulls out a box. "Painkillers. Take two now and two in four hours. Call me back if you need me." His face creases with sympathy. "I know it hurts, darlin', so you get some rest. Okay?"

Slick slaps him on the back. "Thanks Doc. Dollar will sort your bill out as normal."

As the medic leaves, Jill hovers as though she's not sure whether she should stay or not. Slick doesn't keep her waiting long before saying, "I'll take it from here, Jill."

I don't want her to go, don't want to be left alone with him. But having learned only too well what happens when you speak back to a biker, I'm too scared to contradict him and ask her to

46

stay. My eyes follow her as she departs, lingering for a second on the closing door.

And then return to Slick, who's watching me carefully as though trying to interpret the expression on my face.

After a moment he opens a mini-fridge and extracts a bottle of water. "Here." He offers it to me along with two of the painkillers. I take them, but don't swallow them. I'm sore and tired, and I suspect they'll be strong and probably put me to sleep. And I'm in a strange man's room. *A biker's room.*

He raises his head and closes his eyes, and then comes and kneels in front of me, his hands going either side of my chair. "You had a rough night, darlin'. And the last thing you want is another man fuckin' touchin' you. I ain't stupid, I can see that." Slowly he shakes his head. "Truth is, I didn't have it much easier. I didn't sleep worryin' like fuck about you." His fingers stretch out and gently brush against the bruise on my face. "You don't know how hard it was imaginin' what could be happenin' to yer. I wanted to rush in there and drag ya back out."

He was worried about me? Oh, how I wish he had come and rescued me. *He thought he had it bad?* He should have tried being me. My lips purse and I glare. Quickly I try to hide my expression.

His piercing blue eyes give me such a scrutiny I think he must see down to my soul. "There's somethin' you're not tellin' me."

Trying to deny it, I shrug then wince. "I told you, they were rough." And that's all I'm going to admit. The sooner I can forget what happened, the better. *Forget?* I'll never forget.

"I've spoken to Drum, that's our prez. He and the brothers appreciate all that you've done. And it wasn't for nothin'. Everythin's workin'. Because of what you've done, the Rock Demons will get what they fuckin' deserve. And that's the last I can tell you about that." Standing, he holds out his hand. "I'm

47

fuckin' dead, woman. I just need to sleep. And I need to have you beside me to know that you're safe." He points to a closed door. "That there's a bathroom, go shower or just change. I'll give you one of my shirts to wear and then we're going to bed."

I recoil, and he notices. Both hands go up and smooth over the dome of his head, "Fuck, I'm not a bastard, Ella. You're hurt and sore and fuck knows what else. I'm not takin' advantage of you. I truly just want to sleep."

Scanning his features, there's nothing to suggest he's not being honest. He looks so tired, almost broken, that it makes me believe him. And boy, do I want a shower to wash all the filth away. Hoping I'm not doing the wrong thing, I give in. Unable to ignore the pain any longer, I at last swallow the tablets, then pull my sore body up, pause briefly waiting for the dizziness to go, then, moving crouched over, go into the bathroom. I have the water far too hot and stay under it far too long. My skin looking pruned and covered with his shirt—which reaches down to my thighs—I return to find he's lying on one side of the king-size bed, fully clothed and leaving more than sufficient space for me.

The painkillers and the long hours I've been awake, combined with stress, makes the bed look inviting. Trembling, I lie down beside him. Although he's not touching me, I can feel the warmth of his skin radiating toward me and, despite my trepidation, strangely it's a source of comfort not to be alone. I close my eyes. Quickly flicking them open again to check he hasn't moved. Little snuffling noises show he's already sleeping. Reassured, I give in, unable to stay awake any longer.

I wake to sun blazing through the windows and the sound of voices murmuring.

"What took you so long?" Slick growls, and then speaking over the excuse. "Now get out of here, Prospect." At odds with his angry tone, he chuckles as the door closes. Seeing I'm awake, he walks across with two steaming mugs. Even from here I can smell they must contain coffee. "Got to keep 'em on their toes," he explains. At my look of confusion he continues, "Prospects do shit for us to earn their patch. Keep forgettin' you don't know our world yet, darlin'."

And I never want to. I try to sit up, my ribs seem to have seized during the night.

Putting down the mugs he comes over, his hand reaching out, then stopping in mid-air. "Gonna put my arm around ya, help you up."

The alternative is to lie here as boneless as a jellyfish, so accepting his assistance, I nod. His touch is so gentle, giving just enough support that I can get my butt under me. He places a pillow behind my back and puts a coffee within reach alongside the painkillers.

"I'm not staying here, Slick." My voice sounds weak, even I don't recognise it as mine.

But he's not having it. "We've been over that, darlin'. You're stayin' until we can guarantee there's no blowback from last night. Couple of weeks should do it. And you need lookin' after. Until you're on yer way to healin'."

If I stay I'm terrified of what they might want me to do. I put him straight right away. "I'm not going to be a sweet butt, Slick." Last night with the Rock Demons proved I wasn't cut out to be a whore.

His eyes open wide. "Fuck, Ella. I know that." He pauses, brushing his hand over the smooth dome of his head. "I've told the brothers that too." Pulling up a chair to the side of the bed, he sinks onto it, and puts his head in his hands. After a couple of seconds he looks up. "Thing is, El, we have two types of women here. Ol' ladies and sweet butts. Don't have nothin' in between. If you're in the club you're in one of those categories."

"Then I obviously can't stay."

He gives a half-smile. "Yeah you can."

"Slick…"

"Listen to me. Ella, I've claimed ya."

I straighten up fast, ignoring pain lashing through my ribs. "You *what?*"

"Thing is, Ella, I reckon there could be somethin' between us." He points at himself and then at me, "I liked ya from the first time I met ya. Already know I don't want any of the other fuckers near ya. So I claimed ya as my property so they'll keep their hands off."

I start pushing myself up, wanting to get away. My head swims but I fight through the pain.

"Where the hell are ya goin'?" Slick stands, his hands coming out to steady me. Trying to evade him, I fall back down on the bed, trying to smother the yelp of pain.

"I've got to get out of here, Slick. I can't… I'm not ready."

His eyes narrow. "Hey, hey. I'm not going to push ya. You think I'll take advantage when you're in this fuckin' state?" His hands slide over his shaved head. "Don't reckon you've told me quite everything, but I can tell you're scared. No need to be afraid of me, darlin'. We take this slow, take as long as ya want. Can't deny my cock wants in ya, but I'm prepared to wait. Let your ribs heal. I didn't touch ya last night, did I? I ain't gonna force ya. Fuck!" He seems disappointed that I even thought that he would.

I move my head from side to side. He didn't, and I trusted him not to. But what's he telling me? "What do you mean you've claimed me? If I'm not a sweet butt…" I go back over what he's said. "That would make me an old lady."

"Damn right it does. You're *my* ol' lady. But we'll go at your pace, El. I'm in no rush. But I want you here, in my room. Okay?"

That seems to mean he's given me his protection. What he doesn't understand is the thought of any man touching me makes my skin crawl. Even him.

My lips purse. "If I stay, Slick, I can't give you anything."

"Understand how you're feelin', darlin'. I promise, no pressure. We'll go at your pace." I try to interpret the look in his eyes. *Does he mean it?*

This conversation is far from finished, and I'm still miles away from being convinced. *What if my pace is never?* But it's brought to an end as we're interrupted by the sound of giggling and female voices outside the door. Flicking my eyes to him in surprise, I see the corners of his mouth turn up. "Wondered how long they'd be able to stay away."

"Sweet butts?" I ask him, seeing if I can recognise Jill's voice.

He laughs. "No. You're an ol' lady now and won't be mixin' with the likes of them." Getting off the chair, he opens the door and speaks to the unknown women outside. "Come in and meet Ella, reckon she'd like some company." He ushers them in. "El, this is Sophie, she's our VP's woman, this 'ere is Sandy who's Viper's... Fuck, are all of ya here?" He moves over to give them room. "Come on in. Crystal, she's with Heart, and Carmen who's with Bullet." He stands back as they pile in, and wipes his hand across his head, turning to me with a wink. "Fuck this, I'm out of here. Reckon I'd lose my man card if I stay."

And that's how I meet the rest of the old ladies, of which I'm now apparently one of their number. They're welcoming and friendly, sympathetic, but don't allow me to wallow in my pain. From those very first introductions they take me under their wing, teaching me all I need to know about the club. At first taking turns to keep me company then, as I heal and no longer have a reason to hide in Slick's room, they force me down to the clubhouse. I always stay close to one of them, and avoiding the main room I keep to the kitchen, out of the way of most of the men. The women are good company, and one's normally cooking. Unused to doing nothing, I start to do what I can to help.

After the few times I tried to escape before the men came in for their food, the women make me stay back and start introducing me to the other members. Although I'm treated with respect, deep down I remain suspicious and unwilling to trust any of them. As soon as they appear I try to find an excuse to make myself scarce. There's a deep-seated fear inside me I can't shake, however pleasant these men are to me when the old ladies are around, I remain suspicious what would happen if I was around them without female protection. I've seen exactly what bikers are like.

And that's not how Jill sold them to me. Almost daily I wish I'd never bumped into her or listened to her tall tales. As my wounds heal I blame myself and am angry with her. How easily she'd misled me. But I've no chance to vent my feelings, she stays out of my way, in fact going so far as to walk off in the other direction rather than meet me face to face. *Is she aware it was her overblown stories that got me hurt?* Whatever it is, since that morning she'd taken me to Slick's room she seems to have lost any sympathy she showed for me then. She sticks with the rest of the sweet butts, and when I appear she turns away with a sneer.

Slick makes good on his promise not to rush me into a more intimate relationship. But as the days pass, I notice his hungry eyes watching me more and more. It won't be long until he pushes me for something I'm unwilling, *unable* to give.

One morning, two weeks after I arrived at the compound, I'm in the kitchen at the clubhouse turning some bacon and Slick's arm snakes around me. Unable to help myself, I flinch.

"Fuck, El, I'm sorry. Your ribs must still be tender." Then he lowers his lips to my ear. "If you're on top I won't hurt you." He licks the outside of my ear and I shudder. I pull away without responding, feeling his eyes burning into my back.

He moves closer again, when he speaks I realise he's misunderstood my reaction. "El, the brothers and I are going out." I've heard the gossip of the old ladies more used to club life, and have picked up the men have been planning. It comes as no surprise, and not a little relief that they're going out on a run. "When I get back, reckon we could see what we can do without hurtin' ya."

"When will you be back?" *How long have I got?* Proud my voice doesn't sound as shaky as I feel, knowing my time is now up. *I'm leaving today. Before he tries to pressure me. Before he gets impatient and uses force.*

"As soon as I can. And then we'll have us some fun, eh, El?" He seems pumped up and excited.

About what's happening today, or what he hopes for later? I nod insincerely.

Taking my expected place alongside the other old ladies, I watch as one by one the bikes pull out. Muted conversations show the women are feeling nervous, but selfishly I don't join in. Instead I start making my plans. When the roar of engines fade, the compound seems deserted. Only the prospects— Marsh and Spider—and Adam and Mouse have been left behind. Although most of the men have gone, the women carry on as usual, only the worried looks they're exchanging showing something's different about today. Following Carmen and Sandy into the kitchen where they start preparing a casserole, I continue plotting how soon I can leave. *I need to summon a taxi…*

Lost in my reverie, I jump as the door to the kitchen bursts open. Men wearing masks and carrying guns rush in. We're quickly surrounded, gloved hands going over our mouths. It all happens so quickly. Like the others, I struggle, pain blasting through my ribs. They're strong men and soon overpower us, injecting something into our veins.

The brothers have returned by the time I've come round, horrified to learn while the other women and I have been unconscious, Adam's killed, Mouse is injured, and Sophie has only just escaped with her life thanks to Spider's sharp shooting.

After Doc gives us all the okay, Slick fusses over me. Nothing I can say will make him leave me alone—until I manage to get rid of him on some pretext, coming up with the idea of sending him up to his room to find my painkillers. The ones I've actually got in my pocket. Although the effect of being drugged is still making me woozy, I pluck up the courage go to find their president.

Drummer looks tired and drawn, having lost one of his men. It seems like he's got the weight of the world on his shoulders. I feel selfish at intruding, and start to lose my nerve. But he sees me hovering by the door and gives me a weak smile.

"Ella. I'm sorry for what went down this mornin'. We had no fuckin' idea…"

I stop him right there. "It's okay, Drummer. I'm fine. Doc said there'll be no lasting effects, and I know you couldn't have expected it. But…" As I break off and bite my lip he waves to encourage me.

Taking a deep breath I tell him, "I want to go home."

He stares at me for a moment, his eyes open in surprise. "Well, there's nothing stopping you now. If you want to, you can. Any threat from the Rock Demons been removed." As I wonder what exactly they did to know that, he continues, "You know Slick won't like it?"

I nod, understanding that only too well. But if I don't leave he'll only expect more, and I've nothing to give. "I can't stay here Drum, I have to leave."

Another intense scrutiny, followed by a frown. "Look, I know what went down today must have been upsettin'. It's not usual, you know?"

I just return his intense stare and hide my shaking hands by my side. "Ella, don't wanna keep you here if you don't want to stay. But talk to Slick first."

That's the last thing I want to do. "I can't, Drum. Just help me to leave, please? The club owes me, doesn't it?" And this is how I want them to repay me. Letting me just make a clean break and leave, with no messy arguments.

He doesn't look happy, but he nods slowly, realising I'm calling in that favour they promised to pay back. He sighs. "If you're certain, I'll get Marsh to drive you. Boys and I will be in a meetin'," he adds, giving me that window of opportunity I need.

And that's how I escape without saying a word.

CHAPTER 5
Slick

Present Day

Along with my brothers I've reluctantly accepted that Heart being in an induced coma means there won't be any change in his condition anytime soon. Albeit a decision made reluctantly, there's no point in everyone hanging around. With the exception of Shooter, who was first to volunteer—fuck, we wouldn't be leaving my brother alone even if he wouldn't know anyone was there—we all ride away from the hospital, the roar of Harleys shattering the quiet of the early morning. For probably the first time in my life, I resent the solitude of being a biker, the hour-long ride leaving me far too much time to think, to mourn, and to regret. *How the fuck had Heart crashed?*

It's a sombre group who arrive back at the compound, riding in single file through the gate that Marsh, one of our prospects, pulls open. Reaching the clubhouse, we park, backing into a straight line, engines turning off, an eerie silence filling the air. Normally brothers would be chatting and laughing, but it seems all of us are trying to individually process what went down yesterday. Looking up the line I see Heart's usual spot left vacant for him. The sight brings a fresh wave of pain.

The SUV pulls up. Sam gets out with a sleeping child in her arms. Prez, the first off his bike, gives her a quick hug and talks quietly. She responds with a nod and disappears up the compound to the house where they live.

The rest of us dismount, uncertain what to do. Drummer, for once not needing to call for quiet, motions us to gather around him. His steely eyes are filled with pain as he tells us, "Go get some rest, some food. Or fuck if that's what you want. We'll meet for church at eleven. Got it?"

Nods and murmurs of consent are returned, and brothers start walking away. He's only given us a few hours, far too short a period to digest and come to terms with the staggering thought that we may never see our brother again.

I stand undecided. A short nap would probably make me feel worse than having no sleep at all. My stomach growls as though it's making an alternative suggestion. Suddenly hungry, I go into the clubhouse in search of something to eat. But on entering the kitchen I realise I'd forgotten this is the one place that's only going to bring home our great loss. Immediately I take that first step inside and I know something is missing. The quiet reminding me that Crystal is never going to be catering for us again. All at once, I miss her cheery presence, her colourful clothing, her gentle teasing and infectious laughter. Fuck, I even miss that there's no kid getting under my feet. Not that I necessarily think the clubhouse is the right place for children, but Amy? Well, she's actually sweet as fuck, and I know neither myself nor my brothers have a problem with her, or worry that we have to make an effort to act PG when she's around.

I pause in the doorway, bowing my head, overcome by a wave of sadness which slowly turns to a burn of rage. *If I find Heart was run off the road deliberately, I'll tear whoever did it apart with my bare hands.*

Standing, surveying the empty room I try to replace the memories of how I'd last seen Crystal with the image of her in her rightful place, right here in the clubhouse, playing with her daughter.

That visit to the morgue had been hard. Drum had come with me, thank fuck. What I'd seen will haunt me for days. I've seen dead bodies before, of course I have. I've been responsible for despatching them on more than one occasion. But Heart's wife? It was harder than I'd expected to see her lifeless body lying under a pristine sheet, a white bandage hiding the damage to her head. Despite being a hardened biker, I needed all my strength not to vomit.

In life, Crystal had been so vivacious; in death, so unnaturally still. Even with the unnatural paleness of her pallor, I'd waited a moment half expecting her to sit up and talk to us but, of course, she hadn't stirred. And Drum wasn't the only one needing to wipe a tear from his eye. Up to that moment there had been part of me that hoped it was a case of mistaken identification, that it was two different people who'd come off that bike. But the evidence in front of me dispelled my last doubts, along with any lingering hope. It was at that point I truly understood we'd never hear or see Heart's woman in the clubhouse again. It had hit me hard. *Women shouldn't be brought into our war.*

Another gurgle from my stomach reminds me despite my pain, life has to go on. Pulling myself together, I walk to the fridge and pull out the makings of a sandwich. As my hands get busy preparing the snack, my mind refuses to slow. Heart's a fucking good rider, especially with Crystal on the back. For him to land dirty side up with no explanation just doesn't make sense. The more I think on it, the more I'm convinced someone else was involved. But who the fuck could it be? Who was responsible for murdering my brother's wife?

And what's with that odious woman who claimed to be her mother? Not one tear shed for her daughter? How the fuck could someone like that have given birth and raised a girl as sweet as Crystal? It's beyond me how things work out, and the more I think on it, something just doesn't add up.

"It's all wrong, isn't it?" A soft voice by my side makes me turn and look down.

"Yer not fuckin' mistaken there," I tell Sophie, while looking around for our VP, Wraith. Ah, yes, there he is. I didn't think he'd be far away from his woman.

"Slick." He throws me a nod. "Soph, you don't need to be here."

"People need feeding, everyone must be hungry." She chokes back a sob while looking pointedly at my sandwich as if to emphasise the point.

"Need help?" It's a red-eyed Carmen who walks in, followed by Sandy. All three of the women bearing the signs showing they've been crying most of the night. But as befits bikers' women, they know work still needs to be done. It makes me proud of the old ladies in this club.

Seeing they've got things under control, I take my plate, go to the bar and nab a beer. It was a long night, and my suspicions are it'll be an even longer day. When I've eaten my hastily assembled breakfast, I pull out my cigarettes and take one out. Blade appears as if by magic, and I pass him the pack without him having to ask. My usual ribbing absent.

The smell of bacon entices me back to the kitchen. Still hungry, I help myself to a second and more substantial meal. One by one my brothers wander in and do the same. We eat almost in silence, each lost in our own misery tinged with the hope Heart will pull through. It's like we don't dare speak about it, as if by voicing our thoughts out loud we could jinx his recovery.

As eleven o'clock approaches, Drummer doesn't have to summon us to church. Brothers are already walking in without the need to be reminded. And neither, for once, does the prez have to call us to order. All of us quiet and looking expectantly toward him, anxious to hear what he has to stay.

Half-heartedly he still bangs the gavel. "Shooter," he points to the empty seat at the end of the table, "is stayin' at the hospital as we agreed before we left. I've just spoken to him and there's not been a change."

Like others, I nod. With Heart in an induced coma he won't awake, and any difference at this stage could only be a turn for the worse.

"The medics have allowed him into Heart's room."

That's good news. We don't want to leave him alone.

"Will one brother be enough, Drum?" Peg's looking concerned. "If this was no accident, we don't want any mother-fucker able to get near enough to him to finish him off."

"And that's what we're fuckin' here to discuss, Peg." Throwing a scowl at the sergeant-at-arms, the prez continues, "First off, who's gonna be makin' notes?"

I hadn't thought about that. Heart, as our secretary, usually records the decisions we make. Hopefully, I look around the table. Dart's raising his hand. Good, I don't need to volunteer. Writing's not my strong point.

"Okay. Everyone in favour of Dart takin' over for Heart while he's out of action?"

"Only until he's back," Dart quickly gets in, sounding confident he won't be playing the role for long. It's what we've all got to do, focus on him making a full recovery.

A chorus of ayes, Dart gets himself ready with paper and Peg slides the decision book over to him. Anything we vote on will need to be logged in there.

"Let's get fuckin' started then."

Beef raises his hand. "What was it with the heat last night? D'ya reckon they think the accident was deliberate? They know something we don't?"

"Get straight to it, why don'cha," Drum replies with what passes for him as an attempt at a smile. "I have no fuckin' idea. Couple of detectives new to me, don't know what they might think. May be sniffin' around just as Heart's a member of our club."

"You think they'll share anythin' they find?" Beef continues.

"Well, if they think someone ran them off the road, they'll be back after what info they can get about enemies we, or Heart, might have. If they put it down to bad ridin', I doubt we'll hear from them again."

"We're doing our own investigatin' though." Blade scowls, and I know few of us trust the law to do a good enough job. Especially when it involves one of our brothers.

Wraith taps his fingers against the table. "What do we know?"

I wave my hand. "Heart and Crystal went down to Tombstone yesterday. Fuck knows why, but she had a hankerin' to do something different. Wanted to see them acting out the shootout at the OK Corral. Seems she's never been." And ain't that par for the course? Live near somewhere famous and never bother to visit?

Drum jerks his chin toward me. "We've been on lockdown until recently. They just wanted to get out and have some time on their own." He brushes his hand down his beard. "They were on their way back. They left the road just south of Tucson on the I-10 heading north."

No one offers anything else. It seems what we know doesn't add up to a lot.

Blade, our enforcer, creases his eyes. "Heart have a private beef with anyone?"

"Not that I know of," the prez responds. "Anyone know different?"

We all shake our heads. Heart's not one to start trouble. He'll have any of our backs in a fight, but is more peacemaker than a protagonist.

"Okay, so we know where and when, but not why or how." His brow furrows. No one interrupts our prez's thinking, giving him space to get it straight in his head. "He could have had a blow out, something wrong with his bike. We can't rule out that it could have been an accident, his fault or not; another vehicle involved which didn't fuckin' stop. Or it could have been deliberate. An attack on Heart or the club."

A lot of questions and a fuckload of missing answers. And to my mind, if another vehicle was involved, that driver's a dead man whether he did it on purpose or not. They left my brother and his old lady lying dying on the side of the road. Who knows, getting treatment faster might have meant Crystal could have been saved.

"Won't know much more until Heart wakes up." I note Wraith didn't add 'if he does'. None of us want to even acknowledge the possibility.

"Blade, Slick, and I are going to the spot after this meetin', see if there's anythin' to be found."

I nod, mentally noting I'll be looking for skid marks and possibly hoping to find evidence to show that anyone else was involved. Though, presumably, the police will already have done that. I'm hardly going to be lucky enough to find a lost license plate. I point to Drum's cut. "You gonna see if that Hannah woman can give us some answers?"

Patting his pocket where he'd placed her card, the prez replies, "Let's see what we can find first. Time for that when we come back."

"What's gonna happen to the kid?" Marvel, a relatively new member to our chapter with a love of comics is a normally a jovial chap to have around. Today like the rest of us, he's solemn. I'd noticed him having a soft spot for the kid on more than one occasion, and am not surprised when he echoes my concern. "Didn't much care for her gramma from what I saw."

Drum sits forward, his expression fierce. "Heart and Crystal left her in the care of me and my ol' lady. Sam's lookin' after Amy. She ain't goin' nowhere til we know what's happenin' with Heart. And even then I'm not willin' to turn her over. Probably like you, I wanted to kick that woman up her fuckin' ass."

"Looked like she was usin'." Lady drops in, and none of us make any move to suggest we disagree.

There's a moment of silence which I use to spare a thought for the ebullient child being sent to live with such a woman. I suspect my brothers are thinking along similar lines.

"Well, she's not takin' charge of the child. Not if I have anythin' to fuckin' say about it." Prez sounds determined.

"Did Heart and Crystal make any provision for her? Never even heard Crystal mention her mother. Didn't even know she had family." Dart's frowning. He'd joined at around the same time as Heart if I recall rightly. They'd become prospects soon after I'd patched in. I've been here eight years, they've been here what…six? Yeah, that feels about right. Heart had got together with Crystal, who'd come by as a hang-around a couple of years later. It had been love at first sight.

Realising I'd lost myself there for the moment, I bring my attention back to the conversation.

"Yeah, I'll get the club lawyer to check out her will." I must have missed something, but I pick up the gist. Life in a one-percenter club can at times be dangerous, we all know what we're signing up to when we join. When we're patched in Drum sets up a meeting with the club lawyer and we draw up our wills so our affairs are in order if the worst should ever happen. And Drum's down as executor—what's officially called a personal representative here in Arizona—on each and every one, including those of the old ladies. He'll be able to see if she'd given any thought about what would happen to the kid.

"While Heart's out of action, Amy will be stayin' with me and Sam," Drum repeats, then adds almost slyly, "Sam could do with the practice."

The prez just drops it in there, it takes a moment to sink in and Wraith's the first off the bat. "Congrats in order, Prez?" He gives a wide grin.

As Drum returns a chin lift, for the first time this morning there's a cheer around the table. Whether we're congratulating him on getting his old lady pregnant, and so fucking quickly, or laughing at him for the predicament he's in, I'm not sure. It can't be much over three months ago that he'd met the bitch, and she's already carrying his child? Well, fuck, when our prez puts his mind to something he doesn't hang around. If that's what he wants I'm happy for him. Not that having an old lady is something I'd consider. I'll not be getting caught in that trap. Not again. Once was enough.

As my eyes stay on Drummer I see the fucker's actually wearing a smile. Guess this is really what he wanted.

"What can I say? My swimmers know what they're doin'."

And then we all crack up. It releases the tension. Dart gets his cigarettes out and passes them around.

"Anything you need me to do, Prez?" Mouse's fingers are hovering over his keyboard.

"Just check if there's any movement with the Rock Demons. I'm pretty certain they're not reassemblin' around here, but put the word out? They're the only fuckin' one's come to mind who might want to harm us. Oh, and check out that fuckin' woman, the one who said she's Crystal's mom."

"On it, Prez."

Drum puts his hand to his mouth, another sign he's thinking. "Peg, I think we should start being careful about ridin' alone." A collective groan goes around the table. That restriction has only just been lifted. I'm going to miss not being able to take off when I feel like it. I'd been thrilled when I was at last able to go out on my own wherever I want whenever I wanted. "Sorry, brothers." Prez shrugs. "Until we know what we're dealin' with I don't want to risk losin' any more of ya."

Peg's nodding his head. "You only just got in before me, Prez."

"And Joker, you okay to take over from Shooter? I want a brother with Heart at all times."

"Fine with me, Prez."

"I'll take over from Joker," Dollar volunteers. Which starts everyone, including me, saying we'll do our turn.

Prez points to Dart. "You start a list, Dart, so everyone knows what they're fuckin' doin'. Until we know more, one brother will do. But those of you at the hospital, you don't leave Heart for a fuckin' moment. You want to piss, you do it in his bathroom and leave the fuckin' door open. Anything suspicious, call for back up. You hear me?" As we all let him know that we do, he closes his eyes briefly, then opens them and starts to wrap up. "That's all we can do for now. Keep close, and when we get any more intel we'll reconvene."

"We on lock-up?" Wraith asks it as a question, but it sounds more like a suggestion. While Drum's considering, he adds, "Reckon the women will want to stay close. They'll all want to help with Amy and give each other support."

"Okay." Drum reaches a decision. "We won't make it compulsory, but just encourage everyone to stay at the compound. Anyone feels they need space to deal with this, just let me, Peg, or Wraith know. It's one hell of a shock to all of us."

He pauses, then nods at me, and then across to the other side of the table. "Slick, you and Blade stay for a moment and then we'll get goin' to the accident site."

The brothers filter out. I pop through the door for a second to collect my phone, then return and drop back into my seat. I turn it back on and check it. *No messages. Good.* Almost immediately the fucker starts buzzing loudly, shocking me so much it nearly drops from my hand.

Drummer pushes back his chair from the table, puts one foot up against the edge, and looks like he's getting comfortable. He points to me. "Better answer that. In the current situation, we need to know all the shit that's goin' down."

He's right. Heart's situation might be the start of attacks on the rest of the club. The screen's reading *No Caller Id.* Hoping to fuck it's not one of my bitches ringing up to offer me phone sex, I feel my face going red as I take out my phone, connect the call and put it to my ear. "Yeah?"

Oh shit!

"I already told ya. I ain't talkin' to you, bitch. Don't fuckin' ring me again, I don't care what fuckin' trouble you're in." Unwilling to hear her voice one second longer than I need to, I end the call and place my phone in my pocket. I swiftly turn to the prez. "We goin' out then?" The snap in my voice causes Drummer's eyes to narrow.

"Bitch problems?" he enquiries.

Now I'm not thinking straight, so I answer him honestly when I would have done better to keep my mouth shut. "It's that bitch Ella. Second time she's called."

His foot crashes down and he leans forward. "What she want?"

I shrug. I hadn't given her time to tell me. "Fuck if I know. Wanted my help."

His eyes sharpen. "And you didn't think to find out what the fuck she needs?"

I glare at him. "No I fuckin' didn't. You know what happened, Prez. She's fuckin' nothing to me. Four months ago she walked out on me with no word."

"Girl did a solid for the club. We owe her big time, Slick." Blade, knife in his hand, points the tip at me to emphasise his point.

Drum tunnels his hands through his hair. He sounds exasperated. "I don't care what the fuck happened between you and her, Slick. If she needs anythin', Satan's Devils will have her back."

That pulls me up. I hadn't thought of it like that. I was only thinking of what she'd done to me, ignoring what she'd done for all my brothers. She'd enabled us to get intel, which most certainly had saved lives. Feeling a bit of an asshole, I give a slow nod. "I suppose she did do us a favour. But someone else can contact her, find out what she wants."

Drum lifts his head. I can't read what he's thinking, but when he opens his mouth I wish he'd stayed silent. Piercing me with his steely gaze and using the tone that I know would accept no contrary argument, he states, "She's your responsibility, it was you who claimed her fuckin' ass and made her your ol' lady. After we've been to the accident site you go and see her, Slick, and find out what the fuck she needs. And whatever we can do to assist, make sure we fuckin' provide it. You got me?"

I got him. Loud and fucking clear. And no matter how hard I glare at him, he's not going to back down. Yeah, I'd claimed the bitch, but I've never even fucked her, and isn't that the fuck of all jokes? That doesn't make her my old lady. She doesn't mean shit to me.

CHAPTER 6
Ella

Present day

Sitting on my bed with my phone to my lips, I berate myself for even thinking of making that call. Why I thought there was a chance he'd answer the second more civilly this morning than he did the call last night, I don't know, but contacting him had been out of sheer desperation. Whichever way I looked at it, and heaven help me, I've tried, there is no one else I can approach for help. After what I put myself through for the club, I thought they'd be willing to come to my aid. But Slick won't even give me a chance to explain. Oh God, it's been four months since I'd seen him. I hadn't realised that he'd hate me so much. Tears prick in my eyes.

His anger shouldn't bother me. I shouldn't care what he thought about me leaving without a word. And the sound of his voice, and as enraged as it was, shouldn't be causing me to regret the chance I never had. Throwing the phone down, I slap the palm of my hand to my forehead. *Why does his rejection hurt so much?* And why did his cruel words and abrupt dismissal make me want to cry? *I've got to be stronger than this.* I'd done the right thing. The only thing I could have done.

Plumping the pillows up behind me, I lean back my head. Slick. No, I don't regret leaving him. I couldn't have stayed. If he thinks I'm contacting him to rekindle our non-relationship he's oh so very wrong. Four months and nothing has changed. I'm stuck in a prison of my only making, as powerless to move on as able to turn back time and never set foot in the Rock Demons' club.

Angrily I swipe at my eyes, knowing my tears are wasted. Contacting Slick had been a last resort but he isn't even willing to listen, let alone help. It's clear he wouldn't even give me the time of day.

"You fuckin' in there, Els?" The yelling is accompanied by a banging on my bedroom door.

Shit! Quickly dragging an oversized tee over my head and pulling up some jogging bottoms, I go and cautiously open the door to find Bart, my housemate, Tilly's good-for-nothing layabout boyfriend. His eyes rake over me, and a smirk comes to his face mottled from excessive drinking. What she sees in him I'll never know, but for the past month he's been sharing our space. I can only hope that it won't be for much longer. *Surely she'll get tired of him soon.* I've taken to keeping to my room while he's around.

"Whatcha want, Bart?" I ask wearily, pulling my shirt around me and folding my arms over my chest.

Accompanied by a leer that tells me he's being deadly serious, he asks, "A blow job?" As I go to slam my door shut he throws out his hand, stopping it in its tracks. "You're a tight-ass bitch, ain'tcha?" He shakes his head, but the flare in his eyes suggests he might not be far off forcing me.

Compelling myself to stay calm when inside I'm close to losing it, I swallow rapidly to moisten my dry mouth and make my offer again. "What do you want? And sex is not in the cards."

"More's the fuckin' pity." But at least he takes his hand away, leaving me in control of the door once again.

It's not much of a plus, there's no lock on my side. *Where the fuck do you go, Tilly, to find these men? Is there some kind of losers' store somewhere?* It's not the first stray she's brought home. Though Bart's possibly the least house-trained, and that's saying a lot.

"Tilly's fuckin' out. I want breakfast." Yes, she would be out. She's got a job as a barista. She works to support his lazy ass. Biting my tongue to stop myself from telling him to go get it himself, I satisfy myself with rolling my eyes. Luckily, he's chosen that moment to look away, and I'm glad that he did. Tilly's been wearing extra makeup lately and it's not hard to understand why. But this is the first time he's so blatantly asked me for sex, though I'd seen it coming. She and I are going to have a serious chat when she gets in from work—when he's taken her earnings and gone out drinking again.

"I'll come get you something." He scares me; it's easier to give in. "Just give me a moment to wash."

"I'm fuckin' hungry now." Christ! He sounds like a petulant child.

Shaking my head, fearing what he might do if I delay, I step out of the safety of my room, noticing he doesn't move out of the way, which means I have to slide my body up against his, his foul body odour sticking to me like glue. Walking across the lounge that's even more disgusting than normal, I go into the small kitchen. The sink is full of dirty dishes and pans. Someone has had a midnight snack and hasn't bothered to wash up. It could have been either him or Tilly, they're both disgusting wasters. Quickly I wash and rinse plates, putting them on the drainer to dry. Next, I bend down and open the fridge.

For a big man he moves quietly. I don't know he's behind me until I feel the swat to my ass. Trying not to flinch, feeling like bugs are moving over my skin, I summon up strength from somewhere and snarl, "Do that again and you can get your own fucking breakfast."

"Smart-assed bitch," he throws back. But his stomach must be ruling his cock, at least for the moment, as thankfully I feel him move away.

I take out eggs and bacon and get them started, and throw on some waffles to heat. My hand unsteady with the threat of his presence, I've certainly got no appetite myself. As fast as I can, I make him a plate, grab a coffee for myself, and take myself back to my room.

Eyeing my phone, I decide there's no point calling and getting a third rejection. Slick calling me a bitch twice so far today followed by my altercation with Bart has been more than enough. But Slick and his club should listen to me—for what I did for them, and at the high to myself. A debt to repay that no one knows the true extent of. Except for me, that is.

Sitting back on the bed I put my head in my hands, remembering back to the night it all started. That evening when Jill had turned up at my door, the tall handsome biker accompanying her.

After she'd left, Slick had stayed late into the evening, explaining what they'd wanted me to do. A simple job on the face of it, and he'd reeled me in with promises of what was to be my future. Pointed looks around my all too humble and messy abode, countered with descriptions of their compound in the foothills of the Coronado Forest, the clean air they breathe rather than the smog of the city. And he described the men, and the demands they make on the girls. He might not have known, but had he offered to give me a demonstration I'd have agreed to anything he wanted right there on the spot.

I remember only too well the carrot he dangled in front of me, his deep voice drifting over me as he described a perfect life living with the bikers. They'd meet *all* my needs. Sure, he admitted, they could be rough, but to my gullible self the thought summoned up only thrills and excitement, and did nothing to turn me off. To be with a man who knew exactly what he was doing? Not to fumble with a partner who hadn't a clue how to pleasure a woman. They prided themselves on not leaving a woman wanting, he'd said. And I knew then I wanted to experience that. And those heated looks he was giving me? They'd blown me away. I forgot about the other men. All I could think of what Slick doing just what he'd described.

That evening was the last time I found anything about sex to be exciting, or even arousing. Icy cold water had washed away my naïve dreams when I was introduced to the reality of biker loving in the Rock Demons' club. An experience from which I haven't even begun to recover, and suspect that I never will.

"Hey, bitch!" Bart's voice comes loud and clear through the thin door.

When will he realise I've got a name? Grabbing a tissue from the side of my bed I mop up my tears I hadn't realised were falling and blew my nose in a very unladylike fashion. Then I go to see what he wants. Surely he can't want feeding *again?* Glancing at my phone I see that might be the case, I've wasted hours reliving the past.

"What, Bart?" I call out, leaning on the wood on this side, unwilling to face him again.

"You've got a fuckin' visitor. What d'ya think I am, your fuckin' servant or summin'? Come out and fuckin' see him."

Huh? *Him?* I'm not expecting anyone. My brow furrows as I think who it could be. I don't mix with men nowadays—only my boss, and I can't think of a reason he'd visiting. But I won't find out hiding in my bedroom. Blissfully unaware and unconcerned what was about to confront me, I step out into the sitting room to be met with the man I'd just wasted most of the day thinking about. Slick.

Oh. My. God. Why is he here? My first reaction is fear. We hadn't parted on good terms. Actually, we hadn't parted on any terms at all, I'd just walked out. Given his response to my phone calls today, he's the last man I expect to see. Is he angry that I'd contacted him? Had I so enraged him that he'd come to challenge me in person? To tell me never to contact him again? I begin to tremble as I risk a glance at him, only to find he's not looking at me. No, he's looking at the man who's come to stand by my side, and who's just placed a very possessive arm over my shoulder, making me freeze.

"Just tell your fuckin' *friend* to go." *What?* What the hell has it got to do with Bart?

I try to shrug off Tilly's boyfriend's touch, his fingers grip into me causing me to break out in a sweat.

Now Slick looks at me, one side of his mouth turned up. Then he looks to the man by my side who's choosing this moment to put his free hand down his pants and scratch at his balls. Slick shakes his head. "You're with this now? Christ woman." He looks disgusted.

Bart might be stupid, but he knows when he's being insulted. He steps forward, dragging me with him. "Yeah, she's mine. So fuck off, fella." Then it's almost as though a lightbulb turns on. "Unless you want to pay? She's a good fuck."

"What?" Rage gives me the strength to pull out of his grip. "What the fuck are you talking about…" My hand goes to my cheek where he's just backhanded me.

As I stand dazed, with a growl Slick comes forward, pushing Bart away and delivering a punch of his own. Bart screams like a woman and his hand covers his mouth. For good measure, Slick's fist hits Bart in his stomach, then turns him around, holding him by his collar with one arm twisted up his back.

He snarls into Bart's ear, "You never hit a woman. Never mind if she's yours or not."

"I'm not his!" I spit out. "He's with Tilly, my housemate. I don't want him here at all. And I've never fucked him. Never mind what that asshole says."

Slick's eyes open as my words sink in. "You want I take out the trash?"

Best suggestion I've heard all day. I nod slowly. Yes I do, Bart's been getting far too handsy for me today. "Please Slick. And I don't want him coming back." A belated reaction has me visibly shaking. I'd known Bart had been getting worse, but this morning he's shown signs he might go so far as to rape me.

The biker pulls Bart's arm harder up against his back, and I hear a bone snap. The sound makes me wince. "You're leavin' now, and you're never fuckin' returnin'."

Bart's crying like a baby, but Slick is still not letting him loose. "But my stuff…"

"Yer girlfriend can bring it to ya. But yer not crossin' this doorway again. Got it? If yer do I'll find ya and there won't be an unbroken bone in your fuckin' body."

"I got it man, I hear ya. Just let me go." His words are almost indistinguishable through his blubbering.

"Just to let ya know, Ella here is under the protection of the Satan's Devils. It won't only be me. All my brothers will be watchin' out for ya." With that, Slick marches him to the door, opens it with the hand not holding Bart's clearly broken arm, and tosses him out on his ass. Slamming the door behind him he comes back in, brushing his hands briskly, one against the other as if removing all trace of dirt. He moves across to me and turns my head so he can examine my injured cheek. His Adam's apple bobs as he swallows, and seems to choke back what he wants to say.

Instead he settles for, "Well I've sorted your problem. I know his type. He's a fuckin' coward who hits women. But now he knows you've got us to knock back. He'll leave you alone." He lets his hand drop from my face and then turns his back on me. "Right, now I've helped ya, I'll get gone now. See ya... Well, goodbye Ella."

I'm stunned. *He's going to leave?* As his hand touches the door handle my legs are prompted into action. Running across the room, I commit the cardinal sin of putting my hand on his cut and trying to hold him back. He turns around, arms swinging, then manages to stop them in mid-air.

"What the fuck, Ella?"

"I didn't call you here for *that.*" I wave my hand toward the front door. "That was nothing. I could have handled that fucker myself." I couldn't really, but that's beside the point. "I've got a real problem I need fucking help with." Then it dawns on me what he said. "You told me I got Satan's Devils protection. Well now I want some of that."

He's trembling as though he's trying to suppress his anger, his fists clenching and unclenching. Clear signs he hasn't forgiven me yet, and probable indications that he never will.

Even though I know it would be best if he was completely out of my life, I can't let him walk away. Not when I need all the help I can get, and I don't know where to turn except to him and his club.

His breath leaves him on a long sigh, and with one arm outstretched holding the top of the doorframe, his brow resting on his forearm in a gesture strangely reminiscent of the night we'd first met, he asks in a more reasonable tone, "What the fuck have you got yourself into, Ella?"

Now I've got him here and I've got his full attention. Still reeling from Bart's possessive actions and the violent way Slick dealt with him, my hands are unsteady and it's difficult to get my thoughts together. That Slick had acted so viciously shouldn't have surprised me. It's what I've come to expect from bikers. It's safe to say my blinkers have been well and truly removed. I'd been such a fool to believe the things that Jill had told me, and to think it would be a dream to live with them. They are all brutish thugs. And that includes the one standing in front of me. I need to be very careful how to proceed, and not make him any angrier than he already is.

"Spit it fuckin' out, Ella. I ain't got all fuckin' day."

Knowing he's getting impatient makes my heart beat faster and my palms sweat. *Please don't get a panic attack now.* "Would you like a coffee?" I make the offer hoping I might be able to escape his presence for a moment.

"No, I don't want a fuckin' drink. I want you to fuckin' talk to me."

CHAPTER 7
Slick

What Ella calls home hasn't changed at all since the first time I saw it. If anything it's become even more of a pigsty. The air is tainted with sweat and other loathsome odours of the obnoxious male I just had the pleasure of chucking out of here. Fuck Drummer for making me come. At least taking out some of my rage on the man I expelled has taken the edge off my anger.

When I'd seen him with Ella I was surprised to see how low her tastes had fallen. Bikers aren't high up on anyone's scale, but that man was pure scum. Then I was taken aback by the relief that swept through me when I found she wasn't his, and again by my fury when he dared lay his hands on her. To be honest, he's lucky he left here walking. For a second or two there I thought I'd be calling the club and requesting help with a clean-up. But something in her frightened eyes had tempered my reaction. It wasn't that she was scared for *him*, but on some level for me, and I'd managed just in time to tame my most violent instincts. He'd gotten off lightly. *But if he ever came back?* All gloves would be off.

I'd thought it was over, the man who was bothering her gone from her life. Her problem resolved and I was free to get as far away from here as possible. And then I wished he was still in the room so I had a target for my temper when I realised she wasn't going to let me leave. *Let me go, Ella. Just let me fuckin' go.*

The room's small, a kitchenette off to one side. Once my eyes have roamed all around they're drawn back to the woman in front of me. The girl who now I notice seems a shadow of her former self. She's pale, her cheeks flushed, her breathing is quickening, and she's trembling. *She's scared.* Even though I'd removed the immediate threat, she hasn't relaxed at all. Perhaps she should be afraid. She's done nothing to make me feel friendly toward her. *She made me hate her.* But that hatred was far easier to maintain when she wasn't standing so close. *Fuck it, Drum, why did you make me come here today?*

Reacting to her physical symptoms, I gentle my voice and go to the sagging couch. "Look, darlin', let's sit down and you can tell me what the problem is." Seating myself, I prop my elbows on my knees and, after patting the not very clean cushion next to me, rest my chin on my clasped hands. Sitting here reminds me of the first time I met her, and for a moment I wonder, had I known what I was sending her into would I still have asked her to work for the club? If she'd refused, would I have walked out of this house, out of her life, and never returned? There's not much point thinking about what might have been. It's done and dusted. And we both came out losers. For the first time in months I feel a slight easing of the storm raging inside, a crack in the walls I'd built up to keep her out.

Her eyes are wide, her pupils dilated, but she pulls herself up straight and I see some of the backbone she'd originally shown when, clearly reluctant, she comes and sits at the other end of the couch. As it's only a two-seater and long since lost any springiness it might have had, our combined weights cause it to dip, and her body slips toward mine. Unable to keep my distance, without thinking I unclasp my hands and wrap my fingers around one of hers.

"Speak to me, Ella."

A little frightened glance in my direction, and though it trembles and she tries to pull away, when I grip it tighter she finally relents and lets me keep hold of her hand. I give it a squeeze in encouragement.

My attention is drawn to her slender neck when she swallows a couple of times, then, at last, she starts to speak.

"It's my sister. Jayden."

I sharpen my eyes, unaware she had family. We hadn't spoken about it before. Mind you, we hadn't talked much about anything. And perhaps our lack of communication had been part of the problem. "Your sister?" I prompt.

"Yeah. She's only fourteen and lives with my mom." She shakes her head. "My mom's a piece of work. Wrapped up in herself and in her new man."

Knowing Ella has to be some years older than her sister I ask, "She your full sister?"

"Yes. She was an accident. She's nine years younger than me. Guess Mom got careless." She gives another one of her half-smiles. "Mom never wanted her, but then, she didn't really want me either. She's not got much of a maternal instinct." She pauses and clears her throat. "I've tried talking to her, but she's blind to, or not bothered about what's going on with her younger daughter."

"And what is goin' on?"

She looks down at our joined hands as though only just noticing I am still holding on. "There's something wrong. She's only fourteen, Slick, but I think she's seeing an older man."

"You want I should go talk to him?" That would be easy enough.

Another shake of her head. "I don't think it's as simple as that." She pulls away from my touch, stands, and walks to the window. When she turns around her arms are clasped around her body. "She used to be so vibrant and happy. She's a pretty girl, but now she's lost her sparkle. There's something up, but I don't know what."

"You tried talkin' to her?"

Her head jerks. "Yeah, of course I have. Despite the age difference we used to be close, not so much now. In many ways, I've been more like a mom to her, making sure she has everything she needs for school, taking her shopping for clothes, stuff like that." She purses her lips and then starts speaking faster, the words tumbling out one after another. "I went around there last week, she had a new iPad. She was wearing new clothes, one's Mom couldn't afford. There's no way they came from Walmart."

"Someone's buyin' her stuff," I surmise. "Did you ask who?"

"She clammed up and wouldn't tell me. Tried to hide the iPad when she noticed I'd seen it. Slick, she's not happy, her eyes, they look dead. She's not my happy little sister anymore, something's very wrong." She comes back and sits on the couch, her body angled so she can look at me. "Slick, I want to find out who she's seeing, who's buying her these things, and who's leeching the life out of her." She looks down for a moment, "I've tried following her, but she got picked up in a car and I haven't got transport as Tilly had taken hers that day. I waited for her to come home, she stayed out all night."

"What did your mom say?"

"She shrugged it off. Said she often stays round a girlfriend's, doing homework together."

"But you don't buy that?"

"No. I asked Mom where she was getting her money from. She didn't care. I think she knows something's up, but it's easier if she doesn't admit it." Biting her lip, she raises her eyes to meet mine. "I wondered if there's some way your computer guy, Mouse, could help find out where she's going. Find out who she's seeing?"

A fourteen-year-old kid. And presumably an older man buying expensive gifts for her, no kid her own age would be able to afford iPads and the like. Who's not making her happy. I start to see why she's worried. Mouse might be able to help her. Or perhaps we can put a prospect on her, to follow her and find out where she goes.

"She's unhappy, Slick. And I don't know why. I'm worried sick."

"Can't you just confront her?"

"Don't you think I've tried?" she cries. "I've talked calmly to her. I've tried to reason with her. I've yelled at her. But she won't give me a thing." Her voice drops to a whisper. "I think she's scared. She tries to act as normal, but it's like she's forgotten how to be a young girl."

"I'll take it back to the club." It doesn't sound like it would be too much to ask, and as Drum reminded me, whatever wrong she did me, she did an enormous favour for the club. One that ended up getting her hurt. "I think we'll be able to help you, but I've got to run it by the prez." I offer a small smile. "Hopefully it will just be that she's grown into a normal teenager. Sullen and sulkin'…"

"I've thought about that. But the new things she has…"

Ella probably wasn't brought up the same way as me, so I don't bother suggesting Jayden might have been stealing. And that's another option we'll have to explore, and perhaps knock her life of crime on the head before she gets caught.

"Don't worry, Ella. I'm sure Prez will agree to look into it."

"Thank you, Slick. I just didn't know what else to do." She lets out a sigh of heartfelt relief that at last she's got someone on her side.

I turn and look at her. Really look at her. The way she described her sister, well, the description fits her too. Her eyes are clouded, her face pinched, her hair neglected. Once reaching down to her ass and shining, it's been chopped off—and clearly not by a hairdresser—and is ragged and lifeless, the stunning auburn colour now dull. *She looks like she's given up.* Another crack in the wall as I gaze at my old lady. The woman I'd claimed in front of my club. The woman who left me before I even had the chance to know her. She'd been the only woman I've ever thought I could love, and she'd thrown it back in my face.

I'd ridden up to her door with such a feeling of loathing, detesting the very thought of seeing her again. But seeing her this way, looking so broken, it's difficult to maintain the animosity inside.

Putting my hand to her chin, I raise her face, noticing she immediately pulls away. Ignoring her reaction, I continue with my question. "How you doing, Ella? How you doing, *really?*" I point to her ribs. "Are you all healed up?" Grasping she's uneasy with me touching her, I drop my hand.

She swallows before answering, and her eyes flick away, already alerting me that I'm going to hear a lie. "I'm fine, Slick. I'm just worried about Jayden."

Something tells me what's bothering her is another matter entirely. Sure, she's worried about her sister, but this decline hasn't come in a few days. But why the fuck should I care? She'd walked out and left me. She's not my responsibility anymore.

I stand and grab my sunglasses and gloves from where I left them on the side by the door. "I'll go back to the club, bring your problem to the table. I'll let you know what they say."

She remains on the couch but looks up with a nod. "Thank you, Slick."

Then, at last, I'm able to walk out and leave her.

Fuck! I shouldn't want to help her, shouldn't have this desire to put a full smile back on her face. But for some reason I do.

She'd killed my feelings for her stone fucking dead. But I can see that she's hurting, and while I don't understand the extent to which it's bothering me, I can't bear to see her looking so lost.

When I get back to the compound several of the brothers are already milling around the bar. At my approach, Marsh waves a beer in my direction and I take it with a nod. Drum breaks off his conversation and comes across, his eyes searching my face. He knows full well where I'd been and who I'd been seeing. After we'd done what we could at the accident site, I'd peeled off to ride into Tucson and left him and Blade to turn toward home.

"How did it go?"

I shrug. "We havin' a meetin'?" At his nod, I continue, "I'll tell everyone there." Saves me going through the whole thing twice.

"Somethin' we need to get involved with?"

"Prez, I'm not really sure. Maybe."

"She did a lot for this club. Couldn't have taken down the Rock Demons without the info we got."

I nod in agreement, starting to wonder at just how much she'd sacrificed in order to help us. And whether there are still things I don't know. A picture of a woman so clearly damaged comes into my head. *Did we, I, do that to her?*

It seems Drummer had been waiting for my return, as I've barely emptied the bottle when he calls us all in. We take our seats, and as I wipe my hands over my face and look at my brothers it hits me what a long fucking day this has been. I'm dead on my feet, and I wouldn't be surprised if everyone else was in the same boat.

The prez calls us to order then starts his update. "Blade, Slick, and me, well we've been to the site." I nod as he continues, picturing it in my mind. A broken crash barrier, police tape flapping in the breeze. No skid marks on the road, and the police having removed the bike, only marks in the ground showing where it had laid. Although I'm not religious I'd stood and bowed my head at the spot, hoping there might be a god out there to answer the prayer I'd sent up for my fallen brother.

"Unless the police let us take a look at the bike, or Heart comes around and is able to talk to us, we're still no closer to findin' out what happened," Drum finishes up.

"They're callin' for any witnesses on the local news." Dollar tips his bottle toward Drum. "I just seen it."

"I'll ring this Hannah woman in the mornin'." Drum jerks his head. "Though it probably would be too much to fuckin' hope they'll give us much information. Shooter, any change in Heart's condition?"

Shooter's looking drawn. "He coded while I was there. But they got him back. He's fightin', Prez, but I dunno. I spoke to the doc, she's harpin' on about the fact Heart wasn't wearin' a helmet."

I close my eyes briefly. In Arizona, if you're over eighteen you don't need to wear a lid. Confident in our riding skills, most of us don't. Could a brain bucket have saved him? Who the fuck knows? Desolation rolls over me, the thought of my brother with his life hanging on by a thread almost a physical pain. *What the fuck had happened?* What had made his bike go off the road? He's not a reckless rider, and especially not with his wife riding two up. "There had to be someone else involved."

I didn't realise I'd spoken my thought aloud until Drum responds, "Have to say, that's the feel in my gut too."

And we spend a few minutes again trying to work out who the fuck it could have been. Getting nowhere of course.

Drum bangs the gravel. "Slick, what did Ella want?"

"Hey, you been to see your ol' lady?" Beef laughs, and I scowl. Yeah, it's a fucking joke to them that I put everything on

84

the line and claimed her and she walked out on me not two weeks later.

"Shut the fuck up, Beef." Drum glares at him, and that's all it takes. "Slick?"

I let them in on her worries.

Mouse grins. He always loves a new problem to solve. "Kid that age must have Facebook or Instagram. I'll get onto her stuff and check it out."

"She go out often?"

"Apparently so."

"Let's get a prospect on her. See who's she's meetin'." I nod at Wraith, grateful he's offering the club's help.

"Can she get hold of her sister's phone?"

I raise my shoulders. "I don't fuckin' know. If there's anythin' on it, the girl's hardly likely to offer it up."

Mouse pinches his nose. "I could try and get into her records, but that's not gonna be easy. Havin' the device would be the best by far."

"You tell me where she is and I'll get it for ya." Tongue's grinning, and I remember how he survived on the streets as a boy. It wouldn't be the first time we've used his pick-pocketing skills. I nod, a dual-purpose gesture both to thank him and to let him know I'll find out for him.

"Can you bring her to the clubhouse, Slick? If I'm lookin' at her Facebook page she might know what's kosher and what's not."

"I'll try, Mouse." I can't help wondering whether she'll ever want to set foot in the compound again. And just as importantly, whether I would want to see her in what is essentially my home.

"Right, so we're all on board and we'll help Ella. And you douchebags, we all know what went down, or didn't, between her and Slick. But we might not all be sitting here if she hadn't had helped like she did. We got crucial information from those cameras she planted, and she got hurt for her troubles. She comes to the clubhouse you treat her with some fuckin' respect. And that goes for you too, Slick."

I start as Drum focusses that steely glare on me, realising what a dick I've been toward her. *Was it me that fucked up?* Like a light bulb illuminating, it dawns on me that all the time I've been blaming her, lost in the embarrassment she'd caused me, the hurt to my pride the way she'd thrown my embryonic love for her back in my face, that perhaps I'd been wrong to let her go. *I never actually told her my feelings for her, I just expected her to know.* When she'd left I'd been so hurt and angry I'd not even followed her, let alone questioned her on why she'd gone. Had it been something I'd done, or perhaps something I'd missed? Something other than the danger of my life that she couldn't take? Perhaps it's past time that we had that conversation. Accepting at least some of the blame lies at my door another crack appears, this time a big one, and bricks start tumbling down.

"Slick!" Drum growls, "You treat her with fuckin' respect, you hear me?"

Seeing he's waiting for my response, I give a sharp nod. I hear him loud and clear.

"Okay. We're all fuckin' talked out. Rock, you takin' over for Dart at the hospital later?"

"Yeah, Prez."

"Right, church fuckin' over. Go get laid, sleep, drink or play with your dicks. Whatever the fuck you want and we'll meet back tomorrow." Drum bangs the gavel and the meeting ends.

CHAPTER 8

Ella

The nightmares last night hadn't surprised me. I didn't expect to escape unscathed. Seeing Slick again had not unexpectedly brought everything back. I'd woken with the covers wrapped around me, my body covered in sweat, and had run to the bathroom and retched, straining over the bowl with nothing to bring up.

I'd known it was wrong to contact him when I hadn't yet begun starting to heal. Only the desperation and worry about my sister had driven me. What else could I have done? Go to the police with some vague notion someone might be hurting Jayden, when she could just be going through a rebellious stage? As her sister I see it only too well that there's far more to it than that. But to anyone else she'd probably appear like a normal, grumpy teenage girl. I'm relieved Slick seemed to believe me, and enough to try to get his club involved.

Seeing him again though, well, my nightmares showed me I was paying the price.

I go through the motions of getting dressed, throwing anything on that comes to hand. I'm just making a coffee when the sound of a motorcycle coming up the street causes me to catch my breath. And when it stops outside my house, I put my hand to the wall. *Is it him?* I don't want to see him. *He might have brought news.* And if he has, I can't avoid talking to him. I need to hear anything he has to say for Jayden's sake. I've started this now, and must follow it through.

My heart's in my mouth when the knock comes at the door. And yes, it's him, Slick, who's standing in front of me once again. I take a deep breath, about to stand aside to let him pass, and then I notice there's something different about him. Yesterday his cheeks had been reddened, his eyes narrowed, deep creases lined his forehead, and his mouth had been fixed in a scowl.

Today his brow is smooth as he gives a nod and his lips curl into a hesitant smile. "Gonna let me in, darlin'?"

Bemused by the transformation, and realising I'm standing with my mouth hanging open and my body blocking the doorway, I step out of the way. He puts a helmet on the side and tucks his sunglasses into his cut. *When did he start wearing a helmet?* His hands come out tentatively, hovering in the air for a moment, and then land on my biceps. My automatic reaction is jump free and back out of his reach.

His eyes narrow fast. "Can we talk, darlin'?"

"Have you news from the club? Are they going to help me?" If so, he can tell me and leave. It hurts too much to be this close to him, unable to prevent my body's automatic reaction, my head fighting my mixed emotions, wanting him to draw me to him and wanting him to stay far away. As I wait for his answer, I wrap my arms around my body as though giving myself comfort.

Observing my every movement, he doesn't keep me waiting and puts me out of my misery fast. I don't think I knew how much I'd been counting on their assistance until he gives me his reply, a simple nod and a yes.

"Oh, thank God!" My hand covers my mouth as I gasp with relief that I'm no longer handling this alone.

"Mouse needs to speak with ya. Get what you know about Jayden and her habits."

That seems fair enough.

He waves over toward the couch. "Sit with me, Ella. We need to talk."

My nightmares have unsettled me, having been forced to relive that night in my dreams I don't want to be close to any man today, especially a biker. What he needs to know I can tell him right here. "Just ask what Mouse needs to know. Then you can go."

He shakes his head, still watching me carefully. "Naw, that's between you and Mouse. He wants me to bring you to the club so he can sit down with ya. There's somethin' I need ya to know first."

While I go cold at the thought of going back to the club-house, he ignores the escape route I offered him, brushing past me to take a seat. Realising he intends to stay, I close the door and turn around, for the first time noticing how tired he looks.

"Are you alright, Slick?" Now I'm concerned for him rather than me.

He shakes his head, the corners of his mouth turning down. "No, Ella, I'm not."

As his hand smooths over his head, it seems to be trembling. *He's hurting.* I tamp down my fears about visiting the club enough to ask, "What's the matter, Slick?"

He looks at me with over-bright eyes, moisture making them glisten. "Heart and Crystal were involved in an accident on Saturday. We don't know what happened, but they came off their bike. Crystal..." His voice breaks and he clears his throat before continuing, "Crystal didn't make it, and it's still touch and go for Heart."

I gasp. Crystal was a good woman, lively and happy, and both of them adored their daughter. "Amy?" I ask, unable to think of the poor child losing her mom.

"Amy's fine. Well, as much as she can be. Sam, that's Drummer's old lady—you wouldn't have met her—she's lookin' after the kid. At least until we know what's gonna happen with Heart."

Drummer's got an old lady? That must have happened fast. It's only been a few months since I was last at the club.

My mind starts working. In a flash, I remember what it was like at the Satan's Devils clubhouse. Things I'd blocked out which had been overshadowed by my experience with the Rock Demons. Old ladies and Amy, men laughing and fooling around. And then there's Slick, now sitting in front of me, tears in his eyes as he tells me of the accident. Am I lumping them all in together just because they ride bikes? My hands go to my cheeks and I rub them. It doesn't make sense. *Nothing* makes sense. My head starts to throb.

"Look, I know you don't like the life or the club very much, but Mouse needs you there. I needed to tell ya about Crystal 'cause you'd find out if you went. Another reason for you to hate us I expect."

"I don't hate the club, Slick." My eyes widen, realising it's true. I'm downright terrified of what they represent, but it doesn't translate into animosity toward them. And it wouldn't be Crystal's death, while sad and unexpected, that would stop me going back to the club.

"No?" He looks at me and shakes his head. "I think you made it pretty clear that you do, darlin'." He clasps his hands together and then looks down at them. "I can't really blame ya. That day was fucked up. You were drugged, men killed. Fuck, we lost Adam. One fuck of a lot for a citizen like you to deal with." He pauses then looks at me. "Guess I wasn't thinkin' that way at the time. Just saw you going as a kind of betrayal."

I had left at the very worse time. I worry at my lip as I suddenly understand how much I'd hurt him.

"I hated you, Ella. As much as anything you'd hurt my pride. But I can't hate you anymore. The life isn't for you, I should never have claimed you. I got carried away. I thought I saw a strong woman, but maybe I was wrong."

Now it's my eyes that fill with tears, and I can no longer look at him. There's so much pent up emotion inside I can't stop it from coming out. I sink down on the couch beside him, my face falls into my hands as I start crying. Huge body wracking sobs that make him take me into his arms. Immediately I start fighting, struggling to get away, but he doesn't let me loose. Automatically my hands clutch at his cut, but as I gulp in air the smell of leather and oil invade my senses, and it's too much. My arms start flailing as panic overtakes me.

But he won't let me go. As I continue struggling his arms tighten around me until I give up. As my tears flow he begins rocking me like a baby, holding me without speaking for as long as it takes. When my sobs begin to slow he starts murmuring quietly that everything's going to be okay, when I know that it won't. Nothing will ever be okay, ever again.

"Hush, darlin'. You don't need to come to the club. I'll get Mouse to come here. Don't worry about it. We'll sort out whatever the fuck's up with your sister. Hush, don't cry sweetheart. It will be alright."

My fingers grip onto his leather. My mouth moves as words I never dreamed I'd utter aloud try to escape. I choke them back, not wanting to admit it, not understanding what triggers my confession, why what I'd kept buried so deep starts tumbling out. And once I say it, I know I'll never be able to put it back in the box.

"They made me pull a train," I cry out, surprising myself with my declaration. The secret I'd never admitted before.

He stills and goes silent. Under my touch I feel his muscles tense. It's only a few seconds but feels like a lifetime before he spits out, "Fuckin' what?"

Now that I've started there's no point keeping anything back. "The Rock Demons... All their club. One after the other..." And then I'm crying again, howling in my anguish at my shocking admission. Sliding out of his arms I fall onto the floor, curling up into a ball. I'm shuddering and shaking. He tries to lift me and I scream, pushing him away. Like a physical pain the hurt goes right through me, the memories returning of things I'd tried to block out.

"Ella, Ella sweetheart. Oh fuck, Ella. Let me hold you, let me help you."

The tears just won't stop. I don't know what's happening to me, it's hard to get my breath. It's feels like I'm choking, as though I'm being strangled. I gasp and wheeze, my sobbing unstoppable. It goes on and on with no respite.

"Drum. I need Doc here, at Ella's. Yeah, I'll give you the address. She's just told me the fuckin' Rock Demons pulled a fuckin' train on her."

I'm barely able to hear him, but he sounds distraught.

I can't stop bawling or shaking as though I'm having a fit. I curl up tighter when he touches me, flinching away. I hear wailing and I think it's coming from me. My throat feels sore and I attempt to heave in breath with large gulps, unable to get sufficient air into my lungs.

I come round to find myself lying on my bed. My eyes seem glued shut but my hearing still works and the sound of voices speaking quietly reaches me. "The motherfuckers, Drum. I didn't even fuckin' know. She's been livin' with this and she never fuckin' told me. No wonder she doesn't like being touched."

"They're dead, Slick. We blew up the clubhouse with them in it."

"Not all of them. Two of the fuckers escaped. I want to find out who they are. I want to kill them, Drum."

"I hear ya, Slick. I hear ya."

"How am I gonna make this fuckin' right, Drum?"

"Doc, she gonna be okay?"

"I've given her a sedative. She's gonna need help and counsellin'. Keeping somethin' like that to herself? It's probably been brewin' a while, Slick. You comin' back around probably brought it to a head. She's got to start dealin' with it. Keepin' it hidden ain't helpin'."

Making more of an effort, I try again to open my eyes, remembering how I'd lost it. Raising my hand, I rub at the lids, knowing it's my dried tears which are keeping them shut.

"Darlin'."

At last I manage to get them open, and look up to see Slick hovering by my bed, his face looking blotchy as though he's been crying himself.

He's wearing a troubled expression and his hands are fluttering, "Darlin', I wanna hold ya. I don't know what the fuck to do."

Pulling myself into a sitting position, I hold out my arms to him. In seconds he's next to me on the bed, hugging me so tightly I can hardly breathe.

"Why didn't ya say anything, Ella? Why didn't ya tell us?" I glance over Slick's shoulder to Drum, who's also looking distressed, his hands worrying at his hair.

I need to give him an explanation. "I couldn't talk about it. I wanted to lock it away so I didn't have to even think about it." My voice sounds hoarse. "I'm sorry, Slick, so sorry."

"You've got fuck all to be sorry about, darlin'." As a sob escapes him, I know he's sharing my pain. Right now, I don't know if it helps, this strong man being reduced to tears on my behalf.

Doc puts his hand on my shoulder, making me glance up into his kind but worried eyes. "Ella, did you get yourself checked out? Those fuckers raped ya…"

Unable to meet his gaze, I glance quickly away. His question makes Slick tighten his hold. "Yeah. Once I'd healed I got tests done. I knew I had to do that. They didn't all use condoms. I got treatment." Yeah, they'd given me something. I hadn't bothered to find out what.

The three men growl at my admission and the further information. Slick puts his hand under my chin, forcing my head up so I'm facing him. "We killed them all, Ella. You know that, don't you?"

"What about the ones that got away? I heard what you said." I can't suppress a shudder at the thought of two of my rapists escaping.

"We're going to hunt them down. Didn't bother before now as they weren't officers, but we'll find out who they are, Ella, I promise you. And this time we'll finish them off."

"Make them hurt," I whisper.

"We'll do that alright," Slick vows.

"You been strugglin' with this, darlin'?"

I answer Doc. "Panic attacks, trouble sleeping. Nightmares. They were getting better…"

"Until I fuckin' came back." Slick jumps to his own conclusion.

"Slick, it's not your fault."

"Fuck, it is, Ella. I should have come after you. Talked to you. Found out why you ran." Slick's eyes are glistening. "Instead I left you to deal with it all on your own."

"You need to see a doctor, get help, Ella. Maybe some anti--depressants and counsellin'."

"Club will pay for whatever ya need."

I nod at Drum to thank him. There's only one thing I need, and that's impossible. Slick wouldn't want a woman terrified of sex. Involuntarily my fingers tighten on Slick's cut again.

"I've gotta get back." The prez sounds apologetic.

"I'm stayin' here, Drum."

I have to let go of the man I can't have. "I'm alright now. You probably have stuff to do, Slick."

"Not happenin', darlin'. I'll just see them out and I'll be back, okay?"

He puts his hands on mine and reluctantly I release my hold on his cut. It's only a couple of minutes before he's back again. And as I feared, he wants to talk.

"Never stopped lovin' ya." His arms come around me and he shifts us so he's leaning against the headboard and I'm half lying across his lap. Stroking his fingers through my hair, he continues while I'm trying to process his admission. "Thought I hated ya, but I was foolin' myself. I want ya back as my ol' lady."

I pull away, turning my back, unable to look at the man that if circumstances were different, I'd give anything to be with. *He loves me?* But whether he does or he doesn't, or whether he ever did, it makes no odds now. "I can't pick up where we left off, Slick. I can't be your old lady."

CHAPTER 9
Slick

I'd known the bastards had handled her roughly, and that at least one of them had probably forced her, and that had made me angry enough. When I'd collected her from the mother-fucking Demons clubhouse that morning she'd been injured and hurting, but we'd only called in Doc to look at her ribs. She hadn't given any indication anything else was wrong.

Ignorant of just how badly she'd been treated, I'd thought the best thing to do was give her time to heal and come to terms with what had happened. I'd been certain Jill would have told her what to expect. Hell, I'd tried to as well. As prepared as she could be, she'd gone into that club with her eyes open, just like any sweet butt, knowing she was there for one thing only, to be fucked.

That night, as I waited outside in that car, thoughts of what she was going through were swirling around my head. I'd hated it. Already wishing I'd acted on the strange possessive feelings that were screaming at me that I didn't want any other fucker to touch her, particularly not one from a rival club. But equally knowing my brothers came before any bitch. We needed someone to place those fucking cameras, and all we had was her. We'd used her, just like we used the whores at the compound.

I remember asking myself, why was I worrying about some bitch I'd only just met? Even as I sat waiting I argued with myself. I was Slick. I never wanted a woman for my own. I denied my own leanings and bottled them up, refusing to believe I felt anything for her at all. I'd known what she was walking into and didn't do fuck all to stop her. And when she'd walked out the next morning, I knew immediately I'd done everything wrong. I should never have let her take one step into that club.

When she'd appeared, damaged and broken, a blast of unexpected and such strong emotion told me I couldn't avoid or hide it anymore. Those motherfuckers had dared to touch what was mine. With thoughts in my head they were going to die, I'd claimed her that morning. It was too late undo what was already done, but I vowed there and then, no man was ever going to lay their hands on my woman, ever again.

And now as it turns out I never even knew the half of it. Of course it was obvious what had happened in that club there had shaken her, as well as physically hurt her. But what they had done was worse than I ever could have imagined.

Fuck. If any of us had had even an inkling of how she was going to be treated we'd have found some other darn way to get eyes and ears into that club. She was damaged, and scared, so while claiming her as my old lady I offered her space and time to recover, telling myself I wasn't going to push for anything more until she was ready.

But I'm just a man, and she's a beautiful woman. Growing tired of waiting, I'd become impatient. My timing so poor happening just before Sophie's protagonist had found her again, and all went to shit at the club. That very morning I'd started to persuade her, making suggestions about her doing more than just sleeping in my bed. I'm now not surprised that she'd run. I went too far and too quickly. If only I'd known the truth at the time I would have done things so differently.

The motherfuckers made her pull a train.

I never dreamt what had happened had been so devastating. Right now I'm not sure how I'm managing to control myself, keeping my rage locked deep inside so I don't scare her further. I'm actually pleased two Rock Demons escaped when we blew up their clubhouse. The idea of having someone left alive to kill is at least helping me keep it together. And find them I will. Drum's already gone to get Mouse tracking them down.

"I was going too fast for ya, wasn't I, darlin'?"

"Slick, there's no speed you could have gone which would have been slow enough." Her little hand fists and lightly hits me in my chest over and over as if she's trying to get rid of her frustration. "After what happened, I don't want any biker, even you, to hurt me like that again."

She's shocked me. "I'd never hurt you."

"Jill told me all bikers like it rough."

She was frightened of me. "Ella, babe. I can do gentle." At least, I fucking hope I can.

"I don't even want to try. I'm too scared, Slick. Look, just leave me be. I can never be a proper old lady for you."

And there we have it. But she's allowing me to give her comfort in my arms and that, if nothing else, must be a good place to begin. "We'll start over. Take it as easy and slow as ya want." I remember telling her that before, but this time I'll go at a fucking crawl.

"Slick, I can't," she wails. "The thought of sex with anyone makes me feel ill. Please, just leave me alone. I will get some help, but I don't want to lead you on. It wouldn't be fair to keep you waiting for something I won't be able to give."

I ignore her. "We'll go on a date." *How the fuck do I do that?* "Start real leisurely."

"You're a man, Slick, you've got needs. You're better off fucking the club whores. I'm being honest here, I'll never be what you want." Her tightly clenched hand thumps me in the chest again. "And it hurts me to think you're getting, from people like Jill, what I can't give you."

My hand covers hers and I squeeze it strongly. "Give me a chance, El. Give me a chance and I promise I won't fuck whores. Or anyone."

"I can't ask you do to that. What if I never…"

"I'll wait for you, darlin'. And if you're not ready, there's always my hand." Fuck, the promises I'm making here. Already my balls are aching wondering if I really could last. Am I really pledging to be celibate for a woman that, let's admit it, I barely know?

That night we'd met, when I'd first entered this shabby house, there had been something about her. She had a spark, was clearly intelligent, and I'd thought even then I wanted her in the clubhouse, but not for the enjoyment of my brothers. No, I wanted her all to myself. A strange feeling when I've laughed at brothers keeping to one pussy before. She was so fucking brave to agree to do what we asked of her. And it gutted me that I'd misled her about what she was walking into, even if I didn't know at the time. Oh, I'd known they had a reputation as being a bit wild with their women and didn't respect them the way the Devils do, but I hadn't envisaged the level of debauchery to which they would go.

Even the thought that one or two had violated and hurt her was enough for me to feel no remorse when we blew up their fucking club. Now I know it was all the members, it's bringing me to my fucking knees. My guilt in the part I played cementing my resolve. If keeping my dick dry is what it will take to put a smile back on her face, then my self-denial will be a small price to pay.

"We barely know each other, Slick. When you said you'd claimed me as your old lady…"

"I did it too fast, and made you run."

"You claimed me to get into my pants. You wanted to sleep with me."

I can't help but chuckle. "I hadn't planned on there being much sleeping involved. But I'll tell you the truth, darlin'. I didn't want any of the brothers' hands on ya. I wanted you all to myself. And, if you'd told me, let me in and explained, I'd have gone so fuckin' easy on you. I'd have been by yer side and helped ya to heal every step of the way."

A little sniffle comes at my explanation. I need to make this right, and I've no fuckin' idea where to start. "I did everything wrong, darlin'. We never talked. Let's start afresh and take time to get to know each other properly. Just conversation and that. No pressure. No rush. Are you up for that? Ella, babe, say you'll come on a date with me, please? Give me a chance."

She thinks for a moment, and I sigh with relief when her head dips in a tentative nod. I'd give anything to be able to kiss her, but even that step would be moving too fast. Already ideas are building in my head about showing her just how fucking slow I can take this. I'll just have to work at keeping my dick under control.

As she snuggles into me my hands stroke her hair. The repetitive action must be calming as gradually she falls back asleep. While I don't want to leave her alone, I do need to get back to the clubhouse. When I hear the front door slam, I'm relieved, suspecting it's her friend Tilly coming home. She's a bitch I've not met before, so I want to check for myself that I'm leaving my woman, *my woman*, in safe hands. I ease myself out from under her, replacing my body with a plumped-up pillow and quietly leave her room, leaving her door slightly ajar in case she wakes and calls out.

Going along the short hallway, the woman, who I assume to be Tilly, comes into sight. She's older than Ella—either that or has lived a much harder life. She glares when she sees me and halts, placing her hands on her hips.

"You the fucker that gave Bart his marching orders yesterday?" she sneers.

"He had his hands on my fuckin' woman," I growl. "Not gonna let any bastard get away with that. And if you know what's good for you, you won't let him back in this house. Not while Ella's here."

She shrugs. "He's coming around later to pick up his shit."

Ella's mine, and I'm going to do what I should have done before, make sure nothing can hurt her. I take my phone from my cut and select a number. It rings a couple of times.

"Road. Get yourself over to Ella's. I'll explain when you get here." I end the call, replace my phone, then turn to Tilly. "Prospect will make sure he only takes what's his and gets the hell out." I've taken an immediate disliking to the woman Ella lives with, apart from the fact that it's clear she's a slob. When she'd been at the clubhouse, Ella had always kept my room tidy and helped the other women cleaning up. I have no doubt it's this woman who's responsible for most of the shit left lying around. The sooner I can get Ella out of here the better.

Tilly tries to stare me down. It doesn't work. Unable to resist take the few steps down the short hallway and push open Ella's door again, as if to impress the sight of her in my memory. Briefly I watch her sleeping, not missing the way she twitches as though she's having a bad dream. The sight guts me. Now knowing the reason, I vow to do everything that's humanly possible to erase those bad memories from her head—there won't be enough that I can do to try to make things right. If it wasn't going to wake her I'd put my fist through the wall. *Those fuckers raped her.*

When I hear the loud pipes, I go out and brief Road, threatening his life if he lets any harm come to my girl. Then I swing my leg on my bike and ride back to the compound, thoughts of Ella going around my head every mile of the way.

Knowing he'll be expecting an update, I go directly to Drum's office, glad to find him alone.

He jerks his chin as I enter. "Heart has stabilised."

I breathe a sigh of relief at the one good thing I've heard today.

"Take a load off." He waves at one of the chairs in front of his desk. I do so, flicking my eyes toward the Satan's Devils flag hanging on the wall behind him. A shadow of Lucifer hovering over three devils, the same as the patch on our cuts.

"How did you not know? That's what I can't understand." Prez's brow furrows. "They must have cut her up. You must have noticed how sore she was."

Taking a deep breath, I let him in on my secret. "I never fucked her."

His jaw drops and he blinks rapidly. "You took an ol' lady without tryin' her out?"

I raise my shoulders. "I didn't want any other fucker near her, brother or not. Seemed the best way to save her for me." And somehow I'd known we'd fit together like hand and glove. "I was giving her time, knew that they'd spooked her. But hell, my cock didn't want to wait. I started to push her."

"And that's when she took off?"

"Yeah." Running my hand over my head I feel stubble coming through and know I'll need to shave it off soon before it starts to irritate me. "I was so angry, Prez. She didn't attempt to talk things over. I was convinced she couldn't handle the life. You know, when Hargreaves turned up and tried to take Sophie?"

"I can understand that. Fuck, I thought that's why she wanted to go. Mouse gettin' hurt, Adam killed. Ella drugged along with the other women. It made sense at the time. Fuck, who'd have thought she was keepin' somethin' like this quiet?"

"She was shocked, ashamed, hurt. Prez, I can't stand thinkin' what those motherfuckers did to her."

"We all know what pullin' a train means." I nod, we do. It's not unheard of here. But only with the club whores when they're in the mood and willing. All brothers queuing up and any hole fair game. And usually more than one at once. Our girls enjoy it, but even they wouldn't want to be forced to do something they didn't want to do. And particularly not if it got out of hand and violent.

"I meant what I said about the club helpin' out. I don't know what insurance she's got."

Thanking him, I take the opportunity to explain I've put Road on her, and the reason why. I don't trust Tilly, and definitely not that no-good-fucker Bart. Road's good with the women. He works part-time at the strip club and the girls love how he treats them with respect. He's a reliable man to have around her, and competent when it comes to a fight.

Prez doesn't hesitate to tell me he's fine with the shit I arranged, and then he suggests a beer, which sounds fucking great.

Following him to the bar, I'm pleased the deathly silence which had descended last night seems to have broken. None of us have forgotten that Crystal and Heart are missing, and at least one of them won't be coming back, but there's only so much melancholy a body can take—it's human nature to pick yourself up and get on with life. Both will remain in our thoughts, but continually hashing it out doesn't move us along.

But there's one thing that bothers me. "How's Amy doin'?"

Drum looks down at the glass in his hand. "None of us have got any idea how to break this kind of news to a kid. Sam's tried to explain that her mom's gone to heaven, and that her dad's in the hospital in bad shape, but fuck knows if she's taken any of it in. It's not easy, Brother. She's hard to comfort, she just can't understand. All she wants is for her mom and dad to be here."

It's difficult for any of us to cope with. But for a three-year-old it must be crippling. Sam's a fucking good woman to take it all on. I tell Drum so.

"Best fuckin' day of my life when I met her," he muses. And he should be proud. She's stepping up as a president's old lady.

"I've spoken to the lawyer," Prez continues, changing the subject. "Heart and Crystal left everythin' to each other. Doubt they ever imagined they could both be taken at once."

"No provision for Amy?"

"Certainly no mention of anythin' being left to Crystal's mom. And no mention of who would have custody."

I narrow my eyes. "That woman really have a claim?"

"Not while Heart's breathin'," Drummer growls, then reiterates, "Amy's here on the compound and that's where she's stayin'. No one will be takin' her away."

"You got any say, Drum? You bein' the executor and all?"

"Not officially, the lawyer's told me. If the worst happens and we lose Heart, Amy's future will be up to a judge."

But even a judge wouldn't give custody to such an unfit woman. Surely not.

Wraith steps up and get his prez's attention. I move away to let them talk by themselves.

Inside I'm reeling. In just two days my life's been turned upside down. I've lost a good friend and may be going to lose a brother. And on top of all that, all my assumptions about my old lady have done a one-eighty. There's no way I'm not reclaiming that relationship now. I turn my back to the bar and see a couple of the sweet butts sitting ready and waiting—Allie and one of the new girls, Diva—and for the first time in months my cock doesn't even stir. *I'd been trying to fuck her out of my system.* It hadn't worked.

If I'm going to have a chance at winning her back, I'm going to have to be smart. She's agreed to take things slow? I grin to myself. I can do that.

CHAPTER 10
Ella

So now it's all come out and everyone will know my embarrassing secret, the one I'd kept buried deep, hoping no one would ever need to know, so ashamed of what I'd let happen to me.

Oh, I know I didn't ask for it or encourage such debasement, but something I had done had to have encouraged them. *Perhaps just the fact I walked into their club dressed as a slut.* Notwithstanding, I put myself in that predicament in the first place. If I hadn't had been so stupid to believe the rosy picture Jill had painted, been so taken in by the idea of sex with a biker, I'd never have met anyone from the club. It was my own out of character and shocking behaviour that caused me to get into the position I had. The Satan's Devils might have been responsible for setting me up with the Demons, but I wouldn't have been there had my mind not been fixated on my eagerness to sample good sex for the first time. Sex with a biker.

I'm no whore, and I should have known it, it's not just the physical act with a man, but everything else that comes along with it. I might blame Jill, but really all I heard was that I'd have the chance to have one of the bikers as my own. Instead of really listening and thinking things through, I pretended to be something I could never be, and jumped at the chance to escape my drab life. I got exactly what I was after, even though it wasn't what I had wanted. And it ruined my chances with the one man I did desire.

Despite the comfort Slick had given me, and that he'd stayed until I was asleep, I'm perfectly aware he did so only out of guilt. What man would want me now, knowing I'd been violated in every way it was possible for a woman to be defiled? However many times I shower, I can never wash the stain off me. And the thought of ever trusting a man and being intimate with him again causes me to panic. What man wants to be saddled with a broken woman like that?

He said he'd go slow. I don't want him to get started. He'll want sex eventually, and the idea of being touched, *there*, makes me cringe. *Never again.* I might as well go live in a convent, I'll spend the rest of my life as a nun. I doubt the man I'm now coming to know would ever force me, but when I don't put out he'll get bored and move on. He's a man. He's a biker.

I've cried enough tears. Splashing water over my face, I summon up the vision of Jayden. I have to be strong, if only for her. I've got to forget my rash and now much regretted disclosure and concentrate on her instead. *What has she got herself into?* Hoping Mouse will soon be able to find something out, idly wondering how he'll go about it, I wander out into the lounge.

"Wondered when you were going to show your face." Tilly's standing, leaning against the kitchen counter, a mug of coffee in her hands. "Your fucking boyfriend had no right kicking Bart out."

I sigh. I could really do without this now. "Tilly, Bart came onto me…"

She interrupts and shrugs off my attempt at an explanation. "He said you were flirting."

There's no point reasoning with her, not now that he's got his side in first. I've wanted to get out of here for ages, but where else could I afford?

"And another thing…"

This time it's her who's forced to break off by a commotion at the door which swings open, banging hard against the wall. Bart comes inside, along with one of his vicious looking friends. When Tilly's boyfriend's eyes fall on me, he leers, and I step back, poised to escape into my room.

"Get what you came for then get out."

The unexpected deep and authoritative voice has me spinning. I see a man in a Satan's Devils' cut, standing lazily by the doorway. He throws me a wink, then presumably interpreting the look on my face as one of concern, he comes inside, putting himself protectively between me and Bart and his friend. He's tall and well built, and as he crosses his arms over his chest he exudes confidence that he could handle anything they would throw at him. His back turned toward me, I can see the patch saying he's a prospect.

He speaks to me over his shoulder without taking his eyes off any possible threat. "Go to your room, Ella, and make yourself pretty. I'll handle things here. Slick's on his way over and he's takin' you on a date."

What? He meant it?

The prospect risks a quick glance over his shoulder. "I'm Road, by the way. And Slick put me here to watch out for you."

Slick's keeping me safe?

The scene playing out in front of me, now no longer threatening, is amusing, and I linger for a moment to watch. Despite Bart coming with back-up, no one wants to take Road on. Pretending that's what they came for, and not to cause trouble, they're busying themselves carrying out Bart's possessions, armfuls of clothing and then the TV. Wait. What? But Tilly steps forward, she's having none of that. Her vocal objection accompanied by her frown showing she's starting to monitor what they're taking more closely.

Realising all my possessions are safely stored in my room, and that Road's not going to be allowing them anywhere near my domain, I decide to do what the prospect's suggested and leave them to it. *Slick's going to take me on a date? Tonight?* Still unable to compute what that might mean for a rough biker, I sort through my clothes. *Hang on. Why didn't he tell me himself?* I pause. Perhaps I should refuse to go. *Yeah, and if he'd asked me, that's what I would have told him.* The reason for his message being passed on by Road becomes clear. *Sneaky man.*

It might be nice to go out—so long as he's been honest and he's got no expectations. Since I was injured I've had to live off my meagre savings and, even now I'm back at work, it's hard to get by. Going out has been a luxury I haven't been able to afford. And what's the alternative? Spending the evening with Tilly moaning about Bart?

It's that thought that makes up my mind. I restart going through my clothes, realising I have no idea what to wear for an evening on the town with someone like Slick, finding it difficult to imagine where he might take me. In the end, I settle for jeans and a pretty enough floral shirt. I open the bag of makeup I haven't touched in four months, but then pull the zip closed once again. Clean and tidy will do. I'm doing nothing that might encourage him.

By the time I've made myself presentable, Tilly's shouting out, and I go into the sitting room, noticing the TV is back in its rightful place, and find Slick at the door. He's wearing smart black jeans and a button-down shirt under his cut. His head's freshly shaven and gleams under the light. He's looking so good it makes me want to turn and run in the opposite direction.

Ignoring the other woman, he swiftly steps up beside me, the flare in his eyes shows me he likes what he sees, even though I've done nothing to enhance what nature gave me.

"I..."

"Before you fuckin' say you don't think this is a good idea, just listen to me." My eyes open wide, realising he's read my mind. "I'm takin' you out, woman. We'll go have some dinner like normal folks do, and then I'll bring you straight home." As he stares intently at my face, he challenges me. "Has there been one fuckin' time I've given you reason not to trust me?"

My heart's beating fast, but I know that he's right. He's never given me cause to distrust him, why should he now? Those two weeks I'd stayed in the clubhouse, in his room and in his bed, he never pushed me—well, not until the end. And even then it was only a verbal suggestion.

He holds out his hand, I move forward and take it. Swallowing down my panic before it can take hold, I put my fingers in his and take a step toward my future.

As I expected, no car waits outside, just a sleek motorcycle. He opens one of the side boxes and gets out two helmets and passes me a pair of clear safety glasses. He pauses. "Had to borrow this lid from one of my brothers." He puts it on my head and does up the chin strap. "Never had a bitch on the back of my bike before." Patting the passenger seat, he continues, "This spot's for you, darlin'. Only for you."

That he's told me something significant is obvious, and a little warm feeling inside starts to glow. With an ease of long practice, he steps astride the bike, taking it off the stand and holding it steady. This time he holds out his hand to help me get my balance and climb on. Tentatively I place my hands on the little handles which seem to be made for the purpose, and place my feet on the pegs. He reaches back, taking hold of my wrists and pulling my arms tight around him.

"First time?" My trembling body gives him the answer. "Hold on tight and just go with me, okay? Lean when I do, don't fight the bike."

Without giving me a chance to have second thoughts, he starts the engine and we're moving along the road. Suppressing a yelp, I press up against him, needing no further encouragement to hold onto him tight. But as he goes so smoothly soon I feel more confident that he knows what he's doing, quickly finding the experience of riding through the warm late summer evening with the wind rushing past is liberating. Surprisingly I'm starting to enjoy myself, and regretting we've only gone a short distance when he pulls into a car park.

Tapping my leg, I realise he wants me to get off. After taking a second to unlock my hands, I place one on his shoulder and swing my leg around, stumbling a little as I hit a ground which isn't vibrating. He backs into a parking spot and switches the engine off.

"Alright?" His eyes question me, his head tilted.

"Loved it." And my truthful answer seems to bring him relief as his face splits into a smile.

I look around. I've walked past often enough, but never been inside. Slick notices me eyeing it up and gives a little laugh. "I don't know what I'm doing, darlin'. Never taken anyone on a date before. I suppose I should have thought of somewhere else to take you. But fuck, I don't know what you like."

Hurrying to reassure him, I shake my head. "No, here's fine, Slick."

With the faintest of touches he leads me inside and I enter the Wheel Inn for the very first time. It doesn't look like a restaurant owned by bikers, and the clientele look like normal folks, just like myself.

As soon as we enter a woman rushes over. "Got a booth in the corner reserved for you, Slick." I notice she's giving me an appraising look.

"Thanks Marsha." He doesn't say more, just leads me on over.

Slick might not have dated before, I certainly have, so at least I have something to measure it by. And in my estimation, up to this point he's doing alright. As we're seated and drinks ordered, I steal a glance at him over the top of my menu. He's studying his, though I suspect he probably knows it by heart. Suddenly his eyes meet mine and he grins a little sheepishly.

"Know what you're gonna have?"

I fold the menu and put it down. With all the butterflies swirling in my stomach, nothing takes my fancy. "What do you recommend?"

"Steak here is excellent."

"I'll have that then."

The waitress comes over and fusses around with the silverware, then takes our order. One rare, one medium.

Slick leans forward, his elbows on the table, his hands clasped. "We never did do much talkin'."

He's right. How on earth he came to claim me as his old lady when we knew nothing about each other is ridiculous. Feeling brave, unthreatened in this public place, I tell him so. "I never asked you to claim me, Slick. I still can't understand why you called me your old lady."

He closes his eyes briefly. "Truth? When you first came to the club, the arrangement was you were gonna be a sweet butt." He waits for me to agree. While I now know I could never have done that, it had been my intention at the time.

"I don't think I could have gone through with it." Even if I hadn't gone to the Rock Demons club.

"I *know* you couldn't. You're not made that way, El. Heck, I was kiddin' myself as much as you were. Should have gone with it sooner, then you'd never been at that fuckin' place." He looks like he's mentally kicking himself. "Have to tell ya, I never saw myself with an ol' lady, and that was the fuckin' problem. Was tryin' to convince myself you weren't as special as you seemed." He chuckles. "But as soon as the fuckers started talkin' about cha that way I had to shut that shit up, and I found myself claimin' you." He gives me an intense look. "And as soon as I said it, I knew it felt right."

I look down at the table. I don't know what I had expected. Had I hoped he'd say he'd fallen in love at first sight? No, it was baser than that. He just didn't want anyone else to have me.

A finger touches my chin as he gently turns my face up. When he speaks his voice has dropped an octave. "You're so fuckin' beautiful. That first night when I met you? I knew you were brave. It fuckin' killed me to let you go into the Demons' club. To know one of those fuckers was gonna touch what was already mine. If only you knew how much I wanted to stop you."

"I wish you had." My voice breaks.

He shakes his head. "I had my brothers to think of. What you did for us saved lives. I had to let you do it, Ella. But fuck, if I'd have known…"

As guilt crosses his face I wrap my hand around his that's still touching my face. "You didn't know, Slick. It's not on you. It's all down to me."

"You?" He rears back. "You asked for nothin'."

I shrug, knowing I'd set myself up. I look around the restaurant, trying to convey I don't want to continue this conversation.

He gets the hint. "So, Ella. Tell me somethin' about yourself. All I know is you've got a mom and a sister. Yer dad around?"

I raise my shoulders, "Not much more to tell. Dad left Mom shortly after Jayden came along, I don't know where he is now."

"How come yer livin' in such a shithole?"

I flush as he points it out. "Mom and I didn't get along, so I left home when I finished school. I wanted to go to college, but with no support that wasn't possible. A room came up with Tilly and I moved in and been there ever since. Tilly's not really so bad, it's her choice of men that's a problem."

"You don't need to worry about that asshole Bart. Drummer agrees Road will be sticking with ya. And if he's not around it will be someone else. Probably Marsh. Remember him?"

I nod. I'd only lived at the compound for a couple of weeks, but had grown to know the young prospect, usually to be found behind the bar, quite well. In my twisted head he wasn't a true member, and thus not so much of a threat.

"Thank you," I whisper, grateful that they're making me feel safe—and cared for. "Any news on my sister?"

This makes him laugh. "Yeah, Tongue caught up with her leaving school yesterday. I was gonna ask you where she'd be, but Mouse figured it out. Tongue filched her phone. Did some shit that cloned all her information and put some sort of tracker on it."

My hand goes to my mouth. "She's not got a phone? How will I contact her?"

"Don't underestimate us, Ella. Tongue handed it into the school. He waited and watched. It didn't take long before she realised it was missin' and went back and got it."

Now I'm shaking my head and smiling at their audacity. How the hell did Tongue manage to do all that?

"Mouse wants me to bring you to the compound tomorrow so you can go through it with him. See what he can find out with your help. Will you come, El?"

I purse my lips. There's a lot of memories there. And now, it's even worse. "Do they all know?" I hold my breath for the answer.

Now his hand grabs hold of both of mine, his fingers wrapped tightly around them. "Whether anyone knows or not shouldn't bother you. Don't for one second think any of them are going to judge you. It wasn't down to you, Ella. What those mother-fuckers did…"

I try to pull away, but for once he won't let me.

"If you want honesty, everyone's gutted that we set you up."

"You couldn't have known."

His expression suggests they should have expected it.

And then our steaks arrive, putting a stop to the conversation now that the time for eating is here. The chef must be good, the meat's cooked to perfection, and it's not hard to understand why every table around us is filled. I can barely suppress my groan of satisfaction, making Slick grin as he tucks in too.

For the rest of the evening we leave serious subjects behind, Slick regaling me of the antics of his brothers, including that they've apparently got an off-road track set up behind the compound now, and that Sam, Drummer's old lady, holds the current record. They've been holding weekly competitions, but even Road, the new prospect, and who rides in competition, has difficulty beating her.

"She's really bought her own dirt bike?" I wonder if I'd ever like to ride.

"She certainly has."

I ask the question that's always intrigued me. "What's your real name, Slick?"

His eyes narrow, and I don't think he's going to answer, then the corners of his mouth turn up. "Been a long time since anyone's used it. But I don't mind if you do. It's Jeff. Jeff Andrews."

It sounds a strong name, one that suits him. Taking a sip of my drink, I tilt my glass toward him. "So why Slick? Is it because you shave your head?"

His grin widens. "Naw." He chuckles. "Back when I was a prospect I hit an oil slick on the road. Laid down my bike. Fuckers wouldn't let me forget." I smile.

From having no appetite, I've somehow managed to polish off my steak as well as consuming a large portion of utterly delicious cheesecake. I sit back and stare at my empty plate in surprise. The evening's gone fast, Slick being better company that I'd expected.

"Shall I ask for the check?"

And then my spirits plummet down. *What's he going to expect now the evening has ended?* Is he going to be angry when I don't want to give payment in return?

I'm silent as we go to his bike, nervous all the way home, hoping he'll drop me off and ride away. But of course he doesn't. As he follows me to the door, I pause with my key in my hand, worried about what I can say. Last time he didn't take well to rejection.

Summoning up courage, I turn to face him to find him staring down at me. Without touching me with his hands, he lowers his head and his lips brush gently against mine, only for a second before pulling away.

"Night, Ella. I'll call in the mornin' about meetin' up with Mouse." He continues to stare at me. "You know, I've had a good time. Perhaps this datin' thing has somethin' goin' for it."

He turns and goes to his bike, pausing before starting the engine, twirling his hand as if giving me an instruction to go inside. As I open the door, he waves at Road, waiting patiently over across the street, and then disappears into the night.

My hand goes to my lips, which his mouth had barely touched, and it dawns on me how much I enjoyed our date too.

CHAPTER 11
Slick

I'm riding back to the compound with a huge great fucking smile on my face and wondering what that shit is all about? That brief meeting of lips, although admittedly leaving me with a raging hard on, was something so special I don't think I've ever felt this way in my life. Despite the world falling apart around me, this great step forward I've made in repairing, no, starting a relationship with Ella has got me grinning like a fucking kid in junior high. I may not have got completely to first base, but I've made a fucking good start.

Parking up I step into the clubhouse and walk to the bar, a spring in my step that had been missing for months.

"Beer," I demand, rapping on the wood. Marsh snaps quickly to serve me.

"Slick, you and I haven't had some fun together. Wanna give me a try?"

Spinning around I see Diva, and she's right, I've not dipped into that yet. A waft of cheap perfume has me wrinkling my nose, reminding me of the clean, fresh smell of the woman I've just left.

"Not tonight, sweetheart." I let her down gently.

Not easily put off, she tries again. "We could threesome with Paige?"

I glance across to where the other new sweet butt's sitting, looking eagerly across and decide to knock this on the head now. "I've got an ol' lady."

She should walk away, instead she continues to push. "Don't see her around."

"I've got an ol' lady," repeating myself loudly. "Leave me the fuck alone." I turn back to the bar, thumping my hand down, my previous good mood being swept away. There's no doubt my cock isn't as resilient as my brain—he's twitching away eager to sink into any hole. But I know I won't be satisfied if I follow his lead. There's only one woman I want, and I'm prepared to wait. Though taxing as it's going to be at times, she'll be fucking worth it.

Caught up in my inner turmoil, I don't notice Wraith approach, his arm around Sophie, and they're both grinning at me. My VP indicates my, for me, smart clothing. "Date went well I take it?"

"You had a date?" Sophie's beaming from ear to ear. "With Ella? Is she coming back?"

Her innocent enquiry has my good mood returning. "Yeah," I give in and tell them both. "And I fuckin' hope so. Won't be for want of me tryin'."

"Good on yer, Slick." Wraith nods in approval.

Jerking my chin at him in return, I glance at his old lady, who's trying to hoick her butt onto the tall bar stool, noticing she's looking slightly rounded now, their baby starting to show. And suddenly it hits me like a bolt of lightning from one of our Arizonian summer storms that I'd like to see my baby growing in Ella's stomach. The thought so unexpected I turn away and run my hand down my face.

Me claiming an old lady was bad enough, but wanting the real deal with her? Leading a grown-up life with a house off the compound and children? Well fuck me if that doesn't get me as excited as if someone's given me a new Harley, rather than making me want to vomit as it has in the past. But first, a little voice inside reminds me I've got to convince her. I've got to work hard for something I want for once in my life.

Taking leave of my brothers, I walk up to the compound to my room in one of the renovated blocs that used to house guests when this place was a vacation resort. When it had burned out, only a club of bikers looking for a new home saw potential in the shell that remained. And the accommodation provided on site to the brothers was better than in any clubhouse I've ever seen. I enter the building housing my suite and the now redundant Wraith's—as he now lives with Sophie—knowing it will always be mine, even if I buy a house down Tucson way.

I've always had things easy. My parents are still married and living happily together, I wasn't beaten in my childhood or kicked out of home. I served my time in the Army and came back uninjured, and got my place as a prospect shortly after I finished my final tour of duty. Prospecting was hard, I ain't gonna lie, but after I was patched in there was easy pussy on tap and a life free of citizens' rules. I've never had to fight for anything before, it's always been handed to me on a plate.

Until now. For once I've got a challenge on my hands, and fuck me if I'm not looking forward to it. Working to get my old lady back? I'm going to give it every damn thing I have.

Ten o'clock the next morning and we're back in church. Never come to the table as much as we have the last few days, but I can't criticise the reason. Drum's wanting us all to be updated with everything going on. Our businesses running on just a skeleton crew, we're all staying close by in case of trouble.

He raps the gavel down hard, and all eyes are on him. "Who's at the hospital?"

"Viper," Dart confirms. He consults the page in front of him. "Slick, you're on the next shift?"

I nod, happy to do my bit. And fuck, even though he won't be able to talk to me I'm eager to see Heart, even if it's only to see for myself he's still with us.

Drum points at me. "Mouse got some info for ya. You need to stay close and bring Ella here. Rock, can you do a swap?"

"Sure fuckin' thing, boss," he agrees, spinning the gun on the table in front of him.

I sit up in my seat, eager to hear what Mouse has found, apologising silently to Heart and promising him I'll be seeing him soon.

Waving me back down, Prez looks around. "Order of business. Heart, then Ella. Okay? And then Wraith's got some suggestions about prospects."

I toss him a glare. I'd rather it was the other way around, but when he starts speaking he captures my interest.

"Got a phone call last night. Wraith and I went out to meet Detective Hannah this mornin'." He jerks his chin toward the VP. Safety in pairs and all that. Our habit when speaking to the filth. Means no one can be accused of saying something they didn't. If we can't have another brother along, we say nothing without the club lawyer. Nobody, not even the prez, wants to set themselves up for an accusation of being a rat.

"It was odd," Wraith takes over. "She parked around the back of the Wheel Inn as though she didn't want to be seen. We opened it up early to talk inside."

Joker sniggers. "Looks like we've got ourselves a dirty cop."

Drum glares at him. "The opposite, I think. But I've got doubts about her partner."

"We know anything of him, Prez?"

"No, Lady. They're both new to Tucson. But as the VP said, I don't think she's on the take. And if he is, then we're certainly not the ones fuckin' payin' him."

"Somethin' to worry about?"

"Could be, Peg. Could fuckin' be."

"What did she want?" I butt in.

"To give us an unofficial report." Drum taps his fingers on the table, his steely eyes looking around the room. From the expression on his face I get the feeling we will dislike what he's about to say. "They've been over Heart's bike. No mechanical problems to cause a crash. But the rear fender's obviously taken a hit. Something must have shunted them hard."

"Fuck that!" Motherfucker! Though we'd had our suspicions, it's hard to hear that Heart's smash was no accident. Which confirms Crystal's death as murder.

The prez waits for all of us to pipe down. "There was some transfer of paint onto the fender."

"Have they analysed it?"

"Yeah, Mouse. It's a dark green 2014 Ford F-250." Mouse starts tapping away as Drum continues, "Will you be able to find anythin'?"

"I'll look into who's got one registered to them, starting with anyone who's had an issue with us. And at the auto shops. A prang that hard would cause damage needing to be repaired."

"Hannah's checkin' out stolen vehicles."

"Can you look at associates of this Detective Archer?" Something is niggling at the back of my mind.

Prez confirms I'm right to have suspicions. "Good point, Slick. I didn't like the fucker. It's worryin' that Hannah told us he asked for them to be assigned to the case."

"It's clear Hannah is puzzled as to why," Wraith adds.

"Anythin' else she could tell us?" Bullet lights a cigarette and smoke plumes rise above the table.

"Pass one to me." I reach for his pack.

"And me?"

"For fuck's sake Blade!" Bullet all but throws it at him.

Cigarettes lit and burning, I look back at the prez as he carries on after the brief interruption. "No, but at least she's going to keep us informed. She didn't say anythin' about Archer being dirty, but she led us to believe he didn't want us to be given any intel." Drum picks up the beer he brought in with him, making me feel I wish I'd had the foresight to collect one too. "We can expect visitors. They'll want to interrogate us, see if we know any enemies Heart may have had. Readin' between the lines, Archer may use it as a chance to get into the compound. Hannah said she'd suggested they ask us to go to the station, but Archer wasn't fuckin' buyin' it"

Another round of swearing.

Again Drum scans the room. "Don't need to tell ya, anything we know we'll be actin' on it ourselves. Now you've all slept on it, anyone come up with any fuckin' idea who'd want to take out Heart?"

We all shake our heads. Then Mouse puts up his hand. "I don't like the mother, Crystal's mom. Been doing some diggin'. She's an addict, been arrested a couple of times for solicitin'."

"She owe money?"

Mouse smirks at the prez. "Seems likely. But if she does, don't think the types she's owes to keep online accounts." There's sniggering around the table. "But I'll keep diggin'."

"You don't really think she'd put a fuckin' contract out on her daughter and husband, do you?" I'm shaking my head. I didn't like the woman, but surely she wouldn't go that far.

"Doubt it would be worth it. Our businesses are thrivin' and we're takin' home a decent cut, but Heart and Crystal haven't got much to leave anyone. Their house is rented."

Prez knows what he's talking about. We're all in a healthy position, but none of us would leave much of an inheritance to speak of.

Drum bangs the gavel. "As of now, we don't discount anythin'. Keep your eyes and ears open, and Mouse, keep doing your shit. Now movin' along, want to update on what you've found out about Ella's sister."

At fucking last!

Mouse points at me. "I'd like to speak to her today."

"I'll try and get her here." I agree. I'm sitting forward, eager to hear what he's going to say next.

Mouse taps at his keyboard. "I've got into Jayden's Facebook account. And looked at her phone. Thanks for gettin' that done, Tongue." Tongue waves his hand as if to say it was nothing, and to him it probably wasn't. "It looks like she's got herself a boyfriend. Hundreds of text messages back and forth."

"Anythin' odd? Ella said the things she had were expensive."

With his dark hair from his Native American heritage swinging around his head, Mouse shakes his head. "Jayden's quite open in her texts, but the ones from Diego, the 'boy' I'm assumin' she's seein'," he puts two fingers up from each hand giving emphasis to the word boy, "are brief. When he tells her to meet him he just says usual place or same time. Short crap like that."

Drum again taps the table. "We can track her now though?"

"Long as she's got the phone," Mouse agrees.

"What's your readin' of it?"

Mouse shrugs. "It's hard to say. But somethin' doesn't seem right. There's no photos on Facebook, her status is still single. Girls, they like to put shit up if they're in a relationship. If she's got somethin' going on, she's hidin' it from her friends."

I don't like what I'm hearing, something sounds off. Fine, a fourteen-year-old could be in a relationship with an older man that she wants to hide, but according to Ella he wasn't making her happy. "I'll try to get Ella here, Mouse, but if I can't, you okay to go to her?" As he nods I continue, "You can run your ideas past her and pick her brain."

"Appreciate that, Slick. Hey. After hearin' what she went through, don't think anyone could criticise her for stayin' away."

Taken aback I simply stare, and then turn to Drum who shrugs. "Thought it wouldn't hurt everyone knowin' she didn't walk out on you, Slick. She left the club not understandin' there's no way in hell any of us here would force a woman." He pointedly looks around the table at my brothers. "She comes back here, ya'll treat her like fuckin' glass."

My face feels tight, expecting them to think the worse of me for not going after her.

"We got this, Slick," Wraith says, with no derision in his voice. Choked up by his support I can only lift my chin to show my thanks.

"We'll get Marsh followin' this Jayden," Prez announces. "Road's tied up with Ella. You still want him on her I suppose, Slick?"

Pulling my head back into the game, I reply, "Yeah, I don't trust her roommate's ex." Particularly as he wouldn't be an ex if it wasn't for me. Scowling, I remember that fucker's hands on her. No one is ever going to hurt Ella again.

"So that brings us nicely around to the fact we need more prospects. VP?"

Wraith nods and takes over. "I'm proposin' Marsh gets his patch. He's been here fourteen months now. Anyone disagree?"

No one puts up their hands. "Let's take a vote on it."

As Drum goes around the table it's a unanimous round of ayes. As Dart records the decision my eyes flit to the empty chair next to Peg, and I can't help but wonder whether we'll ever see our rightful secretary sitting there again.

Wraith whistles for attention. "There's a couple of guys been coming around. They've been doing some building work for us. Bullet, you want to give an update?"

"Yeah." The treasurer takes over. "Hyde's one, he seems sound. And Spindle."

"*Spindle?*" I can't tell who echoes the name as it's more than one.

"Yeah, skinny fella. But he's only a youngster so he's probably still got some growin' to do."

Viper's nodding. "I'll second them in. They're both dependable." Bullet heads up, and Viper works with our construction crew.

"You spoken to them, Wraith?"

"I have, Prez. They know the score."

And there's another round of voting. We all agree to them coming in. Even with Marsh getting his patch we'll be back to three prospects again. This day's looking up.

CHAPTER 12
Ella

Tilly isn't talking to me when I get through the front door, and I'm not totally sure why, Bart can hardly be a great loss. Hell, she'll be able to find a replacement before too long as she sets her bar so low. As long as it's got a cock she doesn't seem overly fussy. It's probably more likely that I've become the cause of disruption in her disorderly life.

Having had such a surprisingly enjoyable evening, her silence doesn't bother me at all. Ignoring her as I step over yet more trash, go into my room, sling my purse over the chair, and lie back on the bed, my arms folded behind my head.

It had been the first time I'd really sat down with Slick and simply talked. To my surprise, I'd ended up having an enjoyable time—one of, if not *the* best date I've ever been on. He's been so easy to converse with, we'd laughed and had fun. If my mind wasn't so fucked up I'd jump at the chance of going out with him again. But it was, still is. So what should I do? He hasn't hidden his end game. And I'm certain he's not got the patience to wait for the length of time it would probably take before I was ready for an intimate relationship—right now I can't believe I ever will be.

But he's making all the right moves. So far he hasn't put a step wrong.

Placing my fingers to my lips I can still feel his featherlike kiss there. It was hardly a touch at all, yet it still seemed to brand me. A caress so gentle, completely at odds with the rough burly man. He's trying so hard, but how difficult it must be to hold himself back. *He's a biker.* He's used to sex on tap, whenever and wherever he wants it. He'll soon get bored.

But he's trying. And that puts a smile on my face.

I'm woken, after a thankfully dreamless sleep, by my phone buzzing and threatening to vibrate itself off my bedside table. Reaching out I grab it before it falls and, after checking the number, accept the call.

"Slick?"

"Mornin' darlin'. How are ya today?"

I snuggle down in my bed, holding the phone tight, strangely feeling dizzy, like a school girl speaking to her first boyfriend, "I'm good, Slick. And I enjoyed last night."

There's a brief pause and an audible intake of breath before, "Me too, darlin'. Me too. What you up to today?"

"At the moment I'm still in bed." After a sharp breath warns me perhaps I shouldn't have put that image in his head, I quickly continue, "Nothing out of the normal, I'll just be out there looking for a different job."

"Mouse wants to meet up with ya. Can you come to the club?"

My hand not holding the phone twists the sheet, holding it tight. "I'm not ready for that, Slick." The thought of seeing all the bikers again fills me with dread. Leather and motorbikes, sex in the open.

"Okay." He's quiet for a moment. "How about I get Mouse and we'll come to you?"

Remembering the state of the living room last night, I'd be embarrassed to have anyone else seeing the way that I, or rather Tilly, lives. "I don't think that's a good idea, Slick." I could pick up the rubbish but there's no time to wash the stains off the floor.

"Okay. What about somewhere neutral? Have a coffee or a beer?"

I smile though he can't see me. Only a biker would think of beer first thing in the morning. "A coffee sounds great."

We agree that he'll pick me up. As we end the call, I realise it was nice just hearing his voice.

He hasn't given me long to get ready. Throwing back the sheet I get up and go into the bathroom, moving Tilly's mess off to one side before cleansing my face. Drying off with a towel, I glance into the mirror, for the first time in months giving myself a critical examination. Like most Arizonian residents, I've the basis of a tan, hard to avoid unless you stay out of the sun. I don't sunbathe, but my skin browns from the exposure from just walking around.

My cheeks are pinched in, I hadn't realised I'd lost so much weight. My auburn hair is untidy at the ends and has lost its shine. In all I've a haunted look. *What does he see in me?* My fringe is too long and flops over my eyes. I reach for the scissors and give it a trim. *That looks better.* With a shaking hand I pick up a bag, the contents of which I hadn't used last night, and stare at it. Then, finally making a decision, I take my eyeliner out, rimming my eyes with kohl and then lightly applying mascara.

Immediately my eyes look enlarged.

Is it too much? Will he notice the difference? Men don't notice anything. I laugh to myself as I pick up a brush and work it through my hair. It used to be long, reaching down to my ass. But the memory of them pulling on it, using it to keep me in place meant I'd asked Tilly to chop it off. She'd done a fair enough job, but she's no hairdresser. It might be worth spending some of my precious dollars to have it properly styled. Perhaps in a short bob?

Placing my hands on the counter, I lean forward and give myself another critical look. With my eyes highlighted, my fringe trimmed and my hair brushed out, I look more like my old self. My improved reflection gives me a little confidence, and I start to wonder if it's possible to regain some resemblance to the woman I used to be.

Slick arrives on time. He walks in and hands me a helmet. "Got sunglasses, babe?"

I do, and get them out of my purse. *He hasn't noticed.* I turn my laugh into a cough.

I hang onto him without him telling me, and enjoy the short ride to the coffee shop they've chosen, to find Mouse already waiting for us. We go inside and find a table in a corner. I notice both men take seats by the walls, I'm left with my back facing the counter.

Mouse opens his laptop, telling us he's already tapped into the wi-fi in the shop. As he runs his fingers across the keyboard I study him. When I'd been at the club he'd just been one of the leather-clad bikers and I hadn't spent much time watching them, instead keeping my head down so they wouldn't notice me. He's a handsome man, very tall, looks like he has Native American blood, long, straight, almost black hair which is tied back in a ponytail, and slightly flared nostrils in an aquiline face, his skin a shade darker than Slick's.

He catches my inspection when he looks up and grins quickly before becoming serious again. "Ella, I'm afraid you're not going to like this."

I had a feeling I wouldn't. *Is he going to confirm my fears?* "Just tell me, please, Mouse."

"Your sister, Jayden, is seein' someone."

I expected that.

"I've been through her Facebook account and through her phone. You know Tongue was able to get it and clone it?"

I nod to show I'm aware and just wish he'd get to the point. But I'm tongue-tied and nervous, and wary of saying the wrong thing.

"Up to about three months ago, Jayden's Facebook account was exactly what you'd expect from a young girl. Sharing amusing memes about animals, posting selfies with her friends. Then her posts start to slow down, and then stop."

He turns the laptop around so I can see. He's right, the posts tail off. There are posts on her newsfeed from friends, but it doesn't seem like she's interacted with them.

When I indicate I can see what he means, he turns it back around. "There is, however, quite a lot of activity on messenger. He taps a few keys, then once again the screen is facing toward me. "There are messages from a boy she's obviously met. I've checked out his profile, and nothin' seems wrong there. He's sixteen years old, looks his age in his photos. Talks about football and baseball with his friends—fairly normal activity from what I can see. But you see here…" He reaches over and swipes down the page. "They're makin' arrangements to meet in a mall."

I read the conversation.

Sy: Want to meet up this Saturday? At the mall?

Jayden: Mom's working. She told me to stay home.

Sy: She won't know if you don't tell her.

"And so it continues. Now look at this." He swipes down again.

Jayden: Mom told me I'm too young for a boyfriend. And my sister would go ape if she knew.

Sy: Don't tell them. This is our secret.

Mouse taps the screen. "This is what sparked my concern. There's pages of 'don't tell your mom or sister' and 'this is our secret'."

I bite my lip. "You think she's with this boy?" I'm not sure if it's a normal teenage relationship—it doesn't seem too bad. As for keeping it quiet, well, I doubt either Mom or I would be too pleased not having met him and, I for one, would make certain I had 'the talk' with her. But that doesn't account for why she's so unhappy.

"No, I don't. Look here." Again he selects a new part of the conversation.

Sy: "What did you think of my uncle, Diego?"

Jayden: He seemed nice.

Sy: He liked you a lot. He's got a gift for you.

Jayden: For me? Why?

Sy: As I said, he likes you. Will you meet him? Let him give it to you?

Now my eyes shoot up and meet Mouse's. "Oh fuck."

"Yeah. And this is where this comes in." He clicks a few more keys. "These are the text messages I got off her phone. Seems like she met the uncle. Her conversations with Sy stop, and she now starts talkin' to this other man. There's other things here too. Up to that point she's textin' her friends, and then those communications start to slow too. A couple are sayin' Diego's too old for her, but she shuts them up and then stops answerin' completely.

"How old is this Diego?"

"I've no idea, Ella, with just the first name I can't tell you more. But I think we need to find out."

For the first time Slick enters the conversation. "Have you ever heard her mention either of these names?"

I shake my head. "Certainly not. Jayden's always acted quite young for her age. She hasn't had a boyfriend before, I'm sure of that.

Mouse sits back and folds his arms across his muscular chest. His eyes flick to Slick and then back to me. "What I'm findin' worryin' is that this all fits a pattern. You've heard of groomin', haven't you?"

Of course I have. My hands cover my mouth.

The computer guru nods. "Young boys sent in first to get a girl's attention. Isolate her from her friends, get her used to keepin' secrets, then introduce them to an older friend or relative. Use flattery, make her feel special."

"A few weeks ago she was glowing, so happy. As she seemed in a good place, I didn't think anything of it. Oh my God. You think this older man..." I can't say it.

Slick can. "Has raped her? From what Mouse is saying, and what you're describin', yes, I'm sorry to say I think we can assume he has. And it's still going on if she keeps disappearin'."

"She won't speak to me. She clams up. I've tried, Slick, I've pleaded with her, screamed at her to tell me what's up."

"She's probably too frightened. People like this, mother-fuckin' scum that they are, they're the type to use threats to keep girls in line."

Slick sits forward. Reaching over the table he grabs hold of one of my shaking hands. "We're going to find him, Ella. Mouse is trackin' her phone. We can find out where she's going and follow her. We'll sort it, don't worry."

All I can think of is my fourteen-year-old sister being taken advantage of by an older man. Just the thought makes me feel ill. She's so young and should still be innocent. It's too much to take in.

Mouse gives me a moment and then starts talking again. "Last night she stayed home. From the pattern I've noticed, it's normally toward the end of the week she goes to see him. And next time she does, we'll be there and stop it."

"Should I confront her? Now I have a name." I need to do something. Anything. Forbid her to see this man again? But if they're right about him holding threats over her, she'll probably just deny it. I feel so damn helpless.

A shake of Mouse's head. "No. She hasn't confided in you before, I doubt she'll tell you anythin' now. It depends how far this has gone. Or she'll warn him and he might disappear into the wind. Something like this, Ella, I want that fuckin' bastard gone. I doubt she's the first, and if we don't catch him, she's likely not to be the last."

Suddenly my problems seem insignificant. Yes, I was raped. But I didn't have my virginity stolen. At least that hadn't been taken from me. *She's only fourteen!*

"You onboard with our plan, El?" When I don't immediately answer Slick prompts, "Ella?"

I look at Slick, his face set harder than I've ever seen it before. "I could go to the police."

Mouse looks at me sharply. "All the info I have is illegal."

I shrug. "I'll tell them I looked at her Facebook and phone."

"The police ain't gonna do fuck. Or if they do, it will probably go to the bottom of the pile. You know your sister, El, you know there's somethin' wrong. They might look at her and see a moody fuckin' teenager."

Which is why I hadn't involved them before. Biting my lip, I think fast. The quickest way to keep her safe is to let them do their stuff. "Okay, I'll leave it with you." I've got more faith in the Satan's Devils than the authorities anyway. But I don't want to be left out of what they find and what they're doing. "Will you tell me? Keep me informed when you know she's going to meet him?"

"We'll tell you what you need to know."

It's not exactly a confirmation, but it's probably all I'm going to get, now that they've taken this on, doubtless it will come under that dreaded phrase old ladies hate, *club business*. Mouse closes his laptop and leaves us. When he's gone Slick shifts over so he's sitting at my side. He takes hold of my hand again. "I'm so sorry, Ella."

"I don't know why you're apologising, Slick. If anything, this is my fault."

"How the fuck do you get to that?"

I pull back my hand. "Because I've been so wrapped up in what happened to me I've neglected her. While this," for some reason I wave my hand at the table where the laptop had sat, "while this was going on I was wrapped up in myself. You saw those dates? It started just after I'd come back from the compound. I didn't want her to see me hurting, and I was hiding myself away. I didn't see her for a few weeks. It's only recently I started going around again." I cover my mouth with my hand as a horrible thought hits me. "What if this Sy was able to befriend her as she thought I'd abandoned her?"

As Slick shakes his head I continue, "When I felt strong enough to visit, when I was capable of hiding my pain, I thought she was just being off as I hadn't been to see her. Her quietness my punishment for not being there. If I'd been thinking more clearly I might have realised sooner there was something very wrong."

Slick's staring at me. "You take the weight of the fuckin' world on yer shoulders, doncha? Babe, it wasn't your fault what happened to you. And it certainly wasn't your fault what's goin' on with your sister. You got that? You did what you could as soon as you sussed somethin' was off. More than your fuckin' mom has done. You couldn't have done anythin' more."

"I could," I contradict him. "I shouldn't have let what they did affect me so badly. I shouldn't have started any of this. If I hadn't thought the only way I could get a man was to whore myself out I'd have been there for her and maybe stopped this from happening."

Again he makes a grab for my hands, pulling them tight and this time not allowing me to escape. "Ella. Listen to me. I don't know why the fuck you ever thought you could be a sweet butt, or why that was the only way you'd get a man to fuck ya. You're as pretty as hell, and I wanted ya the moment I saw ya. If I'd dealt with my crap then you'd never have gone into that fuckin' Rock Demons club, I should have told my brothers to find someone else. I had my head so far down in the fuckin' sand you'd be quite right to say it's as much down to me." He waits for that to sink in. "But Ella, even if you'd been around, you wouldn't have stopped this happenin'. These types of people are clever, El. They know how to get what they want. She'd have kept it secret from you whether you'd been there or not."

"But I would have seen the signs."

He shakes his head. "The rot had begun the moment she met that boy, Sy. She kept it secret from yer mom, she would have hidden it from you too. Remember he kept tellin' her to keep it quiet? Encouragin' her to hide things? That's the way this groomin' thing works. And I think Mouse is right, there's some threat hangin' over her that is keepin' her tied to them."

I look down to where our hands are joined, grateful that he's here with me, sharing my pain and my worry. I hope he'll stay around at least until Jayden's problem's sorted. Until then I can't think about what I want for myself.

Somehow he senses my feeling of inadequacy. "I'm not goin' anywhere, okay? I'll be with you every step of the way. And we'll get your sister right."

"Knowing what I do now, Slick, how am I going to face her? You said don't alert her, but I don't know how I'm going to be able to do that." All I want at the moment is to hug her.

"All you can do is try, darlin'. Remember, if you let her suspect you know, she'll warn the motherfuckers, and we'll lose our chance of stoppin' them."

"What about Sy? This older one, Diego, I know you'll," I lower my voice, "I'm not stupid, you'll kill him, won't you?"

Slick's face is impassive, he's giving away nothing.

"But what about the teenage boy?"

"If he's involved in this, he'll be treated like a fuckin' man."

It's not much of an answer, but it seems it's the only one I'm going to get.

Slick takes his phone out of his cut and looks at the screen. He shakes his head as he notices the time. "I've got somewhere I need to be, darlin'. But I could come around later?"

I glance sharply his way, gathering my thoughts in a flash. "Slick, I'm so worried about Jayden, I wouldn't be good company."

"You can't do anythin'. You're leavin' it to us. Won't do you no good frettin' on yer own."

"I know, but until things are sorted with Jayden, until I know she's safe, please understand I need time by myself. This," I wave my hand in the air between us, "whatever this is, it's too much for me to handle right now."

He sighs. "You sayin' you want to put us on hold?"

Yeah, I'm saying exactly that. "Just give me a few days, Slick." I hope he understands. I don't want to lose him, I'd like to have the opportunity to at least try. Go on a few more dates perhaps? But the revelations about Jayden have had me reeling. And until I get my head around her problems, I can't sort my own out. I'm guilty enough I wasn't there for her when I obviously needed to be. I can't afford to get distracted again.

I raise my eyes. "Just a few days, Slick. I need to come to terms with what's going on."

He takes my hand and brings it to his lips, placing a kiss on the back. Then turning it over, his fingers trace my palm. His eyes meet mine. "Just a few days," he repeats. "Then you're all mine."

This time I'm unable to interpret the shiver that runs down my spine.

CHAPTER 13
Slick

I don't want to leave Ella with the additional concerns Mouse and I had dropped on her this morning. I'd much prefer to be there for my woman to comfort her, to give her a shoulder to lean on so she knows she's not in this alone. But I really did have to leave, as I'm due somewhere else. And now knowing I won't be seeing her again for a while guts me. In a way it's easy enough to understand, she's too worried about her sister, even though I believe she should be sharing her troubles, not wallowing in them all by herself. It kills me to think of her sitting there on her own, letting her problems fester.

But isn't that just what she does? Or has learned to do because I was a selfish asshole and let her walk away? I gave up all right to insist on inveigling myself into her life when I didn't go after her.

As I drop her off back at her house I insist she keeps in touch and calls me if she gets concerned, or if she just wants to talk. No, it doesn't feel right leaving my woman to cope on alone, but I can't push her, not when she has so much on her plate, and a habit she'd had to develop for taking it all on herself.

As the door closes behind her I spur into action and waste no time getting to the hospital.

The last time I'd seen Heart he was laughing in the club-house, moaning how Crystal was taking too long getting ready to go out, complaining how he didn't want to see "no fight at the fuckin' OK Corral", even as the sparkle in his eyes betrayed he was as eager as his wife. Now he's lying in hospital bed, tubes coming out everywhere, machines constantly bleeping. I'd thought I'd been prepared as to what to expect, I wasn't.

Rock stands as I walk in and I jerk my chin at him. "Rock, I'm sorry man."

"No worries, Brother." Has he not noticed I'm late?

"How is he?" I nod toward Heart, my gut clenching as I watch him, unmoving.

"No change. They're going to start easin' him out of the induced coma tomorrow. The swellin' on his brain has gone down, but it's anyone's fuckin' guess after that." He clears his throat before adding, "They can't guarantee if he's gonna wake up."

Rock and I stare at each other, there's really nothing more we can say. Bikers used to action, we don't know how to deal with something like this that's out of our hands.

My brother leaves and I stand for a moment with my head bowed, then move across and take the chair Rock had vacated, moving it a little closer to the bed. Reaching out I squeeze Heart's hand, hoping in some way he'll know I'm here and that we haven't deserted him. I hold it for a second, but it lies completely still in mine. It's human nature to hope for some sign, the slightest pressure to show recognition. But there's nothing.

"Life's shit at the moment, Brother." I might be talking to a man as still as a corpse, but somehow I can't stop. "You lyin' here like this? It's all fuckin' wrong. And Ella? Shit Brother. Here I am wantin' her back, thinkin' all I got to do is romance her... Hey, you'd fuckin' laugh about that. Me. Courtin' a woman? Not my style, eh? Yeah, you'd fuckin' crease up if you were hearin' me talk. Anyways, there I was thinkin' it would be hard, but I was in it for the long haul. Now she's got this shit to deal with about her sister. How she'll cope with that on top of everythin' else, I've no fuckin' idea.

"You know what? Bet she thought I hadn't noticed, but she'd dolled herself up some this morning. Looked fuckin' fantastic. Didn't want to mention it as I thought I might frighten her off. Now? With what Mouse just dropped on her? Guess we're probably back where we started.

"You want to know if she's worth it? Fuck, Brother. She is, and I ain't givin' up. We'll get there, and I'll have my ol' lady…"

My voice trails off as I realise he hasn't anymore, but it's not my place to tell him that. *What if he can hear me?* And then I wonder who's going to break the news and how he'll take it. Heart's only going to be half the man he was when he realises he's lost his wife. I've no idea how he's going to cope. They'd been so right for each other, their love not starting to tarnish even after the years they've been together. Perhaps having Amy will help. She's the image of her mother, and he'll have to keep it together for her sake. Yeah, he'll have to put the kid's needs first. That must be something. *At least he's got her.* She's part of them both.

Another squeeze to his fingers, still half expecting a response, but none comes of course. "You get well, Brother, and we'll share a bottle of Jack."

I want him to survive, want him to recover. But when he comes round he'll be facing a world of pain. A bit like when I lost Ella, but that had only been my obstinacy holding me back, a suffering I needn't have gone through if I'd used the head on my shoulders. If she had died… Knowing how devastated I'd feel makes me wonder whether it wouldn't be kinder on Heart to just let him fade away. How the fuck is he going to cope when he's told about Crystal's death?

It's hard to make conversation with someone who doesn't talk back. After a while I have no more words to say, so I sit as best I can in the uncomfortable chair and spend the time thinking. Most of it about what we'll do to this Diego fucker when we catch up with him. It certainly won't be pretty—and Ella was right, though I'd never admit it. He won't be left alive to molest any young girl ever again.

Time passes slowly, nurses and doctors drift in and out. At last Lady appears to take over, asking the same question as I'd done on entering the room. I give him the same answer as Rock had given me. Nothing has changed.

Then I'm back on my bike, letting the warm evening air sweeping past, washing some of my depression away. It seems whichever way I look life sucks right now.

When I walk into the clubhouse I see the prez deep in conversation with Mouse at the bar, and I suspect he's bringing Drum up to speed. It's strange to see my brother there. He seems to live in his cave, rarely emerging into the light of day. Nodding at Joker, I walk on by and notice Sam sitting with Viper. I pause as I pass.

"How's Amy?" I surprise myself at how concerned I am about the kid.

As Sam looks up it's hard to miss how tired she's looking. "She's doing okay. Missing her mom, doesn't really understand why she's not coming back. She's wants to see Heart and it's distressing to tell her she can't." She tilts her head toward Viper. "Viper and Sandy are taking her home with them tonight to give us a break. Drum wants a night's uninterrupted sleep."

"You look like you could do with it, too."

Her hand touches her stomach. "I've been telling him we'll have to get used to it."

Viper notices her action and gives her a fond smile. "You've got to take care of yourself until Junior comes."

She smiles. "That's what Drum said. We've already had a discussion about me riding my bike." The droop to her mouth tells me what she thinks about that.

I happen to think he's right to be cautious. If Ella was pregnant I'd wrap her in cotton wool. Then I realise how far I'm getting ahead of myself. First, I've got to persuade her to come back. Oh, and to let me fuck her. Can't make babies without doing that.

As I move on from them I inwardly laugh. I don't even know if she wants children. What I do know is it will be hard enough work even getting her into my bed.

Passing the pool table I see it's in use and balls are in play, but not the ones normally used in the game. I stand for a moment watching Beef's hips bucking as he thrusts in Jill's pussy, and Rock's cock disappearing into her mouth. How the fuck can I ask Ella to come back here and expose her to the real-life porn show that's typically going on?

I view the clubhouse as though I'm seeing it through her eyes. All the girls are in action tonight. Pussy's giving Joker a lap dance, Allie's fondling Dart, and the new girls, Diva and Paige, are either side of Tongue whose jeans are hanging open and he's getting a hand job from one, while his mouth's devouring the tits of the other. Diva notices me being a voyeur and pouts my way, then pointedly redoubles her efforts stroking Tongue's cock. Looks like I might have offended her. Turning away I huff a laugh, not giving a fuck what she thinks. There's only one woman's opinion that matters to me.

Despite the blatant sexual acts on display that ordinarily would have had my balls throbbing, my cock doesn't stir. Maybe being celibate won't be that hard. As long as I keep all thoughts of Ella out of my head.

Drum and Mouse have stopped talking, so I join them at the bar. Mouse raises his chin, "How was Ella when you left her?"

"Fuckin' worried sick."

Drum nods. "She should be. And there's somethin' about this that smells bad. What you plannin' when you know the girl's on the move?"

"Go to the location and snatch her back. And that fucker who's molestin' her."

"That's only conjecture so far, isn't it?"

Mouse shrugs. "Sure, but I can't fuckin' think there's anythin' innocent going on. Best thing we can hope is he's still in the groomin' stage."

I feel a flicker of hope, "Is that possible, Mouse?"

Again he raises his shoulders. "With the timin' involved? I doubt it. These types don't hang around once they've got someone in their clutches."

The prez drums his fingers on the bar. When Marsh pops his head up Drum shakes his head, declining the offered beer. He's still got his shot glass of top-drawer whisky half full. "I don't like this. What if it's bigger than you think? What if there are other girls there? The way you're plannin' it, you could be steppin' into something you can't control."

I know, I have thought about that. "Without being able to ask her, we can't know what we're walkin' into."

"Can you get a bug on her, Mouse?"

"Jayden carry a purse?"

It seems a fair assumption to make. "What girl doesn't?"

"How the fuck do I know what a young teenage girl does?"

Drum smirks and swings around. "Hey, Sam! You carry a purse when you were fourteen?"

"Where else would I have kept my tools, Drum? Yeah, sure I did."

A number of brothers, not otherwise engaged, laugh. Dart yells out, "Bet it was big enough to carry a wrench!"

Ignoring the conversation behind me as various brothers suggest the contents Sam might have carried, I get back to the subject at hand. "I can contact Ella, see if she can slip something into Jayden's purse. You got a bug I can give her?"

Mouse just looks at me as if I've said something stupid. Yeah, he'll have some kind of micro device I can use. Before I can make more of a fucking fool of myself I turn to Marsh and demand a beer. One corner of my mouth turns up as he rushes to serve me. I wait until he moves to the other end of the bar before turning to Drum.

Using my bottle to point at the prospect I ask, "When we patchin' him in?"

"At the next Friday church, unless somethin' comes up."

"We meetin' in the mornin'?" With so much going on, it seems we're coming to the table every fucking day.

"Yeah, feel we need to. I want to bring everyone in on what's goin' down with your woman. You'll need brothers behind you." Fuck, that gets me, hearing the prez refer to her as that. Unlike the others, he doesn't treat it as a joke. Not that he should, it took him less time to realise Sam was the one for him.

And it warms me that I'm going to have the brothers at my back when I sort out Ella's problem. Not that I wouldn't have gone in alone if I'd had to. But having them having my six means we'll be better able to deal with any situation we find.

When I'm back in my room I ring Ella, telling her the latest and confirming Jayden does indeed have a purse to carry her phone. Road will be able to take the bug down to her in the morning, and while she's not looking forward to seeing her sister while having to keep from her what she knows, Ella says she'll make sure she's gets a chance to plant the bug. She even goes so far as to joke she might take up a career as a spy seeing as I'm given her so much practice.

Fuck, this woman gets to me. I go to sleep with a smile on my face.

Next morning I go to the auto shop close to the gates of our compound, and once again throw myself into my work, which has got well behind with everything else going on. I'm in the middle of stripping down an engine when Sam comes over. She stands watching me for a while.

I drop a spanner, made clumsy by her scrutiny. Lifting my eyes to hers, I want to find out what she wants. "What's up?" Rising to my feet I wipe my dirty hands on a rag and then put it back in my pocket.

"I wanted to speak about Ella."

My eyes narrow slightly. "Prez told ya?"

She nods. "I didn't go through anything like she did, Slick. That must have been bad. But when I was taken they stripped my control, and I thought I was going to be raped. That was terrifying enough."

I nod. We'd rescued her just in time.

"I spent a lot of time with the women who'd been through much worse than me." She pauses, and I wonder whether she's getting to the point. "I just wondered whether it would help if I spoke to her? Or just made sure I was here when she comes to the compound again?"

There's a workbench beside me, and I hook my leg over it. "I don't know when that will be, Sam. She's pretty spooked by the whole idea. But thanks for the offer. I'll think on it, okay?"

"Sure." With a smile, she walks away. Fuck, Drum did good when he brought her back to the clubhouse. Viper must be over the moon finding out she is his daughter as well.

Over the next couple of days I keep in touch with Ella, but do as she'd requested and keep my distance. As expected, Heart's taken off the drugs keeping him under, but as of now there's been no change in his condition. Like my brothers, I'm not giving up on him yet, but I just wish he'd give us some sign he's going to be okay. I don't know if there's anyone that can hear me, or fuck it, whether they'd even listen to a sinner like me, but I've taken up praying and I'm not ashamed to admit it. *Heart must recover.*

Thursday evening, Mouse calls me into his cave, a dark hole with the windows blacked out so light doesn't reflect off his screens. I find it depressing. He seems at home.

"Jayden's on the move. Marsh called it in. He's followin', but if he thinks it's too risky we've still got the tracker."

"She gonna meet with this Diego fucker?"

He watches the screen for a moment, expertly rolling a joint at the same time. "She must be in a car the speed the tracker is travellin'. There's not much talking goin' on. Can't tell much yet, but I reckon we can assume she is."

"You keep eyes and ears on it and I'll get the boys together."

Going into the clubroom, I whistle to get their attention. "Looks like Jayden's meetin' the mark."

Wraith, Peg, Dart, and Beef step forward. As we'd discussed in church, they'd volunteered to come along. Drum emerges from his office, tucking his gun into his cut. "I'm coming with, Slick. Wanna see the fucker who's playin' around with kids."

At that moment Mouse emerges, waving his phone. "Marsh thought it was too risky, that they'd notice him followin', so he's on his way back. I kept on trackin' her phone, and now they've stopped movin'. I got the location." When he tells us where it is, it surprises me. It's in a residential area, and not in a seedier part of town as I'd have expected.

Going to our bikes, we waste no time getting rolling, followed by Marsh who's jumped off his bike and is now behind the wheel of the crash truck. It takes about forty-five minutes until we're riding up the right road. Drum waves us to stop a good way down from our destination so the sound of our pipes doesn't raise the alert. We gather around him.

"What you got, Mouse?"

Mouse touches his hand to his ear piece. "I've been listenin' on the way. There's a number of males there, drinkin'. There's a lot of talkin' and laughin'. I can't hear the girl."

At least she's not screaming.

"Can you tell how many?"

"Three, four? Maybe."

"Right. Slick, Peg, we'll go in by the front door. Wraith, you and the others try and find a way in around the back. I want an in and out. We get the girl out of there."

"What about the men in there?"

"Diego I fuckin' want. The others? We'll play it by ear. See what we find. But let's be prepared and get silencers on those guns." He leads us to the back of the crash truck where we open a hidden compartment and take out what we need.

Peg points to the body armour—yeah, we're always prepared. "Think they're gonna fight back?"

"Have to expect it. Hoped we'd just be dealin' with one motherfucker." Drum reaches in and starts passing the protective clothing out.

As I swap my cut for the armoured vest I'm very worried, and starting to dread just what we'll be walking into. *What the fuck is happening to that little girl?*

"Anything Mouse?"

Mouse has his hand to his ear, but shakes his head. "Sounds like they're having a fuckin' party."

"Let's do this thing." Drum leads the way and we follow his lead, carefully walking along the street, trying to avoid crunching gravel as we approach the house Mouse points out. Blinds are drawn, presumably to prevent people seeing in, but that serves our purpose as we can approach undetected.

Drum takes his gun out of his cut, Peg and I do the same. We approach the front door. It's solid. We could kick it in, but…

"Knock?"

"Why not?" Drum answers me with an evil sneer.

As he motions I press my fingertip to the doorbell. To my surprise, it's opened. Drum's arm's rising ready, but the man just gives the three of us a cursory look then waves us in. Surprised, we look at each other then follow him in. What the fuck? Guess they must be expecting more people to arrive. *Bastards.* What is this, a fucking free for all?

We follow him into a living area, open and spacious, but there the normality ends. What isn't normal is a barely dressed young girl, drunk out of her mind, swaying in the middle as though trying to dance to the music playing, while a man stands behind her, holding her up. The man who'd let us in joins two others who are walking around as though inspecting her, their hands coming out to grope her tits. As I watch her top is pushed down, and her perky little breasts are now showing. They've already removed her pants.

"Good girl. I told you my friends were coming tonight, didn't I honey? And you're going to be good to them, just like you are to me." Now the man holding her sees us and grins. "Hey, welcome. Want to inspect the goods?"

Christ! He thinks we more punters. He must be high or something, hasn't even noticed we're wearing bullet proof vests. Just what's going on?

Drum's face has gone black, his eyes sharp and narrowed. His focus on the man holding the girl who I recognise as Jayden from Facebook page Ella had found. My breathing quickens and I roll my shoulders to loosen them up. I flick my eyes to my prez, waiting for a sign that we can put an end to this scene that's making me feel sick. My rage is building as Jayden squeals when a man pinches her tit. If Prez doesn't speak soon I'm gonna…

"Stop what you're fuckin' doin' and let the girl go," Drum's voice thunders out.

All motion in the room ceases as one by one the men turn, seeing our guns pointing at them, a flicker of fear crossing their faces as they realise they're outnumbered.

"I wouldn't do that." The prez focuses his unblinking stare on a man who looks like he is reaching for a weapon. "Take your gun out *carefully* and put it on the floor."

The man starts to obey, then obviously plans on being a hero. I shoot him as he takes aim, a muffled pop from my silencer being the last thing he hears. *That leaves two and Diego.* Whichever one he is.

"What the fuck?" Jayden's captor doesn't seem to know what to do, but the situation's obviously making him regain his senses and fast. "Who the fuck are you?"

"What's going on, Diego?" One of the others looks at the man in the centre of the room, giving Diego's identity away.

"Who are you?" Diego repeats.

Drummer ignores him. "Everyone take out your weapons, now." Seeming like cowards, they're not going to argue. One by one they do as Prez says. Peg collects the discarded weapons. The only man who hasn't complied is the man who's still got Jayden in his arms. "Diego?" Drum asks, his steeling eyes land on the man in the centre of the room.

"Not carrying," he gasps out, looking nervously at the two men who take steps back, as though distancing themselves from him. They can't be friends, more likely customers. Bile churns in my gut as Diego continues, "Just take the girl if you want her."

He gives her a hard nudge and she staggers forward. Without blocking Peg's aim I reach for her and take her in my arms, pulling her top back into place, then push her behind me into the arms of Wraith who, having made a rear entry, is now waiting ready by the door.

"Rest of the house is clear. This one was takin' a piss." Dart pushes one final man into the room. Knowing my brothers, I can trust he'll already be disarmed. Wraith, after taking Jayden outside and leaving her with Marsh, returns. And Beef and Mouse, having completed their search of the house, enter the living room space together.

With us at his back, Drummer walks toward the Diego. The prez stands in front of him, eyeing him up. "So you're the man who likes playin' with little girls."

"Ain't no harm in it. She wanted it. She was begging for it."

Ignoring the statement which is blatantly untrue, Drum continues, "And your friends here? You were gonna share her around?"

The remaining men shuffle nervously and look anywhere but at us. As Diego doesn't answer Drum fists his hand and strikes him hard on the face, ignoring the crunch of bone breaking. He follows up with another cut to his stomach. As Diego goes down Drum goes behind him and pushes him to the floor. Taking out a zip tie he cuffs his hands, then forces him up. "You're comin' with us."

As he pushes Diego out of the doorway Prez turns back around. "These men are all trash. Time we clean up Tucson. Let's get this job done."

Surrounded by my brothers, I walk into the room, paying no heed to the protestation of innocence. "It was all Diego." "We weren't doing a thing." "Didn't mean anything by it". "Weren't gonna hurt the bitch." *Yeah, and I'm the virgin Mary.*

There are five of us, three of them, and I doubt any are expecting this to be their last night on Earth. One even starts smirking, watching as Diego vainly struggles in Drum's hold. I can see another relaxing, believing now we've got what we came for we'll leave them alone. *No such luck, fuckers. You were touching the wrong girl.*

As we line up in front of them, postures change once again, flickers of fear suggesting they're expecting a beating. Oh, I'd love a chance to bloody them up. But Drum wants this quick and clean. It's probably only seconds since we've approached them, but time has stood still for me as I position myself in front of the man on the end, alternatively going from watching their eyes and viewing any slight tensing of their bodies. My trigger finger hovers as I watch hands clench into fists, readying themselves to receive punches just like Diego.

We're here to remove this stain off the face of the planet. I focus and imperceptibly shift the grip of my weapon.

"Just get it done already."

At Drum's terse instruction, I take a deep breath and hold it as I raise my gun up at the same time as my brothers take a similar stance. A bullet to the forehead of each of men in front us, muffled pops as the silencers do their jobs. Bodies hit the floor, not one breathing. Too clean a way to die in my opinion, but too many for us to take alive and deal with back at the compound.

"What the fuck?" Diego screams from the doorway. "That was my brother!"

"You'll be seein' him again soon," Drummer says ominously as he hands him over to Peg, who marches him out of the door.

"We've got a problem," Wraith snarls, pointing up to the corner.

Mouse leaps into action when he sees what it is, pulling up a chair and reaching to take the offending object down.

"They're fuckin' filmin' this shit, the sick fuckin' bastards."

"We need to search this place," I spit out. "They may keep the tapes."

Mouse is examining the camera. He's extracting a SD card and waves it at us. "Look for any of these, and any computer or laptop I want taken back to the compound."

"Slick, get yourself and the girl back to the clubhouse. She needs to be seen by Doc as soon as possible. We'll stay, get it all cleaned up. Send Marsh back with the truck for the bodies and anything else we find."

I'm nodding at most of his instructions, but, "Wouldn't it be better to take her straight home? She should be with family."

"Get her sister there." The prez waves his hand around. "We don't fuckin' know how far this rot goes. We know the youngster, Sy, is still out there. What that girl's been through? I want to make sure she's fuckin' safe."

CHAPTER 14
Ella

Sometimes I wish I could control the way my mind works. It's confusing, even to me. One moment I'm regretting telling Slick to stay away, and the next I'm wishing he was here. He's kept in touch by phone, but I can't help but wonder whether there's things he's not telling me. If he was here I'd be able to see if he was holding anything back.

I'm so worried about Jayden, distressed at what's been going on in her life. Feeling so useless there's nothing I can do. If I hadn't been so wrapped up in my own misery I might have noticed something was wrong and been able to put a stop to it before it had gone so far.

And when I start thinking down that route I'm glad I told Slick to give me some space. I never meant to tell anyone about what had happened to me, now having disclosed my nightmare I've got to come to terms with it all over again.

I'd appreciated Slick taking some of the blame, but at the end of the day, either of us could have stopped it but didn't. And the result was to expose me to animalistic behaviour that I didn't even know humans were capable off, my body used totally out of my control. That I got out with my sanity is a miracle, the level of abuse forced upon me unbelievable. I'm torn into pieces, and I'm not sure it's going to be possible to put myself back together.

Because I'd walked voluntarily, if not knowingly into the situation, I'd been believing I deserved what happened to me. But Slick's reaction has at least made me put that first foot on the road toward considering maybe I wasn't asking for the treatment I'd received. And it certainly doesn't hurt knowing the vast majority of my abusers are dead and will never be able to molest any woman ever again. That fact allowing me to sleep easier in my bed. An extreme punishment, but one I deem fitting. They're gone, they don't deserve to have a place even in my nightmares. My conscious brain knows it, but I've still got to convince myself in my sleep.

This space away from Slick has been necessary to start to process what happened and permit myself to begin to move forward. Will I ever get over it? That's the million-dollar question, and there's no way of knowing. But hiding away, trying to cope on my own hasn't helped much. Perhaps Slick's right, and I should try counselling. For the first time since it happened I'm making a conscious decision that while I can't wipe the slate clean, I can try and work past it. Maybe talking with a professional could facilitate that.

Whichever way I look at it, while I'm taking the first step, it's one hell of a long road I'll be having to travel. And while he says he will now, how much time will it take before Slick gets impatient and gives up? Slick's a man with needs I can't fulfil.

Being left alone has been useful. I've started looking to a future where I can deal with my past. That is, when I'm not worrying about Jayden.

When I went around to see her my heart had fallen. If anything, she looked even worse than the last time I'd seen her. She was sullen and non-communicative, and now I had evidence it's not just a teenage phase. I felt so sorry and useless.

It was easy to drop the tiny bug Road had delivered to me into her purse, far harder not to divulge I knew anything about what is going on. At several points during our conversations I had to bite my tongue, knowing Slick's right. If I let on that I know who she's meeting she'll only clam up. And if they're holding threats over her she certainly wouldn't be admitting it. Limiting myself to gentle probes, I hoped she'd let something escape on her own, but I got little more than grunts out of her.

I wish to God I could lock her away, keep her safe so she never has to see them again. It kills me I've got to let her continue with whatever her plans are for seeing this man one more time so the Devils can do what they do best and deal with the problem in a permanent way.

I manage to hide my distress while I'm speaking to her, but as soon as I leave I stagger as the emotion hits me, and walk home with the tears running down my face. *Oh Jayden, why did you have to get involved in something like this?* How is it possible this Sy and Diego managed to corrupt such a sweet girl? Such things shouldn't happen — it's something you read about, something that happens to somebody else, not a member of your own family. Just how did they manage to reel her in?

Slick listened to me cry on the phone after I'd come back from seeing Jayden, not saying a word as I let it all out. Strangely his silent support gave me strength to go on.

It's Thursday today, getting near the end of the week, and I'm a complete mess. Contemplation of my own problems has become overshadowed with fear for my sister. Nervous anticipation has me hanging by the phone wondering whether this will be the day when their plan to save Jayden is put into action. Now the worry revolves around my dread that something will go wrong and she'll end up getting hurt. I desperately want to call the whole thing off, but Slick is adamant. Their plan, he's told me, is the only way to get her out cleanly and give her a chance at a normal life.

As usual I dress in jeans to walk to work, only changing into the clothes my boss provides for his staff when I get there. Entering the bar I see it's already busy—there's a stag party in, never a good sign. I take a deep breath as I approach their table and, not totally unexpected, as I stand with my tray full of drinks a man tries to grope me, his hand going up under my too short skirt. I jump back in horror, and glasses and bottles go smashing to the ground.

"For fuck's sake, Ella! How many more times?" Of course the owner of the bar has to be in tonight, doesn't he? He continues to shout, "Get this mess cleaned up and then go behind the fuckin' bar. If you can't pull yourself together and serve customers properly you're fired."

As I crouch down to sweep up the fragments of glass and then mop up the liquid, lewd comments fly at me from the already drunk men. I try to ignore them, concentrating on doing the job that I hate. Though I've been trying to find different work for weeks, there's nothing else out there. If I lose my position at the bar I won't be able to afford to live.

"Nice rack there, babe." I'm bent over with a dustpan and brush and can do nothing about the amount of cleavage on display. My cheeks redden and my hands start shaking.

"Nice ass too. Fancy giving me a lap dance?" *Please shut up.*

"What time d'ya get off, sweetheart? Wanna party with us?" I can't even respond. My vision feels blurry, I'm finding it hard to breathe. *Don't let me pass out.* But I can't help it, my legs start trembling…

"Back off. She's under our protection." I hear a deep voice full of menace speaking from behind me. Twisting around I see Road, his face full of concern as he reaches out his hand and helps me to my feet. "Reckon it's time for your break, darlin'."

Throwing a pointed look toward my boss, I dismiss his suggestion. "I've got to clean this up, Road. I'll be fired if I don't. It was my fault I dropped the glasses…"

"It wasn't your fault. It was the fuckers at this table. And now they're gonna clean up the mess that *they* caused."

The men laugh loudly as if he's made a joke. Road flexes his impressive muscles and reaches out to grab the collar of the nearest man, coincidentally the one who'd first groped me. Pulling him out of his seat and easily forcing him to his knees, he indicates the floor. "I said, you're gonna clean up this shit. Understand?"

The man's shirt is bunched round his neck and as his eyes rise to meet Road's, the prospect prompts, "Well? We gonna have a problem? Or are you gonna get busy?" He pulls the dustpan out of my hands and throws it down in front of the man kneeling on the ground.

The other men sit stunned. Compared to Road they're scrawny. It takes a few seconds, but then there's a collective nod. As Road releases him the man picks up the brush and starts sweeping.

"What the fuck's going on?" The bar owner has had his eyes on me the whole time, and now comes over. He looks as angry as hell.

"Road, my job…"

His eyes softening as they meet mine, the prospect gives me a little nudge, "Just go take your break, honey. You can leave him to me."

I don't need much encouragement. While the table of men have quieted and most of them are watching their friend at work, one is openly staring and almost raping me with his eyes with an expression there I've seen before. It promises retribution, and of the kind I wouldn't enjoy.

With Road having my back, making myself scarce suddenly seems a very good idea. Feeling decidedly woozy, I make my way out back, sitting at the table in the break room and putting my head in my hands. This isn't how I used to be. Men such as them never use to faze me. I'd normally have a good comeback to hand when men came onto me. I wouldn't have survived in this job for long if I hadn't. But since going into the Rock Demons' clubhouse, all that has changed, and now my reaction is to panic instead of being able to brush off their approaches. I'd found out what happened when you stood up to a man.

Whatever Road says, after tonight it's probably a certainty I'll no longer even have this job. A tear escapes and I wipe it away, angry at the fuck up I've become. That one night was all that was needed to take my self-confidence away. I'm as much of a mess as the drinks that I'd spilled.

Deep in my self-recrimination, the vibration in my pocket takes a second to register. *Shit, it's my phone.* Taking it out I see it's Slick calling, and my now still hands start to shake once again. He knows I'm at work. He wouldn't be ringing now, unless… *Could this be it?*

"Hi." My greeting sounds tremulous.

And then I'm on my feet as he tells me without any preamble. "We've got Jayden. We're takin' her to the clubhouse."

"You've got her?" That's fantastic. And then his second statement sinks in. "Why there? Slick, just take her home and I'll meet you. Or bring her to my place, that's the best idea. You can't take her to your club." *Not with bikers.* Hasn't she been through enough?

"Babe, look, she's in a bad way. Don't think she's hurt, but she's drunk and possibly drugged. We're gettin' Doc to come in and take a look at her."

No! Oh, Jayden! *What's happened to you?* But whatever it is, "Slick, I can look after her. I'll make sure she's alright. Bring her to me."

"El, you're going to be lookin' after her, but back at the club. You're not gonna win this, so don't even try arguin'. There's very good reason why she can't go home. I know this is hard for you, darlin', but you want to keep her safe, don't you?"

I bite my lip. The thought of being surrounded by bikers chills me, especially after tonight when I couldn't even cope with one table of men. How could I even consider it? *But Jayden's going to be there.* I can't leave her alone. Not in a place like that!

I breathe deeply, unable to think of any alternative. He's basically kidnapped her and is holding it over my head. *I need to be with her.* After a moment I tell him, "Okay, but just for tonight." I'll bring her home in the morning. Then the practicalities hit. "But Slick, I've got no transport."

"Can you get Tilly's car?"

I very much doubt she'd deign to give me the time of day right now. "I don't think so."

There's a pause, then, "Fuck, I don't want to do this, but okay, give me a moment."

He ends the call and I'm left staring at the phone wondering what's going on, the overriding desire to get to my sister as soon as I possibly can taking hold.

It's only minutes later that the door to the break room bursts open and Road's standing there. "Come, hon. Slick wants me to give you a ride to the clubhouse."

He means on his bike. I've only ridden with Slick, and only the one time. I'm nervous about being behind someone else, having to hold onto another man. "I've not ridden much," I tell him, explaining my reluctance. "I can get a taxi." *But I can't afford it...*

"Sweetheart, the quickest way is to come with me. You'll be perfectly safe. I ride in competition. You can trust me." He looks at me earnestly. "Your sister needs you."

Those four words are the right ones to get me moving. Without delaying further, I grab my purse and jacket and we go out into the night. Dressed in my short waitress uniform, I'm not sure how I'm going to do this, but I get on behind him, hitching up my skirt and trying to anchor it under my butt. He pauses to tell me, "Don't have a helmet for you, Ella, just hold onto me tight."

It seems strange to put my arms around a man I don't know, but awkwardly I do so, trying to keep nothing but thoughts of Jayden in my head as we travel through Tucson and head out into the desert. Road goes slower than Slick does, cornering with care, and soon I relax, feeling I'm in good hands. I don't enjoy the ride. It's not like being behind Slick, and I'm overly conscious that my ass is slipping against, and my breasts are pressing into, the back of a relative stranger.

But Road does nothing to upset me. As he pauses for the gates to the compound to open he reaches back and pats my thigh, a non-sexual touch of comfort. And then we're inside. I slide off, trying hard not to flash anyone who could be looking as the prospect parks up his bike. Then with the comforting presence of the big man at my side remembering how he stood up for me earlier tonight, I approach the clubhouse.

Jayden. Just think of Jayden. My heart's in my mouth as I take that first step inside, flashbacks returning of walking into the Rock Demons' club. But the difference is immediately apparent as I step into what seems like organised chaos. There's men standing around, but they're not fucking or partying. Their voices sound angry.

Before I can begin to process the sight in front of me, a woman rushes over.

"Hi, I'm Sam. I'm Drummer's old lady. We haven't met before. Come, you must be anxious to see your sister. Hey, you douchebags, shift yourselves and give her some space."

I flinch, fearing what I expect to happen when a woman speaks sharply to these already riled leather-clad men. But she seems to have no problem keeping the raucous bikers away. At her instruction they part, clearing a path with good natured grunts. Quickly I follow her, trying to tamp my own fear down, focusing on Jayden as it's her who matters now.

Overly conscious that the waitress uniform my boss makes me wear is so short it's all but indecent, I put down my skirt as far as it will go and wait for the leers and crude comments, or the hands reaching out to touch. But as I go through the throng I survive unmolested. Still, my breathing comes easier when we leave the men behind.

Following Sam, I pass the crash rooms where, from my previous time here I know member's sleep or fuck when they can't make it back to their own rooms. Sam stops by a door, her hand on the handle. "Jayden needs you now, Ella. You can sit with her until she wakes up."

She's not awake?

Stepping inside, frightened of what I might find, I waste no time rushing over to my young sister who's lying on a bed. The prospect, Marsh, I remember, is hovering, his face anxious, and Doc's setting up some sort of IV.

"Ella." He offers a quick smile of recognition, but it quickly turns to a frown.

"How is she, Doc? What's the matter with her? Why isn't she conscious?" My words tumble out.

Patiently he explains, "Your sister was barely with it when they found her, and she passed out in the truck. As far as I can tell she's been plied with too much alcohol and probably drugged with some sort of date rape drug. I'm givin' her saline to help rehydrate her, and a glucose solution too. She's gonna be fine, but will probably have one fuck of a hangover when she wakes up."

My voice catches in my throat. "Has she been...?"

His eyes go cold. "I've taken some samples to see what we're dealin' with. But I'd say yes. I'm testin' for pregnancy and STDs."

Oh Jayden. It's not fair. She's so young. Doc steps back as I move to the bed and take hold of her hand. It's feels cold and her breathing seems shallow. As I touch her arm the sheet falls away.

"She's almost naked!" All she's got on is a torn top.

"I was on my way to get her some clothes when you arrived. I'll go grab something now." Then wasting no more time, Sam disappears out of the room.

I look toward Doc. "Are you sure she'll be alright?" It comes out as a hoarse whisper.

Placing a hand on my shoulder, he gives what comfort he can. "As far as I can tell, physically she just needs to sleep it off. But I ain't gonna lie. Something like what she's been through? That would hit anyone hard." His eyes narrow. "I reckon ya know a bit about that."

My cheeks redden as I realise he knows from when he had to visit me at home.

He sees my look of consternation. "Slick's worried about ya. He's spoken to me about gettin' ya professional help." Then he gestures toward Jayden. "Think about counsellin', Ella. She's gonna need it. And if you go too, it might make it easier for her."

And Jayden's the important one now.

Telling me he'll be back later to check up on her, Doc leaves the room. The prospect Marsh is still here, and I'm not sure why he's stayed. As my head tilts he interprets my action.

He coughs and looks embarrassed. "I brought her back," he starts to explain. "She's the same age as my young sister." He breaks off. His hands go up to rest on the top of his head, his fingers interlinked. "If you don't mind, Ella, I'd like to stay to make sure she's okay. Fuck, no one, especially not a young girl, should have to fuckin' suffer like this." His eyes fall on Jayden again. "It broke my fuckin' heart to know what she went through there."

I nod in astonishment, his behaviour not at all what I expected. His palpable concern for my sister means I give my permission. He takes the chair I vacate as I lie on the bed, holding Jayden as best I can while trying not to disturb the fluids running into her.

Shortly after, the door opens again. Marsh leaps up and goes to lean against the wall as Slick comes over and squeezes my arm. When I look up at him my eyes feel sore and must be red-rimmed from the tears that have been silently falling.

"She's safe now." He speaks gently, but his jaw is clenched as he looks at my sister.

I too glance at Jayden, my gut clenching as I again see the IV running into her arms and remember the tests Doc's ordered. What she's been through could break anyone. I lift my face back to Slick and say in despair, "How's she going to deal with this, Slick?"

"With my help," he says firmly. "*Both* of you are going to be fine. It might be a long journey, but I'll get you there." That he sounds so adamant and determined and without a glimmer of doubt, gives me a flicker of hope that he might be right.

I'm feeling uncomfortable, but hadn't wanted to leave her. It's embarrassing, but, "Slick, could you sit with her a moment. I need to…" I point to the adjacent bathroom.

"Yeah, I'll watch her while you take a piss." His mouth quirks.

But when I stand up, trying to pull that darn skirt down, his brow creases and he scowls. "Fuck woman, what are you wearin'?"

Realising he's never seen me at work, I tell him, "It's the uniform I have to wear at the bar."

He closes his eyes briefly. When he opens them again he seems to be biting his tongue, so I rush in before he can say anything. "I'm trying to get another job, Slick, but…"

"I'll find you somethin'. Maybe at the Wheel Inn. You're not goin' back there, El. And before you say anythin' else, Road told me what happened with the fuckin' stag party." He sounds angry, but I'm not going to argue. It would be a weight off my mind if I didn't have to go back. But if I lose that job before getting another, I won't make my rent.

I look down at Jayden, her chest rising and falling, her body twitching in her uneasy sleep. "Let's not argue this now, Slick. Please?"

He looks like he's got more to say but swallows it back down. He glances around at Marsh, who's stayed silent, his arms folded across his chest, his legs slightly apart. "You stay in here, Prospect. Don't leave them alone for a moment. And keep any fuckin' nosy douchebags away. Got it?"

The younger man gives a sharp nod. "Got it."

Slick reaches out his hand. "Go do your business, El, and then I'll have to leave ya for a bit. There's somewhere I'm needed." As his eyes land on Jayden his mouth tightens. I'm not stupid, it concerns her. "Oh, and ring yer mom. She'll be wonderin' where Jayden is. Can you tell her she'll be stayin' with you or a friend for a few days? We'd like to keep the both of you here until we know whether there's gonna be any fallout."

I huff a mirthless laugh. "That won't be a problem. Mom probably won't notice she's gone." Then I realise what he's said.

"Slick, the last thing I want is to stay here. Why can't I take her home? She'll be better off there."

He fixes me with an intense stare. "El, I know how you feel about the club. Believe me, I'd let you go if I didn't think there was any danger. But we can't fuckin' rule anythin' out after tonight." His eyes narrow when I start shaking my head. "Ella, listen to me. You know I can't tell you what went down, but I can assure ya, you'll be safe here. Both of you." It's said as a vow.

Hoping he's right, and unable to delay any longer, I nod then disappear into the bathroom, do the necessary as quickly as I can, and hurry back. As I return the door opens and Sam steps in carrying a bundle. She spares a sympathetic glance for the girl on the bed and then looks at me. "I've got clothes for Jayden, and some for you too." Her mouth twists as her eyes go to my skirt. "Thought you'd like a bit more covering."

"Thank fuck for that!" Slick jerks his chin toward her, then turns to me. "I'm leavin' you in safe hands, darlin'. And I'll be back just as soon as I can."

With Marsh standing sentry, and Sam looking like she's going to keep me company too, I feel safer than expected in this rough biker club.

CHAPTER 15
Slick

Jayden had looked young enough when we found her in that house, but lying there in that bed and hooked up to the IV, she resembled a vulnerable child. Fuck me, I can't understand what leads any grown man to force himself onto a kid like her. I give myself points for keeping my temper, knowing letting all the anger I was holding inside would have frightened Ella had I allowed her to see it.

I'm not blind to the fact that after everything Ella has been through herself, caring for her sister is going to take its toll. Neither of them seem to have any type of support network—no father, and a mother hardly worthy of the name. Straightening my shoulders as I march through the clubroom, I'm determined to do what I can to help the both of them through. Even as I mentally prepare myself for what lies ahead, part of my mind toys again with the idea of buying a house off compound and having both Ella and her sister there, taking responsibility for the girl and the woman. The idea takes root.

Striding up through the compound to the storage room, my fists clench at my sides, and now that I'm nearing my target I allow the rage I was holding back come to the surface and take me over. Focusing my attention on the job in hand, my steps quicken as I approach my destination.

There's no sound coming from the storage room, but it would have surprised me more if there was. It's been soundproofed just for this purpose. I open the door and now shouting reaches me. It's Diego yelling to let him down.

Pausing just inside the entrance, my eyes drawn to the middle of the room where Diego has been strung up, his arms stretched taut above him and his feet scrambling to find purchase on the slippery plastic sheeting under his feet. He's already lost his shirt, and Blade is in the process of removing his pants. None too slowly or gently, but there's not one of us here who'd give a fuck about that.

I take a moment to study him, this defiler of young girls. He appears to be in his mid to late thirties, and though currently his face is twisted in panic, and his nose broken from Drummer's punch, it's still possible to see he's a handsome enough specimen to catch a woman's eye and reel them in. His naked body revealing he's kept himself in shape, trim without an ounce of fat, it's not hard to understand how a naïve young girl like Jayden could easily have been flattered to find she'd attracted the attention of an older, good-looking man.

"Let me down! You can't do this!" He's shouting, but his voice soon tapers off as Blade lays his knife in warning against his chest.

Drum gives me a chin lift, acknowledging my presence. The preparatory work completed, they were waiting for me to arrive before getting started. "You wanna take the lead?"

Like fuck I do. I step forward and stand at Diego's feet, my arms flex and my shoulders pull back as I look eye to eye with the strung-up man. As he stares back at me in confusion and alarm, I decide to introduce myself.

"I'm Slick, and the girl you've been rapin' is my ol' lady's little sister." I let my personal investment settle in for a moment. "You're gonna tell me exactly what you did to her and everythin' else you know." I pause and point at Blade. "This here's our enforcer. I couldn't begin to list the number of ways he can make you suffer without lettin' you die."

Wild eyes flick toward me, his palpable fear giving me a sense of satisfaction.

I'm vaguely aware of the door opening and closing behind me, but don't bother to turn around to see who it is, until I recognise the deep voice as it growls at my side. "And I'm a medic. I'll make sure he keeps ya alive until you've spilt every fuckin' thing ya have to tell."

Hiding both my amusement and surprise, I dip my head toward Doc. He's not technically part of our club, and doesn't normally get involved in the darker side of what we do, though, of necessity he's aware of many of our secrets. Normally he'd want to be far removed from shit like this. The fact he's here now shows his personal level of disgust with this sorry excuse of a man.

Suddenly Diego starts talking, but his prattling doesn't give us anything we want to hear. Ignoring the protests, begging, and offers of money from the man who's struggling furiously against the ties which hold him, Drum steps up and puts his hand on Doc's shoulder. "You sure about this?"

"I want to see him hurt," Doc growls. "That girl's little more than a fuckin' kid."

The exchange appears to have done nothing to make Diego feel easier. His face has paled, his naked body is trembling, and his balls have shrivelled up into his body.

"You can't do this!" he screams. "Lay a hand on me and you're all dead. You won't get away with it."

I pay him no attention, thinking of the questions I'm going to ask. There's so much I want to know, it's hard to know where to start. At last I find my first question, and it's a personal one. "Why did you target Jayden?"

He's mouth purses as though he's not going to speak. Blade stabs him in the side, then trails the tip of the knife slowly downwards, making a six-inch tear in his skin, the looks of concentration on his face showing how seriously he takes his role. I happen to know our enforcer has made a study of anatomy, knowing just where to make it hurt without causing a fatal injury. Well, not before he wants to.

Diego, only aware of the pain and the blood running down, lets out a scream of pain and fear. "Sylas chose her for me."

Sylas? The young kid, Sy? "Sy works for you?"

He shuts his mouth fast. Blade steps close again.

"He's my nephew." Diego's eyes don't move from the blade the enforcer's touched to his skin on the opposite side from the original wound.

"He the kid of that brother of yours? The one that we killed?" Drum interjects.

The man hanging from the scaffolding shakes his head. "No, one of my other brothers."

"Fuck," Drum says in an undertone into my ear. "It's a family fuckin' business. Just how many of the motherfuckers are involved?"

At least three brothers enmeshed in it? One of them dead, one will be soon. And the third will follow soon after if I've got anything to do with it. *It's a family fucking sickness more like.* Staring at Diego, I want to find out exactly who we're dealing with so we can hunt them all down. "What's your family name, fucker?"

That one's easy for him. "Herrera," he yells out. His face twists into a sly smile. "You're fucking with the Herrera family. You're all dead!"

Shit. You don't live in Tucson without being aware of them, they're the city's most notorious crime family. To date, the Satan's Devils and the Herrera's have managed not to step on each other's toes, but now? Drum stiffens beside me, an imperceptible movement giving nothing away.

I'm still in the chair. Keeping my face impassive at his revelation, I walk around him, pointedly stepping over the blood dripping steadily from his side and pooling on the ground. Diego's eyes follow me as well as they can. Back in front of him, I raise my chin. "So how does this work, then? Your nephew, Sy, gets in with a young girl, then brings her to you? What happens next?"

He actually smirks. "I break them in."

The casual way he throws it out there has me moving before I can hold myself back. I punch him so hard in the stomach it steals his breath. As he draws his legs up his body starts swinging and he chokes as he tries to breathe.

I fire more questions, ones he evades, now knowing his answers will draw more punishment. He shakes his head and refuses to speak.

Blade gives me a nod, then jerks his chin over his shoulder and makes a request. "Beef, grab hold of his hand, will ya?"

As Beef steps forward, undoes one side of the chain holding him up, then wrapping him tightly with bulging biceps allowing him no escape, Blade approaches. Armed with tools from his box of toys, he holds a pair of pliers in Diego's line of sight.

Diego struggles harder, his eyes flaring in terror.

"Fuck!" Blade jumps back. "Motherfucker's just pissed himself." I and my brothers remain stoic, it's nothing we haven't seen before, and not the first time we've been forced to smell the rancid odour of ammonia.

Undeterred, the enforcer proceeds with his task and begins to pull out all of the fingernails on Diego's right hand, who quickly starts screaming, his cries and pleas now punctuated with promises to talk. Blade pulls out the last nail and the weeping man's words begin spilling out one after another. Blade signals to Beef and Diego's arm is chained back up.

"Once they get into me, I start training them." He's sobbing with pain, his eyes going to the blood running down his arm from his hand. "We then whore them out to the highest bidders, usually in groups, like last night. Men attracted to young flesh."

It's not just me who sees red at his disgusting revelation. Blade stabs him again.

"Give us the names of the men involved. Your relatives and the punters you contact."

He's howling like a wounded animal. "The family will kill me," he screams.

I give him a pointed look, then start turning my head, giving Blade a chin jerk.

That gets him started again and he screams. "We've got a network all over Tucson."

Further not so gentle encouragement from the enforcer, and it's not long before he's spilling names of his brothers and nephews, and explaining exactly how they groom young girls.

It's hard to stand here and listen to the filth spilling from his mouth. Bile churns in my gut at the scale of this operation and the numbers of paedophiles they attract. What started with Jayden has turned into one fuck of a big mess. And it's all coming down to the Herreras. I'm not even sure where the fuck we'd start shutting it down. There's a reason our paths haven't crossed—our club is a pimple compared with the size of their organisation.

A glance toward Drum shows he shares my concern. He's looking drawn, his hand toying with his beard. Fuck knows how many young girls like Jayden there have been, or will be in the future if we don't put a stop to this. I know he'll be willing, I just don't know if we're able. *We'll have to go head to head with the fucking Herrera family*

"I've heard enough. I can't listen to this poison anymore." The prez looks my way and I raise my shoulders. We've probably got enough, he's told us what he can, he's whimpering but is now just repeating things he's told us before. I hold up my hand, forefinger extended. There's one last thing I want to ask.

"You film them?"

"Of course. It's a good source of money. They go up on the web." Yeah, they'd make as much income from their disgusting practices as they could.

"Jayden? The young girl last night?" My gut rolls at the thought of men watching the depravity they'd put her through. I hold my breath, hoping for a negative answer.

He doesn't want to respond. Blade's knife comes out again. "Yes!" His eyes flick warily toward the enforcer. "There are videos of her," he replies with another screech.

Fuck! As if that young girl doesn't have enough to contend with. A hand drops to my shoulder. "Consider it fuckin' taken down, Slick. I'll find it and fuckin' delete it. And whatever else I can find." Mouse's promise only goes so far to ease me. *Neither Ella or Jayden must ever know.*

"Slick, you ready?" Prez looks as sickened as I feel.

I look at the man hanging, bleeding, knowing he'll never suffer enough, but grateful Drum's leaving the decision to me. I suspect my brothers, like me, are fed up with hearing this shit, and we've probably got all we need or that we're going to get. Raising my eyes toward Blade, I quickly opt for the most fitting end I can think of. "Castrate him, Blade."

With a roguish grin the enforcer moves closer. Diego's eyes flicker this way and that, his chains rattle where they hold his hands over his head.

"I'm going to do this nice and fuckin' slow. Like filletin' a fish. Beef, Rock, hold him steady, will ya?" Going to his box, Blade pulls out some latex gloves and selects a different knife.

Diego's screaming and yelling, begging for his dick and his life. Unfortunately for him even his flaccid cock is impressive and hangs down a few inches, easy for Blade to get hold of.

As he takes it in his hand, Doc steps forward. "There." He points, offering up his medical wisdom. "That's the best place to cut, and do it cleanly and he'll start to bleed out. But not too fast."

As he thrashes and screams, Beef and Rock hold him tighter, and the blade flashes as it comes down to deliver our final retribution. Kept honed and sharpened, it slices easily through the flesh, Blade's brow creasing in concentration as he slowly and steadily completes the castration. The agonised screeching brings solace to my fury at what this motherfucker has done.

Once Blade has finished he stands back, holding testicles and cock in his hand, offering them up to Diego, who lasts just long enough to see what he's holding before he passes out.

I think it fitting the last sight he sees is the instruments of torture he used on young kids. An appropriate end for a child molester.

We leave him to bleed out, some brothers staying to watch. They'll do the clean-up. Me? I want to get back to my girls.

Drum catches up with me after I leave the storeroom. "Some fucked up shit that was."

"Makes me want to puke up my guts." I emphasise the truth of that as my hand goes to my stomach. Watching him in the throes of death hadn't upset me, hearing the words that he'd spoken had.

Wraith takes a place at my other side. "This is a big fuckin' problem. We need to keep Jayden safe. We have no information about what the Herreras might be aware of. If they know about Jayden and that she was there tonight, well, if they get a whiff she's still breathin' they'll know she's a witness to what went down."

I breathe in deeply through my nose. Their customers and two of their family have gone missing. "They'll want to get hold of her to find out what she saw." My body tenses. "The Herrera's are vicious. They'll torture and kill her. She can't go home. She's got to disappear. They've got to think she's probably dead. Until all the risk's over." I'm thinking fast how the fuck that will even be possible.

"We move her and Ella to one of the other chapters. Get them set up in another state."

I can't allow that. I want Ella in my life, not halfway across the country where I might never see her again. "I hear what you say, Prez, but I want Ella here with me." I give voice to the impossible. "I want to take all these motherfuckers out."

He stops, his hand on my arm swinging me around. "Are you hearin' yourself, Slick? You're puttin' us up against the most powerful family in Tucson? Who knows how many of those fuckers have bred. They've got a link with the fuckin' Zetas. It's a big enough organisation by itself—fuck knows what we'll be up against if they bring in the cartel on their side. You prepared to risk this club just to get your dick wet?"

I snap out fast. "What would you do if it were Sam?"

That stops Drum in his tracks, my blunt comparison making my point well. His fingers stroke his beard as he thinks.

The VP suggests, "What if we send the girl away on her own?"

"Wraith, she's only fourteen and she's been through hell. Ella would never stand for that. And she's got a mother who probably wouldn't think much of that solution either."

"Hmm…" Drum's thinking fast. "Would the mother go with her?"

From what I know of her, probably not. I shake my head.

Drum looks worried. "Want the fewest possible people as we can in the know. If the mother can't be trusted she can't be told she's okay, or where she fuckin' is. First place the Herreras would go to try and trace her."

I wipe my hands over my head, realising I may have cocked up. "I told Ella to ring her. Let her think she was stayin' with friends for a while. She'll know she's alive."

"Fuck!" Wraith kicks a rock with his steel toe-capped boot. "I know you did what you thought was right at the time."

I accept that's on me. "I made the wrong call."

"You didn't know what we were dealin' with. Fuck, none of us knew. Fuckin' Herreras," Drum muses, staring off into the distance. "If it gets out she's alive we can't take the chance they won't be stoppin' at anythin' to try trackin' her down. Even if we move her out of state." A moment passes, then, "I'll visit the mother. Get her to see sense. Make sure she reports her as missin'. It might throw up a sufficient smoke screen."

I nod my thanks at Drum. If anyone can put the fear of God into her mother, he can. Thoughts race through my head. We'll have to keep a young girl hidden away when she should be at school, going out with her friends. To recover from what she's been through she should be getting back to normality, not being kept on lockdown at a biker club. But I can't see any other solution, at least not for the moment.

"Look, it's been a fuck of a day. Comin' on top of what's happened with Heart and losin' Crystal, it's fuckin' with all our heads. Let's take a moment to gather our thoughts. Tomorrow we'll bring it to the table and see what we can come up with." Drum tunnels his fingers through his hair. "End of the day, Brother, I gotta think of this club."

I know that. And my brothers come first with me too. It's only just creeping up on me how very close a second Ella's become. And, by extension, Jayden.

When we get to the fork in the path, Drum goes off to his house at the top of the compound and Wraith goes to the guest suite which had been assigned to Sophie when she'd first come to us for our protection, which they now share while they find somewhere to buy offsite. I continue down to the clubhouse, pausing only to nab a beer before making my way out back.

As I open the door, Marsh gets to his feet and I nod, giving him the signal he can leave, before resting my eyes on the girls. It's a large double bed which has seen more action from fucking than resting, but tonight two female bodies are lying in the middle, both fast asleep, Ella's hand holding tight to one of her sister's which hasn't got the drip running in. Doc enters behind me and quickly goes to expertly check the drip and pull the needle out of poor Jayden's arm.

"Sleep will do her the most good now," he says softly, patting my back as he leaves. He's been so efficient neither girl has stirred.

Wanting nothing more than to be close to them, I notice there's just enough room for me if I lie on my side. So, fully dressed and on top of the covers, I cautiously slide down, my arm at first gingerly, then more firmly tucking around Ella.

She starts and turns. I raise my finger to my lips and point toward Jayden. "Hush, let her rest. Doc says that's what she needs. Just let me hold you, Ella. Please, give me this. I need to know you're both safe."

She stares at me for a moment, my desperation to protect her, my distress at the harrowing experience I've just been through must be written on my face. Her hand comes up to place a featherlight touch to my cheek, then, with a nod giving silent permission she turns back around, staring at her sister before closing her eyes.

I stay awake, going over and over what fucking options we've got. One thing's for certain, I'm not able to give Ella up. Shit, I never thought of myself as any kind of family man, but I've made the decision that not only am I going to win my old lady back, but Jayden's going to be under my protection too. Which means I've got to sort this fuck-up of a situation and negate all threats. I must. I'm not letting either of them go.

CHAPTER 16

Ella

Having had a surprisingly deep sleep, I wake disorientated, not sure where I am, but feeling far too hot, surrounded on each side by a warm body. As my eyes fall on Jayden, the events of the night before slam back into my head and, in a flash I'm wide awake, fully conscious of the hardness poking into my ass.

I try to close the gap between myself and Jayden, Slick's arm tightens, and a gravelly voice murmurs in my ear, "Sorry about the mornin' wood, darlin'. Don't let it worry ya. I'm gonna move away now. Want me to get you a coffee or somethin'?"

At the thought of refreshment my stomach growls, making him laugh softly. "I'll see what's doin' in the kitchen."

Which reminds me where I am. "Slick, I…"

"That fucker Marsh came back, seems he's taking his protection duties seriously. Or should be," he throws a pointed look toward the prospect. "I'll kick him awake as I go." As Slick places the most tender of kisses to the top of my head and then rolls and puts his feet on the floor, sliding them back into the boots he must have kicked off last night, I look over and grin at the young man who's asleep on the chair, his mouth hanging open, snoring gently.

"Let him sleep," I whisper. "Poor lad looks knackered out."

"Poor lad? He's fuckin' a prospect. He signed on to take shit." Slick scoffs but his eyes sparkle with amusement and, nevertheless, leaves without waking him. The sound of the door slamming, however, does the trick.

Marsh starts. Coming to himself in an instant, looking sheepish that he'd been caught asleep on the job. He catches me watching him. A corner of his mouth turns up, then he nods at Jayden. "She awake?" he asks softly.

"Not yet," I whisper back. But I can feel her stirring. Now I'd rather she stayed sleeping. The moment she wakes, both she and I have got to start coming to terms with what happened. I'm dreading what she's going to tell me, knowing it will be painful to hear. A shiver goes through me. I'm not letting her get away with it anymore. Whether she likes it or not, now she's going to come clean about everything.

Slick's head appears around the door. "Ella, can you come here? Sam wants to talk to you. She's right beside me, you won't be far."

"You'll let me know if she wakes up?"

When Marsh gives a sharp nod, I step outside. Sam puts her hand on my arm and pulls me away down the corridor. We're only a few steps away, but won't be overheard. Slick walks off in the direction of the kitchen once again.

Sam leans her back against the wall, and mimicking her stance I place myself next to her. She looks down, takes a deep breath, then looks up at me. "I know what happened to you, Ella."

Swallowing down my shame, I stare at my feet.

"Now don't look like that." She frowns. "Two words, 'forced' and 'train'. That's all anyone needs to hear and they'll be filling in the gaps for themselves. And just so you know, if the fuckers weren't dead already, every single man here would mount up and ride to Phoenix to kill them for you. The Satan's Devils have nothing in common with those bastards. If they've got any faults, it's that they can be overprotective."

I'm not sure I believe her, they wear leather and ride bikes. But she seems resolute.

"Anyway," she continues, "I'm not here about that. I just wanted you to know there are no secrets between us. Between friends, which I hope we'll become." Since my ordeal I've let friendships lapse, perhaps I'd like to know more about the president's woman who's done nothing but impress me so far. Though I'm not sure I'm going to be here long enough, I remind myself. As soon as Jayden can leave, I'm taking her home.

She offers a small smile, which I try to return.

"Thing is, Ella. I was kidnapped three months ago. Shortly after I arrived here. To tell the truth, blue clouds and silver linings and all that, it was what made Drum and I get together so fast."

My eyes widen, I didn't know. "What happened?"

"You've heard of human trafficking? Well, I was taken to be a sex slave. They thought I was a virgin, but Drummer had got there first, if you know what I mean." She breaks off and gives an infectious giggle.

Having planted that picture in my mind, I chuckle too.

Then her face becomes drawn. "Because virginity gave me a higher value, they wanted to protect, what they assumed, was my status. That was the only thing that stopped them from raping me soon after they picked me up. But the other girls I was with weren't so lucky." She pauses for a second. "Then I was bought and taken to the home of a sadistic bastard."

"What?" I can't believe what I'm hearing. *Do such things really go on?*

"Yes. To cut a long story short, he tried to break me. I fought back, but it was getting close. Luckily the boys rescued me in the nick of time. I was tied up and naked, and he hurt me quite a lot."

I'm standing, staring at her. Her confidence, the way she deals with the rough men surrounding her, would never have led me to believe she'd only so recently gone through anything so dreadful. I'm completely at a loss for words.

"They rescued a dozen other women too, who stayed on the compound for a couple of days. Because I understood some of what they'd been through, I helped them. They opened up and, believe you me, what I heard wasn't good. Some were better equipped to deal with it than others." She breaks off and grimaces. "Two of them, Paige and Diva, have stayed here. They used to be strippers and they wanted to become sweet butts—probably better than whoring themselves out on the streets. They've settled in well from what I can see." She gives a little scowl which confuses me until I remember, old ladies and sweet butts don't tend to get along. Jill certainly hadn't ever spoken to me again after Slick had claimed me.

She huffs a laugh when she sees me looking puzzled. "I'd like them a lot better if they stopped trying to get their hands on Drum, but I know I don't need to worry, as I can trust him. It just gets wearing having to keep slapping them down. Anyway, Ella, I wanted you to know my story."

Fair enough, and I'm grateful to know I'm not the only one with something to deal with. Is that the reason she told me?

"Look, I'll be honest. Drum's asked me to get involved. There's complications to what's happened with Jayden, more to it than just getting her mind and body healed. It's bigger than they thought, that's all I know. And anything she can tell us might give them a better idea what they're dealing with."

But it's over now, isn't it? Jayden's here and safe. And hopefully, later today I'll be taking her home. But I suppose if it helps the club I don't mind sharing what she tells me. "She's got to get it out. I'm not looking forward to hearing it, Sam. She's only fourteen for God's sake."

Her hand rests on my arm. "I hear you, Ella. I've been thinking, with my experience, and yours too, we could both help her talk. Bottling it up won't help, as I'm sure you've found."

I'd hidden my secret so long, didn't tell anyone until I spat it out to Slick in a moment of weakness as I'd been so ashamed. But now it seems everyone knows what happened to me and no one's passed judgement. Sam's easy acceptance, no sign she's apportioning blame, *and* with her own terrible story to tell... Perhaps there might come a time when I can put it behind me. A concept which didn't seem possible when I kept it all to myself.

Sam's carefully watching me. "The club owes you a debt, Ella. They'll bend over backwards to give you anything you need."

Right now, the person who needs the most help is my sister. And that starts with Jayden getting everything off her chest. And what better than to two people who know what it means to be in someone else's control? She hadn't lost her virginity, she'd had it stolen. In the same way that I hadn't gone into the Rock Demons' clubhouse asking to be abused. And Sam certainly hadn't kidnapped herself. These things had been done to us. Without our consent.

"We're all victims." I breathe the words out, never having admitted it before. Not even to myself, always searching for explanations of what I'd done wrong. Knowing I'll be thinking more on it later, trying to rearrange it all and view it with new perspective.

"Do you mind if I sit in with you? Though I must admit, I'm not a good conversationalist if it isn't about bikes."

As she gives a short laugh directed at what she sees are her own shortcomings, I stand incredulous. In one short conversation she's opened my eyes, giving me things to consider I hadn't thought for myself. And her insightfulness leads me to a decision.

"I'd welcome it. Anything that can help my sister."

Before she can answer, Marsh's face peers around out of the doorway. "She's wakin' up."

My feet are moving in a flash, Sam following. I race to the bed. Jayden's holding her head and looking around, fearful and anxious. Marsh nods at me, then resumes his place against the wall, but standing now, not sitting.

Mindful of the discussion I want to have, I swivel around. "Marsh, could you leave us, please?"

"Sorry, Ella. No can do. Slick told me to stay put so here's where I'm stayin'."

"Can't you stand outside the door? You can guard us from there just as well."

As he's considering it, Jayden grabs hold of my hand and points her other toward the prospect. "You. You were there. You rescued me."

He answers her with quirk of his mouth and a quick nod.

My sister looks at me pleadingly. "Can he stay?" Her eyes flick to him as though he's some sort of hero. Quickly I consider her request. If having him in the room makes her more comfortable and will help settle her, I suppose it doesn't matter.

He walks over to the bed, gazing at her, his eyes widening slightly as if seeing her for the first time. It makes me realise how awful she's looking. There's a dreadful pallor to her skin, her eyes look sunken, there's drool at the side of her mouth and her hair's all over the place. Glancing at the prospect, I see he's showing no sign that he's noticed.

Instead he gives her a quick grin. "I didn't have much to do with it. I just carried you out. Didn't think you'd remember."

She creases her brow. "I don't recall much. Just you. Were there others?" Her hand goes to her head and she grimaces.

"Here, Doc left some painkillers. Can you sit up and take them?" She does with my help. She looks a little green, and she covers her mouth. "Need the bathroom?" As she nods I go to help her up, but Marsh is there first, picking her up in his arms and carrying her through to the facilities. It happened so fast, Sam and I exchange glances.

What the fuck is that? Sam mouths. I purse my lips. Marsh seems almost protective, but she's only fourteen. If there's any interest there I'll have to knock it on the head before either of them get any ideas. But as I get to my feet and go to follow her, seeing her leaning over the bowl with Marsh holding her hair back, I get another glimpse of something else lying beneath the surface of these leather-clad men. A gentleness and caring I never expected.

Finished at last, she splashes water on her face and starts to get more colour back. When she returns under her own steam she takes the Advil, swallowing it down with water. She sighs, then looks around, her hand massaging her stomach. "What's wrong with me? And where am I?" Her senses must be returning as she shows interest at last.

"As for where you are, you're in the Satan's Devils' club-house," I tell her. "They were the people who got you out of that house last night."

Her eyes flick to Marsh's cut. As her eyes widen, "Are you one of them? A biker?"

He gives a boyish grin, and his voice sounds proud. "Certainly am."

Her wide-open eyes come back to me. "Ella? What on earth are we doing here?"

I sit beside her again and come up with the simple story. "Some of the bikers are friends of mine. They helped me find you." As she gives a little frown I continue, "As to what's wrong with you. sweetie, you've got a bad hangover." Immediately her eyes flick to mine in concern, as if expecting me to admonish her, so I hurry to reassure her, "I know you don't drink, honey, this isn't your fault."

Watching her carefully, I see the moment her face falls and then becomes shuttered as memories must be coming back. She reaches over and grabs hold of my hand, tears starting to fall down her face.

My voice breaks as I probe, "You were found with some men, Jayden. And now's the time to come clean about what's been going on. How they trapped you. And what they did to you."

Immediately she pulls her hand back and turns her face away from me. "I don't want to talk about it. You wouldn't understand." Now there's fear on her face as she adds in a whisper. "I can't tell you anything."

It's a similar answer as the one she's been giving me for weeks, and her reluctance to explain fuels my frustration. This time she can't deny there's something wrong, and I'm ashamed to say I want to shake her, get her to admit everything. The tension in my body must give me away.

Sam puts a warning hand on my shoulder and leans forward. "Hi, Jayden. My name's Sam. My old man's the President of the Satan's Devils." As she introduces herself Jayden tilts her head up to face her. "I'd like to share something with you." She parks her butt on the end of the bed and continues, "There are bad men in the world, Jayden. Men who take advantage of women as they think we're the weaker sex." She flicks her eyes toward Marsh and gives a little grin. "I might be a badass, ride a bike and have a gun, but I didn't have a chance when I was kidnapped and sold to be someone's sex slave."

A week ago I wouldn't have wanted my young sister to hear any part of this conversation. Now I realise what Sam's trying to do.

She's caught Jayden's interest, and a quivering of her lips suggests she's getting through to her. "What... What happened?"

"My old man, Drummer, and the rest of the guys didn't stop until they rescued me. Luckily they got there in time." Sam gestures toward Jayden. "Just like they rescued you."

Jayden's eyes open wider, and she glances at the prospect. "So you're the good guys?"

Marsh barks a laugh. "Sometimes," he replies.

Sam smiles, then grows serious. "Somehow they tricked you, Jayden, and we need to know how. It's not only you, sweetheart, they've done this before and will do it again. The club wants to make sure no other young girls are duped the same way you were."

Jayden breathes in, then mumbles something which I have to ask her to repeat.

"I don't know what you mean."

"Jayden, honey..."

"Alright, Ella. I'll tell you. I've got a boyfriend and he treats me real good."

"*What?*" I scream out the question. "What's this crap coming out of your mouth, Jayden? A *boyfriend*. He's a fucking grown man." Normally I wouldn't swear in front of my sister, but I can't believe what she's saying.

She's glaring at me.

"Do you know what happened last night?" I'm grateful Sam's here, her voice sounds so calm and she's giving me a few seconds to pull myself together.

Jayden shrugs in reply, then rubs her forehead.

"You've got a bad headache, sweetie, because you were given alcohol and a date rape drug. You know what that is?"

Sam's caught my sister's attention. Leaning forward, she takes hold of both of Jayden's hands. "Listen to me. This man, Diego. I'm sure he made you like him, but that's what his sort do." She seems to examine her closely. "You knew it was wrong, didn't you? But honey, it wasn't your fault. Just tell us what happened."

Her eyes flicking wildly between us, Jayden looks like an animal trapped in the headlights. She doesn't want to talk, doesn't want to explain. But sharing is the only way to start healing. A message that I should take to heart.

"You're not in trouble, Jayden. I promise you that. Just like Sam, what happened to you wasn't your fault."

Her lips start to quiver and she wipes at her eyes. Her attitude no longer so challenging, I take the opportunity to ask gently, "How did you get involved with them, Jayden?"

Sam nods encouragingly. "It will help to tell someone, I promise."

Jayden looks at me, I add my nod to reassure her. Finally, she starts to speak. "I can't." It comes out as a wail.

Marsh is there almost at once. "Whatever threats they told you to keep you quiet, they won't work now, babe."

Her eyes widen. "You know?"

He shrugs. "It's the way these people work, honey."

Another moment of quiet as she considers his words, and I think on how he knew exactly the right thing to say. He's got a good head on those young shoulders, even though they're covered in leather.

Finally, with a sigh, Jayden starts to speak. "You and me, El, we used to go to the mall on the weekend. Just to browse, have a coffee."

I dip my head. Yes, that's exactly what we used to do.

"When you stopped coming around, Mom didn't care, and I got bored staying in so I went out with a couple of school friends."

I feel my face go tight. As I suspected, so much of this down to me. "Go on."

"A boy came to speak to me. His name was Sylas, Sy. He was so cute. I was flattered he'd singled me out. My friends were jealous." She looks down at her nails. "That's when it all started."

Sam gives me another squeeze on my shoulder, and I know what she wants. "I stopped coming around because I was dealing with something myself. I was raped, Jayden." I never expected to have to make that admission to my little sister, but Sam's right, if we expect her to open up, so must I.

At that Jayden pulls herself up, her hand going to her aching head at the sudden movement. "Ella? You? Why didn't you tell me?" Tentatively she reaches out and touches my arm. "Why didn't I see something was wrong?"

"Oh, Jayden, babe. I was so wrapped up in my troubles, I didn't want you to know. I thought it had been my fault. I stopped coming around because you'd have seen I was hurting. And because I stayed away, I didn't see what was happening to you. And by the time I felt strong enough, you were immersed in your own worries, weren't you?"

Launching at me again, she holds me tightly. "I'm so sorry," she wails. "Ella, I'm sorry." She becomes incoherent as she cries, letting it all out. I'm unable to stop my own tears falling down my face.

When her crying eventually ends on a few last hiccupped sobs, Marsh comes over and tentatively sits on the bed. His hand hovers, and then lands on top of the covers, his fingers squeezing her leg underneath. When he gets her attention, he asks in a gentle voice, "Can you tell us what happened, darlin'? No one's going to judge you, I promise."

Her bottom lip still quivering, she glances at me, then Sam, and then fixes her eyes back on him. Whether it's because he's a stranger or someone closer to her own age, I don't know, but I'm grateful when at last she starts to admit the truth, and the whole sorry story starts tumbling out.

Even Marsh has tears escaping down his face when she finishes.

With cold steely eyes, Sam gets up and leaves the room.

CHAPTER 17

Slick

Once again we're all sitting around the table. Muted conversations cease immediately when Drummer takes the chair.

He picks up the gavel and twists it in his hands, then, with a chin jerk to Wraith begins. "By now I expect you all know who we're fuckin' dealin' with. The Herrera family."

Yes, the rumours have spread fast, but that doesn't prevent exclamations going around.

"Nasty bunch of motherfuckers." Beef puts it into words.

"Don't know that we'll be able to take them on," Dart warns.

Marvel recently transferred from San Diego, and Joker and Lady, patched in from Vegas, look puzzled. Lady's the one to ask, "Who are the Herreras?"

"A family who's got their hands in too many twisted fuckin' pies in Tucson. They breed like rabbits."

"We should leave them the fuck alone." Peg's looking to the club's safety. "If they find out it was us that shot them up last night, killed their punters and two of the family, they'll be comin' for the club. They've got their own fuckin' army."

I want my brothers to have my back. Right now it looks like they're not looking to take on this fight. Banging my fist on the table, I get their attention. "We're assumin' they don't know who hit them last night, so yeah, fuck, we can walk away. But," I hold my hand up as Dart looks like he's going to speak, "it's not just us we need to consider. If they know the girl, Ella's sister, is alive, they'll never stop tryin' to track her down. One word she was rescued, they won't stop until they get their hands on her and make her talk." I shake my head. "Her life's already been ruined, I don't want her livin' under a fuckin' cloud for the rest of her years."

"Slick!" Drum growls. "We said we'd make the decision as a club. I know you want them all taken out so Jayden can have her life back, but there are other ways to keepin' her safe, as we discussed."

"If your answer's to send Ella and Jayden away, I'm going with." I've given eight or more years to this club, it's my home, and I don't want to leave. But my feelings run so deep for my old lady, I can't let her go away alone.

All eyes are upon me, some people frowning at the thought I'd desert my brothers for the sake of a woman. But I can see some support from those with their own old ladies. They're the ones who are nodding their heads.

Drum starts again. "Wraith and I visited Jayden's mother this morning. We didn't give the details, but told her Jayden's got caught up in some shit." He pauses and shakes his head. "Didn't take to the woman, she was more concerned about distancin' herself. More than happy to let us deal with the girls. She has, however, agreed to report Jayden to the police as a missin' person this mornin'. With Herrera's reach I suspect they've got contacts in the department and should soon find that out. Hopefully it should satisfy them that she's gone the same way as the men we killed."

The bodies we disposed of where no one would find them. Another extension to the dirt track. And we'd left nothing incriminating behind, just the empty blood bath of the house, a mystery for the Herrera family to unravel. With Jayden's mother doing her part, no one will know if she's dead or alive.

"You think we can trust her to keep her mouth shut, Prez?"

"I don't think the Herreras will approach her. If she's reported a missin' daughter there'd be no point in them tryin' to track Jayden through her, as it will appear she's got no more knowledge than they do. And she didn't seem overly concerned, more keen on havin' one to one time with her new man. Seems like she's movin' him in. Her daughter not being home suits her down to the ground. I don't know I'd go so far as to fuckin' trust her, but as long as she goes to the police as she agreed, I don't think she'll be a problem. There's no benefit to her in makin' waves."

Dollar's pulling on his fingers, making them click. An annoying habit of his that makes me squirm. "If they don't know who took them out, they might think it's a rival gang who've taken the girl to sell her. Sweet thing like that would attract dollar signs."

"Could Ella's relationship with you be traced back to the club?" This from Peg.

"We've had a prospect based outside Ella's apartment for a while." It's all I need to say. If the Herreras started digging and asking around they'd be able to find that out.

Young Shooter's starting to get more confident with his place at the table. He raises his hand and Drum indicates his permission to speak. "As I see it, Prez, there's a possibility they might join the dots. Slick's ol' lady's sister could be traced back to us. If there's any danger comin' our way, I'd rather we were prepared and ready to fight."

Yeah, Shooter wouldn't want to be surprised all over again, but he did real good when he needed to and protected Sophie. It was his sharp shooting that got his named changed from Spider when we patched him in.

Prez's eyes have widened, and he throws Shooter an appreciative nod. "Good point there." He raps his fingers on the table. "We could hide our heads in the sand, divorce ourselves from this shit. Send Jayden away and lose a good fuckin' member with it," he jerks his chin toward me and I feel warm at the off-handed praise, "and still end up in a fuckin' war."

Wraith's been quiet, and now has his say. "I agree with Shooter. But right now we're going into this blind. We need to find out what we can about this family and see if it's even possible to take them all out. It's gonna be one fuck of an opera-tion. Fuck knows how many we could be up against."

"The way these families work, or how we've seen it in Vegas, is that their foot soldiers have no loyalty. Cut off the head of the snake, the ones who pay their wages, and they'll be too busy lookin' for other jobs rather than seekin' revenge."

Joker's input is interesting. "Don't forget they're family. It might not be as simple as that."

"So we hit all of them." I glare at Wraith. I'm prepared to do anything to keep my girls safe.

"It would make Tucson a lot cleaner." Rock tugs at his ear. His observation is valid.

Drum wipes his face wearily, he looks tired. "We've got Heart in the hospital and tryin' to track down who ran him off the road. And now we're proposin' to go up against a family with far more manpower than ourselves." Breaking off, he gives a little laugh. "And there I was hopin' for a bit of fuckin' peace and quiet."

But his unneeded reminder about Heart stirs rage in all of us, and if my brothers are feeling anything like I am, it will be easy to redirect that anger onto a target that we can at least identify.

"Okay, let's take a vote. All those in favour of takin' on the Herrera clan?" As he goes around the table, it's unanimous ayes. A couple, Viper and Bullet, who both have old ladies, give their answers a little more slowly than the rest.

When it gets around to Peg, and the sergeant-at-arms gives his consent, a wave of relief comes over me.

"Looks like you're stayin' here, Slick. Along with your girls." Ella's not going to be too comfortable with it, but I'll just have to convince her she'll be putting Jayden in danger if she leaves.

Mouse puts up his hand. "Drum, I know what you need from me. But first, as most of you know, the motherfuckers had camera's recordin' in that house we were in last night." He waits for the roars of disgust to settle down. "It's another way they make money. Post it online for paedophiles to pay to download."

"That's sick."

"I know, Dart. Slick, man, this is gonna be hard, but I've found all the shit they taped of Jayden."

"Tell me, Mouse." I know I'm going to want to bleach my ears after hearing what he's going to say.

"Man, I didn't want to watch it. But I felt I had to, to understand what they do. It made me fuckin' sick to my stomach."

There are nods around the table. I don't think any of us would want to watch that shit. Yeah, we're all up for a bit of porn, but not with underage girls who've been drugged and forced.

Wiping my hands over my head, I take a deep breath to give myself strength, then focus my stare on Mouse. "Let me have it."

Drum hits both his fists on the table, his eyes grow dark. "It was one fuckin' thing for Mouse to have to watch it. We're not sick bastards wantin' to relive that shit. Understand, Slick, why you think you want the details, but I don't think the rest of us need to be sickened by it."

He's got a point.

When he sees he's got our attention he turns to Mouse, who, for the first time I notice looks tired and drawn. "Mouse, just give us the headlines."

Mouse nods, seeming relieved he doesn't have to describe the detail of what he had seen. "I found and deleted all the vids on their website. As of this mornin' their business has been taken down. Yeah, Slick, includin' the videos of Jayden."

Again I suck in air and suddenly realise I don't want to know the content. If Diego wasn't already dead, I'd kill him all over again. "Her videos had been viewed?"

The computer expert shrugs. "Hundreds of hits, Brother."

I stand, my chair falling over as I pace around the room. In my mind, I'm seeing perverts jerking off to that shit. My hands go over the smooth skin of my head. "What else? What fuckin' else, Mouse?"

"Slick..." Mouse looks pained as he tries to get the words out. "Jayden wasn't the only one. But from what I could see, we got there in time last night."

"In *time?*" I'm trying to process what he's saying.

Mouse is slowly nodding his head. "Yeah. They were only just gettin' started. In the rest of the shit we got from the house, they had films in different files, all linked by the coded name of the girl. Other young girls had multiple videos, Jayden only had the two. Fuck it, I forced myself to watch a couple. Couldn't stomach anymore." He pauses, then continues, "And it wasn't just young girls... boys too."

He breaks off and breathes in deeply as though it's hard to continue. I wince, realising how hard watching those tapes must have been for my brother. Fuck knows, I wouldn't want to.

Then he says something else. "They fuckin' drug then rape them."

The shouts and roars are deafening. When Drum manages to call us back to order he sits shaking his head. "Can't believe the shit I'm hearin'. Jayden, and presumably the others, went back to their families. Why the fuck didn't they shout out what was going on?"

Mouse briefly closes his eyes. "In groomin' cases like this, they'll use threats to keep them in line."

"How many files, Mouse?"

"A dozen in the house, Prez. But online, fifty or more kids were involved going by the names. As I said, I couldn't watch more."

Wraith's looking stunned and then repeats Drum's question, "And not one of the kids said anything? No one's come forward?"

It's obvious they didn't, but why, we can't answer.

In the ensuing moment of quiet, Drum gets a text. He sends a quick reply and then offers up, "Sam's gonna join us." He looks up and then proceeds to explain why he's taking the unusual step of allowing an old lady into our meeting. "Jayden's awake, been tellin' her story."

Almost before he can finish there's a knock at the door. Shooter gets up and opens it. Sam comes in, confidently striding to the head of the table to take her place by her man. Drum eases back his chair from the table, she sits down on his lap.

As the Prez's arms come around her, she acknowledges us all by raising her chin, and then fills the expectant silence with her voice, unaware she's answering the questions we've just asked.

"Jayden didn't tell Ella, or anyone what was happening. The short story is she met Sy and thought he was her boyfriend. He told her to keep things quiet, as neither of their parents would let them see each other if they found out." She pauses and huffs a laugh. "Jayden was more frightened of Ella's reaction than her mom's. It was an effective threat on a young girl who was enjoying the flirtation of a handsome boy. And she saw no harm in it, enjoying the novelty of sneaking out to see him. Until he introduced her to his uncle. Diego flattered her, and she thought it was great, made to feel so important with the gifts she was given, and enjoyed the attention that was showered on her when she didn't get much affection from her mom.

"Ella was still healing from what she was going through, didn't think it was fair to let her sister see how upset she was. She didn't go around so much and didn't notice Jayden's pain or decline until she was hooked and couldn't get out."

Sam pauses for breath, but seeing we're all rapt, continues, "Diego reeled her in, then alternated his flattering with threats. He introduced her to a couple of his friends and, well, I'm not going to draw a picture. That's when she realised it was wrong, but by then, the promise of intimidation got serious. He told her she was dealing with powerful people, threatening to set her house on fire and burn it down with her mother in it, or making sure her mother or Ella would have a fatal accident. Threats a fourteen-year-old would have no problem believing. Yeah, Slick. They knew all about Ella—threatened to shoot her as she was leaving work one night. One of Sy's jobs was to find out all he could about the girls he entrapped."

So that's how they did it, it was just as Mouse had suggested. And they must have been watching Ella as they knew about her job. If they were watching last week, they'd have seen Road waiting outside. I exchange a look with Drum. If we hadn't already agreed to go after the Herrera's, this would have shown us we had fuck all chance of keeping a low profile.

The ranting and raving blows up, then starts to die down. Drum strokes the arms of his old lady, she relaxes into his touch. Then he turns his attention to the men in the room. "Right. You know what we voted on."

As everyone nods, I notice he's saying no more in front of Sam. That she's a great president's old lady is proven when she shows no indication that she wants to know. Fuck, Drum did well when she rode into his life.

But she's not quite finished. "One thing, Drum, Jayden seems to respond to Marsh. She remembers him from last night. If she needs a man guarding her, I think it should be him. She needs all the reassurance she can get at this stage. She's terrified Diego's men will make good on the threats, or will come here and find her. Giving her protection from someone she trusts could help."

Drum's eyes narrow. "You trust him?"

Sam shrugs. "She trusts him. And at this point I think that's what counts. She's latched onto him as she thinks that he saved her. She doesn't remember anyone else being there."

I was wondering why the unlikely pair had matched up. Now Sam's answered my unspoken question. It does make some warped sense.

"Okay, so Marsh can watch out for her. It could help her ease into the club. Which reminds me. It's a good time to bolster our ranks. We were gonna do it later today, anyway. Let's call in the fucker."

As his words sink in, Dart's first to cotton on. "Patch in party!" Everyone hollers in response.

Sam starts to slide off his lap, Drum holds her tight. "You can be here for this," he tells her with a grin.

Brothers thump the table, and I suspect Drum's chosen this particular moment to lighten the mood. Fuck we've heard some hard shit today, and no one's been affected more than me.

Still holding Sam, Drum sends a quick text, then at a nod from his prez, Wraith opens a cupboard behind him and takes something out. Even I summon up a small grin, knowing exactly what it is.

Within moments Marsh appears, hesitantly poking his head around the door. Like old ladies, prospects aren't normally privy to what goes on in our meetings.

The prez fixes him with his steely glare, the one most of us hope we never have directed at us. Normally it's the last sight a man would see before Drum pulls the trigger. Marsh falters by the door.

"Stand there, Prospect." Drummer points to a spot behind Shooter at the end of the table. Marsh's eyes seem to measure the distance from the prez as though assessing whether he's within range.

Drummer gently pushes Sam off his lap. She stands up and waits at his side, her hand resting on his shoulder, her face as stern as that of any of us. Leaning forward Drum bangs both hands down on the wood. "What's this I hear, Prospect? You takin' advantage of a fourteen-year-old girl?"

Marsh starts. His eyes flick guiltily toward Sam as though wondering what she's spilled. Then his hands come up in a defensive gesture. "No. No, Prez. It's not like that."

"I'll say what it's fuckin' like!" Drum roars, and I swear Marsh isn't the only one to jump. "You're a nineteen-year-old boy, she ain't even legal."

Marsh's cheeks have gone red. "Drum, it's just that she reminds me of my young sister."

Now Drum stands up, leaning over the table. "She ain't your fuckin' sister! You keep your fuckin' hands off her, you hear me?"

Marsh has taken a step back, bringing him up against the wall. His mouth is opening and closing as he seems to realise there's nowhere left for him to go.

"You. Hear. Me?" Drum roars again.

"I hear ya, Prez, I hear ya!"

The prospect is visibly shaking. Drum stays where he is, then slowly sits back down. Lines gradually smoothing away from his forehead, one side of his mouth turning up. "Sounds like you're her fuckin' hero, though fuck knows why. All ya did was carry her fuckin' out into the truck." He points his forefinger toward Marsh. "While she's here you stick with her. Help her adjust. But one whiff that you're takin' it further and you'll fuckin' pay. Got four years to wait, man, before you can go there."

Marsh starts to stammer, Drum shuts him up. "You're her fuckin' champion? Let's go with that. Her knight in armour, her fuckin' Paladin."

"I've had gone for Babysitter." Peg shrugs. Although we're all trying to keep straight faces, a few sniggers escape.

"Paladin is good, Prez," Wraith agrees. I think it's a fuck of a handle, but maybe better than how I got mine. At least he didn't damage his bike.

Marsh wipes sweat off his brow, his eyes are wide open and he's totally confused. Wraith passes what he's got hold of to Drum.

Instead of taking it, Drum just slides it down the table. "Get sewin', brother."

Marsh rears back. Seems it was totally unexpected. Then walking forward, he reaches out a shaking hand and picks up the patches, his knuckles turning white as he holds them so tight, as if worried someone will snatch them away.

Then, slowly, his lips start to curl up. He stares down at what's he's holding, a full grin appearing on his face. He shakes his head, his confusion displaying his complete surprise.

"Meetin' fuckin' over." Drum bangs the gavel, but then holds up his hand. "Paladin, tell the prospect to get another chair in here, will ya?"

CHAPTER 18

Ella

Jayden's story had been so heartbreaking. Since getting everything off her chest she's been quietly crying, clutching onto my body as though she doesn't want to let me go. Sam left a while ago to update Drum, and I'm weeping myself, unable to comprehend people who could target such a young girl, put her through the things they did, and keep her in line with credible threats to her family, leaving her no choice but to go with their demands, believing it was the only way to keep her family safe. Marsh is still sitting at the end of the bed, his face in his hands. It was hard even for a hardened man like him to hear. From time to time he reaches out and pats Jayden's leg — she seems to take some comfort from his touch.

As he notices me watching, he shakes his head. His eyes water as he says softly, "Fuck Ella, she's the same age as my sister."

Shortly afterwards, he gets a summons by text and slips out of the room with a promise he'll be back as soon as he can. Immediately Road enters and gives me a nod, but stands at the wall without speaking. But his expression softens as he looks at the girl on the bed.

I'm grateful for his silence, not knowing what to say either to him, or to Jayden. My guilt lies so heavily; if I hadn't been so wrapped up in my own head I might have been able to save her before it went as far as it did. I'm devastated on her behalf and by the unknowing part that I'd played.

My arm's gone dead and I need to move. Noticing Jayden has cried herself to sleep, I ease myself out from under her and stand up to stretch. When there's a knock on the door Road goes to open it. My hands tremble as he cracks it open just an inch, but I am reassured that he's checking who it is rather than just letting them in. And then relieved when I see who it is.

"Shush, Jayden's sleeping," I tell Slick and Sam, who stand just outside.

"Can I talk to you a moment?" Slick asks.

As I throw a concerned look over my shoulder Sam offers, "I'll stay with her."

"Won't keep ya long," Slick encourages.

I nod and walk out into the hallway. Loud raucous sounds are coming from the clubroom, making me flinch. Slick's hand touches mine and he squeezes my fingers. "Marsh, or rather Paladin, seein' as he's picked up a new handle, has just been patched in," he explains. "Boys will be partyin' later."

My eyes shoot to him in horror.

He turns me to face him. "You've got nothin' to worry about, Ella. They'll be lettin' their hair down, that's for sure, but no one's gonna lay a finger on you or your sister. No woman ever gets forced here, you understand?"

I don't fully believe him. I don't want to remember the last time I saw a bikers party. *But I can trust Slick, can't I?* Or will he be partying along with the rest, fucking a club whore? I couldn't blame him, he'll get nothing from me. *But he promised he wouldn't.* Do I know him enough to believe he's a man of his word?

With thoughts and worries tumbling through my head, I'm only vaguely aware he's still holding my hand, and my feet are moving automatically until he stops in front of another door.

"Drum said we can use his office, so you're not far from your sister. Okay?"

Having been worried he was taking me to where loud voices are getting rowdier, I let go of some of my tension as I follow him into an office. If it weren't for the large flag behind a massive desk, a larger version of the picture they have on their cuts, it could be a manager's office anywhere.

I slide into a seat in front of the desk. Declining to take his prez's seat, Slick pulls up another chair and sits next to me, his body angled so he can take hold of my hands. His fingers caress me. "You doin' okay?"

I breathe a deep breath. "It's so hard, Slick. Listening to her describe what they did to her. How they trapped her."

He nods. "It must have been, darlin'. It was bad enough hearin' it secondhand. But it ain't on her, she was groomed by experts." He breaks off and squeezes my fingers. "Doubt it was easy listenin', babe. All that coming on top of what happened to you."

"Two broken sisters…"

"Never that." He looks fierce as he interrupts me. "Damaged, maybe. But you're both going to be fine."

"You can't promise me that." Right now I'm at the lowest point I've ever been in my life.

"I can," he says firmly. "I'm gonna be there for you, El. Both of you." As I glance at him, wondering how he's going to make good on such a pledge, it's his turn to fill his lungs with air and then to explain some of what's going on. Well, the parts I need to know, the rest falling under that dreaded term, *club business*.

When he finishes I voice my objections. "We can't stay at the club." It's bad enough that I've got to be here. But Jayden is far too young. "Jayden's underage for a start. We can't live with bikers."

He looks down, then back at me again. "Darlin', I don't know what I can do to convince you we're not like that other club." He winces as a particularly loud roar comes to our ears. "Yeah, we're bikers, we drink and we fuck. But Satan's Devils respect women, sweetheart. You stick around and you'll see every man here has your best interests at heart."

Words won't work to convince me. Already I'm a bag of nerves. As I go to refute what he's saying he stops me.

"We're well aware Jayden's underage, and my brothers know what she's been through. Fuck, they'll be walkin' on egg shells around her. But when all's said and done, you've got no fuckin' choice, babe. Your sister's got to stay out of sight. El, no one must know she's still breathin'. If you try to go back home she'll be taken, and…" As his voice trails off, and I see his serious expression, I begin to accept the idea that the alternative might be worse.

"Ella, the brothers and I, well, we'll all do what we can to treat you both right."

My eyes harden. "You're bikers."

"Aware of that, darlin'. But we ain't the Rock Demons. We've got ol' ladies here, and you're one of them now. Brothers fight to protect anyone wearing a property patch. Fuck, we've got Heart's little daughter always runnin' around getting' under our feet. Way we work is the brothers behave themselves until the ol' ladies leave for the night. If you stay after then you might want to close your eyes, but up until then there's not much that's X rated." He laughs softly. "Pushin' an R, maybe." He looks at me earnestly. "Even if you stayed when the party gets goin', there's not one brother here who'd look at ya, let alone touch ya. They'd have me to answer to if they do."

I bite my lip. If we're staying in the room they put us in, we'll still hear enough for it to be disturbing, for me and for Jayden.

As if he can read my mind, Slick puts his finger under my chin. "You'll be stayin' with me." As I go to open my mouth he moves his finger to cover my lips. "You know the setup from before. There are two suites in each of the blocs. Wraith used to have the one adjoinin' mine, but he doesn't use it anymore. You and Jayden can stay there, and I'll be close by if you need me."

My brow creases as I think. If we have to stay on the compound, and Slick's been quite persuasive about the reasons why, at least we'll be some distance from the clubhouse and the worst of the raucousness that goes on.

"For how long, Slick?"

His eyes close as he gives a brief shake of his head. When he opens them again it's to tell me, "I can't say, Ella. It could be just days, but more likely weeks, I expect."

Recognising his expression as one of pain, I touch my fingers to his face—one of the first times I've touched him voluntarily as I suddenly realise how selfish I'm being. I'm not stupid. The only way of removing the threat is for the Satan's Devils to take on the men who got Jayden into the position she was in. They'll be fighting to give my sister her life back. And here I am, refusing to believe anything but the worst about them. Instead, I owe them my thanks. And my concern.

Now it's not just the fears for myself that are troubling me. "Are you going to be in any danger, Slick?"

His hand covers mine and he pushes his cheek into my touch, turning slightly and inhaling, then moving my fingers down and placing a kiss to the tips. "Not gonna lie to ya, darlin'."

Which I take to mean yes. This man who's been so gentle and caring since he'd learned what had happened to me, never doing anything but trying to reassure and support me. Suddenly I realise he's not the enemy, he's not someone I should be fighting. *He's on my side.* And having allowed myself to acknowledge that, it feels good to have him in my corner. "I don't want you hurt, Slick. Or anyone else in the club."

"You just leave that to us." He looks at me intently. "And know I'll being doin' what it takes to keep both of you protected."

Hesitantly he stands, looking down at me. "Come, let's go and see if Jayden's awake, get somethin' for you to eat, and then get you sorted up in your suite."

I get to my feet but pause. My eyes drawn to his, this six-foot-three, muscular biker, Although I'm still not convinced I'd ever be able to be the woman he needs. I'm completely drained from giving comfort to Jayden all morning, now I need some solace for myself, and suddenly I'm not afraid to ask him, no longer scared he'll push for more than I'm prepared to give.

"Slick?"

Having half turned toward the door, he now swings back around. "Yeah?"

"Can you... Can you give me a hug?"

"Fuck, Ella. I'd give you anythin' you fuckin' need. Come 'ere." He pulls me into his arms, cradling my head against his muscular chest. I breathe in *his* smell of leather and cigarette smoke, feeling at peace for the first time in months. Though clothes separate us, I feel the warmth from his skin and hear the beat of his heart. Running his hand up and down my back, he's careful not to hold me too tight. Having allowed myself a selfish moment, I pull away.

"Everythin' will be alright, Ella. I promise. I'm gonna take care of you both."

With his vow echoing in my head, I walk by his side, returning to Jayden. It suddenly hits me that a man like Slick would die trying to keep his promise. The thought makes me stumble, and it's his hand that stops me from falling. He gives me a sharp look, but neither of us speak.

Jayden's awake and dressed in the clothes Sam had brought her, and the sight that greets me as I walk in through the door brings my first smile of the day. Marsh—*Paladin now, I must remember*—is sitting on the bed and the pair are playing cards. Goodness knows what he's teaching her to play. Sam's sitting, watching the youngsters, an amused expression on her face. As we step inside they both turn around.

"Shouldn't you be out of here, Paladin?" Slick asks, with a smile. "Thought you had some celebratin' to do. You're the guest of honour after all."

The Satan's Devils newest member looks sheepish. "Just thought I'd pop in and see how Jayden's doing. The brothers are organisin' some shit for later. They won't miss me for now."

"Can I come?"

At Jayden's innocent enquiry I realise I'm going to have to explain just exactly how things work here, and how she really doesn't need to be at a biker club's party. But before I can open my mouth Slick answers for me. "Sure you can, sweetheart, for a while at least. The ol' lady's will be putting on food and will be hangin' around for a while. But when they leave, you'll have to as well."

Jayden pouts, and what she says next breaks my heart. "I'm not a child, Slick. Surely I can stay?"

This is where big bad sister has to step in. "You're underage, sweetie. If you want, I'm sure we can visit with Sam or the other old ladies. But we won't be allowed here. That's just how it works." I'm uncomfortable at the thought of being in the club-room while the old ladies are still there, let alone stay when they go.

Sam gets to her feet. "Slick told you about where you'll be staying?" I nod, she continues, "Sophie and Carmen have been sorting it out. Sandy's gone in to town with Road, they're going to pick you up some clothing and shit."

Damn, I hadn't considered I wouldn't be able to go home to pack.

Jayden is looking puzzled. "But I've got clothes at home. And why are we staying here? I want to see Mom."

Again Slick takes the lead, giving it to her straight. "Jayden, not going to kid ya. The people you got away from last night are gonna be lookin' for ya. You can't get anythin' from your home, or contact yer mom, okay?"

"They might burn down her house." Jayden's gone white. "They might hurt her anyway."

I hadn't thought of that. Now my eyes find Slick's.

"Don't think you need to worry about that. She's going to report you missin' to the police, and we think that should satisfy them that she doesn't have a clue where you are. But you can't have anythin' to do with her, okay? If you do, then she might be in danger."

"Jayden, I'll be with you. I'll be right by your side, all the time. And it's really important that you don't speak to anyone. No one must know you're still alive." I pause, knowing what I'm going to say next is going to devastate a teenager. "You can't use a phone, iPad, or anything to contact your friends."

To give her credit, she doesn't argue. Those threats must have hit hard. Her doe-like eyes look at me and she gives a small nod. I hate seeing her like this. A girl her age shouldn't have to go through the things she has, *is*. Once we're free to leave I'll need to get her some counselling. I can't see how she can come through this without expert help. One moment she seems normal and more resilient than I'd given her credit for, like when she was playing cards, the next she looks like the weight of the world is going to crush her.

"Come on, let's get you settled." As Slick opens the door and waits for us to leave the sanctuary of the room we'd spent the night in, I take in a deep breath. The rowdy noises from outside reminding me too much of the time I entered the Rock Demons' clubhouse. It's going to take a long time, if ever, before I'm able to relax around these type of men.

Seeing my hesitation, Slick offers me his hand. As I take it he leans down and whispers in my ear, "I won't let anythin' happen to you, Ella. I've promised you that."

Looking up into serious, caring eyes, I know he means every word. Taking hold of Jayden with my free hand, the three of us venture out, followed by the young biker.

"Hey, there's the fuckin' man of the hour! Paladin, come over 'ere."

Slick holds his arm across us, keeping us to the side so Paladin can pass. It's his party after all. We wait for a moment as men throng around him, slapping him so hard on his back I see him stumble. Jayden steps forward, her eyes widening as she takes in the leather-clad men, seeing the club members for the first time. Worrying my sister will be scared, I open my mouth to reassure her, but no words come out. They're not individuals, *they're bikers*, all dressed in cuts similar to those worn by the ones who'd hurt me so badly.

It's me that's afraid. Jayden's just looking curious. Then to my surprise, she smiles and touches my arm. "No one's going to take this lot on, are they Ella? Not unless they're stupid. They'll be able to protect us."

That she's looking at it in such a different and positive way astounds me. *But then she didn't go through what I did.* It's best to keep her in the dark.

"Slick!" Wraith, the VP comes over, his hands holding onto the collars of two men he's pushing in front of him. "Before ya go, thought you'd like to meet our two new prospects. This here's Hyde, and this one here's Spindle."

I notice the second man is quite young, and looks as skinny as a rake.

Slick cocks his head to the side, examining the pair.

An older biker comes up, interrupting. "Naw, not Spindle. If we've got a Hyde we might as well have a Jekyll to go with it."

Wraith's eyes become slits, and then he bursts out laughing. "Don't know how you do it, Viper, you're always comin' up with fuckin' good handles!"

The man previously known as Spindle frowns and shakes his head, but it's clear he hasn't a chance as Wraith yells to the crowd, "Meet our new prospects, Jekyll and Hyde!" Releasing the two men he slaps Viper on the back. "Good one, Brother." Then he spares a nod for me and Jayden. "You two girls settlin' in okay?"

With a dry mouth, all I can do is nod.

The VP's face softens. "You're quite safe here, Ella. Everyone knows what you did for the club, and how fuckin' much we owe you."

I still can't speak, so I rely on my expression to convey my thanks. Jayden's looking surprised, and I know I'll have more explaining to do. As I'm thinking what details I can share about the favour I did for the Satan's Devils, Slick's hand tightens around mine.

"Let's get you to my place." He jerks his chin at Wraith and then takes us through the crowded room, the men simply parting as we make our way past. It's only when we're outside I find I've been holding my breath, and I greedily I indulge in huge breaths of air not tainted with leather and smoke.

Slick's suite I remember, Wraith's is much the same. A large bedroom with a bathroom off to one side. My sister and I will be sharing a bed, but as it's king size that will do fine. The wardrobe's already full of a selection of clothes, and opening drawers I find even underwear hasn't been forgotten. Jayden explores the bathroom and is excited to find women's toiletries and everything else that we'll need, including a selection of sanitary goods. I make a mental note to thank Carmen, Sophie and Sandy. They seem to have thought of everything.

"Have you got everything you need?"

I hadn't noticed Sam had followed us up. Gesturing around I tell her, "Looks that way. Thank you so much for organising it."

Slick's standing behind me, his hands running up and down my arms, and I've only just noticed. Bending forward, he says quietly into my ear, "Get settled in. I'm guessin' you don't want to go to the party, so I'll come back and see ya later. I won't be stayin' long. I'll get some food sent up to you both."

"Slick, you just go and do what you got to do." As I give him his freedom, it hurts to think I could be pushing him into the arms of the likes of Jill.

Another one of his intense looks as he says, "I told ya, El, I don't want no other woman. I'm waitin' on you. Waitin' as long as you want. I won't be fuckin' no whores, at tonight's party or any other. Okay?"

The pleasure his reassurance gives surprises me. Much as I doubt I'll ever be ready to give him what he wants, rather selfishly I find I still want this man all to myself.

CHAPTER 19

Slick

Returning to the clubhouse, my mind's full of the women I'd left, no, just one woman—Jayden's only a young girl, little more than a child. You'd have to be a real sick fuck to want a piece of that. We might have tortured Diego, but the shots to the head were too kind for the rest of them last night. As the thought of all that young kid's been through comes to my mind I realise I'd like to be able to dig them up and kill them all over again.

The party's in full swing by the time I get back, but so far, as they should, the sweet butts are staying away. Going inside I push my way through my brothers and grab myself some food and, pulling Road aside, ask him to make up some plates and take them up to my girls. I neither know or trust the new prospects yet, so won't be asking or letting them anywhere near Ella or Jayden until I know what they're made of. That's why we get them to do shit for us for at least a year before getting the patch. At the end of that time they'll have to have convinced every fucking one of us we can rely on them. Just one negative vote and they won't become a member.

I go to the bar, noting it seems wrong not to have Marsh— *Paladin*—waiting to serve me. Jekyll's standing bemused as brothers just stare at him. First thing prospects need to do is learn the drinks the brothers prefer. We won't be making it easy. My mouth quirks.

I rap on the wood. Jekyll comes over. "Yes?"

"Drink," I snarl.

"Er…"

"A fuckin' beer, what d'ya fuckin' think I want?"

He jumps back as I bite his head off. Passing, Dart gives me a wink.

As I take a swig of my draught, I turn my back to the bar, scanning the room, seeing who's here and who's not. The position puts me in sight of the door, which is opening. When I see who it is I stand straight. *Who the fuck let her in?* I tap Drummer on the back and point in the direction of the woman who's entered. It's Crystal's mom. And if anything, she looks worse than last time I saw her.

I hadn't noticed Amy before now, but the little girl's in the middle of the room. She's hopping and dancing to an AC/DC tune, but as the voices go quiet she notices who's entered. She stills and looks like she's shaking. Bullet's closest to her, and scoops her up into his arms. As the prez steps forward, our treasurer takes Amy away and heads out to the back. As he passes me he's muttering, "Fuckin' Hyde's on the gate. Shouldn't have let that bitch in."

The woman's eyes follow her grandchild as she's taken away. She turns to Drummer. "I've come for the kid."

Drawing himself up to his full height, towering over her, Drummer looks about as threatening as I've ever seen him to be. "You shouldn't be here," he tells her, his voice a low menacing growl. Someone's turned off the music, and the room is completely silent as we watch the altercation.

"And you shouldn't be keeping my grandkid from me." She scratches at her arms. I reckon if she wasn't wearing long sleeves track marks would be seen.

"While her father's alive she's fuckin' stayin' with us. Heart can tell us what he wants to do when he comes round." Drum-

213

mer's eyes narrow. "I've told ya that before. I don't know why you've bothered to come here." Then his gaze turns to the doorway, and his expression blackens further. "We don't take fuckin' kindly to uninvited guests in our club."

His words draw my attention to the man who'd obviously accompanied her. I hadn't noticed him before, and take a second to examine him. If anything, he looks more strung out than her.

"Now are you leavin' on your own, or should we help you out?"

"Come, Susie. Fuckin' leave it for now. These fucker's ain't gonna give you the brat."

Ah. Her name's Susie. I didn't know that. Susie is either fucking brave or fucking mental as she tries to stare the prez down. Just as it looks like she's going to say something else, two more people come in through the door. *Fuck! That prospect Hyde isn't going to last a day at this rate.* Strangers are never allowed unaccompanied onto the compound. Is he even guarding the gate or just opening it like a fucking doorman wearing a top hat?

And the newcomers are much worse than Crystal's mom. All around me men freeze as Detectives Archer and Hannah march straight in as if they fucking own the place.

Moving his attention from the woman to the police, Drum jerks his chin. "Detectives." To anyone who knows him the word is not spoken in welcome.

"Detectives?" This makes the woman turn around. "Perhaps you can talk some sense into these thugs. I'm here for my grand-child. They're stoppin' me from takin' her. That's against the fuckin' law, ain't it?"

Hannah looks suspicious, Archer looks eager. "Yes, ma'am," he starts, "if that really is the case. Care to tell me what's going on?"

I see Drummer's fists clenching.

"I'm Crystal Norman's mother. When Crystal died," she pauses to wipe an imaginary tear from her eye, her action marred by the involuntary twitching—*she's overdue for her next fix*— "she'd have wanted me to look after her daughter. Not be left with these bikers." She spits out the last word.

At that moment Sam appears. She's carrying Amy, who's clinging to her, Carmen's close behind, followed by Sandy and Sophie. A show of strength by our old ladies. "What's up, can I help?"

"That there's my grandkid and she should be with me."

I don't know how much Amy understands, but as her grandma speaks, she buries her head tighter against Sam's shoulder. I notice Detective Hannah's not missing a thing.

With a tight face, Drum speaks. "The last request from Crystal and Heart was that we should take care of Amy. In her home where she's been raised. Until Heart is able to give us further instruction, I'm honourin' the arrangement that was made."

He looks at the detectives and addresses them directly. "I'm the executor of both of their wills, their personal representative. No mention was made of who would look after their daughter in the event something happened to them. And certainly, no mention in Mrs Norman's will of her mother at all. Amy stays here."

Archer sneers, "Would be interesting what a judge would have to say about that. Any criminal record would count against you."

Drum shrugs. "Ain't got no criminal record."

I swear Archer says "not yet" under his breath, but I might be wrong. The detectives look at each other. Archer opens his mouth, but Hannah gets in first. "You're looking after her?" As she speaks she's looking at Sam who, as you'd expect, is looking clean, tidy, and respectable. Then she flicks her eyes with a look of disgust toward Crystal's mom, who's looking anything but. When Sam nods she continues, addressing her suggestion to Amy's grandmother. "If you want your grandchild, I suggest you apply for an emergency custody order."

"We can help you with that," Archer drops in far too quickly. Hannah throws him a sharp look of surprise. He shrugs.

Drum shakes his head. "You're certainly not takin' her tonight. So I suggest you get out of here."

Before you're escorted, and none too gently, I think to myself. Though no one's daft enough to say that in front of the heat.

The woman huffs, and without looking at Amy, joins her companion at the door.

"Viper! Check they go straight to the gate. And have a word with the fuckin' prospect while you're there."

Next, he turns to the detectives. "We haven't invited you in. I presume you've not got a warrant?"

Ignoring the question about the official documentation, which confirms they haven't got any, otherwise he would be waving it in the air, Archer addresses Drum. "We wanted to ask you some questions to help investigate Mr and Mrs Norman's accident."

"Well you can make a fuckin' appointment." Drummer's not letting them get away with simply walking in as they please.

Hannah's looking uncomfortable, but I get the opinion it's not down to us bikers. Something tells me it was her partner who might have wanted to come here. She certainly did not.

I'm not the only one to have a bad feeling. Archer's not hiding his interest in looking around. My brothers move together, shoulder to shoulder, effectively limiting what he can see. Not that there's anything here. And thank fuck, Jayden, who's probably listed as a missing person by now, is nowhere in sight. Suddenly I realise the extent of Hyde's crime. He's a dead fucker if he pulls anything like this again. In fact, I'm wondering if we shouldn't part ways right now. Maybe permanently with a bullet to his brain.

Drum's staring them down. Hannah steps in front of her partner, and they seem to have a silent conversation. With a huff Archer turns around and at last walks to the door. Before she follows him, Hannah looks at Drum and gives a little shake of her head. Crystal's mom grabs hold of her companion and pushes him out into the night air. And at last they are all gone. Without being told, Beef and Dart accompany Viper to follow them out.

Tilting my head on one side, I raise an eyebrow at Drum, asking him what that was all about. But he shrugs and lets out an audible sigh of relief. The music starts up, and we're partying again.

Wraith marches across, grabs a beer and turns to Drummer. He looks furious. "What do you want to do about Hyde?"

Pushing away from the bar I join them. "That was close, Prez. What if Jayden had been here? Even if they didn't recognise her, they could see her picture in a briefin'. Wouldn't take much for them to put two and fuckin' two together. Even them dumb fucks."

"I hear ya, Slick. Loud and fuckin' clear." After acknowledging me, he nods at the VP. "Speak to Hyde, Wraith. And the brother who told him to man the gate. I'll go with what you think after you've had a chat. But one more cock-up, he's out. And I'll need some convincin' not to let him go now."

"Got ya, Prez." Wraith's taut mouth and his glaring eyes make me pleased I'm not the prospect he's going to be facin', even if I can't summon up any sympathy for Hyde.

For my part, I want the prospect gone now. It chills me how close it had come to all our plans going wrong. Everything hinges on no one finding out about Jayden. *If she'd been here…*

The thought of how close we'd come to her being discovered makes my desire to party vanish. I stay for one more beer to be sociable, then leave and head on up to my girls.

As it's still relatively early, I hope I'll find Ella awake. Rapping gently on their door with my knuckles, not wanting to disturb her if she's already gone to bed, I stand, waiting patiently for an answer, pleased when I hear movement inside. Ella steps out, her index finger going to her lips, and pushes it to behind her.

"Jayden's asleep," she starts quietly. "She's taken some of the painkillers Doc left. Her hangover's taken it out of her. Poor kid had one hell of a headache when she got up here."

I'm only half listening, my eyes are feasting on her. Ella's dressed in jeans and a baggy tee, and a clean, recently washed face devoid of any artificial enhancement. The girls I'd passed on my way out of the clubhouse were coming in in clothes that barely covered the bits that they should, and heavy makeup adorning their faces, and they didn't make my cock stir. At all.

Ella, though. Ella could make it stand up and beg if she was dressed in a sack. I have an overwhelming desire to take her in my arms and kiss her senseless then sink my dick into her and fuck her until she can't remember her own name. That's what I want. And that's exactly what I can't have. *Not yet.*

"Hey, how you doing?" I keep my voice low, any indication of my craving off my face, and widen my stance so my swelling dick isn't so obvious.

She leans against the wall. "I wish I didn't have to be here, Slick. Oh, up here in the suite is better than in the clubhouse, but we're still on the compound. You'll say it's an irrational fear, but it's one I can't shake. Yet, underlying my anxiety, I know it's safest place for Jayden to be." She glances down at her hands. "I didn't thank you, did I? For rescuing her yesterday?"

"You don't need to thank me. Or any of us. Fuck, El. It sickened everyone to find a young girl being abused. I'm just sorry it's forced you to come to the club before you were ready. I know this is the last place you want to be, but darlin', nothin's gonna happen to you here." And I'm going to keep telling her that until she believes it. She looks so lost standing there. I might not be able to give into my baser desires, but right now, holding her will suffice. "Come into my room for a moment, you can leave the door open in case Jayden needs ya."

She looks back up, her eyes searching my face. *Does she trust me enough?* Just when I think she's going to refuse, she takes a step forward, and I move aside, letting her pass. Inside she hovers as though uncertain what to do.

"Come here." I stand, non-threatening, waiting for her to move closer. When she does I put my arms out and enfold her close. With my hands gently rubbing up and down her back, she relaxes into me and I hear and feel her held-in breath leave her. I'm giving her comfort, and taking some for myself. *It's a fucked-up world we're living in,* I think to myself. *I should be able to make love to my woman. If it wasn't for the fucking Rock Demons that's exactly what I would be doing. Would have already been doing for months.* I rest my chin on her head.

My lips find her hair, and she turns her face up. I feel so nervous, not wanting to fuck this up, knowing how slow I'll have to be if I want to push this along, but unable to resist embarking on this first step. As her tongue comes out and licks her lips I take it as an invitation, lowering my mouth until it brushes against hers. She tenses slightly. I don't take advantage, don't press inside, just extend the touch for a few seconds before pulling away.

As my lips leave hers she relaxes immediately.

Oh Ella, how am I going to get through to you?

Whatever it takes, I'll do it. There has to be some way to give her back confidence in herself, and in a man all over again. Knowing my very male and automatic reaction will scare her, I turn slightly, unable to hold my body up flush against her, hiding the hard evidence of my attraction. Like trying to tame a wild animal, I must make no sudden moves.

It's going to be a long fucking road we've got to travel down.

She's worth it.

CHAPTER 20
Ella

Slick's being so gentle with me. The touch of his mouth to mine was so sweet, and brought back no memories of the Rock Demons. But that's not surprising, they didn't bother to kiss. No, they used my mouth for more unsavoury things.

He's pulled away. *What I should do now?* Go back to Jayden? There's no reason. If she awakes I'll be able to hear her from here. Stay? But by staying would I be giving him the wrong impression? Would he kiss me again, and this time not hold back? *I'm not ready.*

Slick gestures to the chairs out on the balcony. "Come sit with me?" he suggests.

An innocent proposition, the seats far enough apart we wouldn't even touch. As I bob my head in agreement he slides open the doors. Immediately the heat of the evening comes in, a warm but not uncomfortable breeze carrying the perfume of desert flowers along with the loud chirping of the last of the summer's cicadas. As I sit, I notice the sun setting over the Tucson Mountains on the opposite side of the Tucson Basin. After the worry of the last few days the peaceful setting allows me a moment to simply sit and breathe. I hadn't realised how tightly wound I'd become.

Coming to join me, Slick hands me a beer. While not my favourite drink, at least it's refreshing. I take a long sip, and then hold the cold bottle to my forehead. I cast a glance at the man at my side and nod my head, gesturing at the view. "It's so beautiful here."

He looks where I'm pointing. "Not many biker clubs have somethin' like this."

I think back to the shabby warehouse I'd visited, and can't argue his point.

Turning his head, his scrutiny now rests on me. "It's been botherin' me, Ella. Why did you ever think you could be a sweet butt? It was clear from the start that isn't in your nature."

I tilt my head to one side, not quite sure what he's asking, and my insecurity rears its ugly head as I reach my interpretation. "You're telling me your club wouldn't have wanted me?" My eyelids come down as I lower my gaze, and I mumble, "You're right, I wouldn't have had what it takes."

His head jerks back. "What the fuck you talkin' about?"

"The other sweet butts, they've got great figures and they're so pretty."

He huffs an incredulous laugh. "Pretty and shallow. Ella, on looks you beat them hands down."

My mouth gapes. "Slick, you don't mean it. Just look at me, there's no way I can compete." And then I realise I've invited his scrutiny, and my cheeks burn as his eyes trace a path from my head to my feet, lingering just a little too long on my chest.

Grinning as I squirm, he informs me, "El, I had to beat my brothers off with a stick. I've told ya, that's why I claimed ya. If you'd become a sweet butt you'd have been one of the most popular. And that's no fuckin' lie." As I try to digest what he's telling me, he takes a swig of his beer. "So, tell me, El, what made you even suggest it?"

"I met Jill," I start to tell him, shifting my butt to get more comfortable on the seat. "We'd been at school together. Hadn't seen each other for years. She told me about the life." I pause and raise my shoulders. "It sounded fun."

"Fun?" He's eyes narrow. "Did she tell you exactly what being a club whore entails?"

I fidget awkwardly. "I've never had much luck with men, Slick. The ones I've been with, well, let's just say they didn't fulfil their promise. What Jill described sounded exciting." And had backed up what I'd read in my books. Suddenly I sit forward. "She told me being a sweet butt gave her control. She implied they use the men to get what they want." I stare up over at the distant mountains, noticing a flash of lightening, suggesting a storm's approaching. "Sex," I go on to admit. "Mind-blowing sex. And men who appreciate them."

Another firm shake of his head and a chuckle. "Sweet butts ain't got no control, sweetheart. They're at our beck and call, any time of the day or night. When other chapters are here, they can expect to be passed around the members of the visitin' clubs."

I frown. "But the men are grateful for their services…"

"Only because we need a hole to use, darlin'. We might have preferences, but it doesn't much matter which one. I tell you, a man wants to fuck? He'll just use who's available."

My eyes drop again, he's being a bit too frank. I summon up a more attractive reason, "She said it was possible to become a man's favourite, that you could become an old lady."

He spits his beer out of his mouth and wipes his wet mouth with the back of his hand, drawing my attention to his full and very attractive lips. "Almost never happens, darlin'. Sometimes a brother has a liking for a particular girl, but when they start to get ideas he moves on to the next. Ain't one of us gonna start making somethin' permanent with a woman all our brothers have known. And yes, I'm fuckin' talkin' about in the biblical sense."

"Oh." Put like that, I can understand and see just how much she misled me.

"And you're right. Sweet butts like sex. Wouldn't be here if they didn't. They enjoy havin' sex, rough sex even, and like the variety. They're wired that way. What man would want to take the risk of settlin' down with a woman who's likely to get bored then stray and go lookin' for a different cock?"

He's made a good point.

"Don't get me wrong, sweet butts are important to the club. They're like anythin' else that belongs to us, club property. We take good care of them, and protect them. But that's as far as it goes. There's no emotion involved, Ella. And that's where it doesn't suit you. You need your heart involved too. Being a sweet butt? You'd get that broken in minutes."

Yes, my heart. That organ that pumps blood around my body, but also rules my head. I raise the bottle to my mouth and then think on what he said. Sure, Slick's stuck around, still calls me his old lady, but apparently that's only to protect me from the other club members. He's a good man, but he won't want me now, knowing what the Rock Demons did. *He doesn't want a woman all their members have had.* I lower my beer and start biting my lip as it dawns on me he's no threat. I've been used and abused, as he knows all too well. My eyes start to water as I wish I'd never admitted what happened. Despite what he's said, and our one attempt at dating, there's no way he'd want to make this permanent.

"What's going around that pretty little head of yours, El?" Slick leans forward to reach into his pocket. He pulls out a packet of cigarettes and lights one.

After watching the glowing tip for a moment, my lips purse, and glancing into his penetrating eyes, I know I have to explain. "You won't want me now. After the…"

"After you were fuckin' raped? What the hell has that got to do with anythin', woman?" He stands up, and the half-smoked cigarette is thrown over the balcony, then he then turns back, his eyes blazing. "It wasn't like you chose it. Told you before, it fuckin' killed me to even think of you havin' to let even one of those fuckers lay a hand on you. I should have stopped you goin' into that club that fuckin' night." He moves again, this time dropping to his knees in front of me, and rests his palms on my knees. "Ella, I want you as much as I want my next fuckin' breath. That hasn't changed since the moment I met you."

As I flinch away from his caress he straightens and removes his hands. "It fuckin' kills me that I can't touch you in the way that I want to."

And in my mixed-up head instead of reassuring me, the fact that he hasn't lost any desire for me scares me. "It's the smell!" The words burst out of my mouth. His eyes widen as I continue, "Leather, gas, oil, beer, sex, smoke… You're a *biker*, Slick. Everything about you reminds me of them. What if you want to do the things that they did?"

"I probably do," he admits, making me cringe back in the chair. "The difference is I'd be so fuckin' gentle. And I'd do nothin' you wouldn't enjoy."

"This isn't going to work, Slick. I can't take that risk." I'm already trembling just at the idea.

I don't understand why his lips are curling up. "Yes, it is. You've just got to learn to trust me. Take the time to see I'm nothin' like them."

And it's that I've got the most problem with. How can I ever have faith in a biker again? There's something inside them that I don't want to see ever coming out.

What he says next astounds me. "Stay with me tonight, Ella. Sleep in my bed."

I suck in air loudly. *It's too soon.* "No, Slick. And I need to be with Jayden." *I can't.*

"We'll keep the doors open, we'll hear if she stirs. El, I held you last night. Just let me hold you again. Hell, I'll sleep fully clothed on top of the covers, I just want you in my arms." He winks. "And I'll shower first so I don't smell."

A nervous giggle escapes me.

He sucks in air. "That's a fuckin' lovely sound. You know what? Don't think I've ever heard you laugh before. I'd like to hear it more."

My eyes widen. I hadn't thought of it. I'd been dealing with one thing after another since I'd met him, and definitely since he'd come back into my life. I look up at him, realising that my continuous tension and my to and fro swings of emotion must be wearing for him too. I practice a small smile. As he responds I feel relaxed enough to lean back in the chair and kick my shoes off. He sits down again. For a few moments, we just stare at the darkening skies.

"Why did you become a biker, Slick? What made you join the Satan's Devils?" I give another small chuckle. "It's hard to think of you starting off as a prospect, being shouted at and made to do the unsavoury jobs."

"I was in the Army for a while. When I was discharged I was attracted to the brotherhood, and never felt as good as when I was ridin' my bike. And the shit they gave me wasn't much worse than what I got durin' boot camp."

It must be more than an hour and a couple of beers while we just sit and talk. I'm interested in Slick's history, but just as happy to simply hear his voice. At some point we move inside when the mosquitos put in an appearance, but with hardly any break in the conversation. There's no pressure, no suggestions. Just taking the opportunity to get to know each other, a continuation of what we'd done on our date.

"What did you want to do with your life, Ella?" he asks as he gets up to snag a fresh beer from the mini-fridge. "Or what would you like to do?"

Pointing at my half-full bottle to reject the fresh one he's offering, I answer honestly. "I wanted to go to college, but then I had to move out."

"It's never too late."

Picking up my drink, which I'm starting to get a taste for, I dismiss it. "College costs money."

He lets that ride and continues to ask, "What would you study?"

Resting the top of the bottle against my mouth, I think back over the dreams I'd had as a young girl. I open the box and take them back out, mentally blowing away the cobwebs and dust. "I always wanted to be a nurse."

"Hmm." His head tilted to one side, he seems to be interested, but changes the subject to something else once again.

Eventually it seems natural to agree to sleep in his bed. He's made no gesture toward me or suggestion to make me think he'll be other than a man of his word. I check quickly on Jayden, change into sweats and a tee, and then return to his room and slip under his sheets while he takes his promised shower.

Held protectively in his arms, I fall asleep.

CHAPTER 21

Slick

Last night had been the first time I've had a woman in my room and just talked using words, rather than letting my dick take the starring role in the conversation. If anyone had asked me, I would never have expected to enjoy it as much as I had. Nothing was forced, everything easy. Questions asked and answered while we gradually came to get to know each other. For once in my life, I'm taking time to understand a woman before rushing her into my bed. While my cock isn't so happy about the delayed gratification, she's getting inside my head. And I'll be fucked if I don't like her being there.

The first time I'd seen her, my cock wanted inside her, but for the first time ever, a woman has come to mean more to me than just that. She'd inveigled herself into my heart, the emotion first creeping up while I'd been waiting for her outside that fucking club. Had overtaken me when I'd seen how brave she was, slamming into me when I'd seen how they'd hurt her, and I knew she had to be mine. When she'd left me I tried to kill all feeling for her stone dead, rationalised it had been too quick and too soon, the emotion I'd felt fuelled only by lust. Now the affection is growing again, the sentiment running much deeper. I'm respecting the person I'm coming to know the more I hear about the challenges in her life.

And yesterday? I'd felt like I'd won the fucking lottery when Ella agreed to sleep beside me. Even when she'd got up to check on Jayden, she returned to my side, allowing me to wrap my arms around her again. I'd spent the night with my old lady, and while my cock protests he didn't get any relief, when I'd woken this morning I couldn't have been more satisfied. Our sleeping arrangement the first major step to regaining her trust.

And now, entering the clubhouse, I feel on top of the world, unlike my brothers who seem to be nursing aching heads. A grin splits my face—a patching-in party will do that for you. I make as much noise as possible as I walk across the room and into the kitchen where I bark a loud laugh. The old ladies won't be down until the prospects have cleaned up, and in the women's absence they've put Jekyll and Hyde onto cooking some sort of breakfast. When the fire alarm goes off I'm not in the least surprised. Fuck knows whether we'll get something edible today.

I grimace when I try the coffee. *Who the hell can fuck that up?* I settle for cereal after eyeing charred remnants of some-thing I can't even identify, but which I think at one point might have been eggs.

A slap on my back almost has the bowl flying out of my hands. "Bullet, what the fuck?" Unlike the others, he looks bright and breezy. I remember he was on duty at the hospital last night. "Any news on Heart?"

He closes his eyes and takes in a breath. It's not easy sitting by our brother willing him to wake up. "He's breathin' on his own, but he's not reactin' to anythin'. They've stopped the medication inducin' the coma, and it's up to him now."

"Did the doctors say what his chances are?"

"They don't know fuck all. Oh, I pressed them on it, but all they'd say is he could wake today, next week, next fuckin' year. And when, if, he comes round, he might be brain damaged."

I think we were all expecting him to come out of the coma once they'd stopped the treatment. It's fucking unwelcome news, and my previous good mood starts to disappear.

More bodies enter the clubhouse. Wraith, Drum, and Viper all look awake, and as I step into church I realise being a member of that happy band of men with old ladies comes with some benefits. It prevents hangovers, or at least of the worst kind. Doesn't stop us drinking, but like them, I suspect in future I too will be spending less time in the clubhouse.

Even so, Drum looks weary as he takes his seat at the head of the table. He runs both hands down his face and over his beard. He lifts his head and looks around, nodding at Paladin, who's looking excited despite being a bit green at the gills. Well, it had been his party. And now it's his first time in church as a fully patched member.

Picking up the gavel the prez brings us to order. "Another fuckin' church. Anyone else gettin' sick of these?"

"Sure am." Blade opens a pack of smokes. As he pulls one out and then puts the pack away, everyone looks at him with their jaws dropping open.

"What the fuck, Blade?"

"What?" The enforcer notices he's become the centre of attention. "Just agreed with Prez is all. Got a light, Dart?" As Dart snarls and slides his Zippo over, Blade at last seems to realise what he's done. With a sheepish grin, he gets out the packet and passes them around.

Soon I'm inhaling a deep drag, enjoying my first smoke of the day.

"Alright. Let's get started. Mouse, you got somethin' to say?"

"Sure have, Prez." We wait while he opens the laptop. "Ok, I'm going to be coverin' a lot."

"You've got the floor, Brother."

Mouse dips his chin and looks down. "Tried to look more into Crystal's mom. Susie Clyde is her name. Susannah. Nothin' much more than I said before, I'm still tryin' to find out who her dealer is. I'd like to know more about the fucker who was with her yesterday, but I need a name."

"Not the type of woman who'd win a custody battle," Peg remarks.

"No, but would we?"

Viper sits forward. "That's why me and Sandy couldn't adopt. Social workers don't take kindly to our fuckin' lifestyle."

"Worst case, if a judge gets to decide about Amy, she could end up in the fuckin' system."

Though I don't like to admit it, I think the prez has a point. Fuck, that poor kid. *Heart's got to wake up.* I've either spoken aloud or it's what we're all thinking as I hear all the brothers agreeing with me.

Drum squints at Mouse. "You reckon we could buy her off?"

Our computer expert nods. "I'd say we could give it a fuckin' try."

"She doesn't care for the kid. Can't see why she wants her." Joker's shaking his head.

"That's my worry, Brother. And, well, Sam, she's taken to her. If Heart doesn't recover, she and I have been talkin' about adoptin' her ourselves." Prez pauses and points at Viper. "Your point's well made, Viper. Can't see how we could do it legal in front of a judge. But we'll work somethin' out. One thing's for certain, that fuckin' bitch is not allowed back on the compound. And keep diggin' Mouse. Try and find out why she's so keen to get hold of her grandkid."

"Heart might have somethin' to tell us about her."

Drum sighs. "Yeah, Rock, but at the moment he's not sayin' a lot."

Reaching for the ashtray I stub out my cigarette. "Didn't much care for the support Archer offered her. If she's got the cops on her side it might be more of a fuckin' problem."

"Yeah, well we might have fuckin' trouble with him extendin' well beyond Amy." And with that sentence all eyes are drawn back to Mouse again. He taps at his keyboard. "I've been lookin' into him. Archer's mother's maiden name is Batchelor."

There's various versions of uttered and gestured "so whats?".

"Way back when, a Carmella Herrera married Ian Batchelor." Mouse looks up and spells it out. "Archer is a second cousin of the Herrera family. Don't know how close to them he is, but it's one coincidence that I don't like."

And neither do the rest of us. But it doesn't make sense. I raise my hand, Prez lifts his chin. "Archer requested the case, Hannah told us that. But we had no connection with the Herreras until Ella contacted us, and we didn't know about their involvement until we got Diego to talk. Fuck, we didn't even know his last name before he spilled it."

"Anything on the Rock Demons that got away?" Wraith appears to change the subject.

Mouse shrugs. "Got feelers out with their other charters. As we know, the Phoenix chapter had been goin' its own way, breakin' off from followin' national club rules. There was no blowback when we took them out, as they'd become a pain in the rest of the members' asses." I know that, not that we ever admitted responsibility, but we'd have been the first suspects. To our relief, the other Rock Demon charters had turned a blind eye.

"Found out one of the escapees was the nephew of their old VP," Mouse continues.

The prez growls at that. "So he might want vengeance on his fuckin' uncle's demise."

"Might be a problem we need to keep in mind, but he was in Cali when Heart was knocked off his bike. I'm still checkin' out the other, but he seems very low key and has gone underground. No one knew much of him, only recently patched in."

I open my mouth to remind them I want those two fuckers dead for what they did to Ella, but the VP gets in first.

"Think we've got some dots to join here," Wraith says quickly. "If we leave the prime suspects out of it and ignorin' the Rock Demons for now, could it be the Herreras who went after Heart?"

"For what reason?" Drum taps his fingers on the table. "Not sayin' you're wrong, Wraith, but I can't figure out why. As Slick said, we weren't even aware of Ella and her sister's connection to them when Heart was knocked of his sled."

Beef is grinding his teeth, an annoying habit, but a sign that he's thinking. "Herreras run the drugs trade in Tucson and a protection racket. And the bulk of the guns."

And we do the rest. But we've never come up against them before.

Dollar's been quiet so far, now he wakes up. "We don't do so much of the guns now, got enough comin' in legit." He should know. "If they had a problem with us, a conversation would more easily sort it."

Tongue points at Drum. "You said you got the impression this Detective Archer is dirty. Could be on the take from the Herreras."

"Yeah, man, but what's the point?" Shooter's looking puzzled. "If we're no threat to them, why would they be on our backs?"

Drum bangs the gavel. "We're just goin' around in circles. Let's look at what we've got." He pulls at a finger. "One, looks like we've got a dirty cop." He moves onto the next finger. "Two, said dirty cop is overly interested in us, otherwise, why ask for this case? Three, said cop is related, albeit distantly, to the Herrera family. Four, we've got a brother in the hospital and it wasn't an accident. Five, we wouldn't have found that out if it hadn't been for the cop's partner being upfront with us."

When he pauses and before he moves onto his other hand, I take over. "Six, we've got a custody battle for Amy."

Drum jerks his chin at me. "Hadn't been thinkin' there was any link to the kid. Hmm. Okay, we'll add that to the list." He glances down at his hands. "I'm gonna run out of fuckin' fingers at this rate. On top of everythin' I've just listed, and now I've forgotten what fuckin' number I was at, we've got ourselves in deep with the Herreras as we took two of their family out."

"But we covered our tracks so they might not be aware," Peg adds.

The prez stops playing with his fingers and tunnels both hands through his hair. He pauses midway and looks at the sergeant-at-arms. "I don't understand where Heart comes in. Far as I know, neither we, or he, have ever come head-on with the Herreras. At least not until this week. No, Wraith, let me finish." He holds up his hand as the VP goes to speak. "We agreed we need to take them out. Close that fuckin' family down for what they did to Slick's old lady's sister. For now, let's fuckin' concentrate on that. We can sit with our thumbs up our asses tryin' to find reasons or waitin' for them to come to our door. I say we work on puttin' an end to their fuckin' operation. Don't know about everyone else, but I'd rather be out wavin' a pistol around rather than sit on my ass doing nothin'."

Nods of agreement from everyone.

"Let's vote it. We focus on the Herreras."

He won't get any argument from me. When it's my turn I shout out my "aye" fast.

The vote is unanimous, and is recorded by Dart.

Prez looks around, and one side of his mouth turns up. "Let's get some beers in here and start planning this now. Paladin, you want to shout for the prospects to get us somethin' to wet our throats?"

Paladin leaps to his feet. I don't bother hiding my grin. Yeah, he would be fuckin' enthusiastic about that job.

A couple of brothers take a comfort break. Returning, Tongue informs us he took the opportunity for an apparently much-needed dump. Beef slaps him on the back and Joker fucking throws him a thumbs up.

Drum drops his head into his hands. "Honest to God, if I didn't know fuckin' better I'd think you lot only just left the fuckin' school yard."

"At least the meetin' will give the heads a chance to freshen up." Lady gets Tongue's middle finger flipped toward him.

Paladin re-enters the room, a grin on his face.

"Enjoy that?" Looking up, Drum accompanies his question with a wink.

For an answer, Paladin just grins wider. Marvel slaps him on the back. A man has to go through some shit to get awarded a patch. He's earned it, and deserves it.

The door opens again, and Hyde enters carrying a tray. We all sit stoically as he places bottles on the table, and don't say a word as he goes out the door.

Drum watches him leave, then turns to Wraith. "You have a chance to have that conversation yet? We need to take another vote?"

The VP sighs. "Yeah, we've spoken. And not just yet, Prez. See how it goes. Crystal's mom was pretty persuasive that she had a right to be here, droppin' Heart's name left right and centre, and he let the detectives in as they put on a bit of pressure. He now knows not to open the gate to any motherfucker without permission from a patch."

"Keep your eye on him, Wraith. There's no fixin' fuckin' stupid."

"I hear ya, Prez."

I frown. While I trust my VP's opinion, I'll be keeping a very close eye on Hyde myself.

"Right." Drum bangs the gavel and we're back to planning again.

Peg raises his hand. "What exactly are we up against?" As sergeant-at-arms for the club, he'll be concentrating on how to keep us all safe.

"Mouse?"

"Prez, yeah. I've been tryin' to draw up a family tree. Rabbits have nothin' on this fuckin' lot. The way they multiply, don't think they've heard of wrappin' it up." He pauses to allow the brief laughter to fade. "We know from Diego there are nine senior family members, all living in their own compounds. Diego's dad heads up one, his uncles the others. He's got a shit-load of cousins around. Five of those cousins he named as being part of the groomin' ring. Along with the brother we killed, from what he said, that's the lot. He could have been lyin'."

He's interrupted by Blade's growl. "I had my hand on his dick, he wasn't tellin' no fuckin' lies."

But the prez looks concerned. "Notwithstandin' your dick holdin' skills, Brother, ain't no fuckin' way to know if he was tellin' the truth. Groomin' and fuckin' child porn vids could be a main source of family income for all that we know."

Mouse is nodding. "It's big business, whoever's involved. You can see that from the number of fuckin' hits on those videos that were on the web."

"Shit, man. We got that many fuckin' pedos in Tucson?" Tongue's looking shocked. Paladin's eyes open wide too, reminding me all this is new to him.

For the next hour we put our heads together, tossing around ideas.

Finally, we've honed down our strategy. It's risky, lots of margin for error, but it's the best we can come up with. I can only hope that it works. When Drum bangs the gavel I go out to the bar, grateful to escape the smoke-filled room. My head was beginning to ache with the fumes and all the plotting we'd done.

I'm just getting my second beer of the day when I hear a loud high-pitched scream.

"Horse!"

Spinning around I see Sophie moving as fast as she can and throwing her arms around the English biker who's got an affiliation with the club. As she hugs him tightly, Wraith moves alongside, but he doesn't seem unhappy his woman now has her one and a half legs wrapped around another man's waist. But that I can understand. If it hadn't been for Horse bringing her here, it's a pretty damn certainty she wouldn't be alive. Seeing her looking so agile, it's hard to believe she came here in a wheelchair.

"Hey, Horse. Want a beer?" I offer to be sociable.

Untangling himself from Sophie's tight grasp, setting her down and making sure she's steady on her foot and prosthesis, Horse nods and comes over, still holding Wraith's woman's hand. "Slick, how are you, you old bugger?" His free arm comes around me, and I slap him on the back.

I can't tell him everything's peachy. Quickly I fill him in about Heart, but keep quiet on the rest of our problems, him not being a patched-in member of the club.

When I ask how he's doing, he tells me, and the rest of the brothers who've now gathered around us. "Picked up a lot of work in Sturgis, just about finished with that now." He pauses and looks down at Sophie. "It's time for me to go back to old Blighty, love."

Sophie's face falls. "I'll miss you, Horse. When are you going?"

"Next week. I'll be here for a few days."

"That's pants, Horse. I haven't seen you in yonks, and now you're going home?"

"Oh, love. Don't get your knickers in a twist. I'll be back next spring."

I listen to the two English people speaking their own language, and seeing the grin on Sophie's face shows she's toying with us deliberately. Horse is just playing along.

Horse is one hell of a good artist with an airbrush, much in demand. He spends six months of the year in the U.S., and we're happy to offer him a base. This year, however, he's been given so much work he hasn't been here much, and wasn't able to get around to my bike. Just as I'm about to remind him, he pre-empts me.

"Haven't forgotten your ride, Slick. If you want I'll do it before I go."

"Fuckin' ace, man." I slap his back.

"We'll have to have a good old chin wag before you go." Sophie's looking happier again.

Horse sends a fond smile toward her, then turns to Wraith. "Thought I'd have seen you at Sturgis?"

As Wraith explains we'd had some shit going down at the club and didn't want to leave the compound unprotected, I zone out of the conversation and push away from the bar. All the brothers are milling around, starting to relax having come out of church. Sam's over in the corner playing with Amy, Sandy and Viper sitting close-by. When Drum joins them they look like a fucking family unit. And when the prez proudly places a protective hand on Sam's still flat stomach, I feel my gut clench in an unfamiliar feeling. *I'm jealous.*

Just when I'm trying to analyse my thoughts, the clubhouse door is pushed open, and fuck me if it isn't Ella and Jayden entering.

CHAPTER 22

Ella

Having spent the night in Slick's bed, where I slept surprisingly well, I awake feeling nicely refreshed this morning. Slick had dressed and before he'd left he'd placed another chaste kiss on my lips. When he'd I'd laid my fingers against my mouth like a giddy young girl, leaving them there for a moment while thinking how unexpectedly tender such a rugged biker could be.

When I returned to our room I'd just finished showering and dressing as Jayden started stirring. Noticing her eyes looked clearer than the day before, I feel relief that the drugs and alcohol now seem to be out of her system.

"How you doing, Jayden?"

She sits up in bed, making herself comfortable before she replies, "I'm feeling fine, Ella. My headache's gone at last."

Going over, I sit beside her, taking one of her hands in mine. At least now it feels warm to the touch. I tap my finger to her forehead. "How you doing in there?"

She looks down to where our hands are clasped, and I give hers a squeeze. "I don't feel like a kid anymore."

That one sentence makes me want to cry. She's fourteen-years-old for fuck's sake, still only a child. Yet her innocence has been taken away.

"We'll get you some help to put this behind you."

Now she's looking at me, her eyes wide and scared. "I don't want to live with Mom again. She leaves me alone so much. I'm scared. What if they come after me?"

"You won't have to," I say firmly. "You can live with me." But how am I going to support her when I can't even support myself? My job at the bar—if I haven't lost that already—barely provides enough to support one.

"Do I have to go back to school?"

"You're only fourteen, sweetie. Of course you have to go back. But not for a while. We have to stay here for now, remember?"

She frowns, and her teeth worry her lip. "How long for, Ella? I mean, I don't mind it here. Everyone's been so nice. But I can't have a normal life while I'm here."

As I explain I have no idea, I consider again how her view of the compound is so different than mine. She sees protective men when she looks at the bikers wearing their cuts. I see monsters. Then I think of Slick holding me through the night, and a voice at the back of my head asks whether I'm wrong not to even give them a chance?

"I'm hungry."

As if in an answer my own stomach growls. We both look at each other and giggle. If I text Slick I'm sure he'd get a prospect to come up with something to eat. Or... Conscious I need to make an effort, I come to a decision. "Go have a shower and freshen up, then we'll go to the clubhouse. See what we can find to feed us."

Someone's left us some magazines, and I flick through the glossy pages while waiting for her to get ready. When she finally appears, pulling her blonde hair into a messy bun, I stop reading gossip about celebrities I don't give a damn about and stand.

"Ready?"

We step outside into the sunshine, and I breathe in the fresh air.

"It's beautiful here, isn't it? I didn't take much notice yesterday." Standing beside me, Jayden looks in wonder at the scenery. Living in the city we don't appreciate the area we live in as much as we probably should. "You know, seeing the desert around us makes me think of something I've always wanted to do?"

"What's that, hun?"

"Go to the Arizona-Sonara Desert Museum. They've got fossils and rocks, as well as the animals there. Oooh. And snakes!"

Snakes I can live without. "You've never been?" I went once, but way back when.

She jerks her head side to side. "No, Mom couldn't afford it when my class went."

She sounds like an enthusiastic child. "You like fossils, huh?"

Now she's nodding.

"Tell you what, as soon as we can, I'll take you. Okay?"

As she jumps up and down in excitement I realise Jayden's not completely lost, just that the lines have been blurred.

"Come on, let's go eat." I take her hand, trying to keep up as she skips along beside me.

"Ella! Wait up!"

Surprised I turn around, pulling Jayden to a halt. It's Jill trying to catch up with us. But instead of anything anywhere near approaching a friendly greeting, she narrows her eyes and gestures back at the building we've just come from.

"What are you doing back at the compound? And why you stayin' with Slick? And what's *she* fuckin' doing here?"

Taken aback by her vehemence, I wonder how to explain. "Jayden's my sister, the club's giving her protection."

"She's too young to be here. I don't know what Drummer is thinkin' lettin' her stay. And you, what you doing with Slick? You're not his old lady anymore. You ran away and left him. He won't be taking you back. *I* had to comfort him when you disappeared."

Understanding what she's insinuating, which, for some stupid reason makes me feel sick to my stomach, I pull myself up to my full height, which is only an inch taller than hers, and retort, "Whatever he is or isn't is nothing to do with you." *And I'd once thought she was my friend?*

As her head shakes it's clear she doesn't believe me. "I know what went on. It's all the brothers are talking about. How you went to another club ended up pulling a train. Fuck, Ella. You were going to come here and be one of us. That happens here too, you know. If you couldn't hack it you should have stayed well away." She looks at me and sneers.

My newfound confidence starts to ebb fast. For one thing, she's being far too blunt in front of Jayden, and I'm hoping my sister won't understand. Luckily, perceiving the tension between us, she's stepped away and seems fascinated by a lizard sunning itself. And secondly, Jill apparently sees nothing wrong in what the Rock Demons had done. And the bikers force the girls like that here? Rapidly I'm rethinking my decision to go down to the clubhouse.

Jill's face curves into a cruel smile, but as she opens her mouth, presumably to do more damage, a male voice butts in.

"Jill, get lost. Don't think Slick wants you talkin' to his woman."

"His *woman?*" The sweet butt's voice is shrill. "She fuckin' left him. She's not his ol' lady."

"Yeah, she is his ol' lady. So scat."

Paladin might only have been patched for a day, but there's no doubt he's given her an instruction she can't disobey.

Throwing daggers at me, she resumes her way, her hips swinging in an exaggerated swagger down the incline.

"Ella, don't pay her no mind. I heard what she said. Ain't one of us here would force ourselves on a woman."

He's young, what does he know? But he's been here a year or more, which is a longer than I've spent in the club.

"And Slick wouldn't let anyone else near you. You know that, don't you?" He stares at me intensely until he sees some of my tension leave. Then his attention switches to Jayden, and he steps over to her. "Hi little one. How you feelin' today?"

I notice she'd abandoned the lizard and has been watching him instead. She gives a tremulous smile and answers, "Okay." Then she points at me. "Ella and I are going to the Desert Museum when we're allowed to go out."

"Hey, that's great." He grins back. "I might tag along. I hear they've got Gila monsters there."

"Yeah, and mountain lions. There's a huge collection of fossils as well."

As she starts animatedly discussing rocks again, I'm grateful that Paladin came along. Especially when he expresses an interest too.

Still feeling unnerved, my previous confidence rapidly ebbing, I follow the young pair down to the clubhouse and force myself to step inside, immediately noticing it's heaving with bodies. My hand goes to my chest to try to slow my fast beating heart, and I'm finding it hard to draw in air. Curious eyes seem to stare at me from every direction. *I didn't expect to find all the men around.* Why aren't they out working, doing whatever bikers do? It's the middle of the day.

Paladin has his arm around Jayden and is pulling her into the throng, stopping me from escaping back with her to our suite. I put my hand out to hold onto the wall for support. *There's too many of them.*

And when someone touches me. I jump out of my skin.

"Only me, darlin'. I'm pleased you've come down." Looking up at Slick, he must see the panic in my eyes. "No one's gonna hurt ya here, darlin'." He glances around the room. "We've just had a meetin', that's why everyone's around. I think you know most of them from last time, don't you?"

I give a small nod. I recognise the majority, though probably can't remember their names. I'd tried to keep well out of the way last time I was here.

He puts his arm around my shoulders and brings me further into the room, stopping by a couple of men. "Ella, this is Joker and Lady. Don't think you'd have seen them before. They recently transferred from Vegas. And," he taps another man on his shoulder, "Marvel. Marvel's only just come too, from SoCal. Guys, this is my ol' lady."

"Marvel 'cos I'm a marvel."

"Don't believe a word of it, sweetheart. Marvel likes fuckin' comics. Fuckin' kid." The man introduced as Joker laughs and then steps back smartly to put himself out of reach of a playful fist from the comic-loving man.

After the thirty-something kid mock-places a light punch on his friend, he looks down to me. "Pleased to meet ya, Ella."

I want to summon up the courage to ask about Lady's handle, but as I can only manage a squeak of acknowledgement at the introductions, I'll have to remain in ignorance for now. He's certainly a pretty man though, with the type of defined facial features any woman would be grateful to have.

As we walk on through, I get nods and greetings from the men I do recognise, even if I can't put names to the all the faces. Jill's sitting with the other sweet butts, who seem to have increased their ranks from the last time I was here. If looks could kill, I reckon I'd be dead about now.

When we reach a clear space, Slick turns me to face him. "I really am fuckin' glad to see you here, Ella. What made you pluck up the courage?"

"Hunger forced us down. Jayden needs feeding."

"Well if that's the case, let's go get you somethin'." He spins around and whistles. "Paladin, get Jayden over 'ere. She needs somethin' to eat." He heads into the kitchen where Carmen is busying herself with pots and pans.

"Got anythin' edible?" he jokes. "My girls need food."

"There's still some bacon and waffles? I can do you some eggs?"

"Don't go to any trouble," I say at the same time as Jayden licks her lips and says, "Yes, please."

Carmen laughs and waves a pan toward Slick. "Shoo, I've got this. Ella and Jayden can visit awhile."

After a glance down to make sure I'm going to be okay, and my tentative smile showing I'll try, he moves his lips over the top of my head, then heads back to join the rest of the men.

Within moments my sister and I are tucking into plates piled high with food and drinking cups of very welcome coffee. Carmen stops what she's doing and sits down beside us, taking the opportunity to have a break.

"Slick's a good man, Ella. I'm glad you've come back. It destroyed him when you left."

Jayden's eyes are wide open. "You've been here before?"

Briefly I give her the PG story and bring her up to date. Then turn to Carmen. "I didn't think he meant it. Didn't realise he'd miss me. We didn't even…"

As my voice trails off she barks an incredulous laugh and she completes my sentence in her head, then indicates my empty plate and that Jayden's still eating. She gestures with her head. Getting her meaning I stand up and walk to the rear of the kitchen. "You didn't fuck him?" she whispers.

I shoot a quick apologetic glance toward Jayden, glad she doesn't seem to have overheard. I try to explain, "I wasn't ready."

"And now you are?"

"I don't think I'll ever be." I say the old refrain. But part of me wonders whether that's still true. By taking things so slowly, Slick may be wearing down my defences.

Carmen's kind eyes soften. "Give him time," she says. "I've known Slick years and I'd trust him with my life. And that goes for the rest of the men here. Sure, they can be rowdy and rough with the sweet butts, but you won't hear any of them complain. Ella, Bullet's told me you did something important for the club. No one here is going to hurt you. They wouldn't anyway, but seeing as they owe you, that makes you special."

Our conversation's interrupted by Slick entering with a man I haven't seen before. They sit at the table and Slick pulls a piece of paper out of his cut.

"This is what I want, Horse." He starts to sketch.

Jayden leans over to watch—well, she always was nosy.

"That's not what you asked for before," the man Slick addressed as Horse comments in a very English voice. "But there's no problem changing the design."

Intrigued, I walk over—well, if my sister can look I can too. Without consciously realising what I'm doing, my hand rests on Slick's shoulder. Reaching up his, he covers my fingers with his own, and turns his head. "Horse here's an artist. He's gonna paint a design on my bike."

I stare at the paper. I think I know what it is, but...

Without being asked he gives me the confirmation. "It's a phoenix risin' from the ashes." He pushes back from the table and indicates his lap, a question in his eyes. Without giving it a second thought, I slide onto him.

"You and me, our relationship, and Jayden too. Buildin' somethin' better from our past."

Placing my lips on his, for the first ever time I initiate a chaste kiss, and a warm feeling lights me from the inside. As the man with the English accent and Slick continue their conversation, I relax back in Slick's arms, the feeling creeping over me how right it feels to be here like this. I feel safe and protected, and know it's more than that. Soft voices wash over me, Slick's fingers squeeze gently from time to time, giving tactile encouragement even while he's focused on the other man's words.

Secure in my cocoon, I let my mind wander, going over what he said, the design linking him, me, and my sister together, planning for it permanently to be marked on his bike. This isn't fleeting, this isn't sympathy or misplaced guilt. Slick is offering me the real thing. From beneath lowered eyelids I sneak a peek at this beautiful man, finally understanding and accepting that there's one thing I can be sure of. *Slick would never hurt me.*

CHAPTER 23
Slick

Living in the midst of the desert on the outskirts of Tucson, it's often hard to remember that the city, just sixty miles from the Mexican border, is home to just over half a million people. Difficult, that is, until you come into the downtown area where you're surrounded by high-rise blocks. Perhaps not as many, nor as tall as in other cities, but plenty enough for me to be claustrophobic. The air seems hotter here, and dustier.

Peeling off from the rest of our brothers, who meander on past, twisting those throttles causing the loud sound of the pipes to bounce off and echo from building to building, Drum and I come to a stop and, still straddling our bikes, we walk them back until the rear wheels touch the kerb.

"Ready to do this?"

Hmm. It might be what we'd all agreed on in church, but I can't be sure exactly what we're walking into here. Nonetheless I hold onto my doubts and keep my uncertainty quiet. "Yeah, Prez." I'm grateful he's let me tag along. I'm his chosen companion as he knows how much I need to sort things for my old lady.

At that precise moment, another swathe of a dozen bikes rides past, shattering the mid-week peace. Looking across at Drum, it's hard to keep the grin off my face.

Wasting no more time, we enter the glass and chrome doors. We've done this official, set up a fucking appointment. Not our normal modus operandi—normally we don't bother to announce ourselves. As we swagger over to the desk the receptionist's jaw drops to the ground when she takes in our cuts.

"Drummer to see Leonardo Herrera."

Flustered, she hurriedly turns to her computer. Glancing to check our backs, I see a security guard looking concerned. But there's two of us, and only one of him. As I toss a glare in his direction, he gives me a nervous jerk of his chin. Naw, don't think he'll be trying to throw us out. Fucking pansies they employ here, he looks not long out of diapers. Wondering whether he's even started to shave yet, I spin back around in time to see a bemused receptionist calling someone while pointing in the direction of the elevators.

Fuck. I hate being closed in. Those things are worse than riding in a cage.

Giving me a look that suggests he too is not looking forward to the upward journey, Drum steps across briskly and presses the button for the top floor. It fucking would be, wouldn't it?

"Fuckin' hate these things, Prez," I murmur.

"Not so keen on them myself," he replies.

It seems either a very long way up or a particularly slow elevator. Or maybe that's just me, as I know it's only eight floors. We jerk to a halt, then wait for the doors to decide whether or not to open. Stepping out, we find ourselves in another reception area, this one far more opulent than the first. And another girl seated behind a desk, though she's more composed than her colleague in the lobby. She stands as we enter and shows us a pleasant, professional smile.

"Mr Drummer? Mr Herrera's expecting you. This way please. Can I get you any refreshment?"

Declining her offer, I wonder how many times she's said those exact same words, with a name change of course. It seemed smooth and practiced.

She knocks on a door and then pushes it open, standing aside to let us go past.

The windows rattle as yet more Harleys thunder by.

The man seated behind a desk tips his head toward the glass side of the building. "Friends of yours, I presume?"

Ignoring his question, Drummer steps forward. "Drummer, President of the Satan's Devils. And this is one of my brothers, Slick." Drum holds out his hand. After a momentary hesitation, Herrera offers his to shake. Following my president's lead, I do likewise.

Herrera points to the chairs in front of the desk. "Please take a seat."

As we do so, Drum answers what he'd initially asked. "We've got brothers visitin' from other chapters," he explains. "They're takin' in the sights of the city."

Yes, we have other members arriving. And support clubs too. There's over a hundred additional brothers who'll be bunking down at the compound tonight, and will stay as long as it takes. They're the ones driving past in waves today, out to give a show of force. It might give the Mexican family second thoughts about taking us on.

"You asked for this meeting, and I agreed. I can't think of a reason why we should meet, so your request intrigues me. I'm unaware of any problems between our organisations, and I'm a busy man. I'd be grateful if we can get to the point."

Leonardo Herrera, the patriarch of the family, picks up a coffee and takes a long sip. He might be an old man, but his eyes are sharp and intelligent as they focus on Drum before shifting to me. *He's sussing out the opposition.* I keep my face expressionless.

Reaching into his cut, Drum pulls out some pictures, placing them on the desk in front of him.

The old man puts down his cup, then extends his right hand and slides them toward him with his fingertips. When he has them in front of him, his eyes quickly narrow as he scans the photos. His face grows dark as he spits out, "What the fuck is this? You're brave men bringing these to me." He takes off his bifocals and picks up what I assume are better reading glasses and peers at the glossy images again.

"You know who this is?" he points to the first picture.

"It's one of your grandsons, Diego." Drum doesn't deny it. The picture shows a man with a young girl, her mouth open in an obvious scream." Mouse had provided us with stills.

"And these people?"

"We're hoping you can tell us that. But we suspect other members of your family, with their friends or customers." This one was taken from one of the other tapes and shows indescribable acts. And children.

Herrera drops the pictures, and a flicker of what could be disgust crosses his face. Perceptive eyes examine Drummer. "Where did these come from?"

Drum shrugs. "They fell into our hands."

The old man sits back, he steeples his hands under his chin. I notice they're shaking. Whether it's the effect of the photographs or old age infirmity, I can't be sure. "Diego and his brother are missing. What do you know about that?"

Declining to answer the question, the prez leans forward and taps the first photo. "I know I don't care for the subject matter of these pictures. My men might not be choir boys, but we take exception to anyone rapin' young girls."

We'd taken a gamble coming here today. The Herrera family is vast and has its hands in almost every organised crime in Tucson, together with connections to the cartel across the border. Far too big for us to take on, even with the support of the additional brothers. But further investigation by Mouse has found they don't have a name for dealing with the skin trade, that's left to the cartel. Wondering whether his nephews had embarked on a little side business not endorsed by the man at the top, it had been my idea to reach out to the head of the family. A man known for shady deals, but also for some integrity. A strange combination for someone who's the patriarch of such a notorious family.

I'm holding my breath as I wait for a reaction. But he gives nothing away. The silence suggests a lot of wheels are turning in his head.

For a few minutes you could have heard a pin drop in the room. Then the old man raises his eyes. Looking directly at Drum he asks, "What exactly do you want?"

"I want this stopped. Wiped out. Eradicated. No more Tucson kids to be groomed and trapped into this business."

"You're taking a risk coming to me."

"You've a reputation, but not one for this." As Drum waves toward the photos again, another flicker of repugnance crosses Herrera's face.

Proving he's as hard as they say, Herrera queries, "And if you disappear?"

Drum nods toward the windows. "Plenty of others to take our place." He sounds nonchalant, my breathing quickens at the implied threat. "We've got more tapes, more photos. They'll be released. Along with the information there's others involved."

"More family?"

"Yes. We're pretty confident on that." I note Drum didn't say we got the information from Diego. "We will release other photos and you can see for yourself."

Herrera whistles in air through his teeth and wraps his knuckles on his desk, but that's his only reaction. His face remains impassive. Suddenly he gets to his feet, one hand used to push him up from the desk, the other reaching for a walking stick. "Leave these with me. And I would like to receive the other pictures you have."

I notice he doesn't thank us for bringing it to his attention, and that it's impossible to read whether he's already aware of what's going on or has been kept in the dark. I suppose you don't get to be head of a crime family if you haven't perfected your poker face.

"Gentlemen, I have another meeting. I'll be in touch."

Following Drum's example, I stand. Hesitant to turn our backs on this wily old man, we back up toward the door. I reach my hand for the handle as Drum says, "One last thing. Detective Archer."

Leaning on his stick, Herrera frowns. "A distant cousin. One not connected to the family business as I'm sure *you'll* understand." It's a reference to both of our criminal activities. Though compared to the Herreras I reckon we look as white as the driven snow.

After the prez gives him a chin lift we at last escape the room. Alive. I count that as a plus.

We make the reverse journey, getting on our bikes and our engines started without delay, and easing out into the midday traffic. Some of our brothers are waiting just past the next junction, our escort home. We've just pulled the tail of the tiger, and we can't predict how he'll react.

Drum takes the lead, Wraith and Peg behind him. I find my place behind, alongside my brothers as we return to the compound. Hyde's ready and waiting to slide the gate open.

Our places have been left vacant outside of the clubhouse, Road and Jekyll are directing and trying to organise the remainder of the other hundred or so bikes that are still coming in. People are standing, drinking, smoking, or simply sharing a joke. Others are wandering around the back of the clubhouse where grills will have been set up over the fire pits. And I can hear shouts and splashing—when other chapters arrive they often take the opportunity to wash off the dust and cool down in our swimming pool. The prospects will have an unenviable job cleaning it later. Having done my time I know just what it will be like.

Red, the president of the Vegas chapter, and Snake, the prez from San Diego are first to greet Drum, exchanging hugs with the noisy sound of palms hitting leather cuts.

"What the fuck is it with the mother chapter? You need us to protect your scrawny asses again?" But the gleam in Red's eyes suggests he lives for moments like these.

"Can't help it if your life's borin'," Drum replies, good-naturedly, and probably only I can see the relief in his eyes that our brothers from out of state have come to have our backs. He then turns to greet the presidents of the Colorado and Utah chapters, and thanks them for answering his call.

"Sounded fun," the Colorado prez says. For the fucking life of me, I can't remember his name.

"We'll drink and eat," he tells them, "then we'll meet and I'll bring everyone up to speed. After that we'll party!" As he shouts the last word loud cheers go up. Fuck me, the sweet butts will be busy tonight. Don't see any women have come with our visitors.

I spare a glance to my saddle bag and what I'd picked up on the way into town. Ella's my worry. With so many strangers around I need to make sure everyone knows she's mine. With that thought in mind, I spot Paladin. Knowing he won't be far away from Jayden, I go over to him. "Know where Ella is?"

He breaks off his conversation with one of his friends just long enough to say, "Kitchen."

Pushing through men I regard as brothers, whichever chapter they're from, I enter the clubroom, pausing just long enough to snag a beer, and then continue through to where the women are gathered. The table is strewn with salad bowls, dips, and the like. It looks like they're preparing to feed an army. And they probably are.

Ella's looking anxious. When she sees me her face fills with relief and I can almost hear her exhaled breath from where I stand. Crossing to her quickly, I take her hand and pull her outside. The picnic tables are full, and delicious smells of cooking meat fill the air, making my mouth water.

"Did it go alright?"

She knows nothing except I had a meeting, but I'm pleased her first thought shows she's concerned for me.

"Fine," I reply, not able to say more. "How you copin'?"

"It's not easy," she whispers, her eyes anxiously looking around. "There's so many men here. I wanted to hide in my room, but there's so much work to be done. Sam told me to stick by her side."

I'm proud she's fought against her fears and has offered her help. She's gradually improving, baby steps, but each one is in the right direction. I wouldn't have been surprised to find she'd hidden away.

With my hand on the small of her back, I bring her to a quieter corner. As she looks up at me with her big eyes peering up from under her fringe, I can't help myself, and lean down to brush my lips against hers. To my surprise, her hands come up to hold onto my biceps with only a small second of hesitation, her fingers curling into the bare skin of my arms. For once it's her who increases the pressure as our mouths touch. Flicking out my tongue, I lick along the seam where we're joined. She gives a little moan, and opens for me.

Holding myself back, curbing my instinct to take advantage, we kiss properly for the first time. She tastes every bit as good as I'd expected, fresh and sweet with a hint of coffee. My cock twitches and lengthens. We're standing so close I can't hide the effect she has on me. But she doesn't startle or pull away.

I end the kiss first, pulling back until our mouths part, then unable to resist, pass my lips over hers one more time. Bending my six-foot-three frame, I rest my forehead against hers.

I have no words. My first fuck didn't give me as much satisfaction. If the kiss we just shared was anything to go by, when I finally get inside her I'll be lucky if it doesn't blow my mind. I don't care how long I'll have to wait, it's going to be worth it. This woman is going to be my everything.

Any remaining doubts I'd had about claiming her, whether it was fair on her to insist that she's mine, disappear in that instance, and now it seems exactly the right time.

"Ella, I've got somethin' for ya."

As she releases her hold on me she opens her eyes. Her pupils are dilated, and her lips curve into a small smile. The fact we're surrounded by brothers doesn't seem important, their voices seem to fade. It's just the two of us here. *Just as it should be.*

I hand her the wrapped package, she takes it in her hands. A curious glance up, then back down at what she's holding. She pulls the paper apart and peers inside. Understanding dawning as she sees what I've brought her.

I'm still not certain she'll accept it. Worrying if it's too early to take this next step, I'm clear on what I want, my brothers have known for some time. But when she puts this on, she'll be making that statement that she too acknowledges it. A public declaration. I hardly dare breathe as I wait for her reaction.

She pulls out the soft-as-butter leather cut in a feminine style and turns it around. Her eyes flick left then right as she takes in the words, 'Property of Slick'. She's quiet for a moment, and now I hold air in my lungs. Then, *thank fuck,* her arms are going through the armholes as she slides it on.

"You're mine," I murmur softly, my heart beating so fast it's threatening to jump out of my chest.

"All yours," she agrees. And when her eyes meet mine there's a flicker of a flame burning.

CHAPTER 24
Ella

It's been obvious all day that something very unusual is happening, and I'm certain that while I didn't know any of the details, it's got something to do with the meeting I knew Slick was going to.

He and his brothers had left the compound this morning without giving a clue as to where they were going. And he'd either forgotten or deliberately omitted to warn me that others were going to arrive. Many others. Since midday bikes have been pouring in—men from other out of state chapters. Sam had obviously not been left in the same ignorance and already tipped off, she got all the old ladies together to get to work on preparing the mountain of food she'd sent Jekyll and Hyde out to pick up.

To begin with, I had no idea why we were cooking in such copious amounts, but as people began to arrive, it started to make sense.

Sam put the sweet butts to work tidying up, helping the prospects get cots set up in the habitable suites at the top of the compound. Showing her aptness to be the president's wife, she took no shit at all from the whores, who complained loudly that this wasn't what they were there for. But as the new bikers started to ride in I could see them eyeing them up, knowing they'd be working hard tonight. *That could have been me.* The thought gives me chills. How could I have ever thought I could become one of them?

As each new biker gets off his bike my heart begins to beat faster. My hands so sweaty I drop a plate.

The smashing of porcelain makes Sam look at me sharply, a look of understanding on her face, "Ella, do you want to go back to your suite?"

Shit. I thought I'd hidden my rising panic better. I cast a quick look around. Bikers are already three-deep at the bar ordering drinks, and the air seems full of the that scent which so affects me. Rowdy voices speak loudly, bursts of laughter are roaring out. The combination of sight, sound, and odour making my head spin. Suddenly I feel Sam's hand on my arm, fingers holding me tight as though stabilising me, anchoring me to the present. *This isn't the Rock Demons' club.*

I eye the food, still only half-prepared. Jayden's doing her part, she's laughing at something Carmen has said. *I can't leave them to do this alone.* I've got to be stronger than this. *Before* it would never have worried me.

As I give a little shake of my head, Sam increases the pressure in her touch. "Stay close to me, Ella. But there's no need for worry, they're all Satan's Devils. They're not like those bastards who hurt you."

Sophie hears and comes over. "These men, Ella, they went out on a limb for me. Gave their backing to the club to protect me. As Sam said, they're not like the Rock Demons. Sure, they'll fuck the whores, but they will respect the old ladies."

The words should give me comfort, but I'm not wearing a patch. Only my loose-fitting jeans and baggy top making me stand out from the sweet butts.

"Come, let's start taking out the salads," Sam announces, then laughs. "Though I'm not quite sure why we bothered with them. Reckon this lot will be more the carnivore type."

Going out the back of the clubhouse isn't much better. Men have spilled out here too, and are lounging around. Fire pits are burning and grills are heating. Trestle tables have been set up to hold all the food. I stay close to Sam and help her get things ready.

As I carry out the prepared bowls I feel eyes burning into me, but no one approaches other than to throw us nods of appreciation, which I hope is because we're carrying food.

The whores are preparing to do work of a different kind, Jill's already sitting on a stranger's lap, Paige and Diva have been commandeered by a couple of men, and Ally and Pussy are flirting with a tall man sporting bright ginger hair. When his eyes land on us, he gives a wide grin and begins to saunter across. I start to tremble, but he ignores me entirely, going on past and approaching Sophie, who I hadn't realised was behind me.

"Hey, Sophie girl. You're lookin' fuckin' great!" To my surprise, he swings her up into his arms.

"Red! Put me down." She flails her hands and pretends to beat at him as she laughs. Feet back on the ground, she pulls down her top which had ridden up. "It's good to see you. How are things in Vegas?"

As they wander off chatting, I let out my breath.

"Come on, let's bring the rest of the stuff out." Sam encourages me to get going again.

Before I can move I hear a squeal of childish laughter, and to my horror see Amy run straight into the legs of a dour looking man. The beer in his hands sloshes over the top of the bottle. As Jayden runs up to rescue the child I feel a wave of terror, expecting him to react with violence. I'm too far away but nevertheless force my feet forward, my one desire to protect both young girls.

To my surprise, the man chuckles with laughter, reaches down and puts Amy back on her feet, and then winks at Jayden. Without a word, he turns back and starts talking to his brothers again. Amy flies off in another direction, with my sister tearing after her. She's looking so young, and the men seem to view them with nothing more threatening than amusement as they pass by.

Remaining concerned for them, I watch as Amy runs toward the swimming pool, and I'm pleased to see Jayden catch up and pick up Heart's giggling daughter before she gets too close. But that draws eyes to well-muscled men stripping down to their boxers—and oh my God, one's taken everything off. I turn abruptly away and only hear the splash as he jumps into the water to cool off. But I can't resist sneaking a peak—he's not the only one to bare all. And, by the side of the pool I see one man removing a false arm, and another a prosthetic leg.

Sam sees where I'm looking. "Enjoying the view?" She nudges me with a laugh. Then she notices where my eyes are focusing. "Many members are vets," she starts to explain, then gives me a sharp look. "They join the club as it replaces the camaraderie of their units. Some injuries you can see clearly, but others? Not all wounds are visible."

There's a lot of truth in her words. Perhaps the men who join the Satan's Devils *are* different to those at the club where I was abused.

Even that thought doesn't stop me worrying. As more and more men pile in, my anxiety deepens. I don't want to desert the others, but I'm not sure how much longer I can stay. *It would just take one to overpower me.*

Just when I think I've reached breaking point, and am standing in the kitchen trying to pluck up enough courage to take the next load of food outside, I see a face which has me exhaling with relief. *Slick's back.*

He immediately sees how difficult this is for me and takes me outside, somehow finding a quiet corner away from the rest. And then he kisses me. Properly.

Oh God! He's claimed me as his old lady, but odd to say we've never had even this intimacy before. It's strange to admit he's lain beside me for nights but the most we've ever done, and even then I'd only need the fingers of one hand to count them, is enjoy a brief brush of our lips.

As our mouths caress and at last I get a taste of this man, I wonder why on earth I've held out this long. He doesn't push me, doesn't trap me. It's me who's holding on to him, my fingers digging into his arms. I could pull away at any time. *But I don't want to.* It feels no one's ever kissed me like this before, and when his tongue sweeps inside, tentatively I slide mine around his.

He ends the kiss before I'm ready. I open my eyes as his mouth brushes over mine one last time. As I smile up at him in wonder he hands me a package. Opening it up, I spy something inside. I can hear him talking, but my heart starts to pound as I hope my suspicions are right. My hands shake as I pull out the contents. It's a leather vest, tailored for a woman. Impatiently I turn it over. The patch on the back reads 'Property of Slick'.

It's a property patch.

Immediately knowing what it means, wearing this I won't have to worry. I'll be protected, everyone will see I belong to him. And while it will prevent strangers propositioning me or muddling me up with the whores, there's a much deeper reason why I'm so happy to receive it. I understand the immensity of the step that I'm taking, and there's not one doubt in my mind. *I'm committing to him.* My head knows it's time.

Pausing only for a brief second, I slide on the soft leather garment.

I hear his intake of breath, and then he tells me, "You're mine."

"And you're mine," I reply, knowing this works both ways.

He reaches out his hand and lightly touching my chin, turns my face toward him. After looking into my eyes he gives a small, knowing nod. The hundreds of bikers around us seem to disappear. All I can hear is the blood rushing around my head, all I can feel is the hard, eager length of him pushing up against me. The only scent I can smell is that of my man. The only sight I want to see is him naked. *What?*

The thoughts in my head come as a total surprise. That kiss just a taster that's awoken my dormant appetite, and the cut that he's given me showing his commitment. Sensations begin, feelings I hadn't dreamed I'd ever experience again. His touch brands me, goosebumps rise on my skin. *I feel alive.* My eyes open in amazement, and my cheeks flush.

His hand drops from my face and wraps round my fingers. He gives me a full blast of his beautiful smile, and his blue eyes gaze intently into mine. Something he sees then makes him inhale a deep breath. "Are you ready, Ella?" he asks so softly, so gently.

I have no doubt as to what he's really asking, and with only a slight hesitation the answer comes to my lips, surprising even myself. "Yes."

"Come." His voice rasps as though it's an effort to speak.

"What about Jayden?" For a second I'd forgotten about my sister. How could I do that?

Slick looks around, and then points over to a grill manned by Dart, who's started serving food. Jayden's sitting at a picnic table nearby, helping Amy eat her burger.

Dropping my hand momentarily he cups his palms around his mouth and whistles loudly, then shouts, somehow making himself heard over the voices nearby, "Dart! Keep your eye on the girls." He indicates my sister and the child, and Dart nods and yells back, "Sure thing, Slick."

My cheeks redden at his knowing wink.

He doesn't tug me away, doesn't act like a caveman dragging me to his home in the rocks. He takes my hand once again and raises it to his lips, the promise in his eyes setting me alight. "Any moment, Ella. Any fuckin' moment you want to stop you just say the word. Okay? I'll be content if we just fuckin' kiss."

His promise gives me the confidence to walk with him up through the compound. But my bravado starts to ebb as we reach his suite. *What if he can't help but be rough? What if he hurts me? What does he expect from me?*

Unlocking his door, his hand on my back pushes me gently inside. Then he turns me to face him and again raises my head so I'm forced to look into his eyes. I freeze. *I can't do this.*

"Trust me, Ella?" He runs the palm of his hand over my cheek. "I will never hurt you. Never push you further than you want to go. I meant what I said. You can stop this at any time. Right now if you've changed your mind. I'm not gonna force you. We'll go back, sit with Jayden and the girls."

I'm standing rigid as a rock, my muscles just won't relax. But when I don't tell him I want to stop, he reverently removes my cut, folding it and placing it over a chair. And then he does the same with his.

Reaching back, he grabs hold of the neck of his tee and pulls it off over his head. Widening my eyes, I study him, seeing his naked chest for the first time. With a flick of my eyes toward his face, seeing nothing to threaten me there, tentatively I place my hands on his firm torso, feeling his well-defined muscles rippling under my touch. His sharp intake of breath encourages me on, and he stands unmoving as I find myself tracing tattoos I've not been able to examine before. My fingers touch his nipples, and they harden, and my body responds, revelling in the control I have over him.

"My turn?" he asks breathily.

It's phrased as a question, a request for permission, so I jerk my head.

His hands are shaking as they reach down to the hem of my baggy, unattractive top as he slowly bunches the material and gently drags it up. His own uncertainty gives me more confidence, so when it catches on my hair I give him a little assistance, and then I'm standing there in my plain white functional Walmart bra.

I wait for him to discard that too, but he leaves it for now, another wave of relief at the sign he really is going slow. His eyes flare as they settle on my still covered breasts. Mimicking my actions, his hands explore, touching me so gently I hardly feel his fingers trace my collarbone, and down over the top of my bra. Even through the material my nipples start peaking.

"You're fuckin' beautiful," he breathes. That he likes what he sees helps my confidence build.

Then trailing his hands down, leaving my body for a moment, he undoes his button and his zip, toeing off his boots as he does so. I hear a clomp as they're kicked away.

I watch, holding my breath as he pushes his jeans down, revealing his large, swollen appendage pushing at his boxers.

He's scrutinising me carefully as he undoes my own jeans. Copying his actions, I toss off my sandals. He folds to his knees as he pulls my pants down my legs, exposing me to him inch by torturous inch. And then I'm standing in front of him in nothing but my simple and unattractive underwear.

"Fuckin' gorgeous." Returning to his feet, he glances up at my face, his voice husky as he continues, "You're everythin' I expected and more, Ella."

I'm still standing stiffly, my breaths coming fast. I trust him and I don't, both at the same time. My eyes squeeze shut. I want to see him, and I don't. I start to tremble.

"Open your eyes, Ella. Look at me. I'm here. No one else."

The calming tenor of his voice makes me obey to see him back on his feet, standing in front of me. "I'm sorry," I whisper, seeing his brow creased in worry.

"We can stop now. I don't want you to be afraid."

I don't want to stop. It's difficult to get my voice to speak, so I show him in another way, stretching up on tiptoe to put my lips against his. A soft growl comes from his throat as he presses his mouth to mine. As his tongue probes I open, and he sweeps inside. I already know I love his taste, and wanting more, move forward, causing our naked skin to touch, and his hard erection to press against my stomach. A twinge of arousal hardens my nipples even more, and a zing travels down my spine to my clit —a feeling of arousal I've been missing for some time. It's only now I start to believe I might be able to follow this through.

His fingers tangle in my hair as he takes control. I moan as he deepens the kiss, ravishing my mouth, but in such an erotic way. As our tongues slide and dance my arms come around him, holding him to me. I try to tell him everything with my caress— that I love him, that I want him, that I'm not certain I can allow him so close.

Once again, he's the first to pull back, his lips gradually drawing away, his eyes opening as he stands back. As he brushes his hands up and down my arms he leaves tingling in their wake.

"I love you," he tells me. "Don't know when exactly, don't know how. But you mean the world to me, Els. You knocked me off my fuckin' feet."

He speaks so intently I have to answer back. Like him I don't know how it happened, but I know it's true. "I love you, Slick." I wouldn't be trusting him this much if I didn't.

He closes his eyes briefly before opening them again as if he hadn't been expecting my return declaration—and truthfully it took me by surprise. But the words I'd uttered were true. How could I not feel that emotion for the man who's given me so much?

Now he's gripping my arms lightly and pushing me back toward the bed. I make no move to stop him, made confident by knowing I could do so if I wanted with just one word. When my knees hit the edge, he applies a little pressure to my shoulders and I sit.

Sinking to his knees, he reaches for the clasp of my bra, pausing to give me a chance to object. When I say nothing he unclasps it, and my breasts are allowed to fall free. Just the sight of him staring sends a shiver through me.

His eyes narrow as he sees it. "Alright?"

I just nod to confirm I'm doing okay.

He smiles, then requests, "Up." He prods at my hips.

Shakily I rise, letting him pull my underwear down and off. A hand to my chest, and I'm lying flat on the bed, my feet on the floor.

"Tell me to stop and I will." He reassures me again.

Knowing he can see me, *all of me*, excites me. My evidence of my arousal floods between my legs. *Thank God!* I didn't know if I'd be able to respond.

And then he's touching me, *there*. Gently parting my labia, and oh so softly his finger is touching me. Unwittingly I squirm, but it's not to evade his touch.

"Gonna taste you now."

Without pausing he lowers his head, swiping his tongue and lapping at my essence. My muscles tense, but not from fear, and instead feelings I'd thought I'd never know again sweep through me, the involuntary responses of my muscles, my stomach starting to clench. This is nothing like the selfish painful touch of my rapists. He's treating me like fine china, as though I could break.

He prods at my opening with his tongue, a glorious sensation which increases my moisture. Fingers circle my clit, making it tingle and spark. With his other hand he toys with my breasts, lightly pinching and tweaking one nipple then the other, causing tremors down my spine, and that bundle of nerves to throb.

"Fuck, Ella. You taste so fuckin' good." He raises his head to speak, the vibration of his voice and his hot breath makes me writhe and push up to him.

It might be that it's him, it might be that it's been so long, but my body starts to tighten as my orgasm approaches, fast. He notices and doesn't disappoint, nor keeps me hanging. His fingers and mouth work, expertly playing my erogenous zones until I'm trapping him between the taut muscles of my thighs. My head twists against the bed, my fingers grasp the sheets, and I'm going, I'm going... I come. Hard. A scream of pent-up elation escapes my mouth. He licks gently, circling, bringing me down, lifting momentarily when oversensitivity makes me want to evade his touch. And then he's back there, making me peak once again, strong contractions making my muscles ripple.

My pussy feels empty, I want him inside. "I need you, Slick."

Strong arms reposition me on the bed, my head on the pillows. Reaching across to the table he opens a drawer, pulling out a condom. Sliding off his boxers his large cock bobs free. He's as big as his bulge had led me to believe, and I lick my lips in anticipation, and then with concern as I see the Prince Albert piercing on the tip.

"You'll love it," he assures me when he sees where I'm looking, and for some reason I blush.

Then I can't tear my eyes away as he sheaves his big dick. I notice his own hands are unsteady as he smooths the latex down.

Then his eyes meet mine, his pupils already dilated, the dark orbs full of promise.

Gently he bends up my legs, making a cradle for his crotch in between them. He covers my body, one arm bent to support him, the other guiding his cock to my opening.

I grimace and flinch as he starts to press inside.

"Relax, darlin'. It's me. Stay with me, keep lookin' at me."

I do my best, and the tip of his hardness invades me. I'm so wet he slides easily in. I keep watching him, his brow furrows, his teeth clench as he pushes in so slowly, backing out then forward again, using the tiniest of thrusts. Now with his weight on his elbows beside me, I see his muscles quivering and know he's holding himself back.

With small advancements, he takes his time to fill me, the slow, careful movements alighting all my nerve endings, that piercing, although muted by the latex, rubs me in the right spot.

When he's fully seated, his mouth twists in a smile. "Fuck, Ella, you fit me like a glove. Think you were fuckin' made for me." His face contorts with the effort of holding himself back. "Ain't gonna last long, darlin'. You feel too fuckin' good."

What woman doesn't like hearing how much she's pleasing her man? I clench down on purpose.

"Fuck, Ella. I'm gonna move now."

Again I tighten my muscles, which encourages him to start a slow, steady pace. He feels amazing, probably the largest cock I've ever had, and that piercing is hitting me in all the right places. I watch his face and its range of expressions, his lips purse as he keeps up that relentless but controlled tempo, his cock sliding into me, out, and then in again. There's a fire starting to build inside me. I take in a deep breath, then can only manage short pants as he reaches his hand down and strums my clit with his fingers. My stomach muscles contract, sending ripples through my pussy. I see stars in my head as he gasps aloud.

He quickens his strokes.

When I shatter, he stills, then with short jerks reaches his completion with a satisfied shout.

He stays inside my body and lowers his lips, taking mine in a ravishing kiss. Then as his cock slips out he rolls to his side, gathering me up in his arms.

"My ol' lady. Mine," he declares. "Fuck, Ella. Darlin'. That was worth every fuckin' moment of the months I had to wait."

I've no energy to move, I feel like I'm floating. I close my eyes and bury my face in the warmth of his chest.

CHAPTER 25

Slick

From the moment I'd met her, I'd known Ella was special. If I was asked to list what made her that way, it would be impossible to single anything out. It's the whole package—her looks, her personality, and her bravery.

Holding her in my arms, I think back to the day we met, and that day I'd delivered her to the Rock Demons club, torn between the desire to protect her and my club. My club had won out and fuck, I regret that. She'd been mine even then, just neither of us knew it.

If hadn't been focused on what the club needed from her, I wouldn't have been so blind and would have seen she wasn't sweet butt material from that very first night. But the Satan's Devils were depending on what she could do for us, so I'd smothered any doubts, just pushed forward with what the brothers had agreed around the table. And that was the biggest mistake of my life—she's ended up broken. But now, if the last few minutes are anything to go by, she's on her way back.

Making love so gently isn't my style, but fuck, I couldn't call what we'd just done anything else. And if that's the way it has to be to reassure her, even if I can never let my inner beast loose, I'll still be content for the rest of my life.

Running my hands up and down her skin, covered in a sheen of sweat, testament to what's just transpired between us, I relish in touching her, unable to believe what a lucky man I am. She's mine, she's wearing my property patch. She's all I'll ever want and need. No more sweet butts for me. Why would I want them when I've got Ella? All of a sudden my other brother's fidelity to their old ladies makes sense.

The sound of my phone vibrating makes me move, reluctantly taking my fingers from her.

"Gotta get that."

Making no protest, she lets me leave her. I locate my jeans and answer just before it rings off.

"Yeah?"

"Fuck, yeah. I'll be there. Half-an-hour you say?"

"See ya."

I end the call.

"You got to go, Slick?" Her voice sounds melodious, my cock twitches as I turn to see her face, now relaxed and a smile curling her lips.

"Yeah. Sorry." She seems relaxed and content, but it's still important to me to hear the words which will let me know she doesn't regret what we've done. "You okay, Ella?"

She stretches, her arms going over her head, inadvertently offering her breasts to me. It kills me that I must ignore the innocent invitation. I can't get distracted, I've things to do.

She yawns, covering her mouth with her hand. "You wore me out, Slick."

I twist my body so I can take her hand. "You sure you're okay?" I want, need, her to be.

"Better than that." She huffs a laugh.

Good. Seems like I've done my job. A new wave of satisfaction washes over me. But now I've got to get a move on, else I won't be able to leave her. "Going to have a quick shower, darlin'."

"Want me to join you?" She makes the unexpected offer as her eyes fall on my thickening dick.

I put my hand to her chin and lift her face up. "Not sure that's a good idea, darlin'. Unless you can promise to keep your hands off."

"Me?" She looks up in mock disdain, her face wide-eyed and innocent.

"Yeah, you." I huff a laugh. "Else I'm never going to get anywhere."

But of course we end up showering together, and I only just control myself, making myself remember it's been a while since she's had sex, she'll need time to recover. But as we wash each other with no pressure to do more, she seems to stand taller, her confidence growing.

We dry and dress. Proudly she slips on her new cut, her face smiling as she fingers the leather.

"You going to stay here?"

A shake of her head. "No, I need to find Jayden. Make sure she's alright."

She seems to be happier, a little more self-assured, but I want to remind her. "Wearin' that," I point to her cut, "ain't no one gonna bother ya."

I think she believes me when she nods and says, "I know, Slick. They won't bother me as this shows I'm yours."

Fuck yeah she is.

My brothers all know I've claimed her, but as I walk her through the crowded clubhouse with my patch on her back and probably the stupidest grin on my face, something must give it away that I've *claimed* her. I get slaps on the backs, lewd looks, and crude comments. Well, I deserve that, and there isn't anything that's going to spoil my day. I lead her on through and out the back to the table which all the old ladies and her sister have appropriated—Amy's playing with a toy motorbike and getting under their feet.

Sam jumps up as we approach, twirling her fingers. Pulling away from me, Ella interprets Drummer's woman's actions and turns her back, allowing them all to read her property patch. Hollers and hoots come from the women, and I give her a quick kiss, reassured I'm leaving her in safe hands.

I know I have a spring in my step as I go back into the clubhouse and make my way to the bar where I can see Drummer getting ready to address the motley crew around us. I seem to have made it just in time.

Wraith slaps my back and smirks. "I can tell the day's goin' well for ya, Brother. You've fucked her at last, haven't ya?"

My goofy grin is all the answer he needs.

When he goes to say more, Prez puts one hand on the bar, swings his legs up, and stands on the top. Peg whistles loudly, and the various conversations around us die down.

Drummer looks around, nodding at the crowd, giving a chin jerk here and there. Then he starts to speak, his authoritative voice resonating through the room.

"Welcome, brothers. It warms my heart to see ya'all here." He waits while reciprocal greetings are returned. When the murmuring and shouts die down he continues, "As some of you know, the young sister of one of our brothers' old ladies got herself in with the wrong crowd. She's only fourteen fuckin' years old, and those bastards were gonna pass her around, sell her to whoever wanted to use her."

He waits for the growls and expressions of disgust to fade.

"Traced it back to the Herrera family, here in town. Whether the trade has the blessin' of the heads of the organisation, or were doin' it rogue, well, that's what we're tryin' to find out. We could be up against the whole clan, or just a part. And if it's the latter we don't know whether the rest will rally around and protect them."

"Hence the show of force this mornin'. Thanks for that, brothers." Peg's loud voice bellows.

"What he said." Drum waves down toward the sergeant-at-arms, and laughter rings out. "Now I know you can't leave your compounds undefended, or your businesses short, so for most of you, I hope you enjoy our hospitality and stay for the night. But I'd be grateful for some extra hands to stay on to help put these monsters down."

Hands go up as if to volunteer. Red, the president of the Vegas chapter pushes his way to the front. After exchanging a nod with Drum, he gets up beside him. "Far as we're concerned, I'll get a few men to stay. Good food and good women to fuck here." There's a roar from the back, obviously some of his men offering to step up.

Snake waves his hand in the air. "Same goes for us!"

The two other presidents from Utah and Colorado indicate if necessary they'll leave some men too.

Red jumps back down, leaving the floor for Drum.

The prez does another sweep of the room with his eyes. "I thank ya'll. Good to know the Satan's Devils have each other's back. Position is, we've put the ball in Herrera's court after our little ride past earlier today. Even if the bulk of you go home, he knows what he's up against should he declare war on the Satan's Devils."

Predictably, cries go up around the room. "Ride together Satan's Devils. Satan's Devils ride together!" A member from the Colorado chapter who I haven't met before nudges me. "Fuckin' Herreras haven't a fuckin' clue what they'll be takin' on."

I toss him a nod, feeling my heart swell with pride to know there'll be large numbers of brothers at my back, even if I don't recognise their faces or know their names. *This* is what a one percenter club is all about. Brotherhood. I wouldn't want to live any other way.

Having ramped up the support in the room, Drum and the officers from the other clubs go off to have a more in-depth meeting. I shoot the shit with Dart for a while, but don't hang around too long, as I'm eager to get out to Ella again. As I walk outside I see her still seated with the other old ladies. Places to sit being at a premium, Sandy is sitting on Viper's lap, and Carmen on Bullet's. It seems natural to go over and tap Ella on the shoulder. At her quick glance, I make a gesture and she stands, then sits herself down, her ass pressing against my thighs. Something my cock immediately finds attractive. My arms go around her and as she leans back against me, I instantly get the feeling of coming home. My impulsive decision to claim her, all those months ago, was certainly no mistake.

Paladin is sitting next to Jayden, scrunched onto the end of the picnic bench. It might be due to the lack of space, but my eyes narrow all the same. Particularly when he hugs her to him. He's getting a bit too handsy for my liking, but being surrounded by brothers, for now, I'll let it go.

Amy comes over and tugs at Sam's arm. "Wanna go potty."

With an indulgent smile, Sam lifts her into her arms and carries her through the milling bodies. I watch her go. She's pregnant, Sophie's pregnant. And I really wouldn't mind having a kid of my own.

Nuzzling my mouth against her ear, I ask Ella softly, "Do you want kids, El?"

She turns around sharply and looks at me, as if wondering what's the right answer to a question that seemed to come out of nowhere. I leave my face impassive. It has to be her desire as well as mine. After a moment she sighs and rests her head back against my chest. "Yes."

Her answer, spoken so softly, I nearly miss it. I smile against her hair. "Me too," I reply. Then, thinking of the babies due to be born in the clubhouse and wanting to add to their number, whisper, "And soon."

She doesn't protest, just gives a little delighted shiver. The thought of sinking my cock into her without barriers has my cock swelling more, and I feel rather than see her smile.

The meeting must be over. The officers come out and with drinks in their hands. Wraith comes over and in one smooth movement Sophie stands, lets him sit, then plonks herself back down on his lap. He gives an exaggerated "Oomph," making us laugh.

Red's followed him out. He stands at the end of the picnic bench, putting his foot against the back of the seat. Leaning forward with his hands on his knee he asks, "What's the latest on Heart? Fuckin' bad business that."

"Not a lot to tell, Brother," Wraith gives the answer. "Shooter's with him now, but there's been no change."

"Have to say, I'd hoped to hear better."

The VP shrugs. "He's just got to choose when he's gonna come out of it." He indicates Sam carrying Amy across. "We've got to arrange the funeral for Crystal, but keep puttin' it off as by rights he should be there."

"I hear she's got a mother?" Red raises his eyebrow. "She gettin' on with sortin' that out?"

"No way." Wraith scowls. "Fuckin' junky bitch that one. Tryin' to get hold of Heart's kid, though fuck knows why."

Red creases his brow. "You going to organise the funeral without her then?"

"To be honest, Red, we're steerin' well clear. But if Heart remains unconscious we'll probably have to get in touch. It's her daughter we'll be buryin' after all's said and done."

"Fuckin' bad thing to have happened." Then Red shuts up, which pleases me. Anything else would be club business and the old ladies don't need to know about that.

"Hi Red, fancy some company?" Jill's only doing her job, but it's interesting she's homed in on the handsome Vegas prez. Still, if the sweet butts know what's good for them they'll approach the men they like and hope they'll keep them satisfied all night. They're fair game at a gathering like this, and would be out on their ear if Drum got word they'd turned a brother down. Without good reason, that is. We don't tolerate violence toward our whores. My arms tighten around Ella, and again I wonder how the fuck she ever thought she could be one of them.

My gesture doesn't go unnoticed, and Jill narrows her eyes. I stare her down, once again nuzzling my lips against my old lady's hair. It was her fault, selling the idea of biker cock to my woman. She'd certainly skated around the edge of the truth when building up the image of a sweet butt's life. Oh, it suits some just fine, and is definitely better than walking the streets. And then there's that elusive dream of becoming that one special woman to a biker. Jill hasn't got a chance. I smother my laugh.

Red finishes up his conversation with Wraith, puts his arm around Jill, and walks off. Hmm, there's obviously something I don't know or am missing by the look Sophie throws after her, and the laugh Wraith gives as he turns Sophie's face back and proceeds to devour her lips with a kiss.

A distant rumble of thunder makes me look up to see clouds billowing over the Tucson mountains. Unless we're very lucky this party will have to move inside soon courtesy of a late summer storm.

Drummer comes into sight, he stops with his hand on my shoulder. "Slick, Paladin. Want a fuckin' word."

At last giving Jayden some space, Paladin gets to his feet. "Yeah, Prez?"

Drum jerks his head over his shoulder, and we follow him inside as he leads the way to his office. He leans back against his desk and doesn't offer us a seat. For a while he says nothing, but fixes his steely gaze upon Paladin, who starts to fidget and, unable to meet Drum's eyes, looks down at his feet.

"We got a problem?" The prez at last speaks.

Paladin glances up and sees Drum still staring at him. "What? Not that I know of."

He doesn't drag it out. "Jayden's fuckin' underage," Prez states. "She's here under the club protection. I won't have anythin' happen to a fourteen-year-old girl under my roof."

"Nothin's..."

"Listen to me, boy," he growls. "Nothin' might have happened as yet, but I've got fuckin' eyes in my head. I've seen the way she looks at you. And how you look at her."

"I know how old she is, Prez. Same age as my sister. And..."

"And you've been sittin' cuddlin' her for the last half-hour. And I wouldn't even want to see you canoodlin' with any sister like that," Drum interrupts again. Pushing away from the desk he stands up straight, which puts him inches from Paladin's face. "Get any fuckin' closer and you lose your patch."

Suddenly Paladin gets a backbone from somewhere. "It's not easy for her, Prez. She's not a kid anymore. All she knows is what those bastards did to her, but she's part woman, part child. In her mind she's old enough."

I feel myself tense, wondering what exactly he's suggesting. Jayden's under my protection first, and only second of that of the club. She comes as a package with my old lady.

Drum doesn't miss a beat. "And in my mind she's not. Nor to any other fucker usin' their right head. I'm warnin' you, Paladin. I wanted you to watch out for her, not to fuck her."

"I'm not." Our newest member sounds petulant.

"And you're not going to either. You worked fuckin' hard to get your patch. You're going to lose it quicker than you earned it at this rate. Fuck one of the club whores if you can't keep it zipped."

I've kept quiet up to now, but now I step up. I glare at Paladin to show my agreement with the prez, and then turn to Drum. "Once this Herrera business is sorted I'm gonna be buyin' a house, Drum, for Ella and me. Jayden will live with us, go back to school and get her life back on track."

"Can't be soon enough, can it?" Drum tunnels his hands through his hair. "Look Paladin, if you've got a thing for her, you'll just have to wait until she's legal. Four fuckin' years. I don't want anythin' else to happen to that little girl, and definitely not on my watch. You hear me?"

Paladin looks at his feet, and up again. "I hear you, Prez."

"Now get lost. Go find one of the whores. Or two. Hell, three of them if that's what it takes. But that's a fuckin' order."

Paladin nods despondently and leaves us. Drum looks at me. "Am I readin' it wrong?"

"Naw, Prez. I reckon you're readin' it right. But girl's had a taste, had her innocence taken away. I reckon it's as hard on her as it is for him. And keepin' him around her ain't helpin' much. There's an attraction between them, that's for sure."

"Well, we'll see how strong a fuckin' attraction it is when she sees him with the whores."

"Thanks, a fuckin' bunch, Prez," I grumble. A sulky teenager is just what I need. But for Ella's sake, I'll just have to put up with it.

CHAPTER 26
Ella

Despite being surrounded by over a hundred bikers, I'm actually having a good time today. My property patch feels like a shield, protecting me from unwanted attention. I'm staying close to the other old ladies and eating far too much as food keeps appearing in front of me.

As the drinks flow and are rapidly consumed, comments which would normally only raise a smile have me crying with laughter, and the antics of Horse and Sophie trying to outdo each other with terms none of us Americans can understand has us all in stitches.

"So, it was a right bodge job. The cack-handed pillock tried to fix it himself. I told him he was just taking the piss." Horse winks at Sophie as the rest of us try to work out what he's saying.

"Christ, I'm stuffed." Sophie leans back and rubs her stomach, then nods at her English friend. "After you worked on it, I bet it ended up the bees' knees."

"Yeah, just wish I hadn't had to listen to him wittering on while I was doing it. I did what he wanted, but it wasn't my cup of tea."

"A bit naff?" Sophie nods sympathetically.

"You could say that. Then, when I'd done what he'd asked for, the bloody wanker said he didn't have the dosh."

"That's pants! Bet you threw a wobbly."

Horse grins. "I told him what a tosser he was, then spray painted the whole thing black. As he stood there gobsmacked I just sodded off. Went out and got shitfaced and moved on."

By this time most of our table are bent double with wracking belly laughs. It's the camaraderie and the alcohol that makes it so amusing.

Wraith tugs at Sophie's hair, pulling her head back and kissing her. "Didn't understand a fuckin' word of that, darlin'," he begins as he eventually finishes mating with her mouth. "Just assure me, when Horse leaves you'll be talkin' proper English again."

"Proper English?" Her eyes open wide and there's a twinkle in them. "Are you getting shirty with me?"

Another round of laughter. As I'm wiping the tears from my eyes, familiar arms encircle me from behind, and a voice murmurs in my ear. "Havin' fun?"

Once again, I stand up, allow Slick to sit down, and then reposition myself on his lap. "I am," I confirm, knowing it's the surprising truth. I never thought I'd be able to relax in an environment such as this.

The music's been turned up, Wraith jerks his chin at Slick, then raises an eyebrow. They seem to have an unspoken conversation, then as the VP stands, Slick taps my leg and I slide off his lap.

"Come on ladies, time to leave."

What? I'm still enjoying myself. As I go to protest I see Pussy, one of the sweet butts has dispensed with her top and is now allowing her breasts to be fondled by a man from another club. *Ah.* And over against the wall a man's got his butt on display, his hips bucking and oh, is that Jill? Hmm.

I cast a quick glimpse toward Jayden, but she's wide-eyed and staring. Following the direction of her eyes, I see Paladin with his one arm around Paige, and his free hand inside her shorts.

"Jayden, come on. That's our cue to leave."

Turning sad eyes toward me, her hand covers her mouth, and slowly she shakes her head.

"Come on girl, party's over for you ladies." Slick leaves my side and goes to give her a hand to help her up. Then he brings her to me. I can feel her shaking. Fucking Paladin. If he was going to bail on her like that he could have waited until after she'd gone. What is he thinking of, openly groping a girl when he's been fussing over my sister all afternoon?

Enraged on her behalf, I take her hand and follow Slick up to our suite. By the time we get there she's openly crying. Nodding to Slick I take her into our room, sit her on the bed, and rock her in my arms as though she were a child.

"Why, Ella, why?" she sobs, "I thought he liked me."

"Men, Jayden. He's a man. Look, I'm sure he wants to be your friend, but you're only fourteen."

Angrily she swipes at her tears and I pass her a tissue. "I may only be fourteen, but I can give him what he wants. I can give him the same as that sweet butt. Ella, you know what happened to me! I'm not innocent or naïve."

I'm only too aware of that. My little sister has been exposed to things she should know nothing about. How the fuck does she come back from that? She shouldn't be having such feelings about Paladin. Oh, I know some girls mature early and don't give a damn about the age of consent, but that would never have been Jayden before her ordeal. They made her an experienced woman in a young girl's body. How the hell am I going to protect her for the next four years?

I don't know what to say, so I just hold her close, letting her cry it all out. After a while I try to reason with her.

"Jayden, the age of consent is eighteen. And there's a reason for that. What you went through, your body isn't developed enough, let alone your mind. You've got to enjoy your teenage years like any normal girl."

"But I'm not normal, am I?" She clutches my shirt. "I know what they did was wrong. The first time it hurt, but then he made me enjoy it. What's wrong with me, Ella?"

And that's how that bastard had groomed her. Made her think it was what she wanted. And now she wants more. Suddenly I fear this is going to be a very long wait until her eighteenth birthday.

Eventually I persuade her to get ready for bed, and wait while she cries herself to sleep. Leaving the door slightly ajar so I can hear her, I go to see if Slick's in his room. He is, lying in bed with just a sheet covering him. He's not asleep, his arm is up over his eyes, and as soon as he realises I've entered, he sits up.

"Is she okay?"

I shake my head. "No. What Paladin did…"

"Paladin was only doin' what the prez told him to do. He's got feelin's for her which he shouldn't have. Prez told him to knock it on the head. To make it clear to Jayden that he wasn't for her."

Oh… "But he hurt her so much, Slick."

Slick reaches out his hand and I take it, sitting beside him on the bed. "Had to be done, darlin'. She's too young, you know that. But the way they've been with each other, best thing is to keep them apart."

"Those bastards ruined what should be a fun time in her life. She should be laughing and joking, stealing kisses behind the bleachers, not offering to put out. Slick, what are we going to do with her?"

"We," he parrots. "I like the sound of that." He places a kiss on my forehead. "We are gonna buy a house off the compound. Get her into a different school, and watch her like a hawk. We'll get her some proper counsellin'—same for you, darlin'."

My brow furrows. "You're saying she'll be livin' with us?" It's exactly what I wanted, but it's a burden Slick wouldn't want, would he?

"Better than livin' with your bitch of a mother, ain't it?"

He's not wrong there. But does he know what he'll be taking on? "Slick, a teenage girl…"

"El, I'm well aware that it's not gonna be a walk in the park, but you'll want her close by, and fuck, after what she's been through she deserves to have you near. Anyway, I like the kid. And I love you. You wouldn't be happy with her out of your sight, and I wouldn't want you out of mine. So we all live together, okay?"

I hadn't thought how we'd progress from here, but now Slick's offering me a future. And showing what an amazing man he is to take on a problem girl as well. "I love you so much, Slick."

"And I love you too, Ella. You're going to make a wonderful mom one day."

The thought of having his child makes me go gooey inside. How did I get so lucky to end up with this man?

"Marry me, Ella. One day, when you're ready," Slick suddenly says. "Let's make it official in the civilian world as well."

Unable to stop, I fling myself at him and he wraps me in his strong arms, pulling me over him. In that position it's hard to ignore the evidence of his erection beneath me.

"Slick, I want you."

"You've got me, darlin'." He throws off the sheet that's been covering his nakedness and gets to his knees, pulling my tee over my head and dispensing with my bra in one swift move. "Stand," he instructs. When I do he unbuttons and pulls down my jeans.

"We need to be quiet." I point to the door that's slightly ajar.

He smirks. "I can do quiet. I'm not so sure about you."

Suddenly I'm on my back, and he's between my legs. He wastes no time starting to tease me, running his hands up my thighs until he reaches my slit and his fingers start to probe.

"Fuck, you're wet already."

His fingers slide in and curl around, reaching that place no one's found but him. His mouth comes down and mercilessly lashes my clit. It seems only seconds before my stomach muscles clench. As Slick works my body as though he knows it better than I do myself, his hand comes up and covers my mouth as I reach my peak, unable to hold back a scream.

As I try to recover my breath, Slick sits up and watches me with a wide grin while reaching out to get a condom ready. This time there's no fear, no worries or concerns. This is *my* man, and he's going to make love to me.

He applies protection, then places himself at my entrance. "One day I want to feel you skin to skin. Can't wait for that, darlin'. And to put my baby in here." His hand touches my stomach, which clenches at his words. *I want that too.*

His brow creasing with concentration, he starts to push inside, taking care to ease himself through tissue already swollen by my orgasm. Automatically I raise my hips to help him.

When he reaches my cervix he pauses and asks, "How many orgasms do you think you have in you?

How many? I'm sort of hoping for one. But today was the first time I'd ever come with a man inside me, so already sated I'd be okay with settling for what I've already had.

When I don't reply he continues, "Two? Three? Yeah, we'll go for three, shall we?"

What? As I look at him bemused, certain that's not possible and not sure I'd ever recover if it was, he starts to move. Again he's gentle, long strokes in and then out. Over and over again, in, out, in, out. And every time that darn piercing rolls over that spot. It's not long before my muscles start contracting. His mouth covers one nipple, laving then nipping, and a tingle travels down my spine straight to my clit. As my thigh muscles clench he does the same to the other one with the exact same effect.

As his strong hips drive his cock into me, he bends one knee and changes the angle slightly, and then I'm lost. He lowers his head and swallows my cry with his mouth, his tongue sweeping inside as one hand cradles my head. When I start to come down he continues to thrust, an even rhythm, but so deep, and exciting every nerve ending. I've depleted my reserves, I've got nothing left.

But he takes no pity, just keeps pumping in. Totally unexpected, I start to tighten again.

"Fuck, you're stranglin' my cock," he murmurs into my ear. "That's right baby, squeeze it. You're gonna take it for me, aren't you darlin'? You're going to take everythin' that this filthy dirty biker wants."

It must be his words. My body tenses and I'm reaching again. He quickens his pace slightly and, lowering his hand, starts assaulting my clit. I inhale sharply, holding my breath—my body's on fire—and then I release.

"Two," he says softly. "Knew you had it in you, babe. Now let's work up to another one."

It's impossible. But he's intent on proving it's not. Now he powers his hips, thrusting a little harder, bumping my cervix each time he pushes in. I've never felt so alive, so good. My senses are reeling, the intensity of the feelings driving me crazy. I'm just a collection of sensations, and all of them good. Like an overwound clock, everything's taut and I'm shaking, a quivering mass on the bed. *I can't possibly...* But I'm going to. He's pushing me higher and higher.

"That's right, darlin'. Gonna come with you this time. Gonna flood this condom wishin' I was shooting my cum up inside you. Fuck, you feel good. You're grippin' onto my cock darlin', it loves being inside you. That's it. You gonna come for me?"

I can't.

He presses on my clit as though it was a button and that's all it takes. He lowers his head once again, my muffled scream absorbed as I swallow his. He works through his own release, little pumps into the condom.

We both gasp and struggle to get air into our lungs.

Christ. If that's the way bikers make love it's no wonder Jill is addicted. But I've no desire to try anyone else. Slick is the only biker, the only man, I'll ever want.

"Fuck babe," Slick starts when he's at last able to breathe. "Fuck, you were made for me, you hear that? Never. Been. So. Fuckin'. Good."

"Hmm, I think I like biker loving, Slick."

He raises his head and smirks at me. "Babe, I haven't fuckin' started yet."

CHAPTER 27

Slick

After making love—yeah, making love not fucking—last night, Ella went back to be with Jayden. Knowing Paladin's actions had upset the kid, I understood why she left me, but fuck it if my bed didn't feel empty. Another sign I was right to take her as my old lady. Even after just a few nights I no longer want my own space. So different to the whores who I'd kick out of bed as soon as the deed was done.

Poking my head around their door this morning, I'd seen they were still both sleeping so peacefully I hadn't the heart to disturb them, but I couldn't help myself lingering for a moment just watching them. *My girls.*

Laughing silently at myself, I make my way down to the club-house, and wouldn't you just believe it, the first fucker I come across is Paladin. Although it had been his actions that made me end up sleeping alone, there was valid reason for it, so I pause for a second to tell him, "Hey, you did good, Brother."

The pain radiating from his face surprises me as his eyes meet mine, and he says tersely, "Did it work?"

"Sure did."

His hand brushes back the hair flopping over his face. "Hurts like a fuckin' bitch, man. I didn't want to upset her."

I slap his back. "You had to. She's got a lot of things to work through. Best you keep your distance, it's confusin' for her."

He stares at the ground and kicks at a stone. "I know. I know I should keep away, Slick. Fuck, I don't want to make things worse. Thing is, she doesn't act her age, you know? She seems so much older."

"After what she's been through, she probably does."

He nods then walks off. I carry on, entering the clubroom and stepping over bodies. Fuck, there must have been one hell of a party last night. And you know what? It doesn't even bother me I missed it. I've got Ella, and what we did together was better than any party I've ever been at. My mouth twists into a grin remembering her amazement as I'd squeezed those orgasms out of her.

Drum's coming out of his office, weaving his way through the hungover bodies. Reaching me he waves his hand. "Sometimes I wish all the brothers had old ladies. We're the only ones awake and fit to do anythin' today. Come with me, Brother? Hyde's got a problem down at the gate."

Sure, I'll accompany him. I give a chin jerk to agree, and walk down by his side, curious to know what the issue is.

Hyde's learned his lesson. He's letting no one inside unless it's someone wearing our patch. The prospect's standing this side of the entrance, stoically impassive at the ranting and raving from the other side. It's the woman who I've no desire to see again, Crystal's mom, and the same loser with her. Drum and I exchange glances and I'd bet good money we're both thinking the same thing. *Why are they here, and how quickly can we get rid of them?*

With a meaty hand slapping down on the prospect's back, Drum indicates he's done good not letting them in.

"What d'ya want?" He stands at the metal bars, obviously with no intention of opening the gate up.

"I want my grandchild, that's what," Crystal's mom sneers through the fence.

"Nothin' has changed. She's stayin' here until we find out what her father wants," Drum tells her, sounding bored.

"Dale's as good as dead. It's only a matter of time."

Yeah, unfortunately, as the days pass with him showing no improvement that's what I've started thinking, but hearing her say it makes me see red. "You fuckin' bitch…" I start, but the prez's hand shooting out and grabbing my arm shuts me up.

"Heart's still in the land of the livin'. We ain't givin' up on him yet."

"You've no right to keep the kid."

Drum sighs. "Why do you want her? She's happy here." He indicates her clothing which is dirty and worn. "Why would she be better off with you?" He throws a look toward her companion and his face twists in disgust.

"Because I ain't a filthy biker. Fuck knows what you'll do to her. You into kids?"

Now it's me that's holding my prez back. Daring to accuse us of that? The woman's got balls, I'll give her that.

"My wife's lookin' after Amy." Drum spits out the words. "And I've already fuckin' told ya, that's where she'll stay."

She's not giving up. "Crystal's funeral will be on Friday. She ain't doin' no good above ground. I want the kid there."

Fuck! That's only a couple of days away. Drum steps forward, his hands curling around the bars and the look on his face should probably warn the woman she's lucky the gate's shut. "Heart should be the one makin' any arrangements."

"Heart's a fuckin' dead man. He just doesn't know it yet." Now she's screaming. "And it's my daughter we're talking about. It's my right to arrange it and I want this done. Dale's got no say in this. He killed her on that fuckin' bike."

Christ, it's bad enough that we don't know whether Heart will come out of it or not, but what if he does to find his wife dead and already buried? No chance to say a final goodbye.

But what can we do? Drum throws me a look full of emotion, and I know what he's thinking. *This is all wrong.* But while he's the personal representative in terms of Crystal's will, in Arizona that doesn't make him an authorising agent and able to organise her funeral, only a next of kin or spouse can do that, or someone with a healthcare power of attorney, and Drum's none of these. Without Heart conscious, no one can stop her burying her daughter. As I stare at Drummer I see he seems to be struggling for a response. Then, taking a deep breath, knowing there's no point in arguing, he says curtly, "Let me know when and where and we'll come pay our respects."

"I don't want no biker scum there," she screams back. "Your club is the reason she's dead!"

Drum plays his trump card. "You want us to bring Amy. Ain't sendin' her on her own."

Her face twists, but she knows when she's beaten, and then snaps out the time and the place. Once that's done she turns, drags her companion away by his arm, then they both get back into a beat-up car and disappear down the track.

Drum's head drops forward onto the bars of the gate. "Fuck, Brother," he starts, "if Heart doesn't come around before Friday this will destroy him."

Placing my hand on his shoulder, I agree. "I know, Prez, but I don't see we have any choice. We've no claim on Crystal. Not when it's what her mother wants."

"Fuckin' bitch."

And I can't argue with his assessment.

The sound of bikes firing up and revving comes from behind us. The brothers leaving us today are obviously making their move. For the next half hour I stand beside my prez saying goodbyes and thanking them for their assistance the day before, and watching them leave. When the last of those who aren't staying have left the compound, I wait while Drum fills Wraith and the other Tucson chapter brothers in on the funeral arrangements for our fallen sister. No one is any happier than the prez or I, but none of us can see a way around it. As each day passes, our insistence on waiting for Heart to wake up seems less and less rational.

Prez is lingering by the gate, I stay too, wanting to fill him in that his plan to separate Paladin and Jayden seems to have worked. As the others fade away, I ask if I can have a quick word. But before I can start talking a bike comes up the track. Unlike the healthy rumble of a Harley, it's a high pitched annoying whine. Oh, the bike's pretty impressive if you like something like that. To me it looks like a green monster pretending to have street cred. It's a fuckin' Kawasaki.

Drum shakes his head at Hyde as he tilts his head in question as to whether he should open the gate. Nobody wearing one of our patches would be seen dead on such a piece of plastic crap. Except Road perhaps, but even then it would be a trials bike, not a sports bike like this.

The rider dismounts, takes off her full-face green helmet which perfectly matches her bike, and shakes out her hair, which she's wearing tied up in a ponytail. She takes a step forward.

"Drummer?"

Well, I'll be fucked if it isn't that detective bitch, Hannah.

Rolling his head back on his shoulders and sighing as though this day's already brought enough shit, the prez goes to meet her. "Detective Hannah," he snarls, using the tone that normally makes brothers quake.

She shakes her head. "I'm off duty, Drummer. The names Marcia. Marcia Hannah."

"Marcia, Hannah." He waves his hand in dismissal. "Whoever the fuck you are, don't see we've got business with you."

"I think you have," she contradicts. "And I think you'll want to hear what I have to say."

Another deep sigh, Drum looks at me. I raise my eyebrow. Then he nods at Hyde and tells him to let her inside. Marcia steps through, wheeling her bike and putting down the kick-stand just inside.

"Follow me. We'll talk in my office."

I tag along, not really needed, but I'm curious just the same. The clubhouse is at least empty of bodies now, and Road and Jekyll are carrying trash sacks and picking up the remains of last night's party. Drum makes no excuses for the mess as he takes her on through and out back to his office, calling for Wraith to join us as he sees him at the bar. I hover at the door. I'm not an officer, but I'm hoping to be included.

Drum notices and nods. "Yeah, come on in Slick." At least I'll be another witness. None of us want to talk to even an off-duty cop on our own.

The prez pulls up another chair to go with the two that normally are in front of his impressive desk, and takes his seat under the large flag. Marcia studies it carefully for a moment and then looks at Drum, who's tilting his head, waiting for her to speak.

She's a cop in an outlaw biker club, but she returns his stare steadily. "You've got problems," she starts, then pauses waiting for a reaction. When she gets none she continues, "and so have I." Again she breaks off, but this time she's not looking for any comment. She frowns as though she's gathering her thoughts. "I'm squeaky clean, I'm not on the take. And I'm going to stay that way."

"Never suspected different, sweetheart." Drum sneers the endearment.

She picks at her fingernails as if removing dirt and then looks back up. "Look, I wanted to do this the right way, go through the right channels. But the thing is, I'm new to Tucson and I don't know who to trust. My captain might be clean, but who am I to know? I just can't stand by and see things going on that I know are wrong."

Drum pulls himself up straight, leans forward with his elbows on the table, resting his chin on his clasped hands. "And these things that are wrong. They concern us?"

"Yeah." She sits back and folds her arms. "Look, I'll be honest with you. I'm a damn good cop. I got my promotion after I sniffed out something others had missed. Now there's something going on here and I don't like the smell." She unfolds her arms and leans forward. "But I don't need a load of bikers taking the law into their own hands. If I tell you my suspicions, you've got to work with me and inside the law. I need your word on that."

"And if I don't give you my word?"

"Then I walk. And tell you nothing."

Drum sneers. "And forget about the stink?"

She gives a snort of derision. "No fucking way. I'll just do it on my own."

The prez's eyes flick to Wraith, and then to me. I reckon she's caught all our interest.

"Okay, darlin'. You tell us what's up, and *if* we can, we'll do it your way."

It's not a total promise we'll stay on the side that she wants, but it's all that she'll be getting from him. She stares at the prez for a few seconds, then glances at the VP and myself. She takes a deep breath and starts, "I think my partner's dirty."

Drum huffs a laugh. "Not much doubt about that. My nose is as good as yours, sweetheart."

Ignoring him, she continues, "He's intent on Mrs Norman's mother getting custody of her granddaughter. He's helping her with the paperwork, and I can't understand why." She shakes her head, "You've seen the woman. I've never met anyone less fit to look after a small child."

"She brought Crystal up right." Drum's playing devil's advocate.

"Unfortunately I never met Crystal, so I'll have to take your word on that. But however well Mrs Norman turned out is beside the point. Clyde doesn't want the child, that's plain to see. So, why's Archer helping her against you?" She shakes her head as though it's something she can't work out.

"Bikers don't have a good reputation. If Heart dies and it goes in front of a judge, we could lose a custody battle based on keepin' her here." I decide it's time that I contribute to the conversation.

She acknowledges my comment with a slow nod. "That's my concern. And why I thought you needed to know."

"So now you've told us," Wraith puts in, as though me speaking has loosened the sluice gates. "Is that all you're here for? To warn us?"

"If it is, thank you. But you can go now." Drum takes charge again.

"No, that's not all. Look, I don't know what picture this jigsaw is going to make up, but I need someone else to know all of the pieces." She sighs. "Archer wanted in right from the beginning. A simple road traffic accident, and he particularly asked for us to be given Dale Norman's case. Which has now stalled, by the way. The information I gave you, well, it's gone no further than that."

We all keep quiet that we'd done some investigating on our own.

"I suspect you've done more."

That's when I realise she's not stupid.

"Or at least I hope that you have. I've done some digging too." Another moment of silence as if to increase the anticipation and emphasise the importance of what she's going to say. "Archer has connections to the Herrera family."

"He's a second cousin." Drum confirms we already know.

As she smooths her palms down her face, she stares at him, her expression conveying 'of course you do'. I notice she looks tired. Exchanging looks with Drum, I wouldn't be surprised if he's thinking the same thing as I am. That she must be at her wits end to come to the club.

"Do you want a drink, sweetheart."

For the first time, a smile. It transforms her face and I notice she's really quite attractive. Her blond hair, reaching to her shoulders, has kept its style despite having been flattened by a helmet, and frames quite striking features.

"I could murder a coffee."

Drum sends a quick text.

"Okay, I'll put my cards on the table." She seems to be fighting an internal battle, confirmed when she scoffs at herself. "I've never done anything like this before. What I'm going to tell you could threaten an active investigation."

A knock at the door, Road enters with a tray. She's given her coffee, the three of us take a beer.

"One, we've a biker who's been knocked off his bike, and the evidence points to it being deliberate."

We stay quiet, having come to that conclusion ourselves.

"Two," she's counting off on her fingers, unbeknownst to her, mimicking how Drum had summed up, "a member of the Herrera family wanted in on the investigation, and then has done what he can to put it on the back burner. Three," she pauses and looks up, "Susie Clyde, Mrs Norman's mother, is deep in debt. And I mean deep."

Drum's eyes narrow. This is new to us. Mouse hadn't been able to find out the extent of what she owed.

She waits for a reaction, but that's all she's going to get. "Four…"

"Go on," Drum encourages.

She takes a deep breath, "We've got information that there is a gang in Tucson grooming young girls. We raided a house after a tip off, it was empty, no one around. Lots of blood at the scene." Her eyes look at us, We all keep our faces impassive. "We're trying to find out who owned it, but it's buried under all sorts of aliases."

I'm surprised they'd found it so quickly. Perhaps another one of the kids had spoken out, though it sounds like it was anonymously reported. We'd cleaned the house well, but couldn't remove stains from the carpet or furniture. I force myself to keep still, but my hands form fists at the thought of the other kids that had been abused by that fucker Diego, the only saving grace is he and the others are all dead.

It looks like Marcia is having difficulty continuing, but her mouth's working as though there's something else she wants to say.

"Go on." Drum's picked up on that too.

"The tip off…" She clears her throat. "Said it wasn't a one off. Young kids, boys and girls…"

"Fuck." Wraith looks shocked, his eyes go to Drum. This time Drum acts as though she's telling him news. It's the right reaction.

"You're saying they're paedophiles. Muckin' around with young children?"

Marcia closes her eyes briefly, then when she opens them makes an attempt to pull herself together. "Now this is going to sound crazy, and a bit of a leap, but Ms Clyde's in financial trouble. She doesn't want a child. But what if she's been offered money for her? And," suddenly the words start tumbling out one after the other, "why does my partner want to help her? Could the Herrera family be involved?"

She sits back having got everything out, her eyes roaming between the three of us. We give nothing away. Drum drums his fingers on the table. "Bit of a long stretch, darlin'. The Herreras have their hands in many pies, but grooming children? Where's your evidence for that?"

We've got plenty, but he's not letting her know.

"You've got a partner who's a distant relative to the family, a woman in debt, an accident with no identified perpetrator, and a child wanted by her junkie grandmother."

Again her arms fold. "Nothing else adds up. Look, Drummer. I've tried speaking to Archer, tried to tell him I don't think it's a good idea supporting Ms Clyde. Any fool could see she wouldn't get custody. But he's acting so strangely, doing everything to help her get her hands on the child."

She's right. It's all a stretch, but it could fit. And we've been sidetracked trying to trace the surviving members of the Rock Demons thinking it was likely them who ran Heart off the road.

"One thing wrong with your proposal, darlin'. If we put the pieces you've thrown into the mix together, you're saying Crystal's mom arranged her daughter's death."

"She's a meth addict, anyone can see that. Her brain's probably screwed. And I think she had help. A young kid would be valuable. Look, I've seen Amy, she's pretty and cute."

My stomach rolls at her words, my beer churning in my gut. It's only now the implications of what she's saying hit me. They want Amy? To use her? Sell her to a paedophile? It's unthinkable.

"What do you want us to do?"

"Drum. A three-year-old child takes precedence over everything. I want to get the social services involved." Bravely she shakes her head as Prez's face darkens. "I know you mean well, but a club of bikers isn't a place to raise a toddler, and though you and I believe Ms Clyde would soon be dismissed as a suitable guardian, blood relation or not, someone could help her scrub up and present a different picture to the court. I don't want to take that risk. I want to see her safe with foster parents."

The prez rises to his feet, his hands resting on the table. The thunderous look on his face makes even me shrink back in my chair. "Firstly, *Detective*, I ain't gonna see that child put into the system. Fuck knows where you got such a rosy image in your head. I've heard enough from my brothers brought up that way to know how often good intentions turn out shit in practice." His fist thumps down on the table. "There's a body lyin' in the morgue which shouldn't fuckin' be there. And we've got to deal with that. The last thing Crystal told me was to take care of her daughter. And I promised to look after her like my fuckin' own. If Heart doesn't recover, my ol' lady and I will make that permanent. Ain't nobody touchin' a hair of that child's head on my watch."

Hannah's not afraid to hold her ground. "And if it goes in front of a judge? You won't have a choice but to give her up. Look Drummer, I hear what you're saying, and I get it, your honouring the final wishes of a woman who died far too young. But it's her daughter that's most important."

Drummer's still standing. "You gonna go to the social?"

If she says she will, from the expression on his face, she'll be lucky to get out of here alive.

Her hands rub her face as if she's not certain what she's going to do. "What can you give her, Drummer?"

He's quick to answer. "Stability, love. Familiar surroundin's, the place she's always called home. Uncles who'd all give their lives to keep her safe. She'll be protected better here than in any foster home. No one will be takin' her away."

That makes her think. She looks at me, then Wraith, the commitment to a three-year-old girl spelt out plainly by the expressions in our eyes.

After a moment she turns back to Drummer. "You think you can keep her safe here, and out of the clutches of anyone who might want to harm her? If I'm right…" She can't voice what she means, and I've every sympathy. I don't even want to think about the type of things motherfucking scum of the earth could consider doing to such a young kid.

Retaking his seat, Drum throws his reiteration. "A foster family couldn't offer more protection than we can."

Slowly she nods as she comes to a decision. "Amy's safety comes first, Drummer. And I hear what you say. Okay, for now I won't cause waves, I do see your point. And while you're bikers, you obviously have a lot of love for the child. I'll keep on investigating, try to discover who else is clean to work with me."

"You might have it wrong." I'm grasping at straws. Her summation had seemed logical.

"I can't afford not to do anything if I'm right."

"If a judge awards Crystal's mom custody we won't be givin' her up. That's what I mean by keepin' her safe."

"I know. And you'll be breaking the law." The words, spoken in a breathy voice, show that doesn't sit well with Miss Squeaky Clean."

Drum raps his fingers against the desktop. "I'm not tellin' you nothin' bout how we'll do things. But Amy will be safe with her *family*. I can promise you that."

Marcia's shoulders rise as though a weight has been lifted off them. "Thanks, Drummer. And as for the other stuff, please don't take the law into your own hands. I'll do the investigation through the right channels. I hope that I'm wrong…"

Unfortunately, the more I think on it, the fewer doubts I have that she's probably right. And as for us keeping out of it, she's not got a fucking prayer that we'll agree to that.

She throws a stern look toward the prez. It's almost as steely as his. "This conversation…"

"This conversation never happened," he finishes for her.

Another quick text and Road appears again. Marcia picks up her gaudy full-face, gives us a nod, and goes out with the prospect to be escorted back to her bike.

Leaning my head back, I link my hands behind my neck, and stretching out my legs cross them at the ankles.

Wraith raises an eyebrow. "Can't relax with the heat around." He smirks.

"You've got that right, Brother."

Drum stands. He shakes his head. "Fuckin' unbelievable."

"You think she's on the right track?"

"Fuck knows, VP. The thing that sticks out is that bitch of a mother. Could she really have arranged for her daughter to be killed?"

"Who knows how a junkie desperate for a fix would think." Unlinking my hands, I sit forward again, drawing up my knees and resting my elbows on them. "She might have offered the kid up, the fuckin' Herreras might have worked out the logistics."

Perching his backside against the desk, the prez nods. "That sounds more credible if she's deep in debt to them. But she'd still be complicit. All she wants is to get her hands on Amy, no remorse shown for her daughter. She doesn't even seem to like the kid, and Amy clearly doesn't take to her." He stops and points to Wraith. "Get another brother at the hospital. Heart's lingerin' on, don't want him helped on his way. If Amy's an orphan it makes their case easier."

"I'll get on it, Prez."

"What I can't figure out is the Herreras. Sure, they're dirty all right, but snatchin' young kids isn't what I'd expect from them."

"That hit me too."

"What was your readin' when we met the top man, Leonardo?" The VP asks.

I lean my head to one side, then respond. "I'd have said Herrera was shocked."

"Hmm. Me too." Drum shakes his head. "Fuck me, I wish I could get just five minutes around here without somethin' kickin' off. Rock Demons, human traffickers, and now the Herreras and baby snatchin'."

"I hear ya, Prez." Wraith looks tired too. It makes me glad I'm just a normal member and not one of the officers.

"We'll have church in a few, bring everyone up to date. And arrange for a show of force at the fuckin' funeral."

I'd forgotten about that. "You think they'd try to take her then?"

Drum taps his fingers against his mouth. "I wouldn't rule anythin' out at this point." His face gives his twisted grin. "Crystal's a respected ol' lady. Reckon there'll be a lot of us wantin' to show our respects."

CHAPTER 28
Ella

I've only been here six months, and this is the third wake I've helped organise," Sophie comments sadly. Sam's just informed us Crystal's going to be buried on Friday. "Is it always like this?"

Carmen pats her shoulder. "Naw, sweetie, before this it's been a couple of years since anyone died. And that was old, um, who was it Sandy?"

"Digger." Sandy helps her out. "And he was in his sixties, hadn't ridden for years but was still called a member. Died of liver failure."

"I didn't think you could be a member if you couldn't ride?"

"Never said he *couldn't*, just that he hadn't. Probably wasn't likely toward the end, but no one put it to the test." Sandy smiles as she indulges her step-daughter's curiosity.

"Digger?" Sophie queries, always interested in how the men got their names.

As I'm wondering whether he's was responsible for excavating graves, we're given a far more banal explanation.

"Yeah, he kept digging himself into holes he couldn't get out of." Sandy, who's been here the longest, is again the one to reply. "And he'd never admit he was wrong, just kept digging in deeper."

Her moment of inquisitiveness over, Sophie's face falls again. "It's natural when someone dies of old age, but I never expected it to be one of us. Crystal, she had her whole life in front of her."

I think we all understand how she feels, most of us have probably been thinking the same thing. I glance down at Amy playing under the table, placing her naked Barbie on the back of a bike. Biting back my comment her doll should have some clothes on, I notice she's oblivious to the grownup conversation going on around her. It's better for her to stay that way. Her innocence reminds me Crystal should be here, wearing her colourful leggings, laughing, chatting, playing with her daughter, and it's all wrong that we're sat here talking about making funeral arrangements on her behalf.

"I don't like that we haven't waited for Heart." Carmen puts her hands on her hips. "It just isn't right. If something, God forbid, happened to Bullet I'd want them to wait until I could say my goodbyes. How the fuck will anyone tell him when he wakes up that not only has he lost his wife, he can't even see her in her coffin?"

"I'd feel the same about Viper."

As I would Slick. My heart goes out to Heart. Sometimes I wonder whether it would be better for him to quietly slip away without having to know about Crystal. Maybe there is another side where she would be waiting for him. But then, as my eyes again find Amy, I realise her father needs to recover and come home for her sake if for nothing else.

After my ordeal at the Rock Demons' club, the first time I was at the compound I'd tried to avoid entering the clubhouse as much as I could. The one place I had felt the slightest bit comfortable in was the kitchen, and the company of the old ladies. It was them I'd got to know fairly well, and have fond memories of Crystal. She was so bubbly and friendly, and so totally in love with her man. It still seems impossible that she's gone. She's left a huge gap behind. Even now her ghost seems to haunt us. I almost expect her to walk through the door saying it's all been a bad joke.

"Okay," Sam says, clapping her hands. "Are we going to get on with this or what? I know none of us like what we're doing, but the only thing we can do now is to give Crystal the best possible send-off we can. Now, numbers. We got our members, and how many have stayed over from the other chapters?"

Sandy looks like she's doing a quick sum in her head. "Thirty or so."

"Right, so that makes it more than fifty we need to cater for."

"Carmen's mom's arranging the funeral, is she doing anything else?" Sophie's enquires.

Sam sneers. "According to Drum, she doesn't want any of us biker lot there. If she's having a wake we've certainly not been invited."

"Oh come now, she must know we'll want to pay our respects."

Sam shrugs. "I don't think she gives a damn about anyone's feelings, Sophie. She didn't seem to care that her daughter was dead. No, she wants Amy there, but no one else."

"She's not taking Amy," Sandy growls.

We all agree. Amy's relatively settled now, or as well as she can be. She's loved by everyone here, and whatever happens to Heart, this is her home. To me, it seems a strange place to bring up a young child, but even I can see there's not one of these rough bikers who'd do anything to hurt her.

"Come on, let's get our heads together as to what we need and send the prospects out with a list." Sam pulls a piece of paper toward her. Carmen rummages in a drawer and passes her a pen.

Preparing for the funeral is almost as bad as losing Crystal in the first place, opening wounds all over again. And while we, the old ladies are subdued, the men are sombre, and something tells me it's not just that we're preparing a final goodbye. There's more going on, but as women we don't get to know what. Although Slick's said nothing, I've developed a sneaking suspicion they're expecting trouble at the graveyard. Could it be they believe Crystal's mom will try to take Amy by force? Well, with all of them there she won't have a chance.

Slick's cleaning his weapons, and I've caught Blade sharpening his knives and others checking ammunition. The clubroom's been turned into a war room. There's whispering in corners and conversations ending abruptly when any of us old ladies appear.

The night before the funeral Slick seems particularly tense.

I summon up the nerve to ask him. "Are you worried about tomorrow, Slick? Is there anything you can tell me?" I've just made sure Jayden's asleep and have moved across into Slick's room, as has become our custom.

By the way his back straightens, I know my direct question has surprised him. He fixes his gaze upon me and takes a moment to gather his thoughts. "What makes you ask, El?"

Shrugging, I reply, "It would take a deaf and blind man not to know there's something going on around here. Tension's been rising over the past couple of days."

He tugs off his tee, and as usual, the sight of his bare chest and tattoos distract me. Turning my head slightly away, I try to keep my mind on track, but I don't miss his smirk.

"El, darlin', I'd tell you not to worry, but that ain't gonna work, is it?" Closing the gap between us, his hands cup my cheek. He stares into my eyes. "Can't share club business, babe, but I'll tell you this, we're goin' off the compound, and when we do that, we're always prepared."

It's more than that, I know it.

"Will Jayden be safe here, if we all go to the funeral?"

"The prospects are staying here, darlin'. The place will be locked up tight. She'll be fine."

He's saying a lot without telling me anything. *I'm right. They expect the funeral to be disrupted in some way.*

Slick's hands move down, and before I register his intentions my shirt's on the ground and he's undoing my jeans, his actions pushing all other thoughts out of my head. Once I'm naked he carries me to bed and proceeds to make love to me as he's done every night. So gently and carefully, as though I could break. After an hour of Slick's most personal attentions, I'm sated and exhausted and I fall asleep, held tight and close in his strong arms.

The journey to the graveyard takes us through Tucson, and although the reason for us travelling is sad, I smile to myself as I remember the times it was me on the sidelines watching bikers ride past. Now I've got a handsome biker all my own, and I'm the one hugging his waist. I can't help but feel a moment of pride that I'm wearing my old man's patch. Part of me wonders whether there's some girl drinking coffee outside a café, feeling curious about these men riding past.

The Tucson chapter leading the way, bikes thunder behind us, Drum's out in front, Wraith and Peg behind him, the other officers also up ahead. Slick and I are in the middle of the bunch riding behind. It's the first time I've ridden in formation, and I'm awed at the way all the men handle their machines, turning and leaning as one, the gap between each Harley, the ones to the side and those in front, remaining consistent. Tightening my arms around my man I realise how comfortable I feel to be part of this group, my fear of bikers retreating into the distance.

We park up on the road outside the graveyard. Like the other old ladies, I dismount first, then the bikes are backed up and stands kicked down, leaving a neat line of fifty bikes, almost exact equal spacing between them. Slick takes my helmet and safety glasses, putting them into his paniers, then he comes and takes my hand.

It's a quiet group that moves forward, a few muted conversations muttered in hushed tones. None of us forgetting the reason why we're here today. As we approach a freshly dug hole in the ground I bite my lip to prevent myself from crying. It doesn't seem right a woman who found such joy in life is going to have her final resting place there. The world's too cruel to have taken her so young.

Drum and Wraith walk off together and return with tight faces. Drum points to half a dozen of the brothers who disappear for a while, only to return shouldering their burden, a coffin containing the body of a woman that I didn't know very well, but enough to count her as a friend.

My eyes become wet, tears run down my cheeks. Swiping them away, I notice the people following behind the wooden box as it's escorted to the grave. There's the obligatory priest, and who I assume is Crystal's mother, the latter making a token gesture, not wearing black exactly, but a dark coloured cardigan over a flowery dress which has seen better days. Her hair is tidy, pulled back into a bun, and her face looks clean. Two men follow her. I don't know who they are, but the sharp intake of breath from Slick by my side suggests at least one of them is not a welcome addition.

The priest says some words, I don't take much of it in, unable to pull my eyes away from the cheap coffin in front of me. *Is she really inside?* It seems so wrong that she is. Sneaking a peep at Sam, holding Amy in her arms, I notice she's got the little girl's face turned into her chest. Amy is quiet, picking up on our moods, and I hope she doesn't understand what's happening.

Then the coffin is lowered into the ground.

As I watch, Drum hands Crystal's daughter a flower. Sam puts her down and tells Amy to throw it on the coffin. I don't know how Sam's done it, but whatever she's whispering to her is right, as the child looks up, holding tight to Sam's hand, and her little high-pitched voice can be heard clearly in the silence around.

"Mommy's in heaven now." Amy looks up at the prez's ol' lady as if for confirmation.

Sam gets to her knees, and with a serious look, agrees. "Yes, she is, sweetheart."

Her flower thrown as instructed, as quick as she can Amy turns and launches herself back into Sam's arms. Picking her up and turning Amy into her body, cradling her head with the back of her hand, Sam nods at Drum. "I'm going to get her out of here."

I'd been so focused on the child and choked up with emotion, I hadn't noticed the who I'd assumed to be Crystal's step up, one unknown man in a suit by her side, the other, dressed scruffily, is holding back.

"You're not taking her anywhere," the older woman says with a sneer. "You need to give my granddaughter to me now."

The prez places himself in front of Sam, Wraith comes to his side. "Told you before, woman, you're not touchin' one fuckin' hair on her head. Her father left her in our care, and that's where she's gonna stay."

"I'm afraid you've got no choice."

Drum's whole body stiffens as he addresses the suited man. "The fuck you mean? The child stays with us. I can't understand why you're getting involved, Detective Archer. This isn't a police matter."

"I warn you, Drummer, I'm on duty right now. And I'm here to hand you this in my official capacity. Count yourself served." He tries to hand a document over, the prez folds his arms.

"Whatever that," Drum nods at the envelope Archer is holding. "whatever that is, I'm not interested."

"This is a document from the court giving Ms Clyde, Amy Norman's grandmother, emergency legal decision-making authority of the child. Put in terms you'll understand, she's been given custody."

Drum's face has gone red. "And what lies did you tell to get that?"

Archer shrugs. "Some of the men in your club have rap sheets a mile long. With the evidence I produced it wasn't difficult to convince the judge that the child's at risk if she remains with you, or to agree a biker club is no place for such a young girl. He determined that to let her stay with you would seriously endanger her physical, mental, moral, or emotional health." He sounds like he is quoting from a textbook.

"And a twitchin' drug addict is better?" Drum sneers, and addresses himself to Crystal's mom. "You're already jonesing for a fix, ain't yer? You're fuckin' shakin'."

"Just give me the kid." She tries to get around Drummer, but she hasn't a chance.

Leather-clad men move to stand between her and Sam, who's still clutching Amy as though her life depends on it. Slick leaves my side and joins his brothers, making a solid line. Their stance is identical, legs slightly apart, arms held to their sides, hands hovering over their guns.

Archer looks smug. "You can't refuse the order. I'll charge you with kidnapping if you take the child. You'll be breaking the law."

Now it's Drum's turn to shrug. "Won't be the first time. We're takin' her home with us. The club lawyer will be in touch. We'll be contestin' that order, and hopefully will do so in front of a fuckin' judge that you haven't got in your pocket."

In a swift move Archer draws his weapon and points it at the prez. Drum's eyebrows rise at the same time as fifty brothers at his back take out their guns. "Really?"

Crystal's mother grabs the detective's free arm. "Just get the kid, alright." Her eyes look wild, her hair starts unravelling from her bun, and all signs of her attempt at civility disappear. "I want the fuckin' kid." Her voice is shrill. Her eyes flick round to find the other man who'd come with her, but he's taken a step back, nervously watching the bikers.

Archer shakes her off, his look of distaste revealing exactly what he thinks of this woman he's supposed to be representing as a suitable custodian for a three-year-old. He takes a step forward, his gun now pointing straight at Drum's forehead. "*Give me the child,*" he snarls out.

As I hold my breath, Drum looks unperturbed, though a vein pulsing on his forehead betrays his rage.

"I'm not givin' you shit," Drum replies, looking steadily at the detective. "She is goin' nowhere with this fuckin' sorry excuse for a woman."

"I'm warning you, Drummer."

Drum doesn't flinch. "Shoot me. And you'll be dead within seconds."

"You're fucking threatening me now? I'm a police officer."

"Don't give a fuck who you are. And don't doubt I know exactly why you're here, Archer. And the reason why you're so hot to give Amy to her grandmother. Neither of you give a fuck about the child. She's just a commodity to you." He pauses. When he speaks next, I can see the whites of his eyes. "Your game's up, Archer. Don't think for one second we're not onto you."

"Get the kid!" The woman, sounding like a stuck record, is unravelling in front of our eyes.

Archer seems to think for a moment, then steps back and lowers his gun.

"I'll fuckin' shoot him myself!" she screams as she starts to fight him for the weapon. Archer throws her to the ground. She gets up and starts kicking and punching.

Drum makes a sign, and while the detective is trying to evade Crystal's mom's attempts to get his gun, we fade away and get onto the bikes, and Sam briskly gets Amy set up in her seat in the back of the crash truck.

As I get up behind Slick, I see the envelope lying on the ground, being trampled into the mud as the detective tries to restrain the woman who's clawing at him, with her shabby companion standing back, hands in his pocket as though trying to stay out of trouble.

CHAPTER 29

Slick

I've been in touch with the club lawyer. Got fifty witnesses to say the order wasn't properly served," Drum informs us, looking around the table.

Yeah, it's another day, *another* meeting. Fuck knows when this will all die down and I'll be able to get back to doing a full day's work at the shop. Getting so I miss that darn place. Give me a car with a problem to solve any day rather than dealing with all this shit.

"And Crystal's mom, Ms Clyde, wouldn't be counted as a reliable witness in his opinion."

"Are we certain we'd get rejected if we petition for temporary custody?" Wraith seems to wonder aloud.

"Unlikely we'd have any success now that Archer's stepped up and put our members' rap sheets in front of the court. It's obvious to anyone that woman's not capable of lookin' after herself, let alone a kid. But it's only our word that Heart and Crystal entrusted her to us." Drum taps the table. "Have to remind you, boys, Sam and I wouldn't be seen as model parent material. If we prove Susie Clyde isn't suitable, the likelihood is she'll be taken into care. My thinkin' is, we need to keep this far, far away from any fuckin' judge."

"We kill the woman," Beef says, clenching his jaw, offering a permanent solution. "And that strange fucker who's hangin' around with her."

"Yeah, but we'll be the first in the line of fuckin' suspects," Dart counters.

"Drug overdose? Get her some bad shit?" From what I've seen of her, she could even do that herself, a woman as desperate for her next fix as she is.

"At this point I'm not ready to leave anythin' off the fuckin' table. But we'll see how things develop before I sanction that." Drum's looking serious.

"What we need is for Heart to fuckin' wake up." Joker voices the thought that's foremost in all our minds.

Drum jerks his chin in agreement and asks, "Bullet, you and Rock were at the hospital last night. Anything suspicious?"

"No, Prez. But as I told Tongue and Viper when they took over, we should be prepared for anythin'. Makes their case stronger if the father ain't around."

I voice the unthinkable, but as time goes on I think we all must be considering it. "What happens if he doesn't make it?"

"Amy stays with Sam and me. We'll adopt her. Don't know if we can do it legally, but that's what's going to happen. Ain't no question about that."

Unlike other times when the subject's been raised, today there are no protestations that Heart's going to wake up. It's been too long, and it seems I'm not the only one whose hope is slowly slipping away. Instead, there's just a period of silence in which we mourn the absence of our missing brother. Heart's chair sits empty, even the visiting officers preferring to stand rather than purloining his rightful space.

Feeling awkward that I was the one to pose the question, I pull my smokes out and offer them around. Blade's first to waggle his fingers and I roll him one across. Fuck, I'd forgotten how many visitors we have. When the pack's returned I look at it ruefully, noticing I've only one left. Dart winks at me, obviously relieved he hadn't got his out. I flick my lighter and inhale.

Drum narrows his eyes at me as smoke from numerous cigarettes drifts his way. I shrug.

"Now you're all lit up," he starts, and I remember he's probably missing smoking himself. He gave up, what, it must be a couple of years ago? He's got some willpower to be able to resist amongst all the temptation. "Let's move on. I got a call from Herrera earlier today. He wants a meet."

"When, where, and who?" Peg gets straight to the point.

"Me and Slick, as he's met us before, and in the circumstances, you, Peg."

"What circumstances?" The sergeant-at-arms growls suspiciously.

The prez heaves a sigh. "We're meetin' him and what I assume are his lieutenants."

"Fuck! Prez. We walkin' into a trap?" Wraith slams his hand onto the table.

"That's why you're not gonna be there, Wraith. As VP you stay clear."

"I'm not lettin' you go in alone."

Wraith's words are echoed around the table. Fuck, I'm going to literally be putting my head in the lion's den. It's quite possible none of us will be getting out alive.

Drum shrugs. "He's given me assurances." He glances at me. "Slick, I wouldn't be takin' you with me if I wasn't confident he just wants to talk."

"Where?" Peg's not looking happy.

The prez names an abandoned industrial estate, the exact location an old abandoned warehouse.

"I don't fuckin' like it, Prez."

"You don't need to like it, Peg. Just have my back."

Mouse is looking at his laptop. Glancing over I can see he's calling up Google Maps. "It's quite exposed, Drum. You want us to stake it out?"

"I want Tongue there." That's our sniper. Heart was another, but obviously he's out of action. "I'll tell him when he gets back."

"We're still down a sniper." Bullet echoes my thoughts.

"I can do it." A man, Hooper, puts up his hand. He hails from San Diego. Their sergeant-at-arms if I remember right. "Have you got spotters?"

Dollar and Rock put up their hands.

Blade spins the knife in front of him. "I want in on this too, Drum."

"No. He's expectin' three men. I want you and Wraith to be waitin' close by in case of an ambush, but I promised him we wouldn't go in heavy."

"What would be the point of takin' us out?"

"Slick, for fuck's sake. We killed two of his grandsons."

Yeah, okay. We might not have come straight out and admitted it, but a man like Herrera doesn't keep his position if he can't add a couple of twos together and make five. Maybe that was stupid of me.

Drum brushes back his hair. "Look, I don't know how it's gonna go down. Slick, Peg, I can't guarantee what we're walkin' into, but I don't get the feelin' they want a war. With that show of force the other day, they know we can call on the numbers. If they pull any tricks they know what they'll start. And somehow we need to make contact, start gettin' to know what's going on. He made the approach, we take precautions, but for now I'll take it that it was made in good faith."

When I met Herrera I didn't take to him much, but he was definitely old school. Which leads me to lean toward the thought he'd be straight. Honour among thieves and all that.

Peg pinches the bridge of his nose then looks at Drum. "When?"

"Tonight. Ten pm."

We toss around the logistics, who's going and who'll be staying in case it's a ruse to get us out of the compound. No one's forgetting that tenuous link between Amy and the Herreras. After an hour everyone knows what they're doing and where they need to be to do it. Then we adjourn, and I spend the rest of the day with my girls.

When evening comes Tongue and Hooper leave early with Dollar and Rock. The rest of us are going get ready at eight. We ride into Tucson and directly to the now vacant industrial area, Drum pausing to brief Wraith once more before he, Peg, and I continue on to the warehouse. We're the first to arrive and have plenty of time to scope things out.

At ten precisely we hear the sound of engines. Drum's eyes narrow as he looks at me and Peg. We give serious nods back. *Game on.*

Two men walk in and, as expected, they pat us down for weapons. We're not carrying, having left everything with our bikes. Once they give the okay, Leonardo Herrera enters, another five men following him inside. They stand across from us, their stance unfortunately reminiscent of a firing squad. I notice the first pair have disappeared out the door. Foot soldiers apparently, not privy to the inner circle.

Drum jerks his chin. Peg steps forward and they obligingly stretch out their arms. After taking his time, and nodding at the prez, Peg confirms they're unarmed. Don't mean their men outside aren't carrying, but then, ours are too.

The patriarch steps forward. "Thank you for coming." He's all politeness, but doesn't offer to shake Drum's hand.

Drum jerks his chin in acknowledgement, refraining from replying.

With no time for niceties, Herrera gets straight down to business. "We," he points to himself and then nods over his shoulder at the men standing just behind him, "we are the heads of our family." I notice he doesn't introduce them by name, but their similar Hispanic features suggest they are all related in some way, even if he hadn't introduced them. Three are obviously in his age group, and two from a younger generation.

Leaning on his stick, Herrera clears his throat. "We have an arrangement with Los Zetas. We do not step on their toes, nor they on ours."

The three of us stare back impassively. The information he's given us that they have links with the Mexican cartel was something we already knew. Hell, everyone in Tucson probably does.

He continues, "The skin trade is something in which we do not intervene. And," he pauses, "the grooming of young children for the enjoyment of men with that particular taste is abhorrent to us."

He sounds sincere. I'm still wondering where he is going with this.

"We wish to have both a clean house and clean hands."

My eyes go to Drum. *What exactly does he mean?* Well, Prez is prez for a reason, he's cottoned on fast.

"You wish us to take out the men involved for you," he states, his face still giving nothing away.

"We have come tonight to assure you, if these—men," he spits out the word, "disappear, there will be no blowback on your club."

One man, who in looks and age appears to be Leonardo's brother, perhaps a year or so younger, adds, "We can have no part in this, we can't be directly involved."

Drum looks dubious. "You're agreein' to factions of the Herreras bein' taken out. You're a big fuckin' family. How can you guarantee there won't be retaliation?"

Herrera gives a chuckle, but it doesn't sound like it's in mirth. "It's simple," he tells us, "we point to the cartel. Your men do it clean and quick, no witnesses." He shrugs. "Their contacts will know they've been dabbling in the wrong concerns. We'll make it a warning."

"And the cartel?" Peg can't resist. He'll be considering what danger it could bring to the club if Los Zetas think we're setting them up.

"I'm sure you are clever men. You'll have to do it without anyone knowing."

"I don't understand why you don't want to tidy your own fuckin' house?" Drum's brow creases, his steely gaze never wavering.

"We can't be seen disposing of family."

Another of the men behind him coughs. As Herrera turns around they have a silent conversation, which clearly ends up with the man being given permission to speak. "What these factions are doing is profitable. We, the heads of the family, have no desire to continue this trade. But some of our relations might be tempted to turn a blind eye as to the origin of the income. We wish to avoid argument. As Leonardo has said, all of us here are offended by the material you shared." He actually gives a shudder. "And sickened. It's not something the Herreras want or need to be associated with."

Spurred by his companion, another speaks. "We cannot take the risk that it would be openly debated. At the moment what's happening is under the radar, but if the cartel knew we'd broken our agreement…"

They'd be in deep shit. I finish his sentence in my head.

"The money," Herrera decides to take over again, "may be sufficient that some elements of the family would want to take the risk and continue. We wish to give them no choice."

"So the Satan's Devils take out your dirty washin', and are first in line for any possible comeback."

"I have faith in you, Drummer. I'm sure it won't come to that. You'll have what you want, an end to this despicable business, and we won't be attracting the wrath of the cartel. A win all around, I'd say."

"This puts a big fuckin' risk on my members. I'll have to take it to the table for a vote." Unlike the Herreras, who're obviously playing their cards close to their chests.

"Of course, Drummer. And to speed things along…" He nods behind him and one of the men very carefully pulls something out of his jacket pocket. Stepping forward he hands it to the prez. It's easy to see it's a USB key. As Drum takes it, holding it between finger and thumb with all the enthusiasm of picking up a poisonous snake, Herrera nods toward it. "The names are there. And their addresses."

For the first time something which resembles a flicker of regret crosses his face, and as he walks past me, heavily leaning on his cane, he seemed to have aged in the last few minutes. Well, he has just signed a death warrant on members of his family.

The rest of his lieutenants follow him out.

Peg and I gather around Drum, all of us rendered speechless. Eventually Drum pockets the small device he's still holding.

"Well, fuck me," he says. "I did not expect that."

I doubt any of us did.

"Seems like we've become assassins for the Herreras," Peg observes. "And unpaid ones, too."

"We do get our reward," Drum comments sagely with a raised chin toward me. "Your girl's sister will be safe."

"And our streets will be cleaner."

"That too, Slick. That too."

"I still don't fuckin' like it," Peg grumbles.

CHAPTER 30
Ella

The way Jayden's been behaving this morning is making me rethink the idea of having children of my own. First, she was bemoaning that she wasn't allowed to go to the funeral yesterday, though fuck knows why, she didn't even know Crystal. Next, she was complaining that I'd pulled her away from the wake too early and, of course, that I hadn't let her go to the afterparty, which I'd been certain would have turned X-rated pretty damn fast. Then it was that she'd been left on her own, which was rubbish, as I've been here all the time, but I, apparently, am a nobody and don't count. And while I was out yesterday afternoon, Road had been assigned to keep her company as well as to keep her safe. And then she's going on about why isn't she allowed to see Paladin? And then she starts with why was he such a bastard to go off with a whore? *Honestly*.

She wants out of the compound, and while I have every sympathy with her wishes, I try to explain *again* why she needs to stay hidden for now. But apparently, even being captured and possibly tortured would be "better than this". I know she's been through a terrible ordeal, one that's the root cause of her being so temperamental, but nevertheless, my patience is fast running out. By the time Slick returned late last night I was at my wits end. I'm afraid he bore the brunt of it. We still slept together, but didn't make love. This morning he left before I was awake.

Now I'm both worried about Jayden, and that I took it out on my man.

When I tell my sister I'm going to the clubhouse to get something to eat she sullenly replies she's staying in bed. Throwing up my hands, realising the new morning's brought no better mood, I open the door to leave the suite, bumping into Paladin, who's got his hand raised in the air to knock.

My eyes immediately narrow. *What does he want?*

Without me voicing my question, he answers it. "Ella, I've come to see Jayden. There's some things I'd like to get straight. I've been givin' it a lot of thought."

He's not seeing her on his own. "I don't want you talking to Jayden without me there."

"Fair enough." He nods. "I know I've gone about this all wrong. Can I speak to her?"

I consider his request. As long as I'm there to chaperone there shouldn't be an issue. And seeing him might just cheer her up. I'd try just about anything at this point. "Alright."

Paladin follows me back into the suite, and I call out to make sure Jayden's decent.

"Paladin!" Twin expressions of delight and dismay alternate across her face. But she sits up in bed and starts taking an interest.

Stepping inside, the young biker smiles. "I've come to talk to you, Jayden."

She gives him a 'duh' look, and then her eyes flick to me.

"I'm staying here," I tell her.

She's about to protest when Paladin pulls up a chair to the side of the bed and takes hold of her hand, effectively switching her attention from me to him. "Jayden," he starts, then swallows a few times. "I like ya, girl, you know that."

She gives a little nod and gives an eager encouraging smile. What he says next makes me warm to him.

"What happened to ya, Jayden, that was… Fuck it. You were taken advantage of, and whatever they made you believe, you were plied with alcohol and drugs and didn't have a clear head." As she goes to speak he covers her mouth with his hand. "Shush. Hear me out, okay?" When she dips her head he continues, "Jayden, as far as I'm concerned, you're a virgin. No one's ever made love to you the way you deserve."

My eyes fill with tears as I listen to his words. It's exactly the right thing to say.

She frowns, and says with a pout, "But I'm not a virgin. I know what sex is. I want what you said, to find out what it should be like." Her face goes red, obviously embarrassed he's being so frank.

"You've got to put it behind you, babe. You can't pretend it never happened, but you need to move on and get back the time and innocence that was stolen from ya. You've got a few years yet before you need to worry about bein' with a man."

It's clear she sees what he says as rejection. Quickly she pulls her hand away from his and covers her eyes. "You don't want me. You want that whore…"

"Not what I'm sayin' at all, babe. Please listen to me. Hear me out, okay?"

Lowering her fingers, she watches him.

"What I'm sayin' is I can't want you. Not legally. And it wouldn't be right. When you're ready you should meet boys your own age, go out on dates, hold hands, kiss."

She says with a snarl, "I think I've gone past that."

As I smother a gasp he continues to be patient with her. "You might think you have, but you haven't, Jayden. You can get your life back. Ella here will help you, and so will I."

"You?"

"Yeah, by being your friend. But that's all I can be for another few years."

"Another few years isn't going to make my hymen grow back!" Her cheeks glow red. "I'm not an innocent teenager, Paladin. I shouldn't have to wait!"

At the crudeness of her attack I go to open my mouth, but again he gets in before me. "The years will go fast, Jayden, love. This will be in your rearview, and you can start all over again. Discover what it should be like with a man of your choice, and one who cares just for you." He gives her an intense look. "If I'm lucky enough, when you're eighteen, I'd be honoured to be your first."

Will he? I might have something to say about that. But I'll keep my mouth shut for now.

"And in the meantime, you'll fuck the whores?" This she spits out.

He shakes his head. "Didn't fuck one the other evenin'."

"You walked off with that girl!"

He looks down at his hands. "Fuck knows what I was doin', Jayden. Nothin' happened, I swear. Prez told me to make it look like I did. He thought I was gettin' too close to ya. But hell, I don't think that's the right way about it." He pauses, and then looks straight at my sister. "That's why I'm here explainin' things. Look Jayden, I don't know if I can be faithful, hell, you might find you prefer someone else. But for now, I ain't particularly interested in what the whores have to offer." His face twists. "I'm a man, babe. All I can promise is, if I can't shake the urge, I won't rub it in your face."

"You won't wait for me." Of course she latches onto that.

He continues to be patient. "Maybe, maybe not. Maybe it will be you that moves on. But anythin' else would be wrong, Jayden. We can't go there, alright?"

Once more her hands cover her face as she digests what he's said. We both give her some time, and then she lowers her hands and stares in his face. "You think I'm a virgin?"

"I know that you are. Not in the technical sense, but in every other way."

When she sits up and swings her legs off the bed I'm relieved to see she's in a perfectly respectable tank and shorts. Resting her elbows on her knees, she interlocks her fingers and rests her chin on her hands. We give her a moment. I see Paladin's hands clench and unclench, his jaw is tightened but he's holding himself in check. I'm biting my tongue so I don't say the wrong thing. Paladin's getting through to her, where I had failed.

"I was flattered in the beginning, you know? Stupid looking back." She bites back a sob. "And then I couldn't get out, not with them threatening my mom and Ella."

Paladin reaches out and places his fingers gently under her chin. "He was a monster, Jayden, preyin' on young girls."

She thinks for a bit longer. "I've never had a 'first time', have I? Not in the right way."

"That's my point. But you will, Jayden, when the time's right."

"With you?" she asks, hopefully.

"I'll be hangin' onto that idea. Four years ain't that long a time."

"Three years and eight months."

He grins at her correction. "In the meantime, we'll be friends?" He holds out his bunched hand and waits. After a brief hesitation, she bumps it with her small fist.

"Friends."

Paladin glances up at me. I feel like giving him, them both, a hug, but refrain. Already Jayden looks more content and relaxed. Perhaps I will consider having children after all.

Jayden jumps to her feet, showing more enthusiasm than she had earlier. "I'm hungry. Can you give me a minute to change and then we'll go have something to eat?"

I just about manage to not roll my eyes. "Sure, Jayden."

"I'll meet you down there." Paladin gets up, leans over and places a chaste kiss to her forehead. "See you in a few, babe." And with that parting shot, and a nod toward me, he leaves.

As I wait for my sister to do her stuff in the bathroom, my stomach growls, and I wish she'd hurry up. I swear she takes longer than I do. When I'm on the verge of banging on the door and asking what the hell she's doing in there, she comes out. She looks brighter than she has in days. That talk with Paladin seems to have lifted a weight off her shoulders.

Arm in arm, we walk down to the clubhouse. Apart from a prospect tidying up, no men are around, but in the kitchen Carmen's standing, peering into the fridge.

She glances around as we walk in. "Why, aren't you the sight for sore eyes?" She smiles at Jayden, seeming to notice the change in her too. "You two hungry? I'm just getting a sandwich for myself.

"Sure, that sounds great." I go over to help.

Our stomachs filled, I hear the men wandering out, realising they must have been in one of their meetings. As the voices grow louder, I realise I'm still feeling relaxed, when once the sound would have had my heart racing. *I'm getting used to this place.*

Paladin is the first to appear. He crosses over to Jayden, who's leaning on the counter next to the sink. "You're lookin' better."

And the fact it's down to him makes me beam. They start up an innocent conversation about new music they've heard, and I let their discussion wash over me as I drink my second cup of coffee. I'm at one end of the room, so have my eyes on the youngsters and able to see the through the doorway. I can't miss Drummer as he approaches, his face going thunderous as he's just in time to see them bump hips to celebrate a band or something they have a liking for in common.

Rage beams out of his steely eyes and his fists are clenching.

Oh no.

I jump to my feet and rush over to him. When I'm close enough I put my hand on his chest to stop his forward momentum, feeling his hard muscles flexing through the thin material of his tee.

What am I doing? I'm trying to stop a huge biker who's vibrating with anger.

He looks down at my hand, and then at me. His eyes look as cold as ice. "Got somethin' to say, Ella?"

From somewhere I summon the courage. "Yes," I hiss, tapping his chest to indicate I want him to move backwards. I jerk my head at the pair behind me. "This isn't what it seems."

He could push past me so easily, but one side of his mouth turns up. It's ridiculous to think I could stop him doing anything, but my desire to prevent my sister being upset over-comes my fear. When he gives me a quick nod and steps back into the clubroom I sigh with relief. When I've got his attention I give him a rundown of what's gone on today.

"You trust Paladin?"

"Yeah. Out of everyone, he's got through to her, Drummer. The things he said... He showed he's got an old head on those young shoulders. Let them be friends, Jayden needs that."

He brushes his hair back with both hands, staring into my face. "Well, fuck me. Thought I was gonna have to give him a beat down. Lad's done good it seems. I'll lay off him for now. But Ella, the moment he crosses the line..."

"I'll be killing him myself."

A laugh bursts out of him, and my mouth quirks as I realise what I've just said.

"Everythin' alright over here?"

"Yeah, Slick. Ella's got everythin' under control." The corners of his mouth turn up and I realise Drummer's giving his approximation of a smile. "You've got a damn fine woman here, Brother."

Slick pulls me into his side. "Know that, Drum."

As I lean into his comfort, my adrenaline rush fading, I notice the door to the clubhouse opening, and Sandy and Sam are coming in.

"Drum wants to talk to you women," Slick tells me.

"What? Why?" The prez is polite enough, but doesn't usually go out of his way to talk to us old ladies.

But Slick doesn't enlighten me, just takes my hand and starts leading me into their meeting room.

"You're letting us in here?" My eyes open wide as I see the large table and comfortable chairs where the brothers would sit. There's pictures on the walls of members I don't recognise. And when I see Adam's I realise they must be the ones who have passed.

Slick leads me to a seat and sits down beside me. The other old ladies filter in, Sandy's accompanied by Viper, and Carmen with Bullet. Sam takes a place next to her old man. Lastly, Wraith comes in leading Sophie by the hand.

"To what do we owe this honour, Drum?" Sam relaxes back in her chair and raises an eyebrow. Her easy manner helps ease some of the tension in the room. This isn't normal, and looking around, I'm not the only one to feel confused and decidedly out of place in this male-oriented room.

"We've just agreed somethin' in our meetin' that concerns you ladies." Drum pauses, and his gaze lands on each of us in turn. "You were at the funeral so already know. Yesterday the fuckin' heat tried to serve me with a custody order for Amy."

We nod. Carmen swears, "Fucking cops interfering. Anyone could see that woman's not fit to raise a child."

Sam's face has gone tense. It's easy to see how much she cares for Amy. She couldn't be doing more for her if she was her own flesh and blood. "She's not taking her, Drum."

The prez lays his hand over hers and turns to face her. "No worries, darlin'. She's stayin' with you."

"Us," she corrects, her head tilting to the side.

"That's what we've got to talk about." He takes a deep breath. "Now they've got the custody order and they might come to try to take her, we're bettin' Archer will come with a fuckin' search warrant next, so we're plannin' on gettin' you, Sam, and Amy out of here for a while."

Sam's head goes back and her eyes widen. She's as much in the dark as the rest of us.

"And you, Ella," Drum jerks his chin toward me, "if the police come search the club, Jayden needs to be kept out of sight too."

I give a slow nod, he's answered the question I was going to ask.

"Now you ladies know we don't share club business, but we've been thinkin' it's best if Ella, Jayden, Carmen, Sophie, and Sandy, are off the compound too."

The three old ladies named last look surprised now. Carmen opens her mouth then snaps it shut again, realising Drum won't be divulging the reason, however much we plead.

"Where we going, Drum?" His old lady's accepted it, now she just wants the details.

The prez looks at Sam, and then winks at Sophie and smirks as he replies, "To Vegas. Red's chapter."

"*Vegas?* Really? We're going to Las Vegas?" Sophie's eyes light up, and she's all but bouncing in her seat. Then her face falls. "Will we be on lockdown there?"

Wraith laughs. "Want to get out and see the bright lights?"

"Yeah, I've always wanted to go to the strip." She looks excited and hopeful as her eyes silently plead with her old man. Her smile's infectious. Vegas sounds like it could be fun. And a break is just what Jayden needs If we're allowed to go out.

"We do this right and no one knows where you've gone. I reckon we can relax things a bit. Let you out on the town."

Us women look at each other, and then back to Drum. From the expressions on all our faces I reckon all the women are thinking the same thing. It could be like going on vacation. Then it hits me. It's not just Vegas we're going to, but another biker club.

Slick understands when I still, and squeezes my hand. "Red's a good man, Ella. And the brothers in Vegas are just like the brothers here. They'll respect that you're mine and won't lay a finger on you."

"Same goes for everyone," Wraith agrees. "Red knows the score. He'll keep you safe, and if you want to paint the town red," he gives a quick laugh at his unintended pun, "he'll make sure you have good brothers with you."

"How long? I've got my business."

"I hope only a few days, Carmen. When it's safe you come straight back."

"The restaurant?"

"Marsha can handle it, can't she?" Wraith waits for Sandy's nod.

Sophie's narrowing her eyes. "If you're keeping the women safe and out of the way, what about the sweet butts? Will they be coming too?" If the answer is yes, it doesn't look like she'll be happy about it.

Drum and Wraith appear to be having a conversation, but no words are spoken, just a few uninterpretable grunts and chin lifts. *How do they do that?* After a moment, the prez gives his assent with a nod.

"Yeah, we'll get all women off the compound. They can provide their services to the Vegas boys for a while."

Wraith puts his arm around Sophie. "They won't bother you, darlin'. Red will put them to work."

The casual way they're talking about loaning out their whores chills me. I feel a moment of sympathy for the girls, but it's only fleeting. They like and want this life, though I've no idea how they can do it. I shudder.

"Whores might like the change."

Sandy nudges her old man. "And what are you going to do with no whores and no old ladies?"

That Viper gets blow jobs from the sweet butts is no secret, but that doesn't stop his face going red, and everyone laughs.

"When we leaving, Drummer?" Sam asks the practical question.

"Tomorrow. So make what arrangements you have to and take enough stuff for a few days. If you need to get more, you can buy it in Vegas."

And I'm not the only one whose eyes light up at the thought of shopping in the city that never sleeps.

CHAPTER 31
Slick

The women have taken their enforced sojourn off the compound surprisingly well, but of course, knowing the destination had done much to smooth the way. We'd had considered an alternative option. Snake had offered for them to go to San Diego, although that was quickly dismissed. The Cali chapter has indeed redeemed itself lately, but none of us can forget, or forgive them for offloading Buster on us, and there's a lingering fear in the back of our minds that they might not treat their women as well as we do.

Yeah, Red is a much better choice. Wraith knows him well and that he runs a tight ship. Joker and Lady, who'd patched over from Vegas, had given us a rundown of their brothers there too, and vouched that they'd be hands-off the old ladies. Perhaps not so much the sweet butts, but then, that's their job.

Vegas seems to sound attractive to the girls, and I make a mental note to give Ella some money so she can enjoy herself while she's there. It could be the break and a change of scenery that both she and her sister need. Maybe when all this is over we'll stay on for a bit in one of the fancy hotels. Hmm, that's an idea.

If it wasn't for the fucking Herreras we wouldn't be having to send them away. While I might trust Red and his crew, I'd rather have my girls close and protect them myself. But the meeting last night and the bizarre request from Leonardo had unsettled us all. Essentially, it seems we've been employed as a hit squad to take out rogue members of their family. An assassin for a crime family? Never could have seen myself being that.

As well as planning how we're going to take the Herrera men out, we also have to prepare on the assumption that the whole thing's a sham. Brothers were vocal around the table, many convinced it was a set up. The likelihood of a police raid on the compound combined with the possibility that the Herrera's want to catch us wrongfooted had led to the unanimous vote in favour of moving the women and Amy away from Tucson. If we had a fight coming to us, we'd breathe easier if we didn't have to watch our old ladies as well as our backs. The plain truth of the matter is none of us know who we can trust. The idea that Leonardo is using us to take out the trash, and then set the cartel on us to enact revenge cannot be dismissed. While the Satan's Devils and Herreras have jogged along well enough up to now, keeping our businesses separate, we're still the second power in Tucson. It might be a way for him to get us out of the way. On the other hand, there are indications he's told us the truth—the names on the USB key had matched those given to us by Diego. The additional information, their addresses, will save us time trying to find them. Although Mouse has been digging, all their properties are in the names of corporations.

While we kept it upbeat with the women around, all brothers are aware that this is one fight where we might not be coming back. But, fuck, we knew the risks when we entered this life. The most we can do is ensure our loved ones are safe.

I might not be able to tell Ella why she has to go, but knowing she'll be worried about staying in yet another biker club—fuck, she's only just becoming more comfortable here—I try to give her the reassurance that she'll be safe. Personally I have no worries on that score, especially after I saw her taking on Drum. Fuck me, that was a sight I hadn't expected to see.

She'd been like a mama bear protecting her cub when she'd seen him advancing on Paladin and her sister. The spark I originally saw in her is starting to come back. Yeah, she might not appreciate it yet, but I reckon she's going to be just fine.

But I'm still worries, she's only just starting to fit in here and now I'm sending her away.

And in the meantime, I'll be getting paperwork sorted. The club lawyer's coming around later, a chance for us all to update our wills, Heart's omission to mention Amy in his a timely reminder that it needs to be done. I'll be changing mine, to ensure Ella's provided for should anything happen to me.

Walking out of the meeting with my hand on the small of her back, I feel the tension radiating through her clothes. Shaking off my sombre mood, I smile, knowing there's a way I can comfort my woman and ease her concerns, and my very willing cock twitches, showing he's entirely in agreement. I give her fair warning, leaning down and whispering in her ear, "Gonna fuck yer babe." As I feel the shiver run through her, and know she's on board, probably thinking like me, we need to make the most of the time we have together before she has to leave.

"I need to check on Jayden." Yeah, she's going to make a great mom, her first thought is always for the youngster in her care.

I glance around the clubroom, seeing her sister and Paladin in the small area off to one side that holds the pool table. Nudging Ella in that direction, we wander on over. Paladin and Jayden are standing, leaning with their backs against the wall.

"What are you two up to?"

"Waiting to play pool," Jayden replies to her sister with a grin.

"Waitin'?" I can't see anyone else playing.

Paladin can't stifle his laugh. "Yeah, soon as Hyde's finished we can start."

Now I see what I hadn't noticed before—Hyde's crouched on the floor with a bucket, carefully washing the balls with a sponge. He's got a cloth beside him, and each one he polishes carefully as he dries it off.

I give a chuckle. "Really, Paladin?"

From the look he gives me, he's unrepentant. Hell, let him have his fun. When he was a prospect we gave him all kinds of shit jobs.

"Never seen balls cleaned before."

Ella's innocent comment has us all cracking up. "You can wash mine anytime you fuckin' like," I whisper, but not quietly.

Jayden's hand covers her mouth. "Ewh," she exclaims. "Too much information, Slick." As she gives another girlish giggle I realise she's not had much enjoyment of late. I throw Paladin a chin jerk.

Ella's gone bright red and seems incapable of speaking. "Jayden, we're going on up to the suite for a bit."

"I'm happy down here. I'll give you some time."

"Jayden, we're not…"

"Ella, I'm not stupid." She laughs at her sister. "Just let me know when it's safe to come back."

And at last I get my embarrassed as hell woman to myself. Or, then again…

"Hang on, Slick." Ella's holding me back. "Jayden, guess what? We're going to Vegas! Us and the other women. What do you think about that?"

Jayden's mouth drops open and it takes her a moment to process the news. Then she squeals. "When?" She's jumping up and down with excitement just like the kid she is. The sight doing some to ease my frustration at the delay.

Ella shares the details she knows and we leave Jayden with eyes bright and glowing, and regaling poor Paladin all the things she wants to do while she's there. Poor lad isn't quite sure what to do with an over-enthusiastic teenager. Throwing him a sympathetic grin, I lead Ella away.

And, finally, I have my old lady to myself.

Knowing I'm going to miss her like fuck, I'm determined to make good use of this time when the whole bloc is empty and I won't have to smother her cries. Fuck, I'm planning on making her scream so loud they'll hear her down at the clubhouse. Yeah, I'm going to give my lady some good loving. And then I'll do it all over again tonight. Any plans she's got about going out on the town in Vegas will need to be put on hold until she can walk properly again. Hmm, that will be my fucking send off.

I'm grinning like a loon as we walk out into the sun. She snuggles into my side, her hand wandering under my tee. Any worries about going to another chapter seem to have dissipated some with the delight of her sister and, hopefully, the promise of what she's got coming.

As we walk into my room she turns toward me and lifts her face. I don't disappoint, my lips come down and meet hers, taking her mouth in a ravishing kiss. My tongue swirls with hers, but as always, trying to be gentle, wary, and unwilling to come on too strong and scare her or push her away.

We undress each other, both equally eager to dispense with our clothes, and naked we fall onto the bed. I twist so I'm on the bottom, taking her weight on mine. She sits up and looks at me boldly, her small hand tries to encircle my thick dick. Lifting my head, the erotic sight has the predictable reaction as my cock swells and jumps under her touch.

"Hmm," she says cheekily, her eyes on mine. Then as she glances down, seeming to take delight in the way he stirs in her hand, "I love my biker's cock."

"Just a cock darlin', ain't no biker makin' love to you. Just me."

Her eyes narrow, and her head tilts to the side. "What do you mean, Slick?"

I sit up, my hand curls around the back of her neck, and I bring her head forward so I can kiss her again.

"We make love," I explain. "I don't fuck you. I don't need to." At her look of concern, I hastily reassure her, "I'm your man."

She's quiet for a moment and is biting her lip. After a few seconds, something flares in her eyes as realisation sets in. "You've been holding yourself back?"

"Yeah, but ain't no fuckin' problem, babe, so don't worry your little head about it. Makin' love with you is fuckin' out of this world. I don't want, or need, anythin' else."

Her teeth worry the rim of her mouth again, and I wish I knew what was going through her head. After staring at me for a few seconds, she swallows. "What if I wanted you too?"

"Wanted what?" *Is she saying what I think she is?*

A slight hesitation, then, "What if I want you to fuck me like a biker?"

Fuck! She doesn't know what she's asking for. To ask me to fuck her the way I like to fuck? Hell. *To let loose my inner beast?* "You're not ready for that," I reply through gritted teeth. *Fuck, but she's tempting me.*

"If I'm not now, I'll never be." Suddenly she shoots her arms out to the sides causing her breasts to jut out. She leans back her head and grins wider. "Take me Slick, I'm yours."

Fuckedy fuckedy FUCK! Oh yeah. Still trying to restrain myself, I look for the signs that show she really wants this and is not simply trying to give me what she's not ready for yet. Her eyes are wide and her nostrils are flaring. Her chest's rising and falling faster than normal, there's a pink flush to her skin, and every breath I take in is tinged with the scent of her arousal. Yup. She's glowing with excitement, and there's nothing to suggest fear. *Fuck!*

Giving a wicked smile, I ask, "You wet for me, darlin'?" As she dips her head I continue, "Show me."

Jesus! Without needing any more prompting, she slides her fingers through her slit and raises her slick fingers as though in an offering. I grab her hand and bring it to my mouth, sucking her salty tangy essence onto my tongue. Her flavour on my taste buds has my cock weeping. The grin on her face broadens.

It's like she's challenged me, and I'm going to pick up that damn gauntlet. Normally keeping my movements slow and gentle, this time I shoot out my arm, grabbing her hair and twisting my fingers in the strands. I bring her head down and onto my cock.

"Suck me," I demand.

I'm monitoring her so carefully, if she makes any protest I'll let her up, not wanting to force her, but fuck, her mouth takes me in and she's sucking and laving. I push her down harder, and she takes more of me in. I let her up when she gags, ready to stop, but she's pulling against me, moving her head down until she can take me in once again.

Her mouth feels wonderful, so different from the whores. She learns fast by my reactions, my gasp as she licks the sensitive part under the head has her going back and finding that place once again. Now her tongue's found my piercing and she's toying with that.

My hands jerk and push her down, an unconscious reaction, which makes her gag once again. As I use her hair to pull her away ready to call a halt to something she's finding uncomfortable, but fuck me, she gasps out, "I don't know what to do, Slick."

"Breathe through your nose," I rasp back. If my woman wants instruction I'm all for complying.

And fuck, she tries my suggestion. Taking me in as far as she can, her hands massaging my balls. *Fuck, shit.* I can't take much more. "Wanna come inside you, babe." *If she doesn't stop right now...*

I twist her hair and she stops. Now I take hold of her, lifting then roughly slamming her down on her back. And fuck me, *she laughs.* I grab a condom and sheave myself fast, then forcefully pull her legs up, putting them over my shoulders. As my body leans forward she's totally exposed. Glancing down I see her slit's ready and weeping.

Precum dripping from my slit, I can't wait any longer. Placing my tip to her hole, I push inside her, bottoming out in one thrust. Her gasp of delight is all the encouragement I need to let myself go. Powering from my hips I hammer inside her, my piercing hitting her sweet spot every single time.

There it is. She's screaming my name.

"Slick, Slick. Oh my God, *Slick!* Slick! Don't stop."

I have absolutely zero intention of doing so. *Holy Christ she feels fantastic.* I lean my weight on one elbow, moving one leg so my body twists and I can get deeper. She sucks in air and there's my name again. Another loud cry.

I tweak one of her nipples, and then the other. She thrusts her breasts toward me so I pinch harder, rolling each nipple between my finger.

"Slick, God, Slick!"

Continuing to jack hammer inside her, I fuck my woman until I'm just God as she screams out, "God, *God!*" and her body goes rigid. Her muscles tighten around me as she stops breathing and holds in her breath. And now she's spasming, and *oh fuck* what her muscles are doing to my cock. Quickly reaching my hand down I squeeze the base tightly, willing myself to stop from shooting my load too quickly. I'm not finished yet.

I slide out and turn her over, pulling up her hips so she's face down on the bed. Without wasting a second I plunge back inside her. She cries out in amazement as I push through her now swollen folds.

Now it's back to Slick, and I have aspirations to be a deity again. I put one arm around her chest and pull her to me as I sit back on my heels. She's on my lap, my cock as deep as possible inside her, her back tight against my chest.

I start pulverising that sweet pussy, my hips working like pistons, jerking up inside her, nailing that sweet spot with my piercing over and over again.

Her cries are almost continuous. *Yeah baby, let everyone know I'm fucking my woman.*

My movements are automatic, my fingers pinch her nipple, then with my free hand I encircle her neck before I realise what I'm doing. But fuck me, her muscles squeeze my cock harder in response so I apply a little more pressure, just to show her who's in control, not to restrict her airways.

With her pulsating cunt I've got little chance. But fuck, she's with me, those tell-tale signals she's coming again. I try to hold off, and thank fuck I'm God all over again as she screams her release, her cunt squeezing and releasing as waves of ecstasy roll through her.

I don't have a chance. I let go, flooding the condom, my hips bucking as I give her all I've fucking got.

Gradually my arms relax my hold and she collapses face down on the bed. Slipping out gently, holding the condom in place until I'm out, then tie it and chuck it in the trashcan. Manoeuvring us both, I lie down beside her, pulling her into my arms. She's breathing fast as though she's run a marathon, and my lungs are heaving in time. Fuck, I can't remember a time when it's ever been so good. The things I did...

Yeah, the way I'd held her, used her... "Ella, are you alright?"

Her breathe hitches as she answers, "Alright?"

I try to read something into that one word. Nervously I ask, "Did I hurt you? Scare you?" Fuck, I got carried away.

She turns over to face me, placing her hand to one side of my face. Her skin's shining with sweat, her cheek's reddened with effort. "I think you darn near killed me, Slick."

I'm still uncertain. "Are you okay?"

"Okay? O-fucking-kay?" She chuckles, and her eyes twinkle. "You can give me biker loving anytime you like, Slick. Wow."

I roll my head back as I sigh with relief. "You know," I start, looking at her once again, "I was going to give you spendin' money to take to Vegas." Her brow creases and her eyes narrow as I continue, "But now I don't think I'll bother."

"What are you talking about?" Confused she gives a little shake of her head.

"Another few bouts like that darlin', and you'll be unable to walk for days. It would be a waste as you won't be able to go out."

She pushes me and I roll onto my back, then she sprawls on top of me. "Oh yeah? Can you keep your promises, biker?"

Oh fuck yeah. Just watch me babe.

I run my fingers through her hair—it's grown a bit, still jagged at the ends though, and just touches her shoulders. I remember how long it was when I'd first met her. Idly stroking the strands I ask, "You gonna grow your hair back long again babe?"

She shudders, her mirth disappearing and a heaviness comes over her as she gives me the chilling explanation. "No, Slick. Never. They... They pulled my hair and used it to control me."

Oh fuck. And I'd been dreaming of doing exactly that.

"Shit babe." I tug her into me and hold her close, hoping I haven't completely destroyed the mood. "Babe, keep it as short as you like." And then I kiss her, she begins to respond and, as my dick stirs, I know what to do to wipe all thoughts of the Rock Demons out of her head.

CHAPTER 32

Ella

As the crash truck draws up to the clubhouse I bend to reach for the bag at my feet, giving a little wince as I do. Slick smirks and gets to it before I can. I punch him on the arm.

"Shut it," I growl, but there's a smile in my eyes. He'd made good on his promise and muscles I didn't even know I had are certainly making their presence known today. It's a glorious feeling, a reminder of last night, which is sure to stay with me all day.

"Listen up." Drummer steps out of the clubroom and gets our attention. "Right, ladies. Sophie, Sandy and Carmen, you'll be ridin' up behind your men. Ella, you, Jayden, and Sam will be in the back of the truck with Amy. Bit of a squash I know, especially with the child seat, but it's important no one sees you leave. Once you get out of our territory you can stop and someone can go in the front. No one will think twice about a prospect drivin' the crash truck and followin' the bikes."

"Jayden can sit on my lap, no problem." I'm not going to protest a bit of discomfort if it's going to keep us safe."

"What about the sweet butts?" Carmen asks, her mouth twisting.

"They'll travel tomorrow."

I'd ask why, but I don't particularly care, just feeling relieved Jill won't be coming with us.

Slick's worked so hard at keeping my mind and body occupied, that it only just dawns on me when Drummer starts indicating it's time to get going, what this might mean. Getting all the women off the compound can only indicate one thing, they're expecting serious trouble. Trouble my man is going to be right in the midst of. Grabbing hold of Slick's leather I stand on tiptoe and curl my hand around the back of his head. As our lips press together I kiss my man as though I'm never going to see him again.

"Hey, you'll see me at rest stops, and I'll be stayin' overnight. No need to say goodbye just yet, darlin'" But his hands linger on the side of my face, and his eyes flare with emotion.

But yes, he's coming too. Along with Blade and Dart and Joker as Road Captain, making it look like a standard run to visit another chapter. Drummer and Peg will be staying at the compound. I'm happier knowing that Slick will be there to at least get me settled in the Vegas club, as there's still a big part of me that's nervous about meeting new bikers. At least he found a way to stop me worrying about it last night. By the time he'd finished showing me just what he can do with his biker cock I was too exhausted to do anything but sleep.

But in the cold light of day I start feeling guilty, knowing Jayden and I are somehow at the heart of what's ahead, something so dangerous they're shipping out the old ladies and disrupting their lives. As Slick holds my hand until I'm settled in the truck, I can't help fearing what might happen, that maybe I won't be able to come back, or that something will happen to Slick. The compound has slowly started to feel like home, and the thought that this could be the last time I'm here with my man is sobering. But the way it's all been organised, like a well-oiled machine, I know there's no point in me protesting. I have to go along with what they've got planned.

There's no lingering now that we're ready to get going. The gates slide open and the crash truck follows the bikers out.

Four hundred miles is a long way for the old ladies who are riding. Even with numerous stop offs they walk around with stiff bums. We're not much better off, being confined to the truck unless it's to nip out for an unavoidable visit to the restrooms. They take every precaution to make sure we're not seen. At one stop a patrol car pulls in, and Sam covers Amy as Jayden and I sink down to the floor. It pulls out without giving us a second look. But each mile we travel makes detection less likely, and our spirits rise. At last, early in the evening, we arrive at the Vegas chapter's clubhouse.

To my disappointment, it's out of the city, on the edge of the desert that looks brown and dry without the vegetation and cacti of that surrounding the Tucson club. I suppose it was naïve of me to have visions of their base being within walking distance of the strip with its over-the-top hotels and gaudy light displays. Like Jayden, when I'm able to put my worries to the back of my mind I'm quite excited, hoping it won't be long before we'll be able to get out and see the famous fountains at the Bellagio. Oh, and I want to go to the Venetian as well, and Sophie wants to have a gondola ride. That sounds fun. There's so much to do and see. And then my mood changes again when we arrive at our new temporary home.

The compound is protected by ten-foot-high steel gates and, as they slide open my stomach drops as I see what looks like a warehouse in front of the truck, masses of bikes parked to one side. As Wraith and the men position theirs in line, the truck waits and then pulls into a space alongside. While realising how spoiled the Tucson chapter is with their amazing and unusual setting, I hadn't expected the Vegas clubhouse to be so different and, unfortunately, there's much similarity between this place and the Rock Demons' club.

As I stare at the building that looks frightening familiar, causing memories to slam into my head, Slick comes to help me out of the truck. When he takes my bag in his hand I hold back in reluctance.

He urges me forward, glancing down with a furrowed brow. "Hey, you okay, Ella?"

"It's like…"

"No, it's not," he says firmly, quickly realising what I mean. "Come on inside. It's not much to look at out here."

As he puts his arm around me I tug the sides of my cut together, hoping it will be sufficient to protect me from what I expect to find when I take a step through the entrance and let him lead me on over. I'm holding my breath as we walk through the door…

And into a brightly lit large area which I can immediately see is clean and welcoming. A couple of, who I assume to be, old ladies are laying out food on tables, and there's not a scantily clad woman in sight. Red, the president, who I remember meeting at the Tucson compound, is stepping forward and enveloping Wraith in a bear hug. He then lifts Sophie and swings her around, giving her a smacker on her cheek, before setting her back carefully on her feet.

Wraith growls, then laughs.

Red next greets the men with us, and then turns to us females. "Ladies, welcome." He indicates the women, who come over, one with a bowl of salad still in her hands. "I'll get the introductions started. This is Rosa." He puts his arm around an older woman. "She's the mother hen here and keeps us all in line."

Rosa tosses him a quick look of disbelief and gives us a wide smile.

"And this is Tiffany, she's Fox's ol' lady." As I return her nod I wonder why he didn't say who Rosa's old man was.

Sam starts the round of saying who we all are. The men drift off, following Red. When I notice Slick's left me, I feel panic rising, but I'm not allowed time for my mind to conjure up fears as Sophie touches my arm and brings me back into the conversation. Soon we're going outside to where grills are grilling, and the two Vegas women start introducing us to the bikers.

Despite my concerns, the men we meet seem polite and respectful, and tolerant of Amy who, fed up with hours in the truck, starts running around. Sam tries to keep hold of her but she might as well be trying to catch a greased monkey. Amy thinks it's a great game and goes running off.

"Leave her be," says a grey-haired biker who'd made known he goes by the highly inappropriate handle of Titch, being closer to seven-foot-tall than six and towering over most of the others. "Out back here is all fenced. She can't go anywhere. And look, she's found Tom and Trist, Rosa's twins. They'll look after her."

Turning my head, I see he's right, and she's now being introduced into a game of baseball with two boys who look about twelve. At my side, Sam sighs with relief.

Jayden tugs at my sleeve. "Want me to keep an eye on Amy?"

It's Sam who answers, "Jayden, yes, please."

I watch my sister, who's soon chatting with the two boys who look slightly younger than her, but probably close enough in age to have things in common.

There's so many men here that apart from Titch, who stands out above the others, I know I'll have difficulty remembering everyone's names. In the end, I give up. The Vegas chapter seems to have more members than Tucson, and it had taken me long enough to learn theirs. At least I'll be able to rely on the names on their cuts.

Meat's soon ready and served, and the bikers carry overflowing plates into the air-conditioned clubroom and set it out with the rest of the offerings. Plates are filled and refilled, drink starts flowing, and when Slick returns to my side I'm surprised to realise I've completely stopped worrying about being in a different club. Jayden seems happy too, taking her role as babysitter seriously, and Carmen and Sandy are talking with Rosa.

I'm rubbing my stomach, unable to take another bite, when Slick's voice murmurs into my ear. "I think you're wanted."

Looking around, I see Rosa is standing and beckoning toward me and my sister. Leaving Slick, I go over to see what she wants. Tiffany's with her, and they're waving to summon Carmen, Sam, Sophie, Sandy, my sister and Amy too.

"Let's leave the boys to it. The sweet butts will be coming in soon. Come with me. I think you're going to like this—I don't believe you have anything like this at Tucson."

Intrigued, we follow Rosa away. She takes us out past the kitchen and into an enclosed part of the warehouse. As we step inside I think we all give a collective gasp. It's a comfortable bright and airy room with floral covered sofas and comfortable, colourful cushions lying on the seats, a big flat screen TV on the wall, and a small bar set up to one side. There's no need to point out this is the women's area.

"Wow! We need something like this." Sophie looks around with interest.

"You haven't seen the best bits yet," Rosa notes smugly. She closes the door and shows us the bolts on this side. "It's reinforced steel, and those inside can control who gets in or out. Keys, our security guy, put in a hidden camera so we can see what's going on in the clubhouse. There's bulletproof shutters we can close if we have to as well."

"And here," Tiffany pulls aside a curtain, "is another way out of the compound. It leads to the back of the parking garage. If it's safe we can escape by car, if not, there's another exit that's hard to spot."

They really seem keen to keep their women safe here. "Have you ever had to use it?"

"No." Rosa smiles at me. "And there's no particular threats that we're aware of. When we suggested a room for us the brothers built it and went a bit over the top. And we have the comfort of knowing our security is important to them."

Jayden puts her hand over her mouth to try and not very successfully stifle a yawn. "Sorry." She shrugs. "I'm tired." Sometimes I forget she's only fourteen and needs the sleep of a teenage body. And the long journey was fatiguing.

Amy's already asleep in Sam's arms.

Rosa suggests she shows us our rooms, and then those who want to can come back down for a drink. My plan of staying with Jayden is thwarted when she suggests we leave Amy in with her so we can all go down and enjoy ourselves. As she seems happy enough, I'm content to leave her. And that's how, an hour later, I find myself coming under the spotlight.

We've already discussed Heart's non-improving condition and the lengths his mother-in-law is going in trying to get her hands on his daughter, and Jayden's story has drawn disgust and compassion from the Vegas women. As they show their concern for my sister, having now had the results back from Doc, I'm able to reassure them that luckily everything came back clear, so she'll have no lasting physical reminders. Rosa suggests they'll do all they can to turn her mind to different things while she's here. You can't be depressed in Vegas, they tell me. Unless, that is, you lose all your money.

In the company of the women, I'm able to completely relax, particularly as we ignore the elephant in the room and avoid any discussion of what will happen when our men go back to Tucson.

I'm just thinking about what good company they all are when Sophie turns to me and asks, "What I don't understand, Ella, is why you ever wanted to be a club whore?"

My mouth drops open at Sophie's seemingly innocent question. At my surprise, she seems to know it all. She shrugs. "Jill's got a loose tongue."

Shit. Now everyone knows. I really don't know what to say.

"She was ranting the other day. She doesn't like you monopolising Slick, or that's how she put it. And when he gave you your property patch I thought she was going to explode. She was spitting out you were a whore, just like them."

Sam glares at Sophie and puts her hand on mine. "We know you're not like them, Ella."

"Huh!" Rosa laughs. "Might not know you as well as the Tucson crowd do, but it's easy to see you're no slut, Ella." She curls her legs underneath her on the sofa and sits back, getting herself comfortable. "There sounds like there's a story there, so why don't you spill?"

I could keep my mouth shut, and probably should, but the cocktails I've been drinking have loosened my tongue, and even the new women I've met seem friendly enough. Slowly I nod. "Okay, I'll try to explain, but I need another drink first."

Obviously eager, Tiffany jumps to her feet and gets me another glass of something blue and decidedly alcoholic.

I take a deep swallow and then begin. "I was living a deadbeat life, you know, hand to mouth, just surviving. I've had a few boyfriends, but nothing to write home about, and wasn't in a position to meet the kind of man I was on the lookout for." I pause for another gulp of the blue drink. It warms my throat going down. Looking around at my rapt audience I continue, "I knew Jill at school, we were cheerleaders together, we used to get along well and had a few laughs, but lost touch after we left.

Then, a few months ago I bumped into her. We began to meet up regularly for coffee. She told me what she did…"

"She what?" Sam's eyes open wide. "She should be more discreet about that."

Rosa growls. "She shared club business."

I do defend her. "I doubt she tells everyone. A biker approached her and eventually she ended up telling me how she knew him. We'd met a few times by then and had rekindled our friendship."

Sam doesn't look mollified. "Still…"

"Anyway," I move swiftly on, "I was amazed. Part intrigued, mostly disgusted, so I asked her how she could do what she did."

Sophie's sitting forward. "I always wondered how the girls started out. Go on, Ella, it's fascinating."

I nod and go on to explain what she'd told me that long ago morning before all this had started.

Carmen's looking at me oddly. "So, the thought of biker cock on tap excited you? You obviously weren't afraid of bikers then, honey. But when you came to the club, you were fuckin' terrified."

Sam shoots her a look, and then stares at me intently. I remember she hadn't seen me the first time. I throw her a silent plea for help. *How much should I disclose?*

"Ella, there's more to it," Carmen insists. "What happened to make you so scared?"

I look down at my glass, which is now empty again. "Look, it's club business. But Slick came to see me. Told me if I'd do something for the club they'd let me in as a sweet butt."

Rosa's gazing at me. "Did you really understand what it means to be a club girl, Ella? They're here to do anything and everything the men want. Any time, day or night. When your girls come here tomorrow, they'll be expected to service our men too. It might suit a nympho, but you don't seem like someone who just likes sex and doesn't care who it's with."

I give a shiver. While I liked Titch, for example, he's got to be sixty if he's a day, and the thought of deep throating an old man's cock fills me with disgust. "No, I don't think I understood that at all. Jill made it sound glamourous."

Now they all laugh. Sam's frowning. "They must enjoy it. They can leave at any time, but they don't, they stay."

"It's not just the sex, they like feeling wanted and needed. Jill said she had control over the men." I'd had plenty of time to think it through. "Let's face it, being somewhere I'd be appreciated sounded good at the time. I had no prospects, no man. It would have been a roof over my head, food, and company who wanted me. Jill said there'd be a chance that one of the bikers would take a particular liking to me and I might become an old lady." Which as it turned out, was exactly what happened. Just not in the way I'd originally expected.

"They all think that. One of the main reasons they do it. But they'll be disappointed. It's very rare a man wants a woman all his brothers have already dipped their cocks in every hole." Now everyone nods sagely.

I nod at Rosa. "I know that now. But then?"

Carmen is still like a dog with a bone. "So you weren't afraid of bikers at that point, when Slick came to see you?"

Giving a small smile I reply, "No, and I even thought if they were all like him it wouldn't be a hardship at all."

"You liked Slick?"

I admit it. "Very much. I was attracted to him from the start."

"What happened?" Now it's Sandy who probes.

My voice drops to a whisper, and I glance toward Sam again. "I went into a biker club…" My voice breaks. I hadn't noticed her get up, but Tiffany brings me another drink. I take a hefty swallow and find the strength to continue. "They made me pull a train."

"Why the fuck did you agree to that?"

Sam jumps into my rescue. "There wasn't agreement or consent, ladies. And the whys and wherefores come under club business. Ella here did the club a favour, and it's thanks to her all the men are alive. Let's just leave it at that."

"I wasn't meant to get hurt." I give a small smile of thanks at Sam's concise explanation.

"But you did."

"And that's why they wanted to look after you," Sandy puts in. "I did wonder. Oh honey, I'm so sorry what you went through."

Tiffany comes and sits down next to me. "So that's why you looked like a lamb going to the slaughter when you arrived? You thought the Vegas chapter was going to be like the club you went to? Oh honey, you've nothing to worry about here. The brothers are pussy cats. Wouldn't dream of hurting a woman or making her do something she didn't want to do. Anyway, you're wearing your property cut. Ain't no one gonna touch you with that on."

I start to thank her, then change my mind as a term she used registers. "*Pussy cats?*"

"Perhaps sometimes they can be tigers. Or maybe that's just Fox. Mmm mm." Tiffany laughs, and the amount of drink we've all consumed makes that one of the most hilarious things we've ever heard.

"Talking of sweet butts, when are your lot coming up?"

"Tomorrow," Sam answers Rosa. "The prospect's taken the truck back tonight and will be driving them here in the morning."

"Hmm. Well there's rooms on the upper floor where they can bunk with our club girls." She waves her hand around the room. "Don't worry, this is an old lady's only retreat."

That's good to hear, and as they seemed to have finished with me being the topic of conversation, and I'm let off the hook, I start to relax once again. I finally discover that Rosa was married to the chapter's old president, who'd died of cancer a couple of years back. That she's still got a home here and they've made her feel wanted is the final nail in the coffin of my fears as I at last understand I can't tar all bikers with the same brush.

Having had a relaxing evening, I go to bed, sliding in next to an already sleeping Slick. But he's only dozing as though he'd been waiting. The bed dipping wakes him up, and he turns and pulls me into his arms.

CHAPTER 33
Slick

I hated leaving Ella in Vegas. It just didn't seem right. I cursed having to abandon her now we've reached such a good place in our relationship. Oh, I'm confident enough that this short break won't harm us, but I don't like that I'm leaving her alone. *I miss her already.* My comfort is that she seems to be settled in the Vegas club, not overly concerned by the brothers now she's met them, and surrounded by old ladies whom I can see have become her friends.

On the long ride back to Tucson, all I could think about is that night when she allowed me to let my inner beast free, the memories rolling around my head on a loop. Fuck, once I'd got over the shock of her asking, I'd let myself go and she'd taken all I had to give. I'd certainly fulfilled my promise, and couldn't hide my smirk when I saw her walking stiffly the next morning. Yeah babe, that's what biker loving does to you.

Last night at the Vegas compound I'd changed pace once again, making love to her so gently, cementing the depth of my love for her in my actions as well as words. If this was to be a final goodbye, then I wanted to leave her something to remember me by.

It's not my intention to die, but who the fuck knows what lies ahead? Each and every one of us would lay down our lives for our brothers and for our club. It's impossible to predict what's going to happen, and not out of the question that some of us might not be coming back.

At least the women are safe. If anything happens to us, Red will look after them.

Arriving back at the Tucson compound, breathing in the familiar smells of home, I've got to put Ella out of my mind and concentrate on securing a future for us. Now I need to give one hundred percent commitment to my club while we deal with the Herreras and whatever Archer's going to throw at us. Oh, and to track down who ran Heart and Crystal off the road. There's no doubt with the women away, and no sweet butts to distract us, we can get down to business without worries of them in our minds.

But fuck does it feel wrong to lie alone in my bed, my hand resting on the side where she usually lies, my head on her pillow just to breathe in the perfume she left, remembering the promise I made that I would be returning to her, having to deal with the knowledge it was a pledge that might be beyond my control to keep.

The next morning the clubroom seems eerily empty with no women around. Smells of burnt bacon are wafting through as the prospects do their best at serving up an edible breakfast. They fail, but I grab something, knowing I'll need it to keep me going. When I walk into church it's to find my brothers equally subdued.

Prez is toying with the gavel, but with mostly silence around him there's no need to bang it. He twists it between his fingers before giving a half-hearted tap on the wood.

"I don't need to explain what we're all gettin' into," he starts with no preamble. As he looks from one of us to another, I wonder if he's burning the image of us all into his brain in case some of us don't come back. His action reinforcing my notion we've no idea what we'll be stepping into today.

Mouse gives a slight wave of his hand. "I've done everythin' I can, Prez. The link between the Zetas and the Herreras is still strong, and as we all know, that cartel's on its way back. They're gainin' ground all the time, and while still weakened, a direct attack from them would be more than we could handle."

"They're better armed for a start," Peg puts in. "But my gut feel is we have closer enemies to deal with. Leonardo Herrera wants us to take out the trash. I'm worried that not everyone in the family will appreciate us cleanin' their house."

I nod, he's right. And the Herreras could take us out, with or without the cartel. It's just a simple question of numbers.

"Leonardo is the head. His son will be takin' over when he goes."

"And what do we know about the son, Mouse? Apart from the fact he wasn't at the fuckin' meeting you had?"

"Yeah, that's my worry, Dart." Prez glances down the table. "We don't know how long the old man will last. His son might have a different way of doin' things."

Dart points with the glowing tip of his cigarette. "Way I see it is Leonardo is worried about the Zetas. Sure, there's a relationship there, but the Herreras have been muddyin' that by dippin' their toes into the skin trade."

"They've been clever, they're not shippin' the kids out of Tucson, just keeping them for the *entertainment* here in the city." This from Beef.

"It's still skin trade," says Joker. "Herreras can expect blowback if the cartel gets to know."

"And if the cartel finds out we've launched an attack on the family they're protectin', I don't give much for our chance of stayin' in the clear." Beef voices one of my worries.

"Could we talk to the Zetas? Get them on board?"

A dozen heads swing around to look at Lady. He clears his throat. "Just a thought."

"Lady's right, we should look at all options." Prez rubs at his forehead. "But the cartel's always bloodthirsty, and they don't like loose fuckin' ends. Likely result is they'll go for the Herreras and then come after the club."

A voice comes from a man leaning against the wall at the back, Red's VP, Crash. "Have we got enough manpower if they do?"

"Probably not right now," says Drum. "Not if the cartel comes for us. The Herreras, maybe. If I can get a warnin' out in time and we can call on the support offered by the other chapters. What worries me most is if we go ahead with what Leonardo wants, we could be walkin' into a trap and won't have that time to prepare."

Lost, Snake's VP, folds his arms as an ominous roll of thunder sounds right overhead. Before he can speak there's a round of nervous laughter. He looks up. "Fuckin' weather. Can't wait to get back to San Diego. Thought Arizona was a desert!" Again a few chuckles. "What I was gonna say before I was so fuckin' rudely interrupted was, we've talked this all out, agreed on a plan. I say we just fuckin' go for it."

"Lost's got a good point. We can talk around this all day. We up for a vote on whether to go ahead on the assumption Leonardo's straight and we'll do what he's asked?"

"Don't like being used by anyone." Peg's grumbling again.

"Truth, Brother?" Wraith sits forward and leans his elbows on the table. "We'd have gone searchin' for the addresses, which was giving Mouse a headache. He's sped things up by givin' us heads on a fuckin' plate. And the names tally with the info we beat out of Diego, so we can be sure we know all our targets. Yeah, we take it at face value. We could be on to a winner. Just have to take the risk that there's no hidden agenda lurkin' beneath."

Drum bangs the gavel. "Let's take a fuckin' vote. All in favour of proceedin' as planned? Or do you women want to gossip about it some more?"

Another rumble of thunder coincides with our laughter. It's a fairly quick vote. Being men of action, and not women as Prez pointed out, we feel better moving than sitting around.

Prez starts to run through the plan. "We've got five men that we're targetin'. *If* we can trust Leonardo, they'll be completely unaware."

"And if he's not trustworthy, they'll be ready and waitin'."

Drummer glares at Peg. The sergeant-at-arms shrugs then waves to indicate he'll shut up. "We go in heavy, prepared for whatever we might meet. Five teams. I take one, Wraith, Peg, Blade, and Slick will lead the others. Lost, you and your men will be with me. Slick, you'll have Crash and the Vegas boys with you." Prez goes on to assign the rest of my brothers to the teams. Everyone's going except the prospects, who'll be left at the compound. We're hoping to find each man on his own, but plan in case they're heavily protected.

"What about collateral damage?" Rock asks, tugging at his ear. "You want us to limit that, or what?"

"Women, kids?" Prez asks Mouse.

"Lucas isn't married, couldn't find a connection to a woman at all. Pablo and Miguel have wives, but no kids. Pedro's got a woman and a couple of youngsters. Arturo has two teenage boys."

"No women or kids to be hurt," Drum announces, then stares everyone down to ensure we're all on message. "We take them out clean."

"What about any men they have with them?"

"Tongue, I think it's safe to assume they're on the wrong side. If they get in the way, remove them." Drum sits back and puts his foot against the table, tunnelling his hands through his hair.

"Brothers, this ain't the way we work and it's fuckin' killin' me to do this. But we ain't going out to murder innocent men. Even if it wasn't at the whim of fuckin' Leonardo Herrera, we'd still need to clean out this town. What happened to Jayden can't be allowed to happen to any others if we can help it. These five men are scum and need to be taken out."

"I hear ya, Prez. But can't stop that sort of shit forever. Supply and demand, someone will step up to fill the void."

"Yeah, Peg, that's the risk. But doing this, we'll have saved some young kids. If anyone has doubts just ask Mouse about those fuckin' videos he watched."

"I'd rather you didn't." Mouse grimaces.

I know what the prez is doing. He's winding us up on purpose. But fuck, I need no such encouragement. Jayden's *my* family. "I'd do it alone if I had too."

Steely grey eyes come my way. "You don't have to, Brother."

A murmur of agreement, then another fucking crack of thunder so loud it makes all of us start. I guess all our nerves are stretched tight today.

"We leave at midnight. Now we all got our skills. Use them."

Peg raps the table. "And leave your cuts behind. We don't want anyone clockin' us."

As everyone nods there's a knock at the door. Drum rolls back his head. "What the fuck now? Come in!"

Road looks pissed off when he opens the door. "Got visitors at the gate, Prez. Those two detectives, and a number of squad cars full of cops too."

Prez gives a little grin, it wasn't exactly unexpected. "Everything hidden?"

"Squeaky clean, boss." Wraith returns his smirk.

"Then let's let them in."

I'm not the only one who follows him down to the gate, partly out of curiosity and partly to offer support. There's a crowd of us waiting when Hyde opens the gate. The rain has just stopped and puddles glisten in the emerging sunlight.

Archer's the first in and steps up to Drum, a piece of paper in his hand once again. "You've been served!" He almost spits out the words and lets the letter fall on the ground.

Drum ignores it. "If you've come for the kid she's not here."

The detective's face goes red. "I don't believe you. We've got a fucking warrant to search this rat hole."

Prez stays calm. "Knock yourselves out."

Archer waves to the men behind him and about a dozen flood in. A couple peel off and go into the auto shop, and from the racket, they've started tearing it apart. Fuck knows why they'd be looking for a three-year-old in there. Seems they're using the opportunity to cause as much trouble as possible.

The detective himself leads the others up the compound, some brothers go with them, but all they'll be able to do is watch. I stay where I am. If the auto shop is an example to go by, it's going to break my heart to see the damage they'll be leaving behind.

Detective Hannah has remained. She steps up to the prez and says grimly, "I'm so sorry, Drum. I couldn't stop him."

Turning his stare to her, Drum looks impassive. After a few moments he says, "The kid's not here, Marcia. She's safe." He's being gentle with her, understanding her frustration. And at least the information she'd given had provided us with a heads up. It's Archer we've got an issue with, not her.

The detective looks relieved. "I'm trying to find evidence, but he hides everything well." Her eyes look in the direction her partner had gone then come back to Drum. "Any news on Heart?"

"No change."

Her hands bunch at her side. "He's got to come around, then we can put an end to all this farce."

"It won't end," Drum replies sagely. "Men like Archer don't give up once they've got their sights on somethin'. He just won't be able to do it legally anymore."

She stares down at her feet as though she's got nothing to say.

"Hey." Drum's voice has her raising her head again. "We know you've nothin' to do with this."

Her back straightens. "I'm a cop, Drum. And you're a criminal."

"Never been convicted."

"You've never been caught." Her mouth twists.

"Innocent until proven guilty?" he challenges, making her give a half smile.

Two hours later the fucking cops leave. There's not one bloc, not one room that hasn't been overturned and left in a mess. All the bottles are broken in the clubhouse, fridges pulled out and searched behind, leaving their contents defrosting and water puddling on the floor. In the clubroom there's great holes in a wall, when challenged Archer shrugs and says they were looking for a secret room.

But they found nothing at all, and certainly not the little girl they were after or anything else incriminating. Veins were popping on Archer's forehead when he eventually left.

Hannah pauses before following her partner, her eyes surveying the ruined clubroom, her mouth pursed.

"Criminals, eh?" The prez's face is stern as he tells her, "We got no redress, you and I both know that. But who's in the wrong for causin' this mess? I don't think you and I are far off the same side."

She's got nothing to say.

First things first, Hyde and Jekyll are sent to replenish the bar stocks. Freezers and fridges plugged back in and hopefully most of the contents are salvageable. As Road mops up, the rest of us right the furniture that we can, and start removing that which can't be repaired, which includes a number of the mismatched, but comfortable chairs in church. *Fucking bastards.*

When the last of the police leave the compound, the prez calls everyone around him. He stands on one of the few remaining tables that has all its supporting legs. With all eyes upon him, he starts to speak.

"Brothers. This," his arm indicates the damage, "was nothin' more than an act of revenge. We thwarted Archer's plans by movin' Amy. A little girl's safe. All we've lost here is furniture and possessions, which can be fuckin' replaced. We'll come back from this better than before."

"Could do with some new sofas, Prez."

A ripple of laughter goes around, and I grin. Yeah, those sofas had seen more than enough action, and I don't even want to think about the kind of deposits that had been left on them. I almost feel sorry for the cops who had to touch the surfaces they'd shredded.

"We start building again tomorrow. But now, put this to the back of your heads. We've got bigger things to deal with tonight. Peg, get the weapons back out of storage, and everyone make sure you know what you're doing and that your guns are clean and loaded. Don't want none jammin' tonight. And Slick, you make sure your toys are ready."

I nod. I know what I have to do.

"Prospects will be restockin' the bar, but go easy. I want everyone with clear heads." He looks around, making sure everyone's on board. "Right, let's continue getting things straightened where we can, then go play with yourselves or whatever you do to relax."

A few chuckles greet him as he jumps back down to the ground. Normally he'd say go fuck, but with no whores or old ladies, those that need to will be reduced to using their hands.

As the brothers from San Diego and Vegas offer to make good, or as far as possible, the communal areas, I go up to my suite to see what damage has been done there. Nothing seems to be broken, but every drawer's been tipped out and searched. I do what I can to tidy mine, and then Ella and Jayden's room. Fuck knows which of their stuff goes into which drawer. I feel like a voyeur handling their panties and shit. Holding each item gingerly between finger and thumb, I put all the spilled tampons back in the box. Fuck, a man shouldn't have to do this kind of thing.

By the time I'm finished it's late afternoon and I go to the bunker hidden in the old swimming pool. The disguised and dirt covered top is already slid back, and Peg is sorting out weapons and ammunition. I go to a special pile and take out what I need, collecting my handguns and knives from where I had them stored, noting Prez's precious Linn Sondek turntable is covered in bubble wrap and placed here for safe keeping, along with his treasured record collection. Shaking my head, I smile. Trust Prez.

The mood in the clubhouse remains subdued, and one of the only times I can remember when the whores aren't around to provide their services. Men sit checking their guns, putting ammunition handy in the pockets of their cuts, and strapping on sheaves for their knives. Blade comes over and takes a seat beside me, the chair rocking, and he gets up fast turning it over to inspect it, then swearing when he sees the loose leg. Tossing it aside he pulls up another.

"Fuckin' fuzz," he snarls.

I shrug. There's nothing more to say.

"Who you got, Slick?"

"Lucas. Should be easy. He's not got a wife, hopefully he'll be home all alone."

"You got your special toys?"

Yup, you could say that. I like to blow things up. I nod.

"Tongue and Wraith have got Pedro."

That makes sense. Tongue being a sniper, if he gets a clear shot it should be easy just to take one man out. "Who you got, Blade?"

"Pablo. I'll slit his throat while he sleeps."

"Sounds fuckin' simple."

He grins broadly. "What could go wrong?"

One fuck of a lot.

CHAPTER 34

Slick

As midnight approaches, conversations around me falter, each of us in silent reflection, going over plans in our heads and, probably all the same as me, eager to get out and get this shit done. Looking across the room I can see Wraith impatiently bouncing his leg and Drum tapping his fingers on the table where he's sitting with Lost and Crash. At last the prez glances at his phone to check the time, then stands and gives us the signal it's time to get this job started. *Finally.* Wasting no time, I call my team together and we go over the arrangement once again. And then it's time for the first team to head out.

Men slap each other's back and exchange hugs, cries of "good luck" and "watch your fuckin' backs" abound. I give one last look around the ruined clubroom and then gather my crew.

We're third lot to leave. Crash, the Vegas VP, I quickly discover doesn't mind following orders despite the fact he outranks me and rides alongside as we head to our designated address. I'm well prepared, as usual, Mouse has given us all the details—where to park up and how best to avoid security cameras. Stowing our cuts on our bikes we approach the house and it's then I get my first clue things might not go as smoothly as planned. There are lights on inside, when I'd hoped to find the single occupant asleep.

Crash waves two of his men forward, Rope and Cuff, who I've been told, do everything together. And apparently that means *everything.* "Go see what's goin' on." After instructing them, he turns to me. "Those two move like fuckin' ghosts."

I'm quite happy he's offered their services. Neither Shooter or Viper are particularly light on their feet. Now I'm unable to do anything but stand with my foot impatiently tapping the ground as I wait for intel that will give us suggestions as to how to proceed.

Within moments they're back. "Fuckin' party inside," Cuff tells me. From the expression of disgust on his face, I've got a pretty good idea what he means.

My heart beats faster. "One of their specials?"

"Yeah, fuck it." Cuff spits on the ground. "Fuckin' perverts."

"How many fuckers in there?"

"Seven that I saw. Could be more. And two girls."

"Your move, Slick." Crash shows he respects my lead. "How do you want us to play this?"

I'm for being cautious, so I query a bit more. "How much could you see? Is it possible they're ready and waiting for us?"

Rope shakes his head and gives a disgusted snort. "Man, we could see in through the side window. Looks like they're fully occupied with their entertainment to me."

I'm still wary this could be a trap. "We need to get the girls clear." I hesitate, but only for a moment. "Brothers, we were here to take out one man, but from what Rope and Cuff say none of those fuckers in there are innocent. I say we end them all." And even while it seems unlikely, I can't take any chances. This could still be a trap. At the back of my mind hovers the thought that the Herreras have set us up and, while it looks genuine, it could be anything but.

And we're outnumbered. My team numbers six. It's good to have the Vegas boys here, who'll I just have to trust know what they're doing. Part of me wishes I had more of the brothers I know.

I make my decision. "We go in quiet, quick and clean. We don't give them a chance to draw their fucking weapons. Shooter, your aim still good, Brother? Think you can take two of them?"

Without a pause he gives a quick nod in response. I stare at him for a moment, remembering how shaken he was when he'd make his first kills, but he seems to have his head on straight. Under my examination he raises his chin. I slap my hand on his back.

"Won't be a problem, Slick. They're not men, they're animals."

"You got that right, Shooter."

Cuff lifts a semi-automatic into my line of sight. I nod at him, I've set mine to single shot, having eyed up nearest residences, not too close, but near enough to disturb me. If we need to change to rapid fire we'll do so, but for now, "We use silencers if possible." No point getting the cops here too quickly. Cuff nods in understanding.

Once I know my message has gotten across I continue, "Right, rear, and front entry." Fuck, we're becoming practiced at this, but it had worked for Drum when we saved Jayden, hopefully it will work again now. Though this time I won't be knocking on the front door. "Once those fuckers are dead we get the girls out."

"What's the timer on that?" Crash nods at the device I'm checking before putting it back in my pocket.

"I can set it for whatever we decide."

"Three minutes will give us enough time to get clear." And the house will be blown sky high. Each of our hits tonight will be via a different method. Make it less easy for them all to be linked to the same group.

The time suggested is reasonable, so I indicate my agreement. It's a fucking shame we can't do this as planned. Make sure Lucas was inside, sneak inside to find him sleeping, a quick shot to the head, and then get away clean. But the presence of the girls and other men changes all that. Luckily we've come prepared with the larger team as we'd all known we were going into the unexpected, and quite possibly an ambush situation. We'd tossed around many a scenario during church. And now I'm fucking glad we had.

"I'll take the back with Cuff and Rope."

I lift my chin to Crash, Shooter and Viper nod to show they'll be with me. Giving a chin jerk, we slip on gloves then start to move forward, crouched down, keeping down behind a conveniently placed low wall. Reaching the front door, I check out the lock, then use my useful skeleton key to open it silently, then send a quick text to Crash, immediately receiving one back. They're inside too. The party's going on in the front room. So far nothing has changed, no one's watching out for our arrival and our entry seems undetected.

We head down the short hall. I pause to let Crash come alongside, then burst through into the living room. Shooter's quick on the draw, two men drop by his hand. I get a third. Others are falling. One man's enjoying an almost comatose girl on the ground, while the other young kid is slumped over a chair. Holding my fire, as I don't want to hit the girl, the last man looks around in surprise, pants down by his ankles. As he rises he tries to pull them up when he sees dead bodies around him. I take aim then pause. *Fucking hell.* I'm about to become a cop killer. My arm comes up and quickly pushes Crash's weapon down. He looks at me sharply, and I shake my head.

"Not him." I say tersely to Crash, and then address the man abusing the girl. "Hands up!" He's probably got a weapon to hand. As he raises his arms his pants fall down again, the clang on the wooden floor confirming my assumption was correct. Crash quickly steps forward and seizes his gun.

Detective Archer's eyes open wide, and lines appear on his forehead. His cheeks have gone pink, but when he looks at me his expression slowly changes and the worry lines fade. He looks around at the fallen men, then scoffs, "You're fucking lucky you didn't pull that trigger. Kill me and they'll never stop coming after you if you shoot one of their own."

Does he mean his professional colleagues or the Herreras? If it's the latter and Leonardo's straight he's wrong. If the former he may have a point. But his words have no power to sway me. I only have to glance at the girl lying on the floor crying to realise whatever he says, his remaining life is now measured in hours.

He follows the direction of my eyes and must realise he's not got me convinced as he tries to offer up something more. "I'll lay off the Norman kid. Make the paperwork go away. Just let me walk. You can keep the brat."

"What's goin' on?" A deep voice speaks by my side.

"This, here," I point with my gun, "is a dirty cop."

Crash's eyes open wide. "Fuck."

Yeah. Fuck. "Watch him." Taking out my phone I move out of the room. I try a number a couple of times, but Drum doesn't pick up.

"Ringing Prez?"

"Yeah, but there's no answer," I tell Viper tersely, who's followed me out into the hallway.

"Reckon Prez will want to question him himself."

Viper's got a point. "Yeah, that's what I thought. I'll get a prospect here with the truck. We'll truss him up and take him home." I make a second call, this time one where there's a reply. And while we're waiting for transport maybe I'll get some information myself. Returning to the main room, I quickly update Crash.

"Good call, man. From what you say, your Prez will want to hear what he's got to say. We'll use the waiting time to clean up." He nods towards one of his men. "Cuff?" When he gets his attention, he jerks his head toward Archer. "We're takin' him back to the compound."

"Wrapped?"

"Oh yeah." Crash smirks. "With a pretty bow on top."

There's a reason why Cuff has his name. As he reaches around to his back pocket and takes out of pair of handcuffs I hold back a laugh. While Archer watches in horror, Cuff nods his Vegas brother who takes hold of the cop, roughly pulling his arms behind his back. The cuffs are on before he can blink. Then I watch as Rope walks around to his front, sneering at the immobilised man. The cop tries to back away, forgetting his pants are around his ankles and falls on his ass. Rope laughs, then quick as a flash kneels, leaning his weight on the man to keep him from moving, then takes the belt off the pants and wraps it tightly around Archer's shins, keeping them tight together so he can't kick off his pants. It's a ridiculous sight. Especially when he pulls the detective to his knees and he has difficulty balancing and his flaccid cock's flapping in the air.

"You can't kill me." Archer might be trussed like a turkey, but he doesn't sound particularly worried as he basically repeats what he said before. "I'm a cop. And you need me." Suddenly he's smirking as if he thinks he's got the upper hand. "Kill me and you lose the kid. Now the order's been served social services will get involved. She'll be taken away unless I put a stop to it. Only I can do that. I know the judge. Let me go now, I'll say nothing of this, and I'll make your problem with the brat disappear."

I don't trust him. But it will be Drum's call. He's got a vested interest in keeping Amy safe. For now I'll stick to my plan.

"While we're twiddling' our fuckin' fingers, think we ought to be gettin' them out of here." Crash points to the girl on the floor, and then indicates the one on the couch.

"You can't touch me. Untie me, let me go now."

Tuning out Archer's continuing protests, I focus my attention on the girl lying prone on the floor. I'd thought she was totally out of it but she seems to have recovered at least some of her senses. Although she's surrounded by dead bodies, she isn't looking at us in horror, she's looking at us like we're her saviours. And she's not even a woman, can't be much more than twelve. Knowing Drum will want to take the lead on Archer, with great difficulty I resist the urge to thrust my fist into his face and send his teeth into this throat. *We caught him raping a fuckin' kid.*

Instead, I throw a nod at Shooter and then incline my head in the girl's direction. As he approaches her, his arm reaches out to touch her and she flinches away.

"Hey, we're not like them. I'm gonna get you out of here, pet." I'm impressed how he keeps his voice gentle. "Can you stand? Where are your clothes?"

Her eyes flit around wildly, eyeing the corpses as though they might get up and abuse her all over again. Shooter sees her looking. "They can't hurt you anymore, sweetheart. But you've got to get dressed, else I won't be able to get you home. It's over now, pet, I promise. They'll never hurt you again." As he looks at me I see his face is tight.

But what he'd said to her though? That, right there, is why we've done good here tonight. The men lying dead aren't going to abuse any more young girls.

Viper's calling my name. When I focus my attention on him he's cuddling the other girl. She can't be more than ten, if that. He's obviously calmed her, she's got her hands clasped in his tee. I lower my head into my hands. Archer's still going from complaining to threatening and then back again. If he had any sense he'd shut up. Finding him here with these girls? He's lucky not to have broken bones.

Shooter and Viper have got the girl's moving, and somehow they've found their clothes. When she puts hers on, Spider's girl looks younger than ever, her tee having a sparkly unicorn on the front. The other's even worse, her sleep shorts and tank have kittens on them. My stomach churns with the need to vomit, but I swallow it down. We can't leave any DNA here.

"We'll take them home and meet you back at the compound." The girls throw a look at each other, and then nod. Going home must seem like a fucking good idea to them.

I turn to Viper and Shooter, wary there might be something going on in Tucson tonight that we're still unaware of, and wanting to take every precaution. "You travel together. Drop the younger one off first. Fuck, how do her parents not know she's missin'?" And how would you groom such a young girl?

Viper seems to know what I'm thinking. "We'll get Mouse to look into their backgrounds, but for now, let's get them back to their folks. They'll be safe enough there for tonight.

"Discretely though, Brothers. No ringin' of door bells. Just let them get inside."

Archer's still immobilised, so Rope and Cuff start cleaning up, looking for spent bullets or anything else that would show we were here. While they do their bit, I stare at the man kneeling on the floor. Suddenly I can't keep a rein on my curiosity any longer.

Going to the cop, I put my hands on his skull, pulling his head back so I'm staring into his face. "What's the story with Heart's kid? Why the fuck are you so intent on putting her in the hands of a fuckin' junkie?"

Archer tries to pull his head out of my hands. "You're going to have to let me go," he screams, "I'm the only one who can put a stop to her being taken away from you. You want the brat, you let me loose."

Is that true? Not sure Drum's going to like it if it is. Fuck, I wish I'd been able to get through to him on the phone. Releasing Archer, I try to call him again. Still no fucking answer. And the prospect and the truck will still be some ways out.

"You haven't answered my question."

"Want me to give him some incentive?" Crash is rubbing his hands together.

I nod. It wouldn't' hurt. Drum will be fine with that, as long as we don't damage the goods too much.

Seeing a stranger approach with a knife in his hands, Archer panics and tries to get away, but trussed as he is he just falls on his ass again. Crash moves fast, moving behind him and putting his knife to Archer's neck.

"Don't hurt me!" the coward cries as the blade presses in and a trickle of blood starts to run down. "I'll tell you, alright? The bitch of the grandmother, Clyde. She's well into the Herreras for drugs. Couldn't pay up. She said she had a grandkid she'd be willing to give up."

I step closer, Crash digs his knife in some more. "Kid's got parents." I watch as Archer swallows, his Adam's apple bobs precariously close to Crash's knife. *He's hiding something.* "How could a junkie give you a kid that wasn't hers to give?" I'm starting to smell a strong odour of fish. My heart misses a beat. *It couldn't be. Could it?* And then the more I think about it, the more it fucking adds up.

I move closer to the man lying back on his ass. "When did she make you the offer?"

Archer stays quiet.

"I asked you a fuckin' question." I nod at Crash who presses the knife in again. Archer tries to jerk away. I take another step toward him and say, menacingly. "Drum might want the kid, but whether she stays or goes makes no odds to me." I'm lying through my teeth but he doesn't know that. "And I don't give a damn if I take out a dirty cop. So *tell me! When did she make the fuckin' offer?*" Yeah, I can do intimidating when I need to.

"Six weeks ago!" Archer cries out.

Fuck it! I'm right! But I still need to make sure. "Yeah," I prompt, "you got fuckin' lucky when Heart and Crystal had that accident which made that the kid all but an orphan." Taking a step forward, I aim a kick into his balls. As he folds over, Crash is only just able to change the position of the knife at his throat in time. He gives me a quick grin, and I can't help smiling back. Wouldn't have bothered me if his throat got cut. Except, I reckon there's more he can tell us. And of course, Drum might object.

"Thing is, Detective, I don't believe in coincidences." Six weeks ago Crystal was alive, and Heart still functioning.

Recovering sufficient breath to speak, Archer looks up and actually smirks. "You fucking bikers think you're invincible, riding around on your death traps, preening yourselves that your gang rules the roads. Two wheelers ain't got much chance against four."

Crash exchanges a look with me, clearly sharing my growing suspicion. He pulls back Archer's head, and now speaks. "Reckon you've got more to tell us, Archer. I might not kill you, but I can put you in a whole world of hurt. You see my brother here? He wants some fuckin' answers. Now either you tell us everythin' you know, or you're gonna lose a fuckin' eye." He places the tip of his knife against Archer's left eyelid. "You've can choose to tell us everythin', or I'll give you another fuckin' choice to make. Left or right."

Archer goes white, the threat more than sufficient. He quickly starts spitting it all out. "I put the word out on Heart, got the patrols looking for him. It was only a matter of time until he left the compound. Officers called it in one Saturday afternoon.

He was getting onto the I-10 at Tombstone, and there was only one direction he could be heading."

If it was up to me, Archer would be needing an eyepatch by now. But I force myself to remember Drum will want him whole. Like a scab I can't help scratching, I probe for more. Even though every word out of this bastard's mouth is making me sick.

"You arranged for him to be taken out?"

A prod with the knife's tip and Archer keeps spilling. "It took me by surprise, didn't have time to arrange anyone else to do the hit so I did it my-fucking-self. Fucking piece of cake. Grabbed one of the trucks off the Herrera compound, easily big enough to take out a bike. He didn't suspect a fucking thing as I came up behind him, only gave a quick look back as I was coming up so fast. And lucky for me he had his wife up behind him. Thought I was going to have to do it in two hits. But I killed two birds with one stone." And he looks pleased with himself. And then he laughs.

Seeing nothing but red I breathe in and hold it. *"You fuckin' killed Crystal."* So enraged, it's hard to get the words out. And he'd left Heart in God knows what state. Almost without me being aware of it my hand holding the gun rises.

Archer follows my movement with his eyes. "You can't kill me! Not if you want the kid!" He repeats what he previously warned me.

But all I can see is Crystal alive, happy and laughing, that thought juxtaposed with the sight of her coffin being lowered into the ground. My cheeks burn, the room starts to suffocate me.

"Slick!" Crash shouts a warning at me.

But my arm keeps moving, my fingers twitch on the trigger.

"Don't, Slick!" Crash yells again.

But nothing can stop me applying a little more pressure. My aim is sure, a bullet flies out and I shoot straight at his groin. Archer goes white and slumps forward, blood pouring out.

"What the fuck, man?" Crash looks horrified. "Drum could have your patch for this."

Part of me is devastated with what I'd done. The other part feels no remorse, except for the fact he didn't suffer more. I've killed the man who murdered my brother's wife.

The cop's body is twitching. "Christ, Slick." Crash takes matters into his own hands, and slits Archer's throat. There's no way he'd come back from that injury, and no longer any point taking him to the compound.

Fuck. The bloody body on the floor brings me back to my senses. *What the fuck is Prez going to say?* My eyes meet Crash's. "Look, I fuckin' lost it, alright? Heart, fuck. Heart didn't deserve that. And he ran Heart off the road so he could get hold of the kid? That's fuckin' deep shit, Brother. And he laughed! He fuckin' laughed!" Echoes of Archer's proud mirth seem to be all I can hear.

Crash quickly moves across to me, his hand touches my arm. "I understand, Brother. I'd have made the same call for one of our own. Fuck, it was hard for me to hear it and I don't know Heart or Crystal. I'm just fuckin' concerned what your prez will say. What if he was tellin' the truth, and he was the only chance for him to keep hold of the kid?"

Now it's over, it sinks in what I've done, and how much I've cocked up.

Crash tries to be supportive. "Slick, I'll tell Drummer how it went down, and how that fucker wound you up. And at least we did what we came for." He points to a body lying at the back of the room. "We took Lucas out, he won't be torturin' and abusin' any more young kids." Ignoring the dead man without a dick, I look past him to the man Crash pointed out. The VP's right. His features match the photos Mouse had provided, and which I'd committed to memory. Not so much the deep hole in his chest. *I should have checked that first, that we'd killed the man we'd come for...* Fuck, there's a reason I'm not officer material.

"Let's finish up." Crash signals to Rope and Cuff, who've been silent but watching, then leads me outside. As we get back to the bikes Road pulls up in the truck. The Vegas VP takes charge, walking over and saying some words. Road turns around and starts driving back.

On automatic pilot, I lay out the explosives and set the timer. We're riding away as the whole place blows sky high. It will take weeks for them to put the all the pieces together. And yes, I do mean human parts.

For once I don't feel the pride I normally do in my handiwork. *Prez could take my patch.*

CHAPTER 35

Ella

This clubhouse seems strange and my bed feels so empty. No matter how I arrange the pillows I can't forget something, someone, is missing. I've been lying here for what seems like hours, but I can't seem to sleep. Just tossing and turning, consumed with worry about Slick. *What's he doing right now? Is he safe?* Looking at the clock it's only just turned three. *A long time until morning.*

Slick had rung me earlier in the evening, but in many respects I wish I hadn't had that last conversation with him. He'd tried too hard, had sounded too upbeat, was too concerned for my welfare, and took far too long saying goodbye. It wasn't hard to read between the lines. It would take an idiot to be oblivious that there's something happening tonight. Something which my gut tells me could put Slick in danger. He told me he loved me three times during the call, so insistently as though making sure I'd never forget, burning the words onto my brain.

I can't lose him now. He's brought me back to life and back to the living. It scares me just how much I want the opportunity to have a future with him, prepared to go the whole hog, for us to be family, to have our own children. I bite into my hand to smother a cry. In the dead of the night I'm terrified the odds are against us, and the chance I now want might be taken away.

I've never been warned by a premonition before, nothing alerted me when I took that first step into the Rock Demons club. But tonight foreboding has taken hold of me, making believe my chance to make a life with Slick has even now been taken away. *I want to call him.* I can't. What if he is in the middle of something dangerous and I distract him?

The air con's not as efficient as that back in Tucson. It rattles and clunks but still doesn't do its job. I kick off the sheets and put my legs over the side of the bed, giving up any hope of sleep. Slipping into my flipflops, I glance in the mirror, my sleep shorts and tank cover all the important bits, and should be sufficient in this clubhouse, where for the last two days all the men I've met have treated me with respect. But remembering some might still be strangers to me, I slip on my property cut, pulling the leather around me and breathing in the scent which reminds me of Slick. With my nostrils full of his perfume, I leave my room.

The clubhouse is quieter than it is by day, various grunts and groans escaping from rooms that I pass suggesting the sweet butts are doing the jobs they're there for. I grin to myself at the evil thought, that Jill, who deceived me with her trounced-up version of what she does, might be having to satisfy Titch with a blowjob. I smile at myself having the mental image of her head bobbing up and down on his shrivelled prick, working, possibly for hours, until she brings him off. *God, I'm bad.* While it doesn't overshadow my worry, I find the thought amusing and put my hand over my mouth as a giggle threatens to escape.

Walking down the back way, avoiding the main clubroom, I come to the kitchen, a welcoming modern area with stainless steel counters and appliances, and then my feet falter. To my surprise, I'm not the only one here.

Red, the Vegas president, breaks off from his conversation with Sophie and nods as I enter. "Can't sleep?"

"No. I wanted some water." I grasp at a valid excuse for wanting to get out of my room.

Sophie grins at me and raises a glass, making me a far better offer. "How about some wine instead? It may give you a headache tomorrow, but it will help you get some shut eye."

Fuck the hangover. "Count me in." As she tips the bottle over a fresh glass, I notice Red's got his hands wrapped around a beer. Sophie toasts me with her water, being pregnant she's unable to drink.

"You alright, Ella?" He's watching me carefully. Oh yeah, everyone knows I'm a panicking freak.

"I'm fine, Red. You run a good club." After reassuring him, I give him the reason I'm still up. "I'm just a bit restless."

Sophie's sympathetic eyes meet mine, and she nods. "You're worried about Slick. I know how you feel. I'm concerned for Wraith. There's something going on, I can sense it." Sophie stares down into her glass as though wishing she had something stronger in it. That I'm not the only one fretting doesn't exactly help.

Red combs his fingers through his tussled ginger hair and looks exasperated, as though he was having this conversation when I walked in. "Ladies, just trust your men. They know what they're doin'. They'll be in touch as soon as they can." He stares at us, but his words don't really offer much comfort. "You're not doing any good worryin' yourselves sick." He's right, but just saying it doesn't help. He glances between us, then tries another tack. "Ella, Soph, let's talk about tomorrow. Think it's time we got you to the strip, don't you?"

Appreciating his attempt to change the subject, I perch my backside on a stool, glad now I didn't stay in bed. Having company and talking about something different has to be better than stewing on my own. Remembering the money Slick gave me, I start looking forward to spending it. *Maybe a shopping trip?* "That sounds a great idea, Red. Might as well see the sights while we're here."

"Sin City." He chuckles. "No one can resist. Anythin' in particular you ladies want to head for?"

"Hey! This where the party is?" Sandy comes in, closely followed by Carmen whose hand is over her face as she smothers a yawn. "Any more wine in that bottle?"

Playing the host Red gets up and finds more glasses. "We were just discussing what you want to do tomorrow."

Sophie pauses to smile at the newcomers, but when answering Red doesn't even pause to think. "I'd like to go to the Harley store, pick somethin' up for Wraith."

I've always wanted to visit Vegas and know exactly what I want to do. "I want to see the Bellagio fountains. Maybe go on that ride, what's it called, the one that wraps around the high building?"

Red's eyes widen. "The Stratosphere? Best we take Twister with us in that case. He's the only one fool enough to go on that."

"You're on your own there, El." Sophie shudders. "I'd never dream of it. I'd die." Carmen and Sandy agree giving me a horrified glance.

"She might." Red raises his bottle toward me. I grin back, surprisingly I've got nerves of steel on terrifying rides.

As Sophie doesn't looked convinced Red offers another option. "Fancy your luck at the casinos?" He winks.

I shoot him a look. "We're in Vegas, duh, not much point in being here if we don't. Hey, Sandy, any more of that wine?" She gives me a refill and tops off her own glass.

"What's going on, guys?" Sam smothers a yawn as she walks into the kitchen, her eagle eyes spying the wine straight away. "Enjoying yourselves, ladies?" She pouts as she adds, "Shame I can't join you." She opens the fridge, takes out a carton, and pours orange juice for herself then raises her glass in a toast.

"We're planning what to do tomorrow," I explain.

"Great, I couldn't sleep." She hitches her butt onto a stool. "So where we going to?"

Red throws up his hands. "Fuck if I know. It sounds like you girls will have us all marchin' up and down the strip all day."

I nudge Sam. "Better wear comfortable shoes."

Red shakes his head in mock exasperation.

Sam chuckles. "You'll have to forgive us out-of-towners if we're too enthusiastic. Coming from Washington, I've never been to Vegas before."

"Sandy and Carmen have." Sophie points at the women she's named who nod their heads. "But I've come bloody further than you, Sam. A few months ago I couldn't have dreamed of having the chance."

Yup, Sophie's got her beat, coming from the U.K.

We talk about what we might like to do a little longer, listening to suggestions Red makes, then the conversation falters.

Suddenly Sophie puts down her glass and looks intently at the Vegas prez. "How are we expected to do this, Red?"

"To do what?" He sounds casual, but his penetrating eyes staring back suggest he knows exactly what she means.

Sophie shrugs and waves her hand between myself and Sam. "We're three are new old ladies. I've barely been one for six months. How are we expected to wait for our men, not knowing anything that's going on, because it's 'club business'?" She uses air quotes for the last two words.

Red leans on the counter. "You know there are good reasons why you're kept in the dark."

"Well, it's certainly not to keep us from worrying. Not knowing is worse." Sophie sounds petulant.

Carmen comes over and puts her hand on Sophie's shoulder. "Don't think it is, hun. If we knew what was goin' on we'd be just as concerned, and still couldn't do a darn thing about it. What good would it do? It's to protect our men. Think about it.

If you know nothin' you can't say anythin' to hurt them, you know, in case there's ever any blowback from the police."

But Sophie again shakes her head. "You still haven't answered my question. I wasn't asking *why*, rather *how* we're supposed to cope."

Sandy puts her arm around Sophie's shoulder and answers. "By supporting each other. And getting drunk. Well, those of us that can, of course."

I smile at her good answer.

Red's more for action, taking her words as a signal to get another bottle of wine and open it. "Bottoms up then, ladies?" As he fills my glass he adds, "I pity Twister if you're goin' on the Stratosphere tomorrow. Fuck knows what your hangover will be like. Try not to puke on him, he does tend to sulk."

After a brief chuckle, we drink in silence, broken when Sophie asks, "Hey, isn't there a volcano?"

"Yup, that's at the Mirage."

"And a pirate ship." Sandy waves with her glass. "That's a good show."

Red smiles indulgently at Sophie. "That's at Treasure Island." He shakes his head in mock disgust, "You're gonna make us do the full tourist bit tomorrow, aren't you?"

"Oh shut it," Sophie admonishes. "When was the last time you went into Vegas?"

That makes him think. "It's actually a while since I've been to the strip. Livin' here I tend to avoid the more crowded parts. I suppose you'll want to go to an all-you-can-eat buffet as well."

"Oooh! That would be great!" Carmen's enthusiastic comment has us all laughing. She shrugs unrepentantly, "Can't help liking my food."

For a few minutes we talk about other things we can see and do, and the light conversation and copious glasses of wine help me set aside my worries for a time.

Shit, we've drained the second bottle. I'm not sure what Vegas has in its water as Sophie is giggling, and even Sam on OJ is finding it funny and when a third voice joins in I realise it's mine and that I must be laughing too. Carmen and Sandy are holding their liquor better, but even their voices have got quite loud.

"I'm dead on my feet," Sophie announces. "I think it's time for bed." As she goes to stand up she stumbles. It's only then I realise how closely Red's been watching her as he shoots out his arm.

"Steady girl," he tells her in his deep, rumbling voice, holding her until she's got her balance on her prosthetic leg. His eyes are twinkling as he looks around. "Think I better escort all you ladies to your beds, otherwise I'd be worried I'll find you in a heap at the bottom of the stairs come mornin'."

Which sets us off in another round of giggling we just can't seem to stop. As Red escorts us out, Sandy, Carmen and myself try to be quiet, turning to each other with exaggerated cries of "Shush," and fingers held up trying to find our lips. I find it hilarious when Carmen's nail hits her nose, but I doubt I'm doing much better than her.

When Sam, who must be drunk on our fumes, bangs against a door slamming it open Red laughs and tells us, "I wouldn't bother tryin' to be quiet. I think you've already woken the whole clubhouse up." His pronouncement seems to be the funniest thing we've ever heard.

He leaves us at the doors to our rooms, Carmen and Sandy carry on walking unsteadily to theirs. Before he goes off he gives them, and then us one last lingering look. "Now I know why we don't let women join the club. I swear you ladies are more trouble drunk than half of my men."

"Oh, come on, Red." Sophie pulls at his cut. "That's an exaggeration. I've not even been drinking."

"No exaggeration, I assure you." And he's pointing at me. Me? I glare at him, but my expression just makes him smirk. "Most of the fuckers just fall asleep. Anyway, *goodnight* ladies. Off to bed with you now."

He turns to go away, but is prevented from leaving. "What? No Sophie. I'm not comin' into your room. Wraith would kill me stone dead. And then dig me up and do it all over again."

She giggles and blows a kiss at him as he at last escapes to stride away. I give her a curious look. She and the Vegas president seem almost overfamiliar. I wonder why?

"Hey!" she calls out to get our attention as Sam and I open our own doors. "I wasn't gonna shag him. Just wanted some company. I miss Wraith." Her mouth quivers, and a tear drops from her eye.

The three of us look at each other, the reason why we're all awake at this ungodly hour sobering me quickly. "Want us to come in?" I suggest.

And that's how I spend the night, no longer alone, but sharing a bed with two women, and together we share the burden and concern for our men.

CHAPTER 36
Slick

When we arrive back at the clubhouse Wraith's team's already back. The VP's nowhere in sight, but Tongue is standing at the bar with a shot glass in his hand, which seems like a fucking good idea. After having a quick word with Viper and Shooter, I take my smokes out of my cut and wander on over and join him. Putting my own mess aside for the moment, I ask about his night.

"How did it go man?"

"Fucker didn't know what hit him." The stud in his tongue catches the light as he speaks. "Did the typical knock at the door, he comes down and opens it and bang. Got him straight between the eyes. You?"

I evade the question, just give him a quick nod then ask, "Drum back yet?"

"Not seen him."

When I stay quiet, Tongue doesn't bother me, probably knowing it's been one hell of a night and it's not over yet, not until everyone's got safely back. But every time the door to the clubhouse opens I feel sick with apprehension for a reason that's different to his.

Blade's team's back next, and so far we haven't lost a man. Soon after Peg and his crew return to cheers. Now we're only waiting on Drum, and my nervousness increases every second that passes. When he arrives, a roar goes through the clubhouse.

Our meticulous planning has paid off. Every target eliminated, and every man home without so much as a fucking scratch. Oh, except for Beef, who'd caught his fingernail and ripped it. Hardly a case to call Doc. Who'd have fuckin' thought?

Wraith's appeared and has taken Tongue's place at the bar, which puts me beside him as the prez comes over, for once a recognisable look of pure satisfaction on his face.

"Herrera had it right. The fuckers didn't know what they had comin'." He takes the bottle of beer his VP offers him, chugging it back.

"No one seems to have run into any trouble." Wraith agrees. "Went fuckin' smoothly."

With a feeling of dread, I realise this is my opening to come clean. "Er, Prez." It will only be worse if I delay telling him. As he turns his attention to me, Crash comes up alongside. Throwing him a grateful look, I continue, "Got a moment to talk, Prez?"

Drum looks at me, then down at his now empty beer. "Fuck this. Prospect? Get me a fuckin' whisky. No you wanker, not that. There. On the top fuckin' shelf." Jekyll almost drops the shot glass in his hurry to comply. Drum narrows his eyes. "And for your information that's my fuckin' whisky. Don't go lettin' any other douchebag have any. And yeah, of course I want ice!" The prospect's hand shakes as he gets down the correct drink. Drum loses patience. "Jekyll. Just give me the fuckin' bottle." Drum grabs the whisky and the glass. He looks around the room where noisy celebrations have started, and then at the expression on my face. "Let's take this to my office then, Slick. You in on this too, Crash?"

Feeling decidedly uncomfortable, I follow him the short distance down the hallway, and then inside his room. Once we've got ourselves settled. I take a deep breath, look at Crash then at the prez. Knowing I can't put it off, I enlighten Drum as to exactly what had gone down, and what I personally had done.

His face darkens as I tell him, his hand smoothing over his beard as I explain we now know who's responsible for us having a brother in hospital and one of our old lady's dead. His fist hits the desk, making his drink bounce.

"Why d'ya fuckin' kill him, Slick?"

"He was provoked." Crash tries to offer support.

"Shouldn't have been fuckin' provoked!" Drum's as angry as I've ever seen him. I find my eyes carefully tracking his hands in case he goes for his gun. "He could have told us more. Least of all the contacts at the social that he's dealin' with, and the fuckers who want Amy. Fuck, he could have had good intel that we could use. It wasn't your fuckin' call, Slick. And after what he'd done? All the brothers would have wanted to take their turn with them. You fuckin' denied them the chance."

I hang my head in shame.

"Fuck. I should have your fuckin' patch for this." I feel spittle land on my cheek as Drum shouts at me across the desk, grateful for the expanse of wood between us.

I give a miserable nod. "Prez, I acted on impulse. I'm sorry."

"Now you've gone and killed a cop. That could fall back on the club. A bunch of gangsters they won't do too much digging. But one of their own? They'll never stop."

"I'll step up, Prez. If I have to. Won't get the club into it."

"You fuckin' better. Fuck it." He slams his hand down again.

Crash sits forward, his chin resting on a cupped palm. "We walked into hell tonight, Drummer. Two young girls... It was sickening. Slick made some good calls, what I'd have done myself. We got the other fuckers killed cleanly and the girls away to their homes. Hell. I was gonna shoot Archer myself if Slick hadn't stopped me. And at least, he got him to talk."

Crash's input calms Drummer a little. Well, it turns a hurricane into a tropical storm at least. The prez sits back. "He admitted they wanted Amy to fuckin' sell her?" Drum's fingers tap on the wood. "No doubt he deserved what he fuckin' got. But I'd have liked to be the one to take him down."

"I'm sorry, Prez." I repeat my apology. Seems all I can do.

Reaching behind him, Drummer picks up a couple of glasses and pours a shot of whisky in each, pushing them toward Crash and me. "I can't blame you, Slick. Hearin' him tellin' it like that? Admittin' he ran Heart off the road?"

"He fuckin' laughed, Prez."

Drum closes his eyes briefly and takes a deep breath. He lets it out slowly. "Under the circumstances, I can't say I wouldn't have done the same thing."

Am I going to get away with it?

"If it had been one of my brothers, I could see myself losing it like Slick." Crash continues to add his support. "Fuckin' bad to hear it like that."

"He laughed." I repeat. That was what had caused my trigger finger to twitch.

We all drink the whisky, and by God it's good stuff. Nothing but the best for the prez.

"What about the girls? They know anythin' to identify you?"

I'd checked that as soon as I'd got back. "Not accordin' to Viper and Shooter. Girls were half out of it, only just managed to hang onto the bikes. We didn't wear cuts and doubt they'd remember enough for an identification. And we blew up the house. We left nothin' of ours behind. I'd like Mouse to run a check on the addresses. Girls that young shouldn't be out alone at night, want to see what it looks like at home."

"Yeah. And if we find fuckin' anythin' we don't like, I'll pass it on to Hannah. Reckon she'll help if the kids want protectin'."

It seems a good idea, as long as she doesn't ask too many questions. Like what's happened to her missing partner.

Drum hasn't finished. "Slick, I'm not fuckin' thrilled by what you did tonight, but I can understand it. At least the fucker who went after Heart is dead. Christ, I can't believe it. I knew he was on the take, but he didn't seem the type to get his hands dirty."

"Archer hates bikers, doubt he thought twice about taking Heart and Crystal out."

"At least that's one mystery solved."

"Two," Drum corrects me. "We've confirmed who's interested in Amy. And why." He pauses and takes a sip of his beer. "But I don't like that he's got the social involved. That could cause us problems." He picks up the bottle again and points it toward me. "Once we're certain we get no blowback from the Herreras, your girls can come back. Anyone with an interest in them is dead. But Sam? Fuck. She's gonna need to stay away with Amy while we sort things out. And fuck that, I'll miss her. And it's not fair on the kid. She's lost her mom, maybe her dad, and now she's losing us too. I was getting fond of the little brat too."

I wipe my hands over the dome of my head and try to think. "What about Crystal's mother? Could she be persuaded to drop her claim?"

The prez considers. "For her part in the matter I don't want to even see the bitch again. Being prepared to sell her own grandkid for fuck's sake? Let alone getting her daughter and husband killed."

"She's a drugged-up whore. She's probably not even thinking straight."

"I think you're being too kind." Drum's right, but I've seen enough addicts to know there's no limit to what they'll do to get their next fix. Prez hasn't finished. "Without Archer she'll have no support for her claim. But it depends on her debts, and who wants to collect them. She might still be desperate enough to still fight for the kid."

"Could you arrange an accident?"

"Maybe, Crash. That might be the direction we'll need to go. Heck, I don't like harmin' women, but that one's the scum of the earth." Prez looks down at his drink. "Don't think we need to rush into anything, let's see how it plays out for now. We've all done enough *killin'* tonight." And it's his pointed look at me that makes me realise what his emphasis was directed at.

"Fuck, I'm sorry Prez. I shouldn't have shot him." I feel remorse all over again. Now I'm responsible for keeping him and his old lady apart.

His eyes blast his full glare at me, then, after thinking for a few seconds, his face begins to relax. "Bringin' him back here would have caused its own problems. Wouldn't have got him to talk by playin' nice, he would have ended up just as dead. We should have made him suffer a bit longer, but at least he's out of our hair. May well have the fuckin' heat sniffin' around though. They've got a missin' cop who's had his nose in our shit."

He's quiet for a moment then slaps my back and huffs a laugh. "You shot his dick off, you say? What is it with you and fuckin' dicks, Slick?"

Crash smirks. "I'll have to remember not to cross you, Brother."

Drum shudders then chuckles. "Think we'll all need to remember that, Crash." Then he's staring at me again. "Well, the Rock Demons might be off the hook for Heart's accident, but I haven't forgotten, Slick. We'll keep huntin' those mother-fuckers down."

I raise my chin to him in thanks. Yes, every one of those bastards that hurt Ella is going to be punished. But that's for another day. I'm just relieved I've still got my patch.

"Sounds like the party's getting' goin' out there." Prez's head is cocked to one side. "Get out of here, brothers. Everyone did fuckin' good tonight."

Feeling a weight has been lifted off my shoulders, I'm the first to walk out. Crash slaps my back as I leave Drum's office. I try to thank him profusely, but he shakes my gratitude off, and then, spying Rope and Cuff, goes over to speak to them.

I go to the bar, and Jekyll produces a beer. I'm standing, thinking of the night, of Archer, and of what the prez had just said. And...oh fuck! Suddenly his words filter through my tired brain. If the trouble with the Herreras really is over and there's nothing else brewing, Ella can come home, and Jayden as well. With the rogue element of the crime family cleaned out, unless there's any retaliation no one's going to be searching for her anymore. Tossing back my drink I grab a fresh beer, rolling the cold bottle over my forehead as I think through the implications. It's time to start searching for a house. Fuck, that will be strange. I've lived on the compound since I'd joined the club. But for Ella and me to set up a home? Can't fucking wait or think of anything I'd like better. Put a sprog inside her as well, do it all properly.

Yeah. Do it all by the book. Which gives me an idea. And now the ideas taken hold there won't be anything to shift it.

"Another, Slick?"

"Naw, Blade. Got somethin' I need to do. I'm out of here now." The enforcer looks surprised I've blown him off, but I don't want to waste a minute now I've plans to make.

"Your right hand gonna get some action? Don't rub the skin off," Blade calls after me as I walk off.

Flipping him the finger I call over my shoulder, "Very funny." But he's put a smile on my face. For that, I reward him, pausing to add, "I am gonna try something different. I'll use my fuckin' left." As he flips me the bird I move off. No, I'm not going to be playing with my dick. Well, not until after I've done what I've got in mind first.

Slapping my brothers on the back as I make my way through them, I head on up to my suite and open up my laptop, which I'd retrieved from the weapons store. Yeah, I'd hidden my valuable stuff there too. Opening up Google I search for what I need.

And yeah, the idea fucking excites me. Enough so when I've finished I do give my hand a good work out in the shower. *But I ain't gonna be telling Blade that.*

Early next morning I go to find the prez. As expected he's up early and monitoring the local news. Entering his office a little cautiously, I'm met by a nod. Seeing it doesn't look like he's holding a grudge I take a seat, cocking my eyebrow and inclining my head toward the monitor in front of him.

He correctly interprets my gesture. "Nothing about us. They haven't even pieced it all together yet. Explosions and killing all over Tucson. Cops are in a complete mess."

"There's no connection between us and the Herreras?"

"Seems we have no worries on that score." He stares at me for a moment. "Old man Herrera's been in touch. Bit of a coded conversation, but it appears they'll keep to their word and leave us out of it. They're focusin' the family's attention in another direction. Readin' between the lines I think he's confessed to the Zetas, and they're happy someone's done their work for them. They have no trouble takin' the blame for stampin' down hard. Brings the deviant part of the Herrera family back into line, and the Zeta's can build it up that they don't tolerate sharing their trade."

I breathe a sigh of relief. That's good to know.

"Seeing as we've done old man Herrera a solid, I've pulled in a favour." As he stares at me, his lips turn up into a smile. "Whatever Crystal's mom's debts are, they won't take a child in payment. He confirmed anyone involved in that side of the business we took out last night. Clyde's all on her own with paying them off."

Well fuck me! That's great news. "Sam and Amy can come home then."

He frowns. "Not until we sort out the fuckin' social issues. Even if Clyde has no further interest in the kid, now that a judge has got involved it might not be so easy." And we're back to the fact that if I hadn't been so trigger happy, Archer might have been a help there.

"I'm so sorry, Drum."

"Ain't a problem, Slick. After what Archer confessed to, he wasn't gonna live past last night. We'll sort it, don't worry. We'll get the club lawyer involved. And Heart may still wake up."

I fucking hope so. But it seems a long shot.

"You must be breathin' easier. Ella and Jayden are in the clear now."

Yeah, and there's nothing to stop me putting my plan into action. As I nod, my facial expression must give something away.

Pushing back his chair, Drum places his foot against the desk and levels that famous stare at me. "It wasn't just the update you wanted. You want more than that, doncha? So spit it out man, what can I do for ya, Slick?"

I take a deep breath and start to explain what's on my mind. After I tell him he's silent, and for a second I'm not sure what reaction I'll get. It is a fucking big ask after I cocked up so badly last night. Gradually his eyes soften, his mouth gives a twitch, then his lips turn up.

Finally, he bursts out laughing. "Fuck me! That's fuckin' ace." Leaning forward he bangs both palms on the desk. "Want me to get it sorted with Red?"

"That would be great, Prez." I'm grinning like a loon. Seems the plan's a go.

"And who do ya want?"

I throw out a few names. Well, quite a lot of them actually.

"Count on me, Slick. Just what we fuckin' need."

Happy he's got his part under control, I leave him to get busy making that call while I go top off my gas, which I can conveniently do here at the auto shop on the compound. Removing the hose, I look at the work piling up all around, thinking how good it will be to focus on doing a day's work for a change rather than worrying about fucking child molesters. The place seems empty without Sam too. It's not just Ella I miss, but all of the women. Pansy bikers that we are, the old ladies make this a home.

But it seems Sam will need to stay away until Drummer can sort something out about Amy. What the fuck will Drum do without his old lady? She's pregnant as well. Shit, we might have got out of one mess, but I can't see our way out of the other. Still, not a lot to be gained by going over things I can't mend. I can only hope Drum and Sam can work things out.

Not surprisingly as there'd been one hell of a lot of celebrating in the small hours of the morning, brothers nursing sore heads take a while until they feel able to ride. It's not until midday that those of us with women in Vegas at last get on our bikes. Without the old ladies moaning they need the rest stops, and just Road driving the truck, we have far fewer breaks once we get on the road, and make it to our destination in just over seven hours.

As we pull in through the gates I'm almost shaking with anticipation to see Ella and Jayden again. Impatiently I back into line, forgetting to kick down my stand until the last moment in my hurry to get in and see my old lady, just managing to catch my bike before it topples over. Wraith notices, the bastard, and I give him the finger as he smirks. Taking a deep breath, I force myself to wait, curbing my impulse to push my brothers aside in my rush to get through the doors.

Keep it together, Slick.

The women are waiting in the clubroom, alerted by the roar of bikes arriving. As soon as her eyes catch sight of me, Ella's running toward me, her eagerness matching my own. I pull her into my arms, swinging her off her feet and twirling her around. Then I hug her tightly as we indulge in the physical contact of just being back together again.

When we revert to using words, Ella's first to speak. "I was so worried, Slick!"

Not admitting there were moments I'd had doubts about seeing her again too, I just tell her, "I'm here now."

"Slick!"

"Jayden!" Putting Ella down I put my arm around my other girl. "What you been up to, darlin'?"

"We went to the strip! Ella lost all your money." She gives me a cheeky grin along with the news.

"I didn't lose all of it." And that's a big sister smackdown stare if ever I saw one. "We went shopping first, and I *may* have lost a bit after."

"I played slots. And we went on some rides. Ella went on the Stratosphere with Twister!"

I throw her a glare. "She did, huh?" I pretend to be annoyed, but can't keep it up for long. "Did you go on anything, Jayden?"

"Sophie and I went on the Big Apple Coaster. That was scary enough, and then we went on the gondolas at the Venetian. Oh, and we went on some rides at Circus Circus too." Fuck me, Jayden's almost bouncing with excitement as she tells me everything that she's done. It warms my heart to see her acting her age.

As I listen to her prattle I'm pleased that Ella and Jayden seem to have got their fun out of the way before I arrived. I get enough thrills riding my fucking bike, thank you very much. Racing around on a roller coaster? That's not for me. But that she likes it is just one more intriguing fact I've learned about my woman. You need nerves of steel to go on that ride. I file that thought away.

"We couldn't stay to see everything lit up." Jayden's still babbling on. "We had to get back to meet you."

Huh. "Sorry for that," I reply without meaning it. I'd have been fucking annoyed to get here to find they were out. But I throw her a bone. "Red's agreed to put us up another night. Maybe we can all go to the strip tomorrow night?"

"You really mean it? Slick, you're amazing!" She's so pleased Jayden almost pushes Ella out of the way to give me a hug.

"That okay with you, Ella?" As I glance at the woman who's refusing to let me go, even while Jayden's trying to get to me herself, I notice her mouth might be curved, but she's not smiling with eyes. "Ella?"

"How did everything go, Slick?"

I raise an eyebrow.

"Oh, come on, I'm not stupid. I know something was going down. Did it have anything to do with us?"

And now I can give her the good news and hopefully put a real smile on her face. Leaning down, I speak into her ear. "Jayden can come home now. No one's after her anymore."

She sucks in a breath, then just stares at me as the news sinks in. As she looks like she's got more questions I remind her, "I can't tell you anymore, El. So don't ask."

"Club business." Hmm. Seems she's getting the hang of being an old lady. She swallows back down her questions, and I watch as her mouth turns up into a wide grin. "Going out in Vegas with you will be amazing, Slick. Yeah, that's a great plan."

I hope it is. For a second I'm hesitant, doubting what I've set in motion. *Am I doing the right thing?* And then as she turns the full force of her smile on me, I know that I am. I can't resist, my head lowers, my hand curls around her neck, and I raise her mouth to mine. Everything we did was worth it. The result? My woman and her sister are safe to get on with their lives. And I plan on doing nothing but being right there by their side.

Drinks and food flow freely as another celebration gets going in earnest, our Las Vegas brothers joining our Tucson crew revelling that our plans were carried out with no Satan's Devil becoming a casualty. Drum's arm is around Sam as he's talking to Red, Wraith's holding as tight to Sophie as I am to Ella, all expressing and showing their relief that another chapter in the life of the club has come to a satisfying close. The women may be kept in the dark, but every one of the men know we'd faced an adversity larger than us and have come safely out the other side. A cause for rejoicing if ever there was one.

Predictably the party atmosphere starts to change. When the sweet butts appear, our club girls along with Red's whores, it's my signal to get my women away from the party. Going upstairs, we leave Jayden in her room, then I take Ella along the hallway to the room assigned to us.

Fuck, we've only been apart one night but it seems like it's been forever since my hands have touched her smooth, silky skin, and I take a moment to hold her and simply enjoy the feel of her softness under my calloused hands. This woman has quickly become an addiction for me, almost as vital as the air that I breathe. I can't understand why I'd wasted those months when I didn't go after her. What a fool I had been to blame her for running away instead of searching for a reason as to why she had gone. All that lost time had been my fault. If it hadn't been for the problems with her sister that made her get back in touch, I might never have seen her again. Just the thought makes me reel.

But I got her back. And since then, all my running has been toward her. And now that I've got her, I'm never letting her go again.

Reaching around her, I open the door, then wait for her to walk inside. My eyes fall on the small bag I'd brought with me — a fresh change of clothes and, well, she'll find out what else in a very short while. Let's just say on one of our stops earlier I'd spent some time talking to our Vegas brothers and picked up some ideas. Hmm. Some very interesting suggestions.

I can wait no longer to get started. "Strip, baby. Let me see what I've been missin'."

Her eyes alight at my unexpected command, and her pupils dilate. *Good. Me taking charge turns her on.* Quickly she dispenses with her clothes as I take off my cut and place it on the chair, then pull off my tee. Toeing off my boots, I leave my jeans on for now. As her perfect body is revealed I undo the button and loosen the zip to give a little more room to my lengthening cock. *Has any woman ever turned me on like this before?* If anyone has, I don't remember.

She stands before me, naked, her head cheekily angled to one side, hands on her hips. She's smirking, "Like what you see?" Her eyes fall to the bulge in my jeans.

"Very much," I reply, keeping my voice stern. "Now lie on the bed."

She looks at me quickly, but does what I ask, lying flat on her back, just how I wanted. Taking something from my bag and holding it out of sight, I lay my body across hers and take both her hands, pulling them up over her head. I fumble a bit, *I'll need practice at this*, but with a satisfying click I get the hand-cuffs in place and fasten them to the middle rod of the head-board.

Her mouth gapes open.

I give a reassuring smile. "Alright, darlin'?" Carefully I watch her. Her chest's rising and falling as her breathing rate increases, her nipples are already little firm peaks, and a flush comes over her face.

"I've never done this before." Her voice sounds breathless. I look for signs that she's afraid, but she looks more thrilled than scared. *I remember this is the woman who likes scary rides.*

But I'm mindful she's still got to get those Rock Demons out of her head. "Don't worry, I'm with you. You don't like it? I'll uncuff you."

I wait for her nod, then take the second item out of my bag and show it to her. As her brow creases I explain, "It's a blindfold. Will you try it?"

My dick pulsates and I'm over the moon when her chin dips again, and then she lifts her head so I can wrap it around. And now I've got my woman helpless beneath me. Fuck, the sight of it takes my breath away, and I feel pre-cum seeping out, dampening my jeans. *I can do anything.* I don't know where to start.

As my indecision freezes me, she pulls on the cuffs, spurring me into action. Lowering my mouth to hers, I start with a kiss, slowly applying more pressure until she opens and lets me inside. Just her taste has my cock throbbing. For a few seconds I enjoy the innocent connection until the pressure in my pants makes me need to move this on.

Drawing myself up to give myself room, I start to pay attention to her nipples, a suck on one, a pinch to the other, coaxing them to harden even more under my administrations. Closing my teeth around one makes her suck in air in surprise, and as I gently bite down she pushes her pelvis against me, seeking relief. *Not yet baby.*

Knowing I've taken away one of her senses, I check she's okay. "You doing alright, darlin'?"

Frantically pushing up into me again, a moan comes from her lips. "Just get on with it, already." I grin at her impatience and take it as a yes. And I'm suffering too with her grinding against my denim-clad dick.

But first I want to taste her. I take my time, licking her stomach and up under her ribs, circling her nipples and sucking on them again. Her body tastes salty, and I could feast all day. Or could if my dick wasn't being strangled in my jeans. *Have I ever been this hard?*

I move downwards. Oh yeah, her clit's already nice and swollen and already peeping out from under its hood, and her sweet cunt is glistening with her cream. Taking my time, I lazily reach out a finger and swipe some of the moisture, bringing it to my mouth. Her body jerks at my touch.

Then, with my weight on my elbows, I lean over her once more and kiss her again, her own taste on my tongue surprising her. I grin to myself. Yeah, I got some good advice last night. I take a moment just to enjoy the simple mating of our mouths. Another tug at the handcuffs shows she's getting frustrated, and truth be told, I can't hang on much longer myself.

Quickly standing, I take down my jeans, kicking them off on the floor, swearing my swollen dick sighs in relief. Then I kneel over her, my head facing her legs, and huff a warm breath on her clit.

My unexpected action has her hips rising and she wheezes out my name. "Slick!"

I give it a little suck, and then get my mouth and fingers working, then pause and position my cock, holding it steady with one hand and bringing it to her mouth. "Open," I tell her.

She immediately obeys, and her tongue licks the precum off the head, swirling around my piercing. It's all I can do not to start fucking her mouth it feels so good, but restrained as she is I don't want to frighten her or make her feel trapped. Moving my hand away, I leave her playing as she wants. She widens her mouth and I push in further. Her murmurs of appreciation are almost too much for my poor dick, but she laps up the new excretions that have started to leak.

Lowering my head, I put a finger inside her, my cheeks hollowing as my mouth simultaneously sucks on her clit. I apply another finger, curling up inside her. As she works my cock I lick around her hard bud. Fuck, this feels good. She tastes like heaven. Her tight pussy is clutching my fingers and her mouth drawing in my cock. The scent of her arousal is going straight to my head, and those little sounds, slurping noises she's making, echo around my head as well as vibrating around my hard length.

I'm not going to last. I work my hand and mouth faster, applying more pressure to that special spot inside, as well as licking her clit. As she focuses on what's happening to her body, her lips open and my cock slips out of her mouth. Her legs start shaking, her stomach muscles tighten, her breath comes in gasps, and then she drags in one last breath before her body starts twitching and she screams. Taking her over the top, I soften my mouth and remove my fingers, licking at her gently until she comes down.

Now I turn her over, the chain joining her cuffs tightening, imprisoning her further. I pull up her hips and unable to wait any longer, push inside her tight, sweet channel. Fuck, I'm not wearing a condom, skin to skin feels too fucking good. She's so swollen and I have to work at it to get in, stopping only when I bump her cervix.

"You still okay, darlin?" I can hardly speak, the words coming in pants.

"Move, Slick. Move, please."

Her shrill cries encouraging me I don't disappoint her, I start thrusting until I feel her muscles clenching, but before she can come, pull out and then turn her over so she's on her back again. Pulling her legs up and hooking them over my elbows I hold her wide open as I thrust in fast. As she cries out in pleasure I do it again, and again, until I'm hammering away, my hips piston like an engine powering my cock, slightly changing the angle until I know that my piercing is hitting just the right place.

Stretching my hand up I encircle her neck with my fingers.

"Slick, Slick! Oh God!"

And there we have it! I quicken my pace, frantically pounding, feeling that tingle in my spine as her cunt squeezes my cock as she starts those contractions.

"God! Oh God!"

And I'm lost. My balls tighten, I pull out cum propelling from my slit, covering her tits and her stomach, white streams marking this woman as mine as her body continues to give little tremors.

"Slick?" Her question comes as a gasp.

I grin. Blindfolded, my action surprised her. I rub my hands over her skin until her body glistens with cum, massaging it into her tits and her stomach.

"Fuckin' beautiful." I've never seen anything looking so good.

A moment while I get my breath, then quickly move to her head where I take off her blindfold and remove the cuffs, rubbing at her wrists inspecting for any soreness. Then I roll her to me and take her in my arms, ignoring the stickiness joining us together.

She's still breathing rapidly, my own heart beating just as fast. I hold her and let my hands soothe her, smoothing them slowly up and down her back.

When her chest stops heaving she opens her eyes and I swear I can see love beaming out.

"Slick, that was…that was incredible."

"I wondered if you'd like it." For some reason I feel chuffed with myself, and with her that she allowed me to try something new, giving me total control over her.

"You could have done anything to me." She gives a little shake of her head, bemused she permitted it.

"You can trust me." I'll never hurt her.

"I know. Shit, that was a turn on. Not being able to see, or move. I never would have thought…" Her voice trails off, but I can complete it. She's come so far in such a short time.

I smirk. "I can see we'll be tryin' that again, darlin'."

"I hope so." She laughs. "Fuck I hope so."

Placing a kiss to her forehead, I tighten my hold. "I love you so much, Ella."

"Slick, I love you too."

She's quiet for a moment, and then asks, "I didn't know you were into that."

Now it's my turn to chuckle. "Neither did I babe. First time I've ever tied someone up. But I'm glad you liked it, 'cos fuck was it a turn on, havin' you at my mercy."

Her head pulls back so she can look into my eyes. "I loved it, Slick. But if you hadn't tried that before, what made you think of it? Where did the cuffs and blindfold come from?"

My chuckles deepen. "Have you met Cuff and Rope yet?"

"What?"

"They're two brothers from Vegas. I think you can guess how they got their names."

"Slick!" Her jaw drops.

"Let's just say they gave me some pointers earlier on."

CHAPTER 37

Ella

If I'd been asked a few weeks ago whether I would ever be able to trust a man again, the simple answer that I wouldn't even have had to think about would have been no. The fact that I've changed, and just how far I've come, is down to one man, the man who's now lying beside me, gently snoring. Only yesterday I was worried I'd never see him again. Now I snuggle into his warmth, unable to envisage a time I wouldn't want, or need, him by my side.

I'm still a touch nervous around these leather-clad men, but I've come to learn how this club and the one where the members abused me at poles apart. And, being an official old lady, the Satan's Devils are more likely to protect than to harm me. They've gone out on a limb for both my sister and I, and they'd all come home safe. It relieves me to know I don't have to live with any deaths on my conscience.

As for sex, I've gone from not wanting a man to touch me to being more than happy for Slick to restrain me last night. It was unexpectedly freeing for him to take complete control, leaving me no choice but to lie there and take it. And, well, wow. I don't think I've ever come so hard in my life. I'm certainly not adverse to trying that again. *I wonder what else those Vegas brothers suggested to him... Hmm.*

As we walk down the stairs the next morning, my cheeks are burning as I wonder if I'm going to come face to face with the strangely named Rope and Cuff in the club room, worried my face will give away that Slick had followed their suggestions. Damn, from the glow I feel, I think that it might. As we step into the already bustling room, I apprehensively glance around speculating who they might be, or if they're even here. But as Slick inclines his head toward a pair at the bar, and they smirk at me knowingly, I reckon I've found out. Quickly I turn my head away, my blush deepening, and seek out the more comfortable company of the girls.

And there they are, with Rosa and Tiffany, standing in the entrance to the kitchen.

Sophie looks at me carefully, there's a twinkle in her eye. "Someone had a good night," she observes.

As Slick laughs out loud I redden even more, knowing he's giving everything away. He tightens his arms around me and I lean into his touch.

Drummer comes up to us, he also gives me a smirk. *Christ! Have I got what we did written on my forehead?* His steely eyes stare at me intently, but the crinkles around the edge soften his normal glower. "We've made plans for today." He raises his eyes to the man at my side.

Slick rests his chin on my head, "Yeah?" There's a chuckle in his voice which I don't understand.

The prez nods. "We're heading into Vegas about two o'clock if you want to tag along." *Why is Drummer grinning?* "Sam wants to do some shoppin' while we try our hands at the tables."

I look up at Slick. "I don't need to buy anything. Can I come with you?" I quite fancy trying my hand at roulette again. Hopefully I might come away richer this time.

"Naw," Prez turns me down. "Let your man have a moment to himself, darlin'. You girls go buy yourselves somethin' nice."

"And," Slick starts, "from what Jayden's been sayin', you'll only lose more of my money if you play again."

I thump his arm in mock protest, but nod at Drummer, knowing I can't ignore an instruction from the prez. And it does sound like fun. Yesterday we didn't really get around to looking at any stores.

Knowing what we've come out for, it comes as no surprise that some hours later I find myself in a changing room in an exclusive boutique. What is unexpected is that I'm with Sam and that she's encouraging me to buy a dress I'll never wear. Every argument I put forward she dismisses, showing when she wants to be, she's as forceful as her old man. As she takes the one she's chosen off the hanger and holds it out, I fold under her insistence and, despite my objections, find myself getting attired in a short white cocktail dress which sparkles with diamante.

"Sam, this is daft. It's really expensive. And where the hell would I wear this?" I can't see me walking around the compound in it.

"Ella, it really suits you. You look fantastic. I'm getting something fancy too." As I start to open my mouth she continues persuasively, "Look, how often do we have a chance to spoil ourselves? Just buy something for the hell of it?"

But it's Slick's money. "I don't' feel comfortable. Just look at this price tag. Slick would have a fit."

"Slick will love it," she contradicts, nudging my arm. "The boys are taking us out tonight. We thought we'd surprise them, dress up for once. All they've seen us in lately are jeans or shorts."

I glance at the changing room door as though it's my escape route and wave my hand. "I'm okay with buying a dress, but not here and not this one. There must be something cheaper. Something in a more practical colour and not quite so sparkly."

Sam's hands rest on my shoulder and she turns me to face the mirror, then indicates that I should also look at my rear view in the ones behind. "You look beautiful, Ella. It really suits you." Her hands hover just above my skin as she traces my lines. "It emphasises your waist and clings to your butt. You've got a great figure, Ella, and this shows it off. Just look at your cleavage, it's demure but incredibly sexy all at the same time." I look in the mirror and catch a glimpse of her face. Her features are tightening. "If you don't buy this dress, El, you and I are gonna have problems."

Shit! She sounds serious. If it means so much to her... I look at my reflection again. It's not something I'd normally wear, but hell, she's right. If it wasn't for the price tag, Slick would love it.

"No arguments, Ella. When was the last time you treated yourself?"

Never. I buy the cheapest clothes that I can, often second-hand which others have discarded.

"Are you sure it will be alright?" Slick's given me his credit card, but I'm frightened to use it. "I think I should call Slick..."

"Ella, Slick will be fine about it. Don't worry yourself. If he's not he'll have to answer to me." She draws herself up straight and puts on the fiercest face she can, making me giggle. Although I'm still unconvinced.

We continue back and forth for a few moments, until eventually I decide it's easier to give in. She knows she's got me when I say with a sigh, "Okay. But aren't you going to try your dresses on?"

She'd brought a couple in with her. Having sorted me out, she now tries one on herself. It's in a shimmery emerald green that suits her to a tee. This time I'm doing the encouraging, and she keeps it on.

I go to change back, she reaches out her hand to stop me. "No, wear it, Ella. Let's all surprise the men. Dressed like this they'll have to take us somewhere decent."

So that's her plan! Sneaky. I laugh, then agree.

Leaving the changing room, we meet up with the others. Rosa and Tiffany have come along too, and they're standing there with Sandy and Carmen, all looking pretty as a picture in stunning new dresses. Jayden looks just... Well, wow, is all I can describe it, dressed like she's going to her prom. I give her a big smile and nod my head to show my appreciation. Sophie's grinning like a loon wearing a pale blue satin pant suit. I feel fleeting sympathy, knowing she doesn't like showing her fake leg.

But hell, what she's wearing is flattering, so I can tell her with all honesty, "Sophie, you look fucking amazing."

"I know," she replies, doing a twirl. "Do you see what these trousers do for my arse?"

"Yeah, hun, you've got a fantastic arse." Sandy mocks her English using a posh accent which has us all chuckling.

Before leaving we sort out matching shoes. Finally, we go to the cash desk, my hand trembling as I wait for the cashier to run up the bill and I reach for my wallet.

To my surprise, Sam stays my arm as she hands over a card. When my eyebrow rises she whispers, "This one's on the club."

What?

Well, I'm not one to look a gift horse in the mouth, and I'm the only one looking surprised. *Wow.* There seems to be advantages in being an old lady of the Satan's Devils. "I only hope they can afford it after being at the tables," I murmur, making them all laugh.

"Right." Sam looks at her watch. "We've still got time to kill. Hair and nails, ladies."

Automatically my hand goes to my hair. I haven't had it properly cut in ages. I suppose it wouldn't hurt, and it would help show off my new dress. No longer feeling like making objections —*to be honest, I'm totally enjoying this*—like an obedient lamb,

I follow Sam and the rest of the women as she leads us into the salon at the Venetian.

It's nearly two hours later, and I can't stop looking at the way they've styled my hair into a bob. It suits me and frames my face nicely. My fringe has been straightened and feathered a little so it looks softer. I've had an expert apply makeup, and my nails have been painted and decorated with gems.

Carmen's touching her new hairstyle, looking critically at her reflection in a window, and then she turns with a smile and says, "Okay, they've done a fair enough job."

"Do you like it, El?" Jayden's flicking her French plait—pulled back from her face it makes her look older. And beautiful. I tell her so.

With a broad smile, Sam again pays for everything.

Feeling decidedly pampered and special, I exit the salon, still ignorant about where we're going tonight, but I knowingly I can't wait to show off my new look.

Sam takes another look at her watch, then she announces it's time to meet the boys. Feeling excited, wondering what Slick is going to say, I fidget impatiently as we descend via the elevator and go out through the front doors to find tens of Harley's waiting, more than I expected. As my eyes roam the line I'm amazed to see not only the men who'd come to Vegas last night, but also Peg, Dart, Beef, and Blade. Hey, there's Tongue, Rock, Mouse, and Shooter. And behind them, Joker, Lady, and Marvel. It looks like all members of the Tucson chapter are here. The only ones missing are the prospects. And what's unusual is that every man is wearing a helmet. Perhaps they have to in Vegas?

Behind our men are at least a dozen of the Vegas guys too. When my eyes fall on them, Rope and Cuff give me a little wave and a cheeky grin. *What the fuck is going on?*

The other women go to find their men. Rosa gets up behind Red, Tiffany behind Fox. Sam goes to Drummer, Sophie, Carmen, and Sandy walk past me as I'm still looking for Slick, unable to see him in his accustomed space in the middle of our group. Paladin has stepped off his bike and has come to get Jayden, leading her away and carefully helping her onto the pillion. She leans up against the sissy bar and wiggles her fingers at me. A brief wave of disappointment that my man appears to be missing, and then, *finally*, I see him. My panicked heartbeat begins to slow.

There he is. Why's he at the front of the line? Where's the SUV that we came in? I can't ride a bike wearing this! And Jayden, she's never been on the back of a bike before. And her dress could get caught…

"You're standin' like a fuckin' rabbit caught in the headlights, babe. Come on, we've not got much time."

What? I throw Slick a look of amazement. His head's freshly shaved, he's got on a dress shirt under his tee, and his black jeans look new. Of course, he's wearing that sexy as fuck cut over the top. He hands me an item.

"Put this on, darlin'." It's my own property cut. In a state of bemusement I slip my arms inside, slipping it on over my dress, and then with my eyes flicking around at everyone, take the hand that he offers me. He leads me to the front of the line where he's left his bike.

But the prez rides in front.

I cast a worried glance behind me as I get on, trying to sit on as much of the short dress as I can. I catch Drummer's eye, and he nods reassuringly.

"Jayden…?" I ask as I put on the helmet he's handed me.

"Paladin's got her. Don't worry yourself."

I'm out of my depth, not knowing what the on earth's going on, but my arms automatically go around Slick as he starts his engine. Looks like this will be one hell of a party tonight. *But why are we in the front?*

The roar of more than thirty bikes starting makes me look around. I see Joker, the Road Captain, and one of the Vegas brothers moving out and stopping the traffic. Slick revs his engine and pulls away, and everyone follows us. I hold on tight as we drive down the strip, seeing tourists pausing to watch us, some even taking pictures at the sight. I only hope I'm not flashing anyone and the photos won't be pictures of my bare ass. *I knew this skirt was too short.*

It's a different feeling, leading the pack, knowing everyone's following us. The familiar feel of the leather beneath my fingers, and the smell as I rest my cheek against Slick's back helps both calm and excite me, even if I haven't got a clue what's going on.

We drive over the tarmac, not going fast, taking our time. Pipes rumble behind and I feel pride that I'm part of this show they're putting on. I'm no longer the girl on the side lines watching bikers pass from out front of the coffee shop. I'm holding onto my man, with the engine vibrating between my thighs. I'm on top of the world. *What could be better than this?*

And then we come to a building with a sign saying 'Wedding Chapel' written over the top. Slick uses his indicator, and while he reduces his speed he doesn't stop.

The roar behind us quietens, but we're waved on in through wide open doors. Slick drives slowly and carefully down the aisle, and only at the end applying the brakes and putting the stand down.

My jaw drops to the floor as he taps my leg, indicating I should get off. Carefully balancing on his shoulders and, as demurely as I can, conscious of all the men behind me, I dismount. Slick gets off after. Someone comes up and hands me a beautiful bouquet of red roses.

With my mouth open I turn and look at my man. He's trying to fasten a matching boutonniere to his cut. Then his eyes bore into mine and he watches me intently. As the seats behind us become filled with Satan's Devils, Jayden, Sophie, and Sam come to stand by my side, Drum, Wraith, and Dart stand beside Slick.

Suddenly Slick drops to one knee and holds out his hand.

Bewildered I place my palm to his.

"Darlin'." His voice is hoarse, he coughs and starts again. "Darlin'. Perhaps I should have asked you earlier, but fuck, you gonna marry me babe?"

I don't need to think about it as everything drops into place. "Yes," I squeak.

"Thank fuck for that!" Slick leaps up and pulls me into his arms, his lips crashing down on mine to hollers and shouts echoing around us.

"You're supposed to wait to do that." A stranger's voice sounds amused.

But Slick takes his time before he pulls back.

Fog swirls up around us as the officiate starts to do his stuff. I'm so engrossed in my man I can't concentrate on the ceremony, only hoping I say yes in the right places. I'm trembling with happiness, goosebumps rise on my skin and tears prick in my eyes as I gaze at Slick in disbelief. He's saying some beautiful words about us riding through life together. Then it's my turn to speak.

I only manage to stumble out something about how much I love him.

Then he places a ring on my finger and we're announced as man and wife. *Man and fucking wife!* I'm married! *To Slick!*

Jayden rushes up and throws herself into my arms. "I'm so happy for you, Ella! Slick's so good for you."

I hug her back. I'm so choked up it's difficult to speak. "You knew about this?"

She grins. "Yeah, Slick told me this morning."

How the hell did she keep it secret?

The girls are crying, the men cheering and shouting. Slick's slapped on the back so many times I think it must hurt. I'm kissed by everyone, then we pose for some photos. *My husband* sorts out some money-type business and then we're handed some prints.

We lead the way outside, Slick clutching the licence. Then he turns me and I look up to see emblazoned in lights, SLICK AND ELLA. My hand goes to my mouth and I start laughing, bent double as the chuckles come forth. Like every girl, I used to dream of getting married, but I never thought I'd end up with a biker wedding in Vegas. But it couldn't be more perfect.

Slick's looking at me in concern at my odd reaction, so I wave at the sign. "Slick, this is absolutely mindblowing. You couldn't have made it more special. This is the best wedding I could have dreamed of."

As we kiss under the sign the guys are taking photos on their phones.

He hands me the helmet and glasses once more, and now we're heading off again. I'm expecting to go back to the club, and guessing there'll be a party, this time one I'll really enjoy. The new weight of the ring on my finger is a constant reminder that I'm now this man's wife. It seems unbelievable.

But we don't go back to the Vegas compound. Instead we stop at a steakhouse. Going inside we're shown to a function room. There's dance floor and a DJ who's currently playing bland music. A table's been set up at the top where Slick and I sit, Drum, Wraith, Sophie, Sam, with Amy on her lap then Jayden next to her.

The rest of the brothers settle down at the side tables. I'm in a complete state of bewilderment, unable to believe we're the stars of this show, or that along with the wedding Slick's arranged a reception. I couldn't say what I ate, but I think it was delicious.

Drum stands and gives a speech, I try to listen. He makes us double up with some of the things that he says. And then my man, Slick, stands, and, well, he's just amazing. I fall in love with him all over again at his flowery words. And then crack up as he starts to get crude and makes a throw-away comment that only I, Rope, and Cuff would understand. My face burns.

When the rattle of silverware dies down, a freaking cake's wheeled in. On the top, a pair of bikers riding a Harley. *What else could I have expected?*

"Take a pic, Slick," I say, nudging him, coming to my senses, knowing I want to remember this day for ever.

Slick laughs and points at Mouse, who's got a camera in his hand. I hadn't noticed him recording everything. When I catch his eye I give him a little wave and he lifts his chin in return.

After cake's cut with the normal entertainment, and then passed around, the DJ puts on a record and invites Slick and I to dance. As Paul Weller starts singing, '*You do something to me*', my eyes start to water, and I relax into Slick's arms and gently sway with the music. *God, is it possible to love this man anymore?*

CHAPTER 38

Slick

Ella's got my ring on her finger, and she's in my arms. I'm surrounded by my brothers. I'm on top of the fucking world. Nothing could be better than this. Absolutely fucking nothing. Not even riding my Harley.

We're taking centre spot, dancing to the music, and I'm holding her body so close to mine. I love her so fucking much, and she's become such an important part of my life I've no idea how I lived without her. And soon, if I have my way, she'll be carrying my child. *She's mine.* My old lady. My *wife*.

With more than a little help from Drum and the rest of my brothers, we managed to get everything set up in record time, luckily getting a free spot at the wedding chapel which does Harley weddings, and finding this venue with an available function room. The girls were on board as soon as I'd told them, and even Jayden had managed to keep it a secret.

And the fuck if it hadn't all gone so smoothly, that was just the icing on the fucking cake. And talking about cake, where the fuck did that come from? I suspect it was probably Sam's doing, perhaps with some help from the local old ladies. Now I truly know anything can happen in Vegas.

When Ella appeared in that sexy-as-fuck dress I didn't know if I was going to be able to keep my hands off her during the ceremony. Speaking of which… I let my hands wander down and cup that cute ass, which is all mine, not giving a damn who's watching. Yeah, so what? I'm fondling my *wife*. I'm allowed to. No one fucking else is touching her. Ever. My cock starts swelling at the thought of her in my bed, every night. For the rest of our lives.

The song comes to an end, far too soon. I could have held her forever. I'm not ready to let her go. *I'll never be able to let her go.* Raising my eyes, I see Peg talking to the DJ. *Uh oh.*

When the blistering sounds of ELO's '*Roll over Beethoven*' start to scream out, I have to laugh. *Trust Peg to liven things up.* Drum comes onto the dance floor and, fuck it, they're all getting up. Wraith's gently twirling Sophie, carefully making sure she doesn't lose her balance, and all the other brothers are boogying out with their old ladies, and those without women are dancing by themselves.

Ella gives me a cheeky grin and pulls back, and now she's shaking her fucking booty. I'd never seen her dance, and wow. I realise I'm standing still in the middle of the fucking dance floor looking like an idiot just watching her shimmy to the music. What a sight! And she's all *mine!*

She reaches out her hand and pulls me in to her. Coming back to myself I take the lead. We're dancing together. From the flare in her eyes she likes the moves I've got too. *Fuck, I can't wait to get her under me tonight.*

Now she's dancing with her sister. And now with the rest of the girls. Fuck, Satan's Devils know how to choose their women. They're twirling and bopping, what a sight for sore eyes. Even Amy's jumping around and hey, that three-year-old's got the dancing talent of her mother. *I hope Mouse is filming this shit.*

Someone puts a beer in my hand. I've never been happier in the whole of my life.

I'm just lifting the bottle to my lips when the music stops, abruptly switched off in mid beat. Automatically my hand goes to rest on my gun…

Drummer steps up to the mic, tapping it once, twice, the sharp amplified sound shattering the mood.

All the men step up. All eyes upon him. All of us ready for the call to action.

The prez rolls back his head and wipes his hand over his beard. He shakes his head as he stares out over the club.

"Sorry to interrupt the proceedin's, but you need to hear this. Fuck…" His voice breaks with emotion. As I tuck Ella into my side he continues, "I thought nothin' could top this day, seein' our brother Slick and his ol' lady tie the official knot. But fuck…" He shakes his head as though he can't believe what he's going to say. "I won't draw this out. But, please, take a glass."

Surprised, I notice waiters walking around with trays. I take a champagne for me, and pass one to my *wife*.

Drum surveys the room and picks up his own glass. "I've just had a phone call." He pauses, and you could hear a pin drop as we wait to hear what troubles are on our way.

He takes a deep breath and again turns his head from side to side. "Can't fuckin' believe what I've just been told…" He pauses. *Just spit it out, will ya?* After clearing his throat he continues, "I've just had word from Road, who's at the hospital. Heart's conscious and fuckin' lucid." The prez's voice cracks on the words I'd given up all hope of hearing.

After a brief moment of silence as the incredible news sinks in, a deafening wave of roaring sweeps through the room. Men stamping their feet and cheering, women screaming with joy. *Heart's back with us?* Un-fucking-believable! Best. News. Ever. Only rivalled by Ella saying yes.

Prez taps the mic to get our attention. "So raise your glasses everyone. To Heart! And, of course, to Slick and Ella."

Feet are stamping, hands thumping on tables, and thunderous roars that crash and roll through the function room.

"Heart! Slick and Ella!" "Slick and Ella. Heart!"

Drum's watching me, he lifts his chin and gives me an exaggerated wink while beaming towards Sam. Immediately I know what that means. Amy's getting her dad back.

I couldn't imagine anyone getting a better wedding present.

My brother is coming home.

Targeting

DART

SATAN'S DEVILS #4

Dart

When Alex auditions to work at the Satan's Devils MC strip club, a more unlikely dancer I never expected to see. Knowing she's been left with no other option but to become a stripper, I want to help her out and make her life easier. She's so unlike the other women I'm attracted to, it's no hardship to follow our strict "hands off the dancers" rule. But that was before I came to know and admire her and understand the challenges in her life. And then I lose her before I can admit how much she's come to mean to me.

Alex

Running from an abusive husband I come to live with my sister and somehow end up taking my clothes off in a club owned by bikers. I'm just settling into my new life when my ex finds me and takes me away. Tortured, hurt and left to die, I hope and pray that someone will come and rescue me.

SATAN'S DEVILS #4: Targeting Dart

OTHER WORKS BY MANDA MELLETT

Blood Brothers
A series about sexy dominant sheikhs and their bodyguards

- *Stolen Lives* (#1 – Nijad & Cara)

- *Close Protection* (#2 – Jon & Mia)

- *Second Chances* (#3 – Kadar & Zoe)

- *Identity Crisis* (#4 – Sean & Vanessa)

- *Dark Horses* (#5 – Jasim & Janna)

SATAN'S DEVILS MC

- *Turning Wheels* (Blood Brothers #3.5, Satan's Devils #1 – Wraith & Sophie)

- *Drummer's Beat* (# 2 – Drummer & Sam)

- *Slick Running* (#3 – Slick & Ella)

Coming soon:
- *Targeting Dart* (#4) (2017)

Sign up for my newsletter to hear about new releases in the Blood Brothers and Satan's Devils series:
http://eepurl.com/b1PXO5

ACKNOWLEDGEMENTS

A massive thank you to Brian Tedesco, my amazing editor for all his work on this book. Really enjoyed working with you, and apologies for the part which made you cringe. Your input and suggestions were very useful.

Cover design and formatting by Freeyourwords. Lia, what can I say? Your cover design is excellent as normal.

My dear husband, Steve, was once again great reading and picking up stuff which I'd missed. I'm so lucky to have someone who encourages and supports me so much.

And my son must get a mention, even if it's only because he tells me he's proud of his mum.

And of course, I'm grateful to everyone who's taken the time to read the books in the Satan's Devils series. If you enjoyed this one, please leave a review – writers write in a vacuum, locked away in their lonely towers. We love to know what you think of our efforts and appreciate all feedback we receive.

STAY IN TOUCH

Email: manda@mandamellett.com
Website: www.mandamellett.com

Connect with me on Facebook:
https://www.facebook.com/mandamellett

Sign up for my newsletter to hear about new releases in the
Blood Brothers and Satan's Devils series:

http://eepurl.com/b1PXO5

ABOUT THE AUTHOR

After commuting for too many years to London working in various senior management roles, Manda Mellett left the rat race and now fulfils her dream and writes full time. She draws on her background in psychology, the experience of working in different disciplines and personal life experiences in her books.

Manda lives in the beautiful countryside of North Essex with her husband and two slightly nutty Irish Setters. Walking her dogs gives her the thinking time to come up with plots for her novels, and she often dictates ideas onto her phone on the move, while looking over her shoulder hoping no one is around to listen to her. Manda's other main hobby is reading, and she devours as many books as she can.

Her biggest fan is her gay son (every mother should have one!). Her favourite pastime when he is home is the late night chatting sessions they enjoy, where no topic is taboo, and usually accompanied by a bottle of wine or two.

Photo by Carmel Jane Photography

Made in the USA
Columbia, SC
16 November 2017